THE RUINATION

THE END OF ALL THINGS
BOOK 3

MIKE KRAUS

D1737049

MUONIC
PRESS

THE RUINATION
The End of All Things
Book 3

By
Mike Kraus

© 2023 Muonic Press Inc
www.muonic.com

www.MikeKrausBooks.com
hello@mikeKrausBooks.com
www.facebook.com/MikeKrausBooks

CONTENTS

WANT MORE AWESOME BOOKS?

Find more fantastic tales at books.to/readmorepa.

If you're new to reading Mike Kraus, consider visiting his website (www.mikekrausbooks.com) and signing up for his free newsletter. You'll receive several free books and a sample of his audiobooks, too, just for signing up, you can unsubscribe at any time and you will receive absolutely *no* spam.

Special Thanks

Special thanks to my awesome beta team, without whom this book wouldn't be nearly as great.

Thank you!

READ THE NEXT BOOK IN THE SERIES

The End Of All Things Book 4
Available Here

books.to/BhiYs

CHAPTER ONE

Ryan Cooper
Somewhere Outside East Lansing, Michigan

Jack Willoughby stood in the old couple's dining room, annoyed at how long it'd taken him and his group to get inside. As they were breaking in, the old man had shot at them through the plywood-covered windows, drowning the intruders in wood shrapnel and bullet fragments. Jack had been led to believe it would be an easy fight, but the old man and his wife were much tougher than he could've imagined. Mack Tilly had been the first casualty of their little war, when they'd sent him to scout the barnyard the evening before. He'd never returned, leaving Jack wondering what the oldsters had done to him. That should've been the first warning sign.

The second should've been all the traps that had been set up in the yard, starting with the spikes hidden in the grass, keeping them from taking cover behind the trees as they were approaching. As a result, the old couple had shot Tommy Sloan dead and wounded

Jasper South with a shot that would probably end up killing him slowly and painfully.

He had the old people trapped upstairs, but Jack didn't know how to get to them without incurring even more losses. The old man was an excellent shot, and the barking dogs sounded big and nasty. If he gave up, though, he wouldn't get to their supplies, and walking home empty-handed would lead to a lot of complaints, and it wouldn't be long before he lost the support of the other neighbors. Barb would never let him live it down.

A table took up most of the dining room, and a cabinet rested against the east wall along with a tall chest of drawers next to it. The cabinet was covered in school books, notebooks, older children's toys and various odds and ends, and for the briefest second a twinge of guilt passed through Jack. Rita Tilly stared back at him across the foyer from the great room, a question in her eyes as dust and smoke from the shootout drifted through the moonlight, and the twinge was gone. Ron Jenkins crouched near her shoulder with the same dumbfounded look, the last to charge the grounds and the weakest of the bunch. It was doubtful if he'd even used the pistol he carried – or if he'd be willing to if push came to shove. *Cannon fodder has its purpose, I guess,* Jack mused, the macabre thought lifting his spirits a bit.

Across from the kitchen and dining room, the great room had a TV mounted on the west wall above a gas fireplace, and a leather couch sat in front of the massive display with a pair of recliners on each side. The modest arrangement of common household goods was a fortune compared to what he and Barb had left after all they'd owned had burned to the ground, along with two barns and most of their feed and supplies. If he didn't come through with something soon, they'd be hard-pressed to survive long out there.

"Hey, man. Are we going or not?" Trace Crenshaw whispered as he peered around Jack and tried to see up into the loft area.

He'd wrapped his right hand up in a rag after grabbing the back doorknob covered with razor blades, the cuts so bad he couldn't hold his pistol, the blood soaking heavy through the cloth and running down his arm. He tried to get around Jack, but Jack pushed him back, chiding him.

"Just hang on a minute."

"What are we waiting for?"

"We need to think this thing through. We've already got some people down, and running out there like idiots will only get *us* killed too."

"What's there to plan?" Trace hissed back. "I'll step out there and give you some cover fire while you and Rita rush up the stairs."

"Yeah, we'll take on those dogs by ourselves."

The dogs hadn't stopped barking, the timbre of the notes deep and chesty, giving the impression that they were huge, slavering beasts of war waiting to be unleashed. He remembered seeing Alice Burton walking her dogs one day and thinking how massive and shaggy they were. They'd seemed friendly and dopey as they trotted beside her, but if that was them upstairs, they were more akin to monsters than big, playful household pets.

"Just shoot the damn things." Trace grabbed Jack's shirt with his bloody hand. "Only dogs a bullet won't stop are pit bulls, and those ain't pit bulls."

"Are you crazy? Those're *big* bastards, and it'll take more than one round to kill them!" Jack edged toward the threshold, peering up into the loft through the chewed-up rails, seeing no one before he eased back. "I wonder how bad the old man is injured? I think one of us got him."

Trace shook his head and pushed past him. "Let's just get on with it, man."

"Wait!"

Trace shoved him back with his forearm and crouch-walked into the hallway, glancing up the stairwell before scanning up along the catwalk. "No dogs up there I can see."

"It doesn't mean they're not there. Listen to them!"

Trace slipped into the hallway, staying beneath the catwalk, slowly moving toward the great room, neck craned to look above. As he cleared the edge of the loft, the old woman's voice cried out, and a second later something massive and white flew up and over the catwalk's rail, plunging into him in a blur, paws slamming him full in the chest, knocking him backward, and sending his gun flying as they hit the floor. The shaggy, bear-like dog snarled and flashed its teeth, clamping on his throat, pushing him back toward the front door. The animal was ripping and jerking his powerful head back and forth to tear out a sizeable chunk of Trace's neck and windpipe, the bloody muzzle whipping upward in a spray of blood, Trace's pulsing jugular vein spurting red in a high arc that coated the door like paint.

Jack took a step back in shock and horror, mouth dropping open, fumbling with his pistol in shock, barely catching it before it fell to the floor.

The old woman shouted again from the loft, clearly enough for him to hear, and his blood ran cold. "Attack, Duchess! Attack, Diana! Attack!"

The growls and barks were replaced by paws pounding down the stairwell and another massive beast hit the hardwood foyer with a grunt. Almost a perfect twin of the animal gnawing on Trace's neck, the second one swung its heavy head to the right toward Rita and Ron, who were backing into the great room, gaping at the bloody mess developing in the foyer.

In a scrabble of claws on wood, the dog launched itself, knocking Ron aside and enveloping Rita in one bound. They tumbled into the great room, the dog pinning Rita to the back of the couch, jaws snapping at her arms and face. The dog's enormous frame shook back and forth, shaggy fur rippling as blood sprayed the floor and walls and splattered Ron. Rita shrieked repeatedly, gurgling and gasping in between bites while Ron dropped his weapon, screamed, and dashed into the foyer toward the broken-open window, running headlong into a third dog as it too hit the foyer floor in a tumble of fur and snarls. Legs swept from beneath him, Ron went down on the floor chin first, bone against wood with a sharp crack, then the dog was on him, snapping, grabbing the back of his jacket and jerking backward, tearing its head back and forth.

Jack woke from his surprised daze and took two steps forward with his gun raised. At first, he aimed at the dog attacking Trace, but his friend was gone, so Jack shifted his aim to the beast across the hall destroying Rita. Its paws were spread, its powerful shoulders low to the ground as its maw did its work, and Rita could only cover up

4

with one arm as she punched and kicked weakly at the massive, enraged Great Pyrenees.

Ryan had been crouched back off the rail, holding in a groan from the pain radiating up his wounded calf when Helen clicked the dogs' quick-release leashes and shouted for them to attack. Duke and Duchess spun in a frenzy, almost surprised to be let loose. With Duchess taking up the space around the top of the stairs, Duke bounced off her, reeled, and rushed toward Ryan, jaws snapping. In two bounds, the dog leaped on the rail, his massive claws scrabbling, slipping, pawing at the wood as he propelling himself over, plunging out of sight before Ryan could even think to stop the beast's movements.

A moment later, Duchess flew down the stairs, hitting the hardwood floor in a scrabble of nails. Screams ripped through the house, guttural sounds of raw terror, followed by canine grunts, snapping teeth, and snarls. Ryan came out of his crouch and stepped toward the rail with his rifle raised while Helen finally got Diana turned down the stairs to follow the others, then came to join him.

Curses, exclamations of horror and the primal sound of death itself sent a shudder through Ryan. Soft flesh tore, and the gurgling shrieks of a woman fountained in his ears as at least two people downstairs received the brunt of the Great Pyrenees' rage. Hundreds of pounds of muscles, teeth, and claws unleashed a storm of violence upon the intruders as the dogs did exactly what they were born to do: protect and defend.

Still, even with the dogs turning the tide of the battle, Ryan and Helen had to take advantage of the situation while they could. He nodded to Helen, and they flew to the rail with guns aiming downward, looking for targets. Ryan shifted his barrel to a man wearing a red flannel shirt about to shoot Duke, the dog holding a man against the front door, paws spread, massive body pinning him, jaws clenched on his face. Squeezing the trigger too quickly, Ryan pulled his shot

5

and clipped the man's gun hand, forcing him to flinch with a cry and lose his weapon to clatter on the hardwood.

Helen shot multiple times at a different man crawling across the foyer floor, trying to escape Diana, her shots hitting him in the shoulder, punching through to the floor, and he spasmed and ripped free of Diana's jaws. Flying through the swirling dust, he slammed into the man in the red flannel, the pair shouting and cursing as they tried to get away. Ryan and Helen peppered the intruders, their weapons lighting up the darkened foyer like a fireworks display as Diana crouched, barking loudly.

In the darkness, Ryan couldn't tell who he hit because the men were bunched together and stumbling, though the one Helen was firing on collapsed to his knee with a sudden, crippling weakness. The man in flannel dragged his wounded companion to the broken window while Ryan kept shooting at them, his bullets finding flesh, drawing cries of shock and curses of anger and pain. They fell backward through the window, taking out glass shards and broken wood before landing in the bushes.

"Come on!" Ryan called, turning and hobbling toward the stairwell, wincing and growling as his calf cramped. He fought it, slamming his teeth together, grinding through the pain as he hobbled down the stairs and into the foyer to stand in the middle of the bloody scene. Duke was still locked onto his prey, and Duchess had the woman's neck in her jaws, pinning her to the floor, snarling deep in her throat but holding tight even as the woman's last gurgling breaths bubbled from her lips.

"Get the dogs, Helen! I'm going to chase these bastards off!"

Ryan angled toward the window, limping, slipping on the bloody floor and finally falling to his knee at the sill. Sticking the barrel outside, he tracked the two men stumbling through the yard, the larger one helping his friend stay upright, both of them somehow still able to walk, their adrenaline fueling their escape. He popped off two more shots, missing both times but sending the men into a frenzy to escape. A third squeeze came up dry, and he ejected the magazine and took a second one out of his pocket, almost dropping it from his blood-slick fingers, finally jamming it home. Charging his weapon, he aimed at the fleeing men, slowly lowering the barrel as they got to the gate and clambered over it, the man in the flannel working hard to get his wounded companion up and over before they staggered off into the night.

Helen had set her rifle down and pulled Dutchess off her prey, taking her by the collar and kneeling between her and Diana. Duke was ignoring her, still with the man's face in his jaws, panting through his open maw, growls rippling from his throat as his sides heaved.

"He's not listening," Helen said with strained frustration.

"Come on, Duke!" Ryan shouted at the dog, crossing the foyer and stopping a couple of feet from it. His white coat was stained dark red around his chest and jaws, with streaks along his flanks where the man had tried to beat him off. Duke rolled his eyes and looked at Ryan with animal ferocity, though a hint of recognition showed through, and his tail, previously low, swept back and forth, and he loosened his hold slightly.

Ryan shouted, "Come on, Duke! Let it go, boy! Let it go!"

Duke's tail wagged a little harder and his chesty growls tapered off, though he still had a firm grip on the man's mangled face, fangs puncturing his cheek, the flesh shredded away to expose his bone-white jaw and bloody insides of his mouth.

Equally disgusted and thankful for the animal's effective response to the intruders, Ryan used the Winchester to support himself as he knelt on one knee, wincing at the extreme stiffness gripping his calf muscle. "I said, let it go, Duke! Let it go, *now*!"

The stern note in his voice cut through the animal's instinct, and Duke dropped the man's face, letting the skull hit the hardwood with a thump. The Great Pyrenees turned, tail wagging as he licked his chops, sniffing at Ryan's outstretched hand before shifting to Duchess and touching noses with her. Diana was the most curious, her aggression having been raised but not fed, and she sniffed at her parents with her ears perked up and her tail wagging.

Ryan patted Duke's side. "Good boy, Duke! Real good boy. You, too, Duchess. You're such a good girl!"

Hauling himself up using the Winchester, Ryan turned slowly, gaping at the bloody mess around him. Bullet holes and empty

7

cartridges peppered the floor and there were jagged holes torn in the sidelights, window frames, and even parts of the ceiling. Blood streaked the hardwood and soaked the gray carpet in the great room where the dead woman lay, and arcs of red could be seen halfway up the walls. Some spatters reached as high as the foyer window fifteen feet above them, the red slowly dripping down across the walls. Stepping closer to the big dogs, he gave them hearty slaps on their sides, rubbing their heads to put them at ease as he looked over at Helen who was stepping gingerly toward him.

"Are you okay, honey?"

With a half-smile, she said, "I think so. I'm a little shaken up, but I'll live. What about you?"

Ryan shook his head. "I'm afraid to look. I got hit in the calf."

Helen glanced down and blanched. "Oh, no, Ryan! I didn't even notice you were hurt... everything was moving so fast!"

"I can hardly feel it, though I imagine it'll hurt like hell here soon, once this adrenaline wears off." Ryan held up a hand, watching as it gradually began to shake faster with each passing second.

"Come over to the dining room table. I'll get the first aid kit and take a gander at that."

"That's okay, dear. I'll be fine for now. Let's get these bodies out of here while I can still stand."

He leaned his Winchester against the wall and stepped through the pool of blood to stand next to the dead man. Unbolting the locks on the front door, he opened it a few inches but stopped with a frustrated sigh when the door stopped with a thud on the corpse's head.

"We need to move him first," Helen said, swallowing a nauseous gulp.

"Right. Let's drag him away from the door."

They each grabbed a foot and pulled the body into the hallway, leaving a smear of blood behind. Ryan returned to the door, popped it open with a tug, and returned to the man. In the same fashion, they dragged the man in a circle, his arms hanging wide, face chewed to bits as the curious dogs crowded around and sniffed at him.

"Hey! Get back!" Ryan hissed.

Duke sat at the edge of the pool of blood with his head tilted to the side and his tail sweeping in the smears. Duchess and Diana paced in the hallway, the younger dog trailing behind her mother and sniffing at the blood on her fur. Bumping their shoulders against the door frame, Ryan and Helen got the dead man outside and dragged him off to the side of the front porch, wincing as the man's head thudded and scraped across the hard concrete.

"This is just terrible," Helen said in a trembling voice.

"Would've been smart of them to just back off when they first stepped on those traps out near the trees." Ryan winked at her. "This pair of old folks wasn't quite as easy to take out as they thought we'd be."

Helen only sniffed and nodded, tears glistening on her cheeks as she gripped the man's foot and kept pulling until they had him out in the yard.

"I'm sorry it came to this, dear." Ryan dropped the man's foot and went to Helen, squeezing her tight. "If we could've done it any other way, we would have."

"Oh, I know. I don't blame you for any of this. They pushed us hard and got exactly what they deserved." Her voice dropped for a moment. *"Bastards."*

"Except the part where I got shot, I'm a little surprised at how well it all worked. Thank heavens, though... the way they were coming at us, there's no way they were going to just let us live. The dogs were our trump card, though, no doubt."

"I know." She held him at arm's length. "Could you imagine Duke and Duchess could cause so much damage to someone? I'm shocked at what they did – and I remember what our Shepherds would do to the odd coyote or possum that came after our chickens back in the day."

"They're powerful animals. Pretty well-trained too. The kids did a good job with them."

Back inside, they moved into the great room and stood over the dead woman, her face unrecognizable, red staining her white tank top, and small pieces of her lying around.

"Oh, Duchess," Helen sighed. "You really put her through the wringer."

9

Each taking a leg as they had with the previous corpse, they dragged the woman through the foyer and got her outside, laying her next to the man and dropping her feet in the grass.

"There's at least one more in the yard," Ryan said, gesturing toward a lump out in the grass. "We should bring them over, too."

"No. I want to see to that leg." Helen wiped her hands disgustedly. "I don't want to look at dead people anymore. They'll be fine out here."

"Fair enough." Ryan winced as they went back inside. "Besides, this calf is really starting to stiffen up."

"Your pant leg is soaked in blood. Come on, into the dining room with you."

Ryan shuffled through the foyer and angled toward a dining table chair, then altered course and sat on the floor, stretching his legs out in front of him and lying back to rest his hands behind his head. Helen shuffled off to find a first aid kit as the dogs came up, wanting to lick at him with their bloody maws.

Laughing and more than a little disgusted, Ryan pushed them away. "Not right now. Go on, now. Get away from me."

"Not sure if they'll be hungry after all that," Helen called from the kitchen, "but maybe I can distract them with some food."

A moment later, the sounds of a food bag shaking got the dogs' attentions, and their ears perked up as they trotted away, Duke moving with a noticeable hitch in his step. Helen poured a heavy amount of food into their bowls and joined Ryan in the dining room with the first aid kit, a pair of scissors, some clean hand towels, and a big bottle of saline. With everything bundled in her arms, she crouched slowly, her hips reaching a breaking point before she fell onto her backside. The items she carried fell into her lap, and she leaned against the wall with her hands resting at her side.

"I'm getting too old for this, dear," she said.

"You and me both."

"Okay, let's see the damage."

Ryan rolled onto his left side and scooted closer to Helen, lifting his pained right leg and resting it across her knees. "Here you go. One missing leg and one shot-up leg."

Helen groaned at the sight of all the blood caking his lower pant leg and seeping into his shoe, then she took a pair of scissors and cut the surrounding material, laying it open and leaning closer.

"It's kind of hard to see," she said.

"Wait. I've got a flashlight."

Ryan unclipped the flashlight from his belt, flicked it on, and shined it across his leg, for the first time getting a good look at the damage. The hole had gone through the thickest part of his calf, not quite the center, but toward the back. The hair around the wound was soaked in blood, and the edges were dried and crusty.

"The bleeding seems minimal," Ryan said. "Probably nothing to worry about."

Helen pressed around the wound on his calf, forcing blood to ooze from the entry wound, drawing a wince from Ryan when her finger circled around to trace the exit hole. "Sorry, honey," she said sheepishly. "Oh, my. The bullet went right through, for sure."

"It did? Good. At first, I wasn't sure. Did it nick an artery or anything?"

"It's bloody, that's for sure," she replied, "but it couldn't have hit anything vital or we'd see a lot more blood. I do wish you would have let me look at this before hauling those bodies outside, though."

"Oh, no," he said. "Not sure I'd be able to at this point." He held out his hand, which was shaking noticeably more than it had been before. "Pain's kicking in more now, too."

"Is it a lot?" Helen asked with a raised eyebrow.

"Heck yeah, it is." Ryan tried to get comfortable. "What do you recommend, Dr. Cooper?"

"I'll grab some water to go with some pain meds."

Ryan held out his hand. "I'll swallow them dry."

After giving him two white pills and two green ones, Helen took a towel in one hand and squirted saline on the wound where it drained onto the carpet, Ryan wincing and grinding his teeth.

"Oh, shoot. I should've put something down. Now the carpet is ruined."

Ryan laughed. "If anything, I think you just made a clean spot. I wouldn't worry about it too much. There's a lot more to deal with than just some stained carpet. Probably best to just cut it out before it dries into the padding."

"Alice might have some good stain remover that'll get the blood-stains out. Let me work on it before we go cutting."

"Well, we'll worry about it later. Most of the blood's on the hard-wood, and we can soak up the big puddles tonight, then actually clean tomorrow." Ryan winced as she continued dousing the wound. "Do you think I'm going to need stitches?"

"That's a definite yes on the stitches. Alice has a suture kit down-stairs with their supplies. I should probably go get it before I get too deep into this." Duke walked up, blinked at the two, and laid down with his legs stretched in front of him, licking along both sides of his upper jaw, dog food crumbs caught up in the bloody fur. Helen sighed. "And before I pass out from exhaustion."

After Helen had shuffled away, Ryan laid next to Duke, reaching over to rub the clean spot between the dog's shoulders, the dog stretching his mouth wide in a yawn and resting his head between his legs.

"We certainly got ourselves into a brawl, didn't we, boy? You did so well protecting us. Alice and James are going to be so proud. Might make up for destroying half their house... I hope."

Duke's tail swished back and forth.

"And I hope you're up for a bath tomorrow because the two of you are going to get soaked. And I don't want to hear any fussing about it." The tail swished harder, sending droplets of red flying back and forth. "We're not going to worry about that right now. I'm the one who's going to be howling in a few minutes as soon as Helen puts the stitches in me. Not sure if that makes you feel any better."

Duke emitted a low whine and rolled on his right side toward Ryan, craning his neck to lap at Ryan's face.

"Whoa, boy!" he jerked, setting off an ache that coursed up the back of his leg. "You almost crushed me."

The pair lay there for the few minutes it took for Helen to come upstairs with the suture kit, and when she got there, Ryan was nearly passed out with Duke snuggled by his side, his arm thrown over the big, red-stained dog.

"Are you ready for this, dear?"

Ryan's eye opened, and he gave a slow and tired nod. "I guess so. Are you any good at this?"

Helen sat down in her previous position, pushing Duke aside to make room. With a towel covering her lap, she motioned for Ryan to put his leg back and turn so she could see the wound, and he complied by rolling onto his stomach and resting on his elbows.

Helen prepared the needle. "Well, there was that time I stitched Alice's finger myself during that big winter storm when we couldn't get to the hospital. Do you remember that?"

The memory hit him hard; Alice in her brown pigtails sitting at the kitchen table, sniffling, cheeks wet with tears as she rested her arm on the table with her index finger sticking up. The cut ran beneath the second knuckle from where she'd been playing out on the farm with her cousin and cut herself on glass in a pile of junk out at the back of the property.

Ryan grinned wistfully. "I told her and her cousin not to play in that pile of junk."

"But they did it anyway," Helen nodded. "Never was one to be locked inside the house."

"She had the whole farm to roam, but they chose that damnable pile for some reason."

"It was mysterious to them. I'm going to spray some topical anesthetic on this. It'll feel a little cold." There was a hiss as the cold spray hit his leg. "Okay, first stick coming right up."

"I'm ready for it." Ryan squeezed his fists tight. "Are you going to count down - ouch!"

"That's the first one through," Helen replied with a frown. "Sorry, dear, but if I'd counted down, you would have flinched."

"True." Ryan sucked air through his teeth as Helen continued stitching. The pain medication he'd taken, plus the topical anesthetic, took the edge off, but the needle's sharp tip sent pinpricks of pain through his leg regardless.

"Now shift a little to your left so I can get the exit side of it."

"Okay." Ryan clenched his teeth, eyes squeezed shut all the way through until the last stitch was placed.

"That exit wound needed an extra pair." She gave him a light tap on the back of the knee. "I'm all done, but I'm going to clean up a little more and get some antibiotic cream on it."

"You're the doctor."

"Back to your previous point. Remember the time when Alice's cousin cut her knee on a creek rock? Well, I stitched that, too."

"Your brother was so mad at you for letting them play in the woods unsupervised."

Helen shrugged. "We were always allowed to roam the neighborhood, but it was different times back when we were young. You didn't have to worry as much about things. I was just trying to give Alice a place to use her imagination and play with no boundaries."

Ryan looked down as she finished cleaning the wounds and putting bandages on top, smoothing them out with her long, graceful fingers. "And that's why you were such a great mom."

Helen scoffed. "I did the best I could. We both did."

"All done, Doc?"

"All done," she replied and started putting things away, rolling up the towels to put in the laundry bin and giving Ryan's leg back. "I don't know about you, but I could go for a cup of coffee right about now."

"I'll brew it up." Ryan started to roll to his feet.

Helen got up as fast as her sore legs would allow. "You'll sit at the kitchen table, and I don't want to hear any arguments."

Ryan got up with her help, limped in a circle, and hugged her. "Great work, honey. My leg's as good as new."

Helen chuckled and took his hand. "Quit goofing around and stop putting so much weight on it."

"I'm not," Ryan complained as she guided him into the kitchen. "Well, maybe just a little."

Leaning against the wall in the kitchen, Ryan looked out into the great room and under the catwalk at the mess that lay before them. Helen was humming next to him, quietly heating water, pouring it over grounds in a French press, and pulling out some milk from the refrigerator. A dejected sigh from Ryan drew her attention, and she slipped up next to him.

14

"What's wrong?"

"Just... all of *that*." He gestured at the mess. "It's a *lot* to try and think about dealing with, on top of keeping watch and everything else."

"You want to work on it some tonight?"

"Kind of, yeah. Mopping up the worst of the blood, maybe getting some vinegar on the carpeting and using some towels to get some of the stains mopped up." He groaned. "Laundry's going to be a pain in the butt, too."

Helen wrapped an arm around his waist, pulling him in tight. "It'll be okay. We're through the worst of it. At least for today."

"I hope so."

"C'mon. Let's have some coffee and catch our breaths. I'll get to work on the worst of the blood while you figure out a way to keep the door closed for the night and get some plywood over that broken window. An hour of work and then we'll get some sleep and get back at it first thing in the morning."

"What would I do without you?" Ryan smiled at her, giving her a kiss on the forehead before she turned to pour the coffee, adding a splash of milk to each mug.

"Still have a hole in your leg, probably. Can't imagine you stitching that up yourself, you big baby." She gave him a wink and he laughed, the stress, tension and shakes from the fading adrenaline beginning to melt away. Relaxation was a distant goal, but safety, a loving companion and a cup of something hot to drink would be good enough for the time being.

CHAPTER TWO

Alice Burton
Omega, Georgia

Alice walked outside to an unusually brisk morning with groups of birds landing in the yard to hunt for insects and seeds before flocking to a tree or another part of the yard. There were two rockers on the front porch to sit on, though she ignored them in favor of standing at the edge and rocking on the balls of her feet as the rich aroma of freshly brewed coffee drifted from her cup.

"I've just about got the horses ready, Mom," Jake said, coming around the corner and dusting his hands off.

"We just woke up and you're already dirty," she replied, reaching to wipe a smudge from his cheek.

"Hey," he said, drawing away. "I like getting dirty!"

"The work suits you." She stared admiringly at his shoulders, which seemed to have grown several inches since their whole ordeal had begun. "You've come a long way since we left the beach house."

Jake shrugged noncommittally. "Let me know when you want me to bring them around front."

"Give me a couple of minutes."

"You're the boss." Jake stepped toward the front door. "Just let me know. I think I might have some coffee too, in the meantime."

Alice smiled and turned her attention back to the Nielsen's property. She'd only learned their last names at breakfast the day before, and they continued to be the consummate hosts. On the previous two nights, Nate had relieved her early, insisting Alice and the kids had a long road ahead, and they'd need all the rest they could get. Nate and Elaine had talked the trio into staying for an extra day, as well, and while Alice had argued at first, the hospitality, delicious meals and rare opportunity to relax were too much to pass up.

In return, everyone doted on Elaine and little Ethan, helping out around the house with chores and cooking while Elaine and Ethan recovered. By then, Elaine had gone into the master bedroom with him, leaving the living room remarkably peaceful and giving Alice the best couple of sleeps she'd had in days, free of bad dreams and constant worries about James and her parents. While they had a long way to go, the road seemed a little less dark and foreboding thanks to the Nielsen family.

The front door opened and Sarah stepped out, hands wrapped around a big blue mug of coffee, mirroring Alice's grin. She'd found a brush somewhere and untangled her brown hair so it fell halfway down her back, covering her thin neck and shoulders.

"What are you grinning about?" Alice asked with an elbow nudge.

"I guess I'm still giddy after the other day. The baby is *so* cute."

"He is, isn't he?" Alice's smile spread. "I'm so proud of you, Sarah. You were so strong throughout the whole thing. Didn't even flinch when things were touch and go there for a minute."

"I saw how you handled it and wanted to be the same way. I'm so happy they're both healthy. They're going to be okay, right?"

"Baby's perfect as far as I can tell, and Elaine's in the clear, I think. They'll be fine, especially with a guy like Nate looking after them. He has a lot more skills than we figured. Great cook, too."

"Are you kidding? Scrambled eggs, leftover pork chops, bacon… biscuits and butter." Sarah took a deep breath of her coffee's fragrant aroma and smiled. "I'm almost tempted to suggest we stay here forever."

"Uh huh. Nice try, but we need to get back on the road. Your brother has the horses ready."

"I know we have to get home to Dad and Grandpa and Grandma. I can't wait to see them, but I'll never forget this place. Maybe after all this is over, we can come back."

"Maybe." Alice wrapped her arm around her shoulders. "Right now, two days is more than we can afford, and it's important we don't lose sight of where we need to go and what we need to do to get there. It was a nice rest, but it's time to move on."

"I'll get our things and put them on the porch. Then I want to say goodbye to little Ethan."

Alice nodded and let her go, taking a deep breath of the fresh morning air, watching as the sun rose across blue skies for the second day in a row. "This is the perfect time to go. It's a nice day, and I've got a good feeling about it."

Finishing her coffee, she called for Jake to bring up the horses and nodded at Sarah when she came back out. They placed their packs in a row across the porch and reconfigured things to ensure their supplies were stowed properly, and Jake brought the saddled horses around.

"They're all ready to go," he said. "I saddled them up just like Sarah taught me."

"Good morning, Stormy." Sarah patted the blood-red horse's muzzle, getting a pleased snort in response. "Look, Mom, he's bonding with me! They're *so* great!"

"Probably because they know we love them. I'm sure they appreciated getting brushed out last night."

"Oh, they loved it," Jake agreed with a pat on Rocky's neck. "I can't wait to get riding again."

Nate stepped out. "I'm truly sorry you folks have to go. You're welcome to stay as long as you want. Heaven knows we could use the company."

"We really appreciate that," Alice replied, "but two days was perfect. We rested and got to help around the house and snuggled with Ethan. You guys make a fine family."

"Thanks." Nate held his hands clasped in front of him, eyes glassy with emotion. "We're going to miss you guys."

"We're just glad we could help. I'm pretty sure you all are going to be okay."

"We will. Elaine will be fine, and Ethan is pretty strong for a little guy." The storm door came open, and Nathan turned. "Hey, honey. We were just talking about you. You shouldn't be out of bed, though."

Elaine stepped outside, her shoulders wrapped in a coverlet with baby Ethan in her arms, swaddled tightly as he cooed and grunted. Nate gazed lovingly at his son and put his arm around his wife, hugging her close and kissing her on the forehead.

"I'm weak, but I can't let you all leave without seeing you off. I hope it was all good talk," Elaine laughed.

"It was," Alice grinned back. "And let me say, you're positively beaming. You look beautiful."

"Thanks. I feel a *lot* better, in spite of everything." She released an exasperated breath. "That's the second hardest thing I've ever had to do – well, besides giving birth to Missy, of course. The hospital and epidural made it a lot easier on me, though."

They stood in silence for a moment with Elaine bouncing Ethan gently on her chest, staring sadly into the expansive front yard and their gravel driveway that stretched way down to the main road. "I wish you guys didn't have to go."

"Us too," Alice stepped forward and hugged her, then cooed at the baby, smelling deeply from him, reminded of the way Jake and Sarah had smelled when they were newborns. "Thank you for sharing the gift of this little guy with us."

Elaine blinked back tears. "And thank you for spending so much time with us and rescuing us. You didn't have to, but you did. Not many people would've done that. At least not from what you told us."

"It's been a hard road," Alice agreed, "but we've met a few good people. Enough to keep hope alive. You're part of the proof of that."

Alice backed up as Sarah hugged Elaine and Ethan, kissing both, sniffling, and wiping away tears. Jake gave Alice the horses' reins and jumped onto the porch to say his goodbyes, shaking hands with Nate before the older man wrapped his arms around Jake in a strong embrace. Alice and Sarah hugged Nate as well, patting his back as tears flowed down their faces.

"You're going to do great, Nate," Alice told him. "Remember what we talked about and do the best job you can. It's all any of us can do."

He nodded assuredly. "I will. And, before you go, we've got some gifts for you."

"Oh, that's not —"

"Nope, no arguing!" Nate turned and held the door open, reaching and calling to Missy. A moment later, they both stepped out holding pillowcases with the bottoms bulging.

"What's this?" Alice asked.

"Just a few supplies to see you on your way. It's not much. Some canned food and water you can put on Hercules there."

"We can't take this stuff." Alice drew back. "You've got two little ones to feed. That's no small task, especially with things how they are."

"Believe me, we've got plenty. The biggest problem will be protecting it, and you gave me the right advice. I'm heading out today to look for weapons at some houses that I know are abandoned. Should be able to scrouge up something."

"Be careful, Nate, okay? It's not just you who you need to worry about."

A faint smile tugged at the corner of his mouth. "Yes, ma'am."

"Bye," Missy held Nate's hand and waved. "I'll miss you."

"What do you say, honey?" Elaine asked.

"Thank you!" Missy grinned sheepishly. "Thank you for my little brother!"

Sarah laughed and kneeled to hug her, and Alice swooped in and wrapped her arms around both as Jake came up and tousled the little girl's hair. "I'll talk to you later, you little knucklehead."

"You're the knucklehead," Missy said with exaggerated toughness before breaking into laughter.

Jake leaned down and tickled her sides, sending her retreating behind Nate in fits and giggles, peeking around his leg. Disturbed by the commotion, Ethan made a soft mewling sound and began stirring in his mother's arms, his face going red, mouth coming open as he shook and squalled.

"Welp, he's getting hungry," Elaine sighed. "I better get him inside and feed him. Y'all take care, okay? Be safe. I mean it."

Alice nodded while Jake sniffled and led Rocky away by his bridle. Nate was holding the door open for Elaine when Sarah suddenly rushed forward and embraced them one more time, planting a soft kiss on Ethan's head. With a half wave, she mounted Stormy, turning away to wipe away her tears. Elaine watched her go with a loving look, a smile, and a tear racing down her cheek as well, then the door swung shut as she and Nate headed back inside, leaving Alice and Jake standing with sad smiles.

Alice nodded to the backpacks and sacks of food on the porch. "Jake, help me get these loaded onto Hercules."

They had their supplies loaded in less than a minute and were mounted up when Alice handed Jake his tether. "Take Hercules, would you?"

"Sure, Mom."

While Jake and Sarah began trotting down the driveway, Alice patted Buck's neck, watching the shadows of Nate and his small family walking around in the living room. With a faint smile, she nudged Buck and turned him toward the road, kicking him into a gallop to catch up.

After catching up with the kids, they joined the main highway heading north, moving along at a leisurely pace on the roadside, seeking soft grass for the horses to ride on, looping far around the first two wrecked vehicles they came across and keeping their eyes peeled for chunks of debris. The skies were still blue, and the sun cut brilliantly across the sky, coating everything in a vivid brightness. A two-day break had been more of a delay than Alice wanted, but she couldn't argue with the results. She felt more invigorated than she could remember, and her mood and motivation to get home were sky-high.

"I'm so stuffed." Sarah held her belly. "I think the food was just about as good as that baby of theirs."

Alice laughed. "It didn't seem like you ate all that much."

"Are you kidding, Mom?" Jake snorted. "She was sneaking bacon the whole time. Ate darn near half of it!"

"I did *not*, Jake," Sarah replied in mock offense, then stretched back with a yawn. "Now the biscuits and butter maybe...." When Sarah finished her yawn and stretch, she took on a more sober demeanor. "Where to now, Mom?"

Alice reached into a saddle pouch and pulled out some maps Nate had given her, old dogeared things he'd pulled from an old cabinet from before the age of phone apps and built-in navigation systems. She unfolded one and put the others away, holding Buck's reins in one hand as she spread the map and held it steady. "The general idea is to head north but let me see where these roads lead... Can you tell where we are now?"

"No idea." Jake scanned ahead. "This is just some old country road. We could be going anywhere."

Sarah held up her compass. "But at least we're going north."

"This might be Omega Road we're on," Alice said as she traced the stained map with its many interconnecting highways. "But this thing looks old. They could've built it out over the years. I guess we'll just have to keep following this and hope it takes us somewhere we can use to get a better sense of location."

"As long as it keeps going north, can't we just keep following it?" Sarah angled Stormy off the road into a long stretch of soft green grass. Flat woodland pressed in around them, with crowded clusters of saplings standing or leaning against each other, vines hanging from the high boughs like brown drippings. Hooves crunched on the deadfall and forest debris, nuts and twigs, and small branches lying everywhere, and the rustle of small creatures in the trees and undergrowth was constant as they scattered from the approach of the four horses and their riders.

"More or less." Alice folded the map and put it away, straightening, and sighing. "We'll keep going until something makes us turn off. It's a beautiful day, but let's not be lax. Keep your eyes open, especially along the highway."

They rode for most of the morning, leaving Omega Road only when they had to. One large section was covered with a tremendous car crash, several vehicles smashed in a metal lump with sharp debris scattered across the pavement and lying in the grass and woods on both sides. Not long after that, they passed a burned–down farmhouse with twisted vehicles blown to bits in the circular driveway, parts having rained down on the road, forcing them to divert around through a clearing.

Returning to the highway, they rode more miles past edged fields with beautiful straight and curved patterns cutting into the reddish-brown dirt. Some land had been harvested before the disaster while other areas suffered with rotting, drooping crops, and Alice kept a wary eye on every farmhouse they passed, on the lookout for anyone who might leap out as Nate had done, only with different intentions. They swept over more miles, the horses walking with a sense of purpose after two days of rest and near constant attention.

Eventually they passed beneath Highway 82 running east and west, and from their position on the road Alice saw spots of wreckage in the distance. Blown-out glass and metal shards glinted in the sun, smoked-out car interiors with matte black soot stains on the hoods sitting like ancient relics of some bygone time and Alice tried to imagine what they'd look like in five or ten years.

Omega Road branched into Cottle Road, though they kept riding straight ahead to stay on a northerly path, passing through the front yard of a still-standing home with no signs of people anywhere. Dogs barked in the distance, a frantic sound beneath the bright blue sky and off to the northwest, storm clouds loomed, big round puffs of billowing darkness suspended in the sky. They avoided the main roads for the rest of the morning, opting to take back roads and country byways. Stretches of straight gravel roads cut between pure green fields with waving grass while at other times they were on curving avenues crowded with sturdy oak trees and tall white pines that broke up the winds and left only soft breezes fluttering through the branches.

They crossed bridges over thin, trickling streams that smelled like mud and wet moss, vegetation growing thick up to the road, making the horses work hard to cross the soft areas. When things became too swampy they ventured into the fields where the dirt was firmer and the horses steps surer. Farther north, they saw their first people in a lonely patch of low hills on a farmstead in the middle of a broad curve of trees, the family out in the front yard working gardens with ripe tomatoes glinting in the sun and long stalks of corn stretching as high as the tallest child.

"What a beautiful setup," Alice commented as they rode on the edge of the woods outside the tree line.

"It looks peaceful," Jake replied. "Let's hope we have something like that to look forward to when we get home."

"If I know your grandparents, things will be well taken care of. I bet they've got the place looking beautiful right about now."

In the farmstead yard, a girl spotted them and pointed, and an older child stepped in front of her and fixed Alice and the kids with a stare, lifting his shirt to reveal a pistol on his hip before shouting something over his shoulder. A few seconds later, their father rushed around the corner of the house and the front door flew open, and the mother came out to stand on the porch, wearing an apron and wielding a shotgun, studying Alice and the kids.

"Come on. Let's get out of here." She flicked Buck's reins and galloped along the tree line with the kids behind her, putting the farmstead behind them.

A deer path cut north through the woods, and she turned Buck onto it, grinning as he quickly took the sharp dips and sudden twists in stride, flying through cascading vines and brush until they came to another stretch of green. Somewhere up near Tifton-Worth County Line Road, they spotted a few businesses still set up, a simple vegetable stand with three people on guard with shotguns. They waved at Alice and she waved back, but she and the kids still continued on with haste.

By midday, the road was getting long, and when they came upon a glimmering pond secluded in a forested area, Alice called for a lunch halt. They dismounted and let the horses drink at the water's edge while they sat on a grassy slope and broke out their provisions. Sarah stuck to peanut butter-flavored snacks while Jake removed an MRE and put the main course in a heating pouch and Alice went to her favorite meal, a brown sugar and maple multigrain package.

"Can you believe we still have some of these old rations?" Alice opened the package and poured a measured amount of water inside, chuckling at herself. "Look at me, calling this stuff 'old' as if we've had it for more than a week."

As they ate, the storm clouds she'd seen earlier appeared above the treetops, and a brisk gust of wind blew through to rustle the leaves. The tree branches arched over them, protecting them from the drizzle that made ripples on the lake and caused Buck to shake his head and look back at Alice in annoyance.

"Hey, don't look at me," she shrugged and fed herself a spoonful. "If you want to stay dry, you'll have to come up here away from the water." The horse snorted and lowered his head for another drink.

Lunch passed quickly, and as soon as they were done, they stowed their garbage and mounted up again. Checking her compass, Alice guided them around the pond to find another deer trail continuing northwest. They picked up the pace, and she began sweating as the drip from the forest canopy trickled on them. The woods went on longer than she'd figured until the trail ended at the top of a rise overlooking a vast field that was littered with rusted farm equipment and the remnants of old barns and sheds long forgotten. At the bottom of the slope was another highway and small blocks of farmhouses burned to the ground. They sprinted past the charred ruins, letting the horses run hard through fields and glades, searching for some sort of path running north.

Slowing to a walk, Alice hunched over the saddle and tried to protect the map from the raindrops, tracing the multicolored lines with her finger. "There should be something up ahead. If we keep heading north, we'll cut right between Macon and Columbus and hopefully avoid both those two towns."

"Should we pick up the pace a little?" Jake asked.

Alice looked upward. "I'm tempted to, but we don't want to run the horses too hard. We've still got a *lot* more miles to go. A little wet won't hurt us."

Jake stood in his stirrups and twisted in his seat to stretch his back. "That's probably the smart way to do it, but I just want to fly so fast on Rocky. I can feel he wants to run."

She self-consciously pushed Buck to go faster, getting well ahead of the kids and forcing them to catch up, feeling the mountain of muscle moving beneath her. "They do seem like they want to run a bit, huh? We should save their energy for when we're in trouble and need to move fast, but I guess a few minutes wouldn't hurt!"

As the shadows grew long and night began to fall, the drizzle finally stopped and Alice called for a halt, catching sight of a tall, dilapidated structure way off in the gloom surrounded by clusters of waving trees. She angled Buck to the right, leaving the highway and cutting across a short field to reach the old, disused barn.

"This old place should do us just fine. Let's tie the horses out back and give them enough lead so they can graze on some of this long grass."

Alice dismounted and gave Jake her reins, then circled to the other side to inspect the place. It was of moderate size, the original color blue by the looks of things, but weather had stripped the wood bare and much of it was broken off or rotten along the bottoms. The roof was intact for the most part, though, and aside from one wall looking particularly rickety, it seemed in decent enough condition to serve as a temporary shelter. Alice leaned in close to peer through a crack in the boards and a field mouse squeaked and dashed past her feet to burrow through the brush and disappear into a hole.

Alice put her hand to her chest. "Jeez! You scared me, little guy."

She met Jake around back, where he found a short section of old wooden railing to tie the horses to. "You think they'll be okay out here?"

"We'll let them graze for a while and bring them in before we get some shuteye." She gestured to several puddles on the gravel lane and overgrown yard. "They've got plenty of water to drink."

Once they had the horses tied up, Alice explored the rear barn opening, but it was packed with stacks of old rusted machinery. They circled and entered through the wide entrance, where a mud puddle spread about ten feet inside. The smell of old musty hay filled the air, touched with the remnants of horse manure and something – or somethings – dead. Alice flipped her flashlight on and shined it around from left to right, illuminating old crates, wood and iron farm implements, tractor hitches, and field tools.

"Wow, this place is a museum," Sarah said.

Jake jumped over the puddle and walked past the thick wooden beams holding up the roof. "What's with this stack of stuff?" he asked, using his own light to highlight the pile of junk blocking the rear exit.

"No idea, but this back corner looks pretty dry and clean," Alice said, following them inside. "There's some decent-looking hay lying around we can make into beds. Hey, there's an old lantern over here, too." Alice stepped between the piles of rust to the back corner where the crates and boxes formed an L-shape. On one of them sat an oil lantern, and she gave it a shake, hearing the splash of liquid inside. "I'm going to light this."

"Someone's been here," Sarah said, stepping in and pointing to a soda can and discarded chip bags and candy bar wrappers, all of them covered in dust and dirt.

"Could be some local kids used this as a hang out before. In any case, it looks like a decent spot to spend the night."

"It's not nearly as good as Wilford's stable or Nate and Elaine's place," Sarah chirped as she stood in the middle and looked around. "But we can make it work for a night."

"You read my mind," Alice replied. "Jake, go grab our stuff, and Sarah and I will clear a spot for us to lie down for the night."

Together, the two got the place straightened out, making soft beds from the non-moldy hay and moving the boxes and crates to create a barrier to help keep them protected in case someone wandered in. When Jake returned, she found a lighter and lit the oil lamp, grinning as she set it in the corner and brightened the place with warm, ambient light.

"That'll draw some attention," Jake said.

"If anyone's even out here, yeah, but we need some light to see by and I'd rather use this than try to start a fire in this old place. The lantern's enough of a fire risk as it is. We'll just have to hope it's gloomy enough outside to keep us hidden."

"It's getting pretty foggy out there. I think we're safe." Sarah said, peering through a crack in the wooden walls. Outside, a heavy mist had descended over the area, filling the cracks between the trees with soupy gray. The sound of frogs and crickets intensified in the fog, adding to the eeriness of the place and sending a shiver down her spine. "As safe as one *can* be when you're in an abandoned barn in the middle of nowhere...." She mumbled as she turned back to her mom and brother.

They broke out their blankets and placed them over the hay beds, patting them down and making pillows out of rolled clothes, then sat cross-legged, with Sarah facing Alice and Jake. Packs in front of them, they pulled out some food, and the sounds of packages tearing replaced their talking.

A weariness passed through Alice as she ate, the food settling in her belly to make her eyelids droop. "Wow, that was our first really long hard ride. I'd say it was a resounding success, though. We kept out of trouble, stayed hidden as much as we could, and generally did a great job of moving with both speed and stealth."

"Creeping around sure takes a lot out of a person," Sarah sighed.

"You should eat something more than just those candy bars."

"You said they were high calorie, though."

"It's the nutrition part I'm talking about," Alice said. "Those things have tons of sugar and not much else, so get a meal, please, Sarah."

"Okay, MRE mac and cheese it is."

Alice rolled her eyes and sighed. "Good enough. I'd cook some canned food, but, well... that lantern is making me nervous enough as-is."

"Hey, this is why we have these," Sarah broke open the package and placed the components on the blanket at her feet. She read the directions, took out the entrée, and put it into the heating pouch, then she poured water in and sealed it. While it heated up, she examined the other contents of the MRE, brightening and holding up a bright red pack of multicolored candy. "Score!"

Alice shook her head and laughed. "I tried to get you to stay away from sugar, and you still managed to find it."

"There's some beef jerky, crackers, and jalapeno cheese spread here, too," Sarah said. "Never know what you're going to find in these things."

Alice had a strawberry-flavored multigrain meal, the contents filling enough, though the watery milk-like drink didn't quite substitute for the real thing. "Jake, you should be eating, too."

He shrugged. "I'm going to finish some of this jerky. We've got a bunch of bags of it with crumbs and stuff. I'm not that hungry; I just want to get something in my stomach and get some sleep more than anything."

"Fair enough."

Jake took a bite of his jerky and gestured toward the front door of the barn. "How far do you think we got today?"

Alice grabbed her map and placed it in front of her. "I was keeping a close eye on the signs as we rode, and it seems like we're somewhere between Macon and Columbus, closer to Columbus, though we're heading a little too far west for my taste."

"Take an immediate turn north?" Jake asked.

"Yeah. We'll get back on this highway in the morning and take the first left-hand turn we come to."

Sarah opened her package of mac and cheese began to eat, dripping cheese sauce down her chin. She caught it with her finger, then licked it off. "This is great, Mom. Thanks for the suggestion."

"Oh, yeah, sure. I've got plenty more recipes where that came from," Alice replied dryly.

After they'd finished eating, they put their garbage away, curled up on their makeshift beds and whispered about what might be happening back home and what Ryan and Helen were up to.

"I bet they're having a movie night or something," Sarah said.

"Definitely taking it easy," Jake added.

"I can't wait to get home. I'm going to hug Grandma so hard when I see her."

"I'm going to hug everyone," Jake said, his voice growing sleepy, "especially Dad."

Just before drifting off, Alice woke up, picked up her rifle, and stepped outside into the cool evening. She went out to bring the horses inside, tying their leads to some of the heavy metal pieces at the back of the barn, removing their saddles, and brushing them down. In between caring for the animals, she walked outside and took in some air, leaving churning eddies of fog as she passed.

The highway crossed west to east, framed by fields of long grasses and gnarled trees beneath a misty, green-tinted sky. Nothing moved, no lights blinked, and there were no shouts in the darkness. A glowing ambiance bathed the place in full moonlight, though its round shape was merely outlined in the puffy cloud cover. As the light passed through the fog, it created a brilliance that illuminated the ground and even cast shadows across the field. Alice turned and circled the barn, slowly counting down the hours before she had to wake Jake up to take his shift.

The following day came swiftly with the distant crowing of a rooster, then another and another after that. Sarah woke up Jake and Alice and the trio had a quick breakfast, then gathered their things with little fanfare. The fog still surrounded them, though the morning sun was rapidly burning it away. Jake got the horses saddled up, and they soon found a pleasant strip of soft grass along the road-side to travel on. Alice guided them northwest, looking for a satisfactory route to turn north on, the miles passing beneath them as they moved from one side of the road to the other, using grass and fields whenever they could, depending on the amount of debris and junk in the way. Every intersection was clogged with destruction, though, and campfires and house chimneys trailed smoke through the tree-tops, making her leery about going offroad.

"Are these actual neighborhoods or something, Mom?" Sarah asked.

"Some of them might be," Alice responded, "but I'm not interested in wandering into someone's backyard to ask them about it."

The farther they rode, the more the side roads seemed to be purposefully jammed, with piles of garbage and appliances dragged out and stacked up to form obstructions. Poorly cut trees stretched across the road with construction materials thrown on top, spilling onto the shoulders.

"Shouldn't we be turning north soon, Mom?" Sarah asked with a nervous glance.

"Yeah, probably best to get out of here as soon as we can, but I don't see a spot where we can get north very easily. I was hoping to stay out of the deep woods today, but we may need to cut through some fields."

"Too late for that." Jake pointed at the black railings running along the roadsides. "Unless you want to jump the rails, we have to go forward or back."

It was a detail Alice hadn't thought much of, as such fences usually ended after a mile or so, and there were often breaks. The ones they were riding along, though, stretched as far as she could see, and any potential breaks were filled with unnaturally stacked piles of debris. She cursed silently for not seeing it sooner. "You're right, guys. Something doesn't feel right about this."

"Mom, we need to get out of here," Sarah sat stiff in her saddle, head on a swivel. "How about that street up ahead? It's mostly open."

The lane's entrance was conspicuously lacking any obstructions, and narrowed into a series of driveways that wound downward into a side yard. "No way. That looks like a trap to me... heck, *all* of this looks like some kind of trap. Let's ride on through as fast as we can. There's bound to be something up ahead."

Jake moved off the left-hand shoulder and onto the road, kicking Rocky into a gallop. Alice and Sarah came right behind him, raised in their saddles, searching for a way through the fencing ahead when an engine revved, sending growling echoes over the treetops, causing chills to shoot up Alice's back, punctuated by a tailpipe backfire and *boom* that startled the horses enough to make them whinny and rear up. A cloud of smoke rose into the air from off to their right and behind them, and something massive moved toward them behind the trees, angling in their direction, trundling on wheels that sounded as though they were crushing everything in their path.

Alice swallowed hard and gathered her breath. "Ride, kids!" she shouted. "Ride hard!"

CHAPTER THREE

James Burton
Frankfurt, Illinois

Rain fell in fat drops that struck the brick walls and cobblestones in rhythmic sheets, hammering everything in their path, feeding rivulets that fed streams that in turn fed large torrents of rushing water. It flowed along the alley's edges, dumping its crimson-stained liquid into wide puddles that eventually poured into sewer grates. Garbage had half-blocked many of the grates, and with no one around to unblock them or monitor and maintain the complex sewer system, the tainted water was at risk of becoming a full-blown flood.

Beneath the towering buildings in a back alley reeking of wet trash and urine, splashing through puddles and tripping over wet cardboard, James Burton fought for his life. Amber lay a few feet away, a bullet hole in her head, her sides heaving one last time, a final breath before expelling a long, quivering exhale and lying still, James unable to give her even a second's attention as the life bled from her and mixed with the rushing water.

He took a punch to the gut and staggered back two paces, straddling the dead man at his feet who was bleeding out from several head wounds James had inflicted with his aluminum staff. The remaining assailant – a tall, sinewy man with sores and scars on the insides of his arms – looked like he weighed eighty pounds soaking wet, but fought like a demon, shoving James back and going for a revolver tucked into his waistband. James swung his staff one-handed, grunting as he aimed for the man's head, gore and bits of flesh whipping off the end of the stick before it struck the man in his rising forearm, cracking hard and drawing a pained grunt, but not stopping him from getting the gun out.

With his free hand, James lunged and seized his attacker's wrist, keeping the gun pointed at the ground. The man jerked backward to escape, but James went with him, stumbling forward and digging his fingernails into the man's wrist, pressing with his thumb and nail into his tendons to make him drop the gun. His staff flailed as he nearly lost his balance yet somehow remained on his feet, staggering, throwing himself backward, staying upright at all costs.

The assailant screamed with rage as rain poured off his nose and chin, his lank black hair plastered to the sides of his temples. James held on, pulling him closer to gain more leverage even as the man punched him in the face with his left hand. James grunted and returned the favor by cracking his staff into the man's ribs, and as he was drawing back for another strike, the assailant twisted frantically, his limbs like rubber, breaking free, grinning as he raised the gun to fire.

James was already swinging, his stave cracking the man's gun hand, knocking the weapon off-course as it popped off with a muzzle flash and a bang that echoed through the alley, the smell of gunpowder immediately washed away by the torrential rain. James' backhand sweep with his staff caught the man in the jaw, a glancing blow that snapped his neck hard enough to buckle his knees, and James charged in with his head low and feet driving. Just before impact, he held his breath and locked his jaw, shoving the man's arm aside, planting his head on his hip, and tackling him with his right shoulder. Driving forward and lifting, James picked the slighter man off the ground, held him suspended in midair, then slammed him hard on the wet pavement.

The man landed with a grunt, air shooting from his lungs. James lost control of the man's gun arm and felt it angling in to shoot him in the side, but he caught the skinny arm and pinned it to the ground. Keeping the wiry man from squirming beneath him, James raised the staff to strike, but he was too close to get any sort of momentum built up. With the man wiggling like a wet fish, James tossed his staff aside with a clatter, balled his bloody fist, and struck the junkie across the jaw. The man shook his head and grinned with bloodstained teeth, his drug-fueled glare filled with undaunted fury—he had nothing to lose.

The rain picked up in a rush, lightning cracking overhead bathing the dark alley in a sudden burst of light. James was slipping and sliding on the cobblestones as he tried to balance atop the squirming man, and for a moment the two were grappling like awkward, exhausted wrestlers. The attacker clenched a fistful of James' jacket and shoved him, almost flipping him off onto his back, but James leaned into it, thrusting his right arm and grabbing the loose material of the man's hoodie around the shoulder area, leveraging him to the ground with a strained groan.

They stayed locked that way for a long moment, James' bruised ribs aching as he gasped to get his wind back. The attacker was weakening, his body shaking, grasp slipping as he tried to angle the gun toward James' head. In a quick shift of balance, James slid his hand down to grip the man's wrist with both hands, and he slammed the pistol on the concrete multiple times, trying to knock it free. Seeing he was losing, the junkie let James go and tried to roll beneath him, bringing his arms together against his chest and curling up on the ground. James found himself mounted on the man's back, and he sank, using his weight to keep the gun arm trapped and pointed at the brick wall. With a frustrated growl, the man fired twice, the bullets cutting deep into the brick, sending a spray of debris that the rain carried away.

Twisting and leveraging himself, James slipped his right shoulder in and got both hands on the attacker's gun arm again, one clenching his wrist, the other grasping his forearm. The man had worked himself into a twisted shape, turned face-first into the pavement with his gun arm stretched beneath him, losing his tenacious hold on the weapon. James pressed his thumb hard into the man's bloody wrist, adding his body weight to it, dirty nails digging into flesh and separating the tendons painfully.

The man groaned and whined, the sound morphing into a strangled wail that grew in volume and intensity even as his fingers loosened on the revolver. With a final smash against the pavement, James knocked the gun free, pounced on it and grabbed it with both hands. The attacker exploded into movement beneath him, punching, kicking, and grasping to hold James back. Once James had secured the weapon, he threw a right elbow backward, hitting the man's jaw with a sharp crack and dropping him backward onto the pavement. Gun in hand, he staggered to his feet and fell against the alley wall where rain cascaded down in a waterfall from the roof above, splashing over his shoulder and into his face. His vision swirled in front of him, water dripping off his eyebrows and down his face, the junkie just a blur as he wailed in frustration, the sound slicing through James' ears. He raised the pistol as the man tried to roll into a crouch but slipped in the water and collapsed onto his backside, glaring up like a wounded animal. James stumbled over with a pained grimace, and when the man tried to rise, James planted his right foot onto the man's chest and pushed him to the ground, pinning him.

"You... killed my... horse." James' voice was ragged as he struggled for breath.

"Never... was... your horse." The man spat blood as he wheezed out a response. "No one owns... anything out here anymore."

"It was given to me."

"Nothing is given, you fool," The man leered. "It can only be taken away. Even if you kill me, someone else will take my place. You're going to die out here, man. You're going to –"

James squeezed the trigger and the man's head rocked back as red sprayed across the cobblestones, quickly washing away into the cracks and crevices. The man fell back with a thud, his body convulsing weakly as some still-intact part of his brain fired off signals to his extremities, his eyes rolling back in his head. James nearly shot him again, but hesitated as there were only three rounds left. While the would-be killer's blood was carried away by the raging torrent, James crouched and found a box of bullets in the man's front pocket, transferring them to his jacket.

He fell away from the dying man, putting his shoulders against the wall, sliding slowly downward until he was squatting in the couple inches of water, gasping for breath as the adrenaline surge ended, staring straight ahead. He listened as he tried to calm himself, trying to pick up any motion, footsteps or changes in the pattern of rain that would tell him that his pair of attackers had a third partner around somewhere, but the only sounds above the rain were distant cracks of gunfire and shouts that echoed through the narrow city corridors.

It had been three days since he'd left Eli's family on the road, and he'd lost almost everything. His M4 and Colt were gone along with half of his supplies, not to mention poor Amber. James stood over the remains of the most recent group who'd attacked him, walking over to kick the other man in the shoulder to make sure he was dead. Rain dripped from James' chin and ran down his jacket as he inspected himself for injuries, finding several cuts on his neck, some facial abrasions, and pains in his knee and hip. His ribs ached from being punched and kicked, and he was probably at risk of infection from whatever was in the water swirling around his feet, but other than that, he was fine.

He retrieved his staff, wiping the last of the gore off on the dead man's shirt, giving him a final look of disgust before staggering away to his former companion. Amber's massive form lay unmoving on her side in a pool of blood, so much of it that the water swirling around her was still bright red. The pair of attackers had shot her point-blank during the ambush, a single round to the head that had sent her crashing to the pavement and thrown James off. He stooped over to ensure she was dead, prepared to end her misery if she was somehow still alive, but the round had gone all the way through her head, her chest wasn't heaving, and her deep black and brown eyes were bereft of life.

"Bastards." James choked out the word, sinking to one knee and stroking the horse's head and snout. "You were a good girl, Amber. Such a good girl. You did so good, carrying me so far and keeping us safe for so long. Rest easy now, girl." He turned his face to the sky, letting the cool rain wash his cuts and sores, sputtering, spitting and crying as guilt flowed through him.

"I'm so sorry, Abram. I'm sorry I got your horse killed. She was the best gift you could have given me and I'm so, so sorry." Squatting lower, falling to his knees, he rested his head against her neck and hugged her one last time, breathing deep of her wet, musky smell before standing back up.

James retrieved his backpack where it had fallen when he had been thrown during the ambush, then tried to get his other supplies, but Amber was lying on them, and it was impossible to get them free no matter how hard he tugged and pulled at the straps or tried to move her heavy, water-logged body. Gunfire came, a staccato burst, and James stiffened, crouching low and pressing himself against the wall, pulling his pack toward him and hefting the revolver he'd taken from his attacker. After a moment, and several more shots, it became clear that they weren't nearby.

Shrugging on his pack, James stood and listened, trying to pinpoint the location of the gunfire and shouts echoing through the city through the noise of the rain, needing to find a spot to rest and gather his wits about him. Checking the compass on the top of his staff – cracked, but still functional – he turned due east, creeping beneath creaking fire escapes and past dumpsters filled with garbage and things that smelled of death, his boots splashing through puddles and clanking on metal sewer grates. The sky was virtually nonexistent thanks to the roiling storm clouds, moonlight piercing through them every once in a while with a glow that gave the city a purgatorial appearance.

Lightning and thunder cracked, the sounds reverberating through blocks of cold brick and empty windows, lightless and filled with shadows moving inside, either from the shifting light or from figures that were hiding from the rain and violence. James felt eyes on him, fearful denizens crouching beneath porch stoops and in alleyways as he staggered past with his jacket tight around his shoulders. Revolver held against his waist, ready to shoot anything that moved, he crept through the alleys in the dripping rain.

What he thought was a small town or the outskirts of something larger, had turned out to be more dangerous than he'd expected. Refugees from Chicago were everywhere, overrunning the town and spreading into whatever buildings could provide shelter. Every nook held potential danger, and shadows swept through the streets to disappear into alleys and narrow lanes. The streets were congested with the remnants of vehicles and flame-ravaged buildings. A strip of small local shops had been defaced, their front windows blown in, glass and brick glinting on the wet sidewalks with the smell of wet ash coming in waves as the water poured over the blackened structures. James was lost in it all, the compass nearly useless as he kept having to change directions in the concrete jungle, unable to follow it while he was wounded, disoriented, and desperate for a safe place to catch his breath.

He went several more blocks, hoping to stumble into a highway that would get him out of the mess and into a more rural area where he could find a secluded place to hide, but the city streets continued with no end in sight. James spotted a small office building wedged between a pair of old warehouses with no lights in the windows and he took slow steps across the street and into an alley, turning to search the street and make sure he wasn't being followed. Satisfied he was alone, he looked upward and spotted a glinting iron structure about halfway down the alley, a fire escape leading to the upper floors. Standing beneath it, he leaped up and pulled down the ladder with a loud creak that set his teeth on edge. Anyone nearby would undoubtedly hear it and come to investigate, so he climbed quickly, drew the ladder up behind him, and continued his ascent up the winding stairwell to the third floor. Flipping on his flashlight — one of his few possessions still *in* his possession — he pointed it through the window to reveal a warehouse room full of junk and machinery with odd-shaped arms that jutted out from their steel bodies.

When he tried to open the window, it stuck, so he put his flashlight down, slipped his fingers beneath a pair of metal tabs, and jerked it upward with a groan of painted wood. Iron shavings and dust swirled past his face as he climbed in and slammed the window shut, cutting off both the rain and the sounds of the dangerous and dying town. James turned off his flashlight and stood next to the window for a good five minutes, staring into the alley, waiting to see if anyone had noticed him or his light, until finally he was satisfied he hadn't been followed.

With a heavy sigh, he turned and faced the floor of machinery, boxes, and crates. It was some manufacturing plant that turned out machine parts and other odds and ends he couldn't identify. In the center of the floor was a massive cargo elevator he assumed led downstairs, though it – like the rest of the city – didn't have power. On both sides of the warehouse were stairwells leading down, and he locked the deadbolts to each, checking through the square windows for signs of people. Satisfied the floor was relatively secure, he continued exploring until he found a side office at the front side of the building with a desk and a plush office chair. James locked the door behind him, shrugged off his pack, and dumped it on the desk next to a dead computer monitor. He took off his jacket and hung it from a coat rack in the corner behind the door before going to the window and checking the street through a crack in the thick curtains, his high position affording him a view across the surrounding buildings' rooftops. It was difficult to make out anything in the torrential rains, but there was an occasional shadow that ducked and moved along the alleys, thin shapes huddled beneath tarps and pieces of vinyl that flapped in the wind, refugees covering themselves from the rain as they sought shelter from the inevitable violence that lurked around every corner.

James exhaled deeply, feeling – at long last – some measure of safety. "Should be okay here for a while. Got to catch my breath... figure out what to do next."

James placed the revolver and staff on the corner of the desk, along with his flashlight turned to the lowest setting. He stripped off his shoes and socks, draping them over chair backs and filing cabinets, followed by his wet jeans and underwear. His skin was clammy cold as he stood there naked, but he found a dry towel tucked deep down in his backpack and patted every inch of himself dry, drawing the cloth down his face with a wince, smearing it with blood from some cut or scrape he'd just reopened.

Tossing the towel on the desk, he put on a loose gray jogging bottom, sweatshirt, and a thick pair of socks he'd gotten from the refugee camp. The garments were too big for him, but their warmth and comfort made his eyelids droop. Shaking the weariness off, he dug out his first aid kit and took care of the wounds on his hands and forearms, the result of the first of the alley attackers who'd pulled a knife on him and got a couple of swipes in before James had managed to use his staff to put a sizeable dent in the man's skull. One cut on his left arm could have used stitches, but he settled for cleaning it out with some antibacterial cream and used several butterfly bandages to press the wound closed before wrapping it in gauze and medical tape.

His knuckles were raw and bleeding from punching the other man's jaw and getting scraped on the cobblestones, and he cleaned those with some wet wipes and applied antibacterial cream and bandages to the more significant cuts while leaving the raw spots alone to save on supplies. As his body began to warm after being out in the cold rain for so long, he started feeling better, and after finding a small mirror in one of the desk drawers, he rested it against a brass lamp, and attended to his facial wounds, covering the end of the flashlight with a sock to further mute the glow.

The man looking back at him had changed. His face was thinner, his eyes dark and ringed with bruises and bags, and a grayish-brown scruff was growing around his jaws and neck, creeping up to his cheeks. He attended to the cuts and scrapes as best as he could, trying to avoid thinking too hard about where each one had come from. He couldn't guess at the miles he'd fought across since Denver. At times, it seemed like fate was giving him a reprieve, but the majority of the time seemed as though it was throwing obstacles in his way on purpose, tripping him up every step of the way, pushing him two steps back for every one he took. *Especially the last few days*, he thought. *What the hell is the world even coming to?*

When he touched an especially bruised spot on his cheek, pain blossomed through to the bone, and he sucked air through his teeth until it began to fade. As James worked against the pain, he thought of Alice and the kids, trying to remember what their voices sounded like. Every wince was soothed by Sarah's laughter, and the burning cuts cooled by Alice's touch. The deep, aching bruises that made him want to quit were eased by one of Jake's jokes or encouragement. Staying positive wasn't for him – it was for them, that simple truth hardening his resolve. No one would stop him from getting home and finding them, even if the entire world conspired to try and foil his plans.

He finished cleaning up and collapsed back into the office chair, listening to the rain and the soft drip of his clothes on the office carpet. When he felt energized enough to stand again, James got the box of bullets out of his jacket and placed them next to the revolver. The box was only three-quarters full, giving him about thirty-five rounds to work with. His staff was still in good shape, though, and he used the already dirty rag to clean the dirt and bits of gore that were stuck in the small gaps between its sections, recalling how many times over the last three days the simple tool had saved his life. The pack had some tears and was covered in dirt, water and blood but was none the worse for wear, and he lined up what remained of his supplies on the desk: another change of clothes, some dry socks and underwear, a pair of boots he'd found in his size, a half-dozen MREs, and a well-used water filtration straw. The first aid kit, a box of assorted bandages and gauze, and a small bottle of pain pills rounded out his medical supplies. As he put everything neatly back, a low growl of hunger rumbled through his guts, and he reached inside for an MRE.

He tore the package open, ripped the inner bag, and placed the contents in a neat row in front of him. He started with the oatmeal cookie, liberating it from its pouch and taking a bite, eyes closed as the sweetness overwhelmed him. After two more bites, he put the beef and beans packages into the flameless ration heater, poured a small amount of water inside, and sealed and shook it, setting it aside.

James contemplated not making the orange drink because he didn't want to waste his remaining water, but he'd been going on empty for days, and the calories of the powdered beverage were sorely needed. Plus, with it raining out, he could stay hydrated with his drinking straw until he found a new source. He mixed a half bottle of water and the orange powder and drank it as he walked around the room with the sock-dimmed flashlight, looking over the generic office paintings, curiously drawn to a display of framed maps showing various parts of the city including marked business districts and famous restaurant spots.

Something familiar piqued his memory, and he squinted at a map of the warehouses. "Hey, I remember a few of these streets. I passed them on the way here."

James placed the beverage pouch down, took all of the map pictures off the wall, turned them over, and removed the backings. He spread them on the desk, taking up the entire surface area, and dug around in a drawer for a pencil. Using his flashlight, he marked the spots he remembered and traced his location to a warehouse on South Winton Street, right in the middle of the warehouse district that stretched several blocks in every direction. The vast spread of buildings that surrounded him was disheartening, but knowing exactly where he was felt like progress, and the trapped feeling lifted from his shoulders as he began tracing potential paths out of the area.

James ate his meal with the maps as companions, chewing absently as he focused on two paths that could keep him off the main streets and out of trouble. He looked them over again and again, checked any potential side routes and marking off odd-shaped corners that might have stores or gas stations. While those spots would likely be destroyed, it was possible there could be some food left lying in the streets or ruined husks of buildings – or perhaps they hadn't gone up in flames at all. *Just need to get out of this damn city,* he thought. *Then I can reassess my situation.*

After he finished his meal, James sat back in the desk chair with the maps in front of him, resting his eyes for a few moments, the time creeping past with nothing but the rain coming down in sheets and the soft sounds of the creaking building as if ghosts roamed the halls.

CHAPTER FOUR

Ryan Cooper
Somewhere Outside East Lansing, Michigan

Ryan wore thick leather gloves as he picked up the last piece of broken glass from the floor and placed it in a bucket along with the rest. He pulled shards of the windowsill off as well, big chunks split by bullets he and Helen had fired down at the intruders the prior evening. A cool breeze blew into the wide-open dining room, whistling through the cracks between some of the boards that he had yet to pull off, blowing his graying hair around his head. An enormous pile of bloody rags sat heaped on the floor, used to soak up the crimson pools that had been on the hardwood, the crusty parts scrubbed off with soft cleaning brushes. The vacuum and wet vac sat to the side along with bottles of cleaner, floor polish, and a bucket of Helen's homemade cleaning formula they had soaking into the carpet.

"I can't believe how much damage we did to the place," he spoke as he put the glass aside and picked up the plywood piece he'd cut to replace the window. "I'm almost tempted to look around town for a new window in some of those ruins."

"That sounds way too dangerous, dear." Helen replied.

"Nah, I'm just kidding. We'll settle for plywood and an apology to the kids when they get home. This is a *lot* of damage to the place."

Helen was repairing the walls with patching plaster, filling in the bullet holes and using a putty knife to smooth them out. "It seemed way worse from where I was standing. So much noise with the gunfire and dogs barking." She wiggled her pinky finger inside her left ear. "If I wasn't hard of hearing before, I certainly am now."

Ryan laughed. "My ears are still ringing, too. Those earplugs we used sucked." Most of the furor of the battle had worn off for the dogs, and they'd gone back to lying on their dog beds after receiving baths in a big tub in the backyard. While Duchess and Diana rested in the living room, Duke got up from his bed and went back to patrolling with a heavy limp, watching the front door and windows, licking his mouth where faint traces of blood still stained bits of his fur.

"Poor Duke," Ryan said. "Big guy hurt his shoulder pretty bad last night. He must've landed wrong."

"Well, he did go flying off the foyer rail and land on that man. I'm surprised he's not got something broken."

"I wonder if we should wrap his leg or something?"

Helen shrugged. "I don't know. He came running when I made him a special breakfast with eggs and extra gravy mixed in with his dog food. I don't think he's as hurt as you think he is."

Ryan gave the dog a skeptical look. "Is that true, boy? Are you just pining for attention?" Duke chuffed and wagged his tail. "I wouldn't put it past him," Ryan chuckled. "He must really think he's a hero after all that."

"He's definitely a hero. And a ham, too."

Ryan picked up the large square piece of wood and fitted it where the window used to be. He put his left shoulder against it to hold it in place, then drove screws in with a power drill through the wood and vinyl sides of the windowframe, moving from the top right corner all the way around, placing twelve screws in total.

"That should just about do it," he said, pressing on the wood.

"It'll be nice to keep the draft out. Been chilly this morning."

"I'll kick the furnace on and get the house warmed up a bit once we finish up. Isn't it absurd that we're sitting here patching bullet holes after everything that's happened in the world?"

"Well, we've always said we should leave a place better off than we found it." Helen focused on the last couple of holes, working in the patching plaster and smoothing it as perfectly as she could. "I'd never forgive myself if we left the house a mess for Alice and James to come home to."

"I think they'll understand if we don't have everything in tip-top shape." He raised an eyebrow. "I think we'll get most of it in order, but these windows are hopeless."

Helen laughed. "I wonder what replacement ones would cost?"

"Insurance'll cover it... well, if there's even insurance left at all."

Helen fell quiet for a moment, her expression turning worried.

"What's on your mind, honey?"

"I'm just... thinking about all the changes we'll be making in the coming months and years if this really as bad as it seems. Especially when all we used to talk about was our retirement, savings, and medical coverage in our golden years."

Ryan took off his gloves and embraced her, pulling her away from the wall and holding her close against him. She put her cheek on his chest and wrapped her arms around him, squeezing him hard as he replied.

"We shouldn't just assume all that's gone now. The world's been turned upside down, but never underestimate the ability for human beings to rebuild. It's just going to take some time. There'll be organization again. I mean, shoot, if anything, you can count on taxes to never go away. Just wait till the IRS wants their money next year... they'll find a way to fix things up, you'll see."

Helen smiled at him, then sighed. "It just seems impossible to salvage anything good in all this."

"I don't care about any of that other stuff anyway." Ryan gave her an extra squeeze. "As long as I'm still here with you, I'm happy. We'll figure the rest out."

"You're right. I'm sorry. I'm usually the positive one."

"We pick each other up, Helen. That's just what we do. Are you okay?"

"I am now." Breaking away from Ryan, she went back to patching, finishing the last hole and shaking her head. "Did you expect the neighbors to attack us so hard like they did?"

"I was a little surprised that they didn't give up after we shot a couple of them. They certainly were tenacious. I guess it's easier when you're attacking strangers. Makes me wonder if we shouldn't have gotten to know the neighbors around here a little better." Ryan scratched his head and glanced toward the front door. "Kinda hard to do that when we only come by for visits once in a while, though. The two dead ones I pulled out of the yard this morning... I've never seen them before."

"Me neither. I guess I expected them to be more like Mike. He seemed appreciative that we helped his family put out that fire in their garage, in spite of how he was watching us. Who knows where they got off to? He wasn't with the ones who attacked us last night, was he?"

"I didn't see him," Ryan shrugged, "but anybody's got the potential to be nice or mean. They can be sneaky and even deadly when a situation goes south." He pointed toward the patched bullet holes that would eventually need sanding and repainting. "And we've got the damage to prove it. Let that be a lesson to us never to underestimate anyone."

Helen stooped to pick up the pile of bloody rags lying off to the side. "Well, I'll take all these dirty rags into the laundry room and start washing them. Do you think we'll have enough power to do that?"

"Let me limp downstairs and switch off the freezers and refrigerator circuits to be sure. The food will be fine in there for a few hours. Should give you enough time to run a few loads through the washer, and I'll hang them up to dry later."

Ryan headed down to the breaker box, with Diana getting up to follow him like usual. Once he'd switched off the freezers and refrigerator, he came back upstairs, wincing with every step as lancing pain shot through his stiff calf. He met Helen in the laundry room, helped her separate out the stained rags, and put in the first load, the washer starting up without any issues.

"It looks like our power plan works pretty well, but I need to get the rest of those solar panels up today. If my napkin math is correct, another row will give us all the power we need to run more things during the day."

"Well, shouldn't we conserve power, anyway? Keeping the refrigerators and freezers off at certain times of the day would be okay, wouldn't you say?"

"Eh, once we've got the extra panels up, we should only have to turn things off at night. They should eliminate power lags or losing it completely when we least expect it."

Helen looked out through a narrow window in the laundry room as they sorted through the rest of the rags and some garments at a long laundry table. "Do you think they'll attack again?"

Ryan laughed morbidly. "After the ass-kicking we gave them, I doubt they'll be by again for a while."

"And you said we shouldn't underestimate people."

"The drubbing we gave them should give us time to rebuild our defenses for when they *do* try again. Replacing or covering all the windows with wood would be a lot better. If I can find enough scraps, I might just do it. It's probably unnecessary right away, though. Another thing..." Ryan stopped sorting and gazed upward.

"What is it?"

"No matter how much we bolster the lower-level windows, they could still climb up and enter through the top floor if we ever had a slip-up in our watch rotations. A nice tall ladder and someone could sneak in and we'd never see them coming."

"Oh, my," Helen raised an eyebrow. "I hadn't thought of that."

"If we have time and materials, I may try to do something there. In any case, I'll head to the barn to get the tractor out and finish hooking up the solar panels. And we've still got to finish a few chores out in the yard before the day is through."

"Should we do something about the bodies soon?"

"Do we have to?"

"Yes, we do. We have to give them a proper burial."

Ryan scoffed. "It just doesn't seem necessary."

"What's not necessary?"

"People come on our property to die, and suddenly it's our responsibility to bury them *proper?*"

She slapped him gently on the shoulder. "Oh, Ryan. I know that, but we have to do it. It's the right thing to do, no matter who they are."

"We'll do right by them," he nodded, "but they take second priority to us keeping the place running. Speaking of which, the animals need to be fed. Can you handle that while I work on the panels?"

"Of course. Let me get this mess sorted, and I'll be right out."

"Thanks." Ryan rested his forehead on her shoulder and hugged her waist. "I appreciate everything you do. We make a great team, and I'm proud of how we fought last night." He sighed sadly. "I'm not happy we killed people; I feel it weighing on my soul already. But they pressed our backs to the wall, and we had no other choice. I'm confident that in my heart of hearts, we did the right thing."

Still with stained rags in her hands, Helen half turned and kissed him on the cheek. "You're my rock, Ryan. I don't know what I'd do without you."

With a lingering smile, he returned to the dining room for his jacket, rifle, and magazines. He'd cleaned the blood off everything, putting one magazine into the gun and the other into his right pocket. His pistol was still holstered, and he carried two spare magazines for that in his left pocket, giving him plenty of ammunition to handle any trouble in the yard. Exiting through the back, he walked past their EV and sacks of harvested food, testing his weight on his injured calf which still radiated a deep ache despite doubling up on pain medication and trying his best to favor it as much as possible.

In the barnyard, hungry animals harried him in expectation of being fed. "It's not my job today, guys," he grumbled, stepping past the bleating sheep and goats who tried to follow him inside the barn. "Go on! Get out of here! Yah!"

Bessie lowed in greeting as he stepped in, and he promised her

Helen would be out to milk her soon. Ryan reattached the forklift to the tractor, then backed it out slowly, waiting for the animals to meander out of his way, then headed through the barnyard gate and closed it behind him so the animals didn't follow him down to the house. Halfway there, Helen came out, carrying her rifle and pistol, her light grey hair pinned back in a tight bun.

"Oh, aren't you a sight?" He called over the steering wheel as she strode by with Duchess on her heels.

She grinned and waved as he pulled up slowly to the solar panels and lowered the forks, then climbed down and grabbed the box of extra panels where they leaned against the house next to the post hole digger and quick drying cement. Taking up where he'd left off the previous day, he spaced out spots to dig more holes, filled them with cement powder and water, mixed it all up, and used tension strings to hold the poles in place.

After a few hours of dirty, sweaty work, he was ready to mount the panels. Helen was still working out in the barnyard, talking to the menagerie as she finished tossing feed to them before giving him a distant wave and going inside to milk Bessie. While the last of the cement dried, Ryan did a quick walk of the grounds, patrolling around the house past the harvested fields where the stalks and vegetation they'd pulled out lay brown and wilting. He strode out front to the trees where he'd placed the area traps and kicked up several spiked pieces of wood and hose with blood on them where the intruders had trampled.

Gathering up the pieces, he placed them back on their respective spots and lifted the wooden garden stakes so they were pointed up again. The attackers knew where the traps were, and Ryan figured they'd try from a different direction next time, but any chance to inflict pain on those trying to harm him and his wife was worth taking. For the next attack, he'd make sure to cover the sides and more of the backyard as well. The only true weakness he saw was that someone could try for the animals first to lure them out into an ambush, and it might behoove them to keep the animals locked up inside the barn at night, unless, of course, that just gave someone an opportunity to get at the animals when they were in a confined space, in which case....

Ryan took a deep breath, trying to stop the torrent of thoughts and what-ifs that kept surging through his mind. "First things first. One thing at a time."

He paused at the front of the house where the four dead bodies were piled up, pale faces staring at the sky; at least the two with faces *left* were staring at the sky. The pair Duke and Duchess had torn into looked like something from a horror movie, flesh flayed off their heads, chunks taken out of their arms and hands from trying to fend off the dogs. Ryan couldn't look at them for too long without feeling his breakfast trying to come up. They were already attracting bugs and starting to give off a foul scent, so he'd have to do what Helen asked and bury them soon. *Course, if I had it my way*, he thought, *I'd put you all on stakes at the front gate to show the neighborhood what we do to thieves and would-be murderers.*

With a sneer at the cluster of corpses, he circled the house and returned to the solar panel work, using the forks to raise each panel into place, finally bolting them to the frame. Once set, he pulled the pin beneath each one, adjusting the angle so they lay in a flat layer with the others, and locked them tight. Stepping away, he checked that they were perfectly level then used the levers at the end of the rows to shift them forty-five degrees toward the south and east and then back flat again, which gave him the ability to angle them as the sun arched through the sky.

Ryan got the bag of cables and crawled beneath the panels, plugging the cables in and running them along the frame system. He clipped them neatly into the wire holders and wiggled on his back, repeating the procedure until he reached the far end and plugged them into the unit's control box. Ryan crawled from beneath the panels, stood, and dusted himself off, then hurried inside and went into the basement to James' workshop with Diana jumping on his heels. A small door built into the west wall led to the cramped battery room, watertight and filled with stacks of batteries against the north wall. A cabling conduit branched up from the batteries and angled to the right where it connected with the main line in from the solar panels. Using a multimeter and a specialized controller James had set up on the battery rack, Ryan tested all the terminals for incoming current and grinned when the indicator shot through the roof on every single one on the very first try.

"That's more input that I thought we'd ever get, girl," he told Diana, who watched him curiously from the doorway. "There should be more than enough juice to keep a solid flow to the batteries. Let's go tell Helen, okay girl? C'mon!"

Helen was just coming in from the chicken coops with a basket of eggs and Duchess by her side when he got upstairs. "The solar panels are looking pretty good. Are we drawing any more power?"

"Absolutely." He grinned. "We'll need to let the batteries charge for a while so we've got power for tonight, but we'll be able to run the fridge, freezers, and lights, and have limited heat through the HVAC, too. And, shoot, it's cloudy out right now. Imagine how much power we'll generate on sunny days!"

"Oh, that's wonderful, Ryan." Helen's grin widened as she stared at the solar panels from the doorway. "Does that mean we'll be able to take some hot showers too?"

"The pump on top of everything else'll push things to its limit, and we do need to conserve the propane unless I can somehow source an electric water heater in the future... but yes, we should be good. Do you need any help with the chores?"

"We could use the tractor or ATV to bring down the milk, but other than that, I've got everything done."

"Great. Want to have a late lunch before we finish up?"

"I'd *love* that."

Before lunch, Ryan went downstairs to turn on the water heater, grinning when the flames popped on and the metal casing ticked as it heated up. Back upstairs, he got cleaned up as Helen got out a pan and a can of soup from the pantry, heating it up before starting on a pot of coffee as Ryan went over his list.

"Here's what I want to do," he said, holding up the notepad. "Bolster the upstairs windows so we have some concealment in case we're shot at again, set some more area traps around the sides of the house and barn, and start putting the animals inside every day."

"Anything else?"

"We'll start with burying those would-be thieves the first chance we get. They're starting to attract bugs and probably animals soon. The last thing we need is coyotes running around here gnawing on the bodies. Wouldn't be good for the chickens."

"And it's the right thing to do."

"Yes, exactly."

"I'll help, of course." Helen finished heating the food and brought two bowls and utensils over to sit across from him. They ate vegetable soup and stale crackers, then Ryan ran the faucet in the kitchen sink, smiling back at Helen as the warm water hit his sore hands.

"Heyyy, we have hot water again, honey."

She rose and squeezed his shoulder. "Thank you so much."

"Don't thank me. Thank James and Alice for having such a great setup. Those two picked a prime spot to settle down on with the well, and they've got a great well-pump." He gave Helen a brief hug, then gestured. "You go ahead. Have yourself a shower. Not a ton of hot water in the heater yet, but it'll be better than ice-cold sponge baths or shutting off half the house just to run the well pump for an ice-cold shower."

"I don't care if it's just lukewarm; a shower sounds like Heaven to me," she replied, kissing him on the cheek and heading for the master bathroom.

Ryan made a quick trip to the barn while she was inside, firing up the ATV to bring the milk down where he placed it just inside the door on the kitchen's gray tiles. Then, he put all his tools away and drove the ATV back to the barn. With gloves on, he dragged the man Helen had shot the previous day to the ATV, straining as he lifted the body and laid it across the cargo tray.

Helen would no doubt be mad at him for not letting her help, but there was no way he wanted her to have to suffer with the images of the mutilated, bloating bodies any more than she already had. As soon as he could, he'd dig the holes for them and drop them in. Helen could help with the finishing touches if she wanted, but he'd spare her the worst of it, if he could.

Ryan drove the first body to the east side of the property and dumped it at the edge of the woods, then went for the others. Soon, all five were piled up next to the woods, and Ryan put the ATV away and walked back to the house with a worsening limp, his calf stiffening and tight.

Back in the kitchen, he poured himself a cup of coffee with shaking hands and sat heavily at the table, a wave of nausea hitting him deep in his gut, more strongly than he'd ever experienced. His whole body was shaking, and he nearly spilled the coffee three separate times as he sipped on it, breathing deeply to try and return a sense of calm. After a few moments, he returned to his notepad, going over his list of things to do, crossing off a few he'd completed and bringing new ones up as priorities, trying to forget the bodies and their gruesome faces. By the time Helen finished with her shower, Ryan was wired from the caffeine and feeling better.

"How was it?"

"Heavenly," Helen replied, moving to the coffeemaker and pouring herself a cup. She'd laid a towel around her shoulders, and her wet, gray hair lay over it. "Water pressure fluctuated off and on, but I could get used to regular showers again."

"Mm... might need to tweak the power, then, if the pump's shutting off a lot." He gestured at his list. "In the meantime, I'll be able to knock a few of these things out before dinner."

She sat across from him with the steaming cup. "First thing we need to do is get you a shower and change that bandage. Trust me, honey, it's worth every second. The warm water will do wonders for your joints and muscles."

"Mm." He continued looking at the notepad. "I don't doubt it."

Helen reached across and placed her hand on the notepad, turning it around to look at it before pushing it back. "With everything we've gone through in the past few days, you should settle down and rest a bit. I don't know about you, but I barely got any sleep last night."

Ryan frowned and tapped his pen on the table. "I didn't sleep that well either, but I can't help but keep working on this stuff."

"We've got plenty of food and water for now," Helen insisted.

"*Hot* water, too."

"Warm," Ryan countered. "And that might not be for all that long unless I can do something to convert from propane to electric."

"That's what I mean, hon. Instead of worrying about the hard things that could take days or weeks or months, why don't you think of one or two things we can do together *tonight* before we start our shifts? Nothing too hard or strenuous. We need to take a bit of a break. I feel beat to heck, and I know you do, too."

"Okay," he sighed, shoulders slumping. "I'll take it easy tonight."

She took his pen out of his hand. "Trust me. You'll feel a hundred percent better, then we can talk about what to do next."

"It might be nice to make it safe to turn on lights in the bedroom. We'd need to put some coverings over the windows to keep any light from leaking out."

Helen smiled and patted his hand. "I'll look for some curtains and blankets while you get cleaned up. Now, get on up there. I'll watch things down here."

Ryan shifted in his seat, unable to give up on the list of responsibilities he'd made for himself, reaching for the list again, though Helen pulled it out of his reach.

"Go, mister. Upstairs. Now."

"Oh, all right."

Ryan finished his coffee, stood, and went upstairs, peeling off the old, sweaty clothes he'd been wearing for days, tossing them in a basket and heading into the bathroom. A mist still clung to the mirror and shower door, and it smelled like shampoo and soap. Ryan peeled off the bandages he'd accumulated, wincing when he pulled the one off his calf, bringing some hair with it. The bullet wound was puckered, pink, and clean, and showed no signs of infection, Helen's stitches still holding strong, but the muscles were stiff, the skin tender and bruised all the way around.

Stepping into the shower, he turned on the hot water and raised his face to the sharp spray, abrasions and cuts stinging as he washed away the dirt and grime, trying to scrub away the memories of barking, snarling dogs, gunshots, and the torn-up, shot-up bodies lying on the east side of the property.

CHAPTER FIVE

Ray Sider
Paris, France

Smoke rose above the streets of Paris, congealing in a thick, desolate fog the midday sun could not penetrate. The once beautiful city, the cultural heart of Europe, bled like a burst abscess, its edges black and oozing dirty water from broken pipes, creating a sludge that spread over everything, clogging the sewer system and giving off a reek so foul that not even scavengers wanted to go near it. The city's buildings lay split open and bombed out by strings of explosions thanks to an endless supply of delivery trucks, public transport vehicles and cars that had crowded the streets. Though most of the two million residents had perished in the flames, the ruins crawled with small groups of survivors, scavenging for morsels to keep them alive.

In the Saint Germain neighborhood, Ray Sider and his new companions were picking through the husk of a restaurant, digging up the rubble beneath an open sky, turning over corpses, checking pockets, and looking for anything edible that might've survived the explosions. They were a mixed group of American and Japanese tourists that had been on a walking tour, along with several French citizens who'd been fortunate enough to make it out alive when the end came.

"Anything, Jiro?" he asked.

Jiro stood from the rubble of a server's station with a broken cash register and a partial wall of shelves. He responded in Japanese and shook his head helplessly, shrugging and holding his hands out.

"I'll take that as a no," Ray replied, looking around as Gemma and Sara picked at what appeared to be a buffet bar with a wilted plastic cover. They were Americans, like Ray, missing a father and husband who'd lost his life when a piece of debris had smashed through a café window and embedded in his face.

Ray walked over, smiling at little Sara as she picked up a metal serving tray and flipped it to reveal a pile of charred biscuits that had turned to charcoal. She looked up at him with smears of soot on her face.

"Not much there, huh?"

"Nope."

"You're standing in mud," Ray said. "Here, give me your hand."

He helped Sara out of the mud and gave her to her mother. "Here you go."

"Thanks," Gemma laughed. "She can't seem to stay clean around here."

Ray gestured at his soiled tennis shoes and smiled hesitantly. "None of us can. No matter how much we try."

Gemma wiped the smudges off Sara's cheeks, stood, and frowned. "We've been at this for hours and have barely found a thing to eat."

"Well, we have to keep trying," Ray replied. "There's nothing else we can do until help gets here."

Gemma rolled her eyes. "It's been days, Ray. There won't be any help coming. The entire world is like this."

The complex Parisian architecture of a church across the square was gone, the lines of gothic arches and stained-glass windows blown to pieces. Pews inside had burned like kindling, spreading glowing cinders for blocks in every direction and helping lay the city aflame.

The sharp spike of the Abby of Saint Germain des Pres two blocks away had split, its top half crumbled, leaving a sliver of concrete and stone jutting up.

Tears brimmed in his eyes as Ray stared at the damaged ruins. "I was just there with Julie the day before everything went up. She loved that place. She... loved all the gothic churches. We were supposed to be here another week."

"I'm sorry about your wife," Gemma said.

"And I'm sorry about Steven."

"Ray!" Another voice cut in.

Jiro was standing on the other side of the restaurant with some of their new French friends. Beside a decorative fountain were a pair of lopsided swinging doors leading to the kitchen, hanging crooked on their hinges. Jiro said something in Japanese, and when Ray only shrugged, he frustratedly mimed putting food in his mouth and pointing at the doors.

"Okay, sure. Bound to be something to eat in there."

Jiro climbed over some garbage to join Paul, pressing on the door but only getting it to move an inch or two.

"Is it stuck?" Ray asked, coming over. The section still had a ceiling, and the walls were intact but crumbling. He didn't see another way in unless they wanted to go around.

Jiro gestured, and Paul said something in French, but pounded his fist against his palm and nodded toward the doors.

"Yeah, yeah. We need to break it down. Stand back." Ray waved them away. "Give me some room."

Ray was bigger than the two men by a foot and a half and fifty pounds, with meatier shoulders and an overall larger frame. As the members of their group gathered around, he laughed. "I was a lineman in high school, and I blocked guys way tougher than these doors."

Jiro and Paul shared a confused look while Ray prepared to charge.

"Don't hurt yourself, Ray," Gemma said.

Yua shook her head, seeming to agree with the gist of Gemma's tone, and Paul and Anna held hands and watched with concern.

"I won't. Don't worry about old Ray."

Ray launched himself at the doors, striking them, knocking whatever was blocking them back a good three inches. He held his stinging shoulder, walking away from the doors while giving them a side-eyed glance. "One more time should do it."

On his second attempt, he gave it his all and slammed the doors hard, plowing the blockage aside so the doors swung fully back, knocking into a cart and banging against the wall. Jiro pumped his fist and grinned, and the rest of the group followed Ray in as he rolled his arm, rubbing it and looking around. It was like any other kitchen he'd ever worked in, except it looked as though a fire-laden tornado had torn through the place.

Toppled shelves and garbage lay everywhere, most of it at least partially burned up, but there were several untouched cans of tomato sauce, olives, and moldy cheese lying around. Paul held out his sack, and Anna started putting things inside while the rest spread out and kept searching. Ray continued to hover near Gemma and Sara, their shared language and country of origin making it far more comfortable to communicate with the pair over the hand signals and charades with the others. Checking in another area of the kitchen back by the walk-in refrigerators, he grabbed one handle and tried to jerk it open, but it was stuck. Bracing himself with his foot against the edge, he tried again, yanking it wide and releasing a belch of fetid air that singed his nose and twisted his stomach with nausea.

"Oh, that's disgusting," Gemma said, waving her hand in front of her face. "Smells like rotten food."

Ray shined his flashlight inside and swallowed hard, shutting the door as they came up. "Uhhh... yeah, that's what it is. Just a bunch of rotten food. Nothing else. Nothing to salvage."

"We should go through it anyway," Gemma insisted, reaching for the handle. "You never know what we'll find."

Ray winced. "You *really* don't want to go inside. All that rotten *food*. Trust me on that."

Gemma mouthed "bodies" at him questioningly and he nodded, then she quickly pulled Sara in the other direction.

"Yeah, you two go over there," Ray said, "and I'll check the rest of the walk-ins."

"Bingo," Jiro called from a pantry area, pointing at a box of crackers Yua held.

Yua dug open the top, frowning as she pulled out a small bag with just a few broken crackers and some crumbs at the bottom. She shook it sadly, then poured the remaining crackers in one hand, crossing the kitchen to Sara, kneeling in front of her and holding them out.

"You don't have to do that, Yua," Gemma said, though she didn't try to stop Sarahwhen she reached for the crackers and ate them hungrily while everyone watched with sad smiles.

"Eat all, please," Yua said in broken English.

Gemma wiped some crumbs off her daughter's chin. "There you go. See, things aren't quite so bad now! What do you say?"

"Thank you!" Sara looked up at Yua as she spoke, cracks of clean skin showing through the thick layers of dirt as she smiled broadly in thanks.

Across the room, Paul and Jiro found several trays of expensive-looking cutlery, stashing them in their pockets and handing Ray the steak knives. He put them in an extra-thick sack they'd picked up specifically for collecting sharp objects and tucked one under his belt. Plates and bowls had spilled across the floor, but they ignored them, having more than enough dishware back at camp.

After a while, they finished picking through the restaurant ruins and were standing back outside again where gray clouds crept across the sky, a distant scream or the sound of an explosion or gunfire occasionally punctuating the city's silence, sounds they'd gotten used to over the past several days. They were only worth worrying about if they got too close, and if that happened Ray had promised to form up a defensive team to go investigate and run off any would-be attackers.

Ray scratched his head and pointed to the sky. "Come on. The sun will be down soon, and we don't want to be out in the dark."

They packed up the meager supplies they'd collected since starting their scavenging earlier in the morning and prepared for another long walk. Ray's legs and shoulders ached, head throbbing from sadness and worry, yet he held it all back behind a grim face. He told himself it was for the others, playing the part of the big dumb American brave enough to run off marauders and show leadership when the others broke down. In reality it was for Julie, the memory of her, and knowing she would want him to keep going in spite of everything, just to help those around him.

Ray was walking point, as he always did, as the sun began to set over the ruins of the city, bringing another deep night when the real predators would come out, the ones that couldn't be frightened off by screaming at them. They were the ones who'd practically gone feral and would stab you and strip your body while you were still breathing for nothing more than crumbs and the fun of it.

"Hanging in there, Ray?" Gemma asked, suddenly next to him with Sara walking beside her.

"Yeah, absolutely." He nodded and smiled, blinking back a wave of emotion and moving faster to get ahead of them as their faces were suddenly replaced by those of his wife and child.

Halfway home, Ray spotted another group encroaching from the west, about the size of their own, but with several big men standing on the periphery as the rest scavenged through the skeleton of a building. He'd seen the group before, skirting the edges of their territory and eyeing their camp in the park. As they learned over the days, attacking a smaller group was not a guarantee of success, and fights had left the combatants bruised and beat up. With basic medical supplies difficult to come by, two people had already died from scratches that had gotten infected. A simple cough could turn into pneumonia, and eating rotten food could bring stomach illnesses that could put someone down for days – or permanently. It was best to avoid confrontation altogether and only attempt to steal or scavenge from another group when the odds were heavily in their favor.

Still, Ray put up a bold front, and he stood in the middle of the road with Jiro and Paul, each wielding splintered sticks or pieces of sharp metal, knives tucked into their belts, glaring at the other group as they stared back, the two parties keeping a respectable distance. Ray was reminded of an old stray cat he and Julie used to feed off their porch for five or six years. They'd cared for the cat as best they could, named him, and got him neutered and kept him well-fed. Still, every night Old Man would come home from roaming the neighborhood with scratches, patches of fur missing, and infections Ray had to get treated and stitched at the vet. Whenever a possum or another tomcat came around, Old Man would stand at the edge of the patio, mewling, hissing, and spitting until his challenger finally gave up. Ray was feeling a lot like Old Man, a beleaguered, beaten-up old tomcat guarding what little he had left in the world, protecting his people and their meager supplies by appearing tough.

It worked, though, and they passed the other group without incident as they walked the Parisian lanes, twelve grubby adults and a couple of kids, carrying sacks of what they'd collected that day over their shoulders, heads down, slouching, feet shuffling beneath the gray skies. Ray took them a different way home to avoid seeing the other group again, and in the narrow cobblestone lanes they stumbled upon a small French market that had escaped most of the burning. The shelves were stripped, and most of the nonperishable goods were gone, but still they spread out through the store while Ray and Jiro kept watch out front. Jiro pointed to the sky with a worried expression, putting his hands together and spreading them.

"I know, man," Ray said. "It's getting late, and we probably should get home. It looks like they're finding a lot of stuff, though. Might be worth sticking around a few more minutes."

Jiro shook his head and formed his arms into a hugging shape, opening and closing the circle, muttering more Japanese.

"Right. We've got to get back to the others soon, or they'll be undefended. I get it, friend." Ray patted him on the shoulder. "Just a few more minutes. It might be the last chance to scavenge this place. We brought in three more mouths to feed, remember?" Ray held up three fingers, and Jiro threw up his hands frustratingly and nodded.

"Ray, look!" Gemma said, coming outside and flashing him a can of expensive French canned meat.

"Fancy." He grinned and held open a sack. "Drop it in. Hey, how much longer do you think you'll be? It's almost dark."

"Just a few more minutes, and we'll call it a day." She went back inside.

Someone found a box of stale animal crackers, which automatically passed to Sara, who ate them on a countertop, grinning and swinging her legs. Just when Ray was starting to worry, his people came outside with the bottoms of their sacks weighted down, smiles on their faces as they finished chewing on bits and bobs they'd found inside, their relief over the found supplies nearly palpable.

Ray had them pick up the pace, marching through narrow alleys and backstreets to reach Rue de Vaugirard. The main thoroughfare circled a massive series of parks and greenery in the middle of the city, the backyard of Luxembourg Palace with its fountains, gardens, tennis courts, and quaint fields of greenery divided by paved walking paths. Turning down Rue Guynemer, they stayed on the left-hand side of the road, where trees grew right up to the road and the brush was overgrowing the sidewalks. Ray watched the thick clusters of apartments and hotels to the west as the last vestiges of sunlight dropped below the horizon, leaving fractal rays of light scattered across the buildings and streets.

Lanterns and flashlights were forbidden for safety's sake, so they took known paths they'd cleared of wreckage and were known to be clear of obstructions. Ray knew the way by heart, and at a certain point, he stepped into the brush, putting his big backside against the rough branches and squeezing them back to give the others room to get by. Jiro led them deeper into the park, and after the last person passed, Ray stayed where he was for a few extra minutes, watching the streets and making sure no one was following them. He dipped inside and took a narrow trail to the main camp, guided by twin points of candlelight up in the tree branches that marked the entrance to their base. If the lights were on, the camp was safe to enter, but if they were out, it meant the camp was jeopardized, and it would be time for Ray and his people to move on. They'd relocated twice before, carrying their supplies to new spots, slipping deeper into hiding each time, starting over and over again.

Ray passed beneath the tree, nodding to the guards in the bushes, drawn by murmuring voices and occasional chuckles. The adults seldom laughed, though Sara and the other children did, the youngest showing incredible resiliency in the face of disaster. Still, the evening's haul had put smiles on everyone's faces, and a giddiness spread through the group like a bolt of lightning in a storm. He hugged and shook hands with several people on the way in, working toward the center of the clearing, the night sky looming over them, the hidden moonlight casting an ambiance that didn't seem hostile for once. Tiny fires dotted the camp, illuminating the field of tents and tarps hanging from poles, raggedy shelters offering a degree of privacy.

They'd opened the sacks and spread them around the camp's central fireplace, a large, circular pit that they made sure kept a low fire going at all times, where they gathered to exchange stories, make plans, and slowly learn each other's languages. A French cook, Gemma, and Anna rifled through the collection, stacking canned goods, separating out powdered meals and giant cans of tomato sauce and processed cheese, and fussing over what to make in the pot. Ray accepted a bottled water from Paul, and the two stood and watched as the meal came together like it often did, most everything going into the single pot, with the French cook standing over it and sprinkling in spices.

At first, Ray had thought there was no way the process could give them edible meals, but the mélange had often made the meal filling and flavorful when the broth was thin and chunks of meat and vegetables were hard to find. Wood went into the fire, and the flames kicked up, bathing the surrounding faces in a warm glow where twenty-five of them sat on old lawn chairs, seats stripped from theaters, bedrolls, bins, stones, and logs. Smudged faces beamed with renewed hope as cans were opened and dumped into the pot and the French cook stood over it, coaxing the flames, bringing the meal to a boil, and stirring it with a big spoon as she sprinkled her spices and worked her magic.

Gemma approached and crossed her arms, keeping watch over Sara as she played with the other camp kids. "We've got a nice little place here for now."

"Yes, we do."

"But we've had to move twice already because bigger groups moved in. What'll we do if they try and come in on this one?"

"We'll keep moving," Ray nodded. "Whatever we have to do to keep everyone alive until help... ah, never mind."

"Do you really think help will come?"

"I have to think the cavalry is coming," Ray grinned hesitantly. "Otherwise, why keep going on?"

"Because it's the only thing we can do?"

"That only gets you through a few days. After that, we need more hope, and we have to get angry and want to do it for those we've lost. Your husband, my Julie..." Ray clamped his mouth shut and pushed away the emotion. "We have to imagine a future where we're not living hand to mouth, and that's all there is to it."

While he hadn't asked her age, he was probably fifteen or twenty years her senior, her like a daughter to him than anything else. She locked arms with him and rested her forehead against his shoulder.

"Thanks, Ray. Sara and I... We can't thank you enough for taking us in."

"Don't mention it," Ray replied, patting her on the arm.

"Water," Jiro spoke hesitantly in English, pointing to a satellite dish in the middle of camp connected to a central pipe that ran to a barrel. Off to the side were several containers they'd filled, though a lot of them were empty, and it hadn't rained hard in a few days. "More buckets."

Paul came up, adding his thoughts in broken English. "Radio says rain."

"Yes, we need some more containers to save water in," Ray agreed. "I saw a bunch of those on the outskirts of our area..." As Ray talked, he made gestures with his hands, using his fingers to draw a perimeter and point to the edge. "Very dangerous past there. We have to be very careful."

"Careful, yes," Jiro nodded, clasping his hands behind his back. "Careful."

"We've been thinking, Ray," Gemma said. "I mean... some of us have been talking."

"Yeah, about what?"

"About what we can do next. You know, the next steps in all this."

"Safety," Jiro nodded in agreement and gestured around.

"Isn't survival enough?"

"It's great, of course," Gemma said, "but some of us wonder how long we can sustain this."

Ray nodded, in fact, had been prepared for such a discussion. "I don't know. This is a pretty good spot. We've got protection and plenty of prime scavenging spots. That's not something we want to give up lightly."

"But people are encroaching on us every day," Gemma pressed. "We keep seeing that same group, and they're getting bigger and bigger. You and I know it's just a matter of time before they attack us."

"We don't know that. We could try to reason with them, join with them."

"Conflict is inevitable, Ray. You know this."

Ray crossed his arms and watched the pot come to a boil, the chef pointing and lining up people to get their share. "Okay, what are you thinking?"

Gemma and Jiro exchanged a look before Gemma continued. "Well, wouldn't the rural areas offer more shelter?"

"Maybe it'll be worse out there."

"It can't be worse. The pickings are getting slim around here."

"Farm," Jiro said, making a square shape with his fingers. "Grow."

"So, you guys want to pick up, head to the country, and start building farms? That tells me you've given up on any chances of rescue."

"Not at all. Look, none of us have a chance of getting home. We haven't seen an airplane or helicopter since all this started. The radio hasn't been helpful at all. For all we know, this thing could stretch on for months or even years. We need to plan for the long haul, not just camp out in the city streets, hoping for a break. We need to make our own breaks."

Ray sized up their expressions of determination, finding an equal measure in all. "All right. Maybe we should get out of the city and find a quiet spot in the country to set up. There's bound to be less competition for resources."

"Farm," Jiro said.

"Right. There's bound to be some good farmland outside the city, but that will be fiercely guarded, too."

"But there would be more of it, and we could use the land to protect it. Hills and valleys and things." Gemma nudged him with her elbow. "Come on, Ray. We could get out in the fresh air and show what we're made of. I grew up on a farm myself, and Paul told me about his family's farm."

"So we're all farmers now?"

"Not farmers yet, but we know enough to get started. You wouldn't have to do anything different. Just keep an eye out on things. Protect us."

A long line had formed, reaching from the big pot to the edge of the woods, the kids all together in a bunch, fidgeting and jostling and laughing with their bowls and spoons clanking. They were happy for the moment but deserved a lot more, and Ray imagined them in a different place, perhaps a barn with a big fire out front, land to play and run in, woods to let their imaginations run wild.

"We'd be packing up and moving everything."

"We know."

"Our supplies are low, so we'd need a lot more to make a journey like that. Possibly thirty or forty miles."

"Fifty, by Paul's estimation. That would put us outside the city and in the surrounding farmlands."

"More danger and more risk."

"You'll protect us."

"You really want to do this?"

"Yes. The parents have all discussed it, and everyone understands what's at stake. We're ready to go."

Ray flexed his arms and shoulders, stunned by the revelation that they all put so much faith in him, concerned he might not have what it would take. "All right. If everyone agrees, we can move to the outskirts. We'll build that farm you want, Jiro."

Jiro nodded and grinned. "Build farm."

"And, who knows, maybe we'll find peace until all this blows over." Looking out across the dilapidated city, Ray had to concede that Gemma was right. It could be months or years more before anyone with any significant resources or power came to help out the people of Paris, and meanwhile the thousands of tourists and residents who had survived would slowly starve and die. "Let's form up a few scavenging groups. We'll need to pull double time if we're going to gather enough food and water to make the trip."

Gemma was beaming at Sara as she came up with a bowl of stew, almost spilling it over the edges before Gemma took it. Around them, other families had taken their food to their seats, sipping on the watery mix of meat and vegetables.

"How long until we can leave?" Gemma asked.

"Inside a week, but we shouldn't wait any longer than that. It's going to get colder before too long, and our chances of making it through this go way up if we find a place before winter hits."

"Sounds awesome, Ray. Thank you." Gemma had a bite of stew and nodded to the French chef appreciatively. "Wow, this is good. I can't wait to start growing our own food. It's just... liberating."

Ray accepted a bowl of stew from another person who held it out to him and they stood in a semicircle, watching the line continue to move.

"All done with mine, Mama," Sara said, holding out her bowl. "Can I have some more?"

The soup spoon was already clanking against the bottom of the pot as the last few people moved through the line, and Gemma shook her head. "Mm. I don't think so, honey. There won't be any seconds today."

"Aww. That's okay," Sara said, lowering her bowl.

Jiro smiled and stepped over to Sara, dumping the bit he had left into her bowl, and the others followed suit, every adult in the group picking a child and offering what they had. Ray took two bites of his own, downing a couple of meat chunks before giving the rest to a little boy sitting off to the side who'd lost his parents.

"Here you go, son," he said, scraping the last bit into his bowl. "Eat up. You're going to need your strength."

69

CHAPTER SIX

Alice Burton
Columbus, Georgia

The engine roared, its exhaust pipes bursting with smoke, belching, choking, and rumbling with diesel fury, but Alice couldn't tell from what direction. Jake and Sarah had already gotten ahead of her, breaking the horses into a sprint with the wind whipping Sarah's hair around. Leaning forward, balancing her weight on her hips and legs, Alice rode hard after them, Buck's hooves pounding the pavement, searching for a way north. She almost missed the service road coming up, hidden as it was behind a thick cluster of brush.

She shouted to the kids before they shot past it. "Jake! Sarah! There's a service road on the side... it's open!"

Alice angled Buck toward it as Sarah yelled at Jake to stop, and they both turned to fall in behind her. Alice turned up the narrow lane and kicked Buck faster toward the curve ahead, hoping to outrun whatever was trying to cut them off. Movement erupted from the tree line to the right where something massive trundled toward them. A white cab with a bright yellow stripe along the side flashed in the trees, followed by a wide steel frame and a big, flat front windshield. Surprised faces stared back at her from the cab as it rounded the bend and cleared the trees, pouring smoke from its exhaust pipe. The street sweeper had two arms with massive round brushes stretching from beneath it, spinning furiously to sweep stones and dirt beneath the frame with a raucous clatter. Large workbaskets had been welded to the sides with four men standing in them, two holding shotguns while the others clung with one hand to crude handrails while brandishing blunt instruments.

She pulled Buck up and rested back in her saddle as the sweeper bore down on them, simultaneously stupefied by the appearance of a working internal combustion powered vehicle and confused that it was a street sweeper. Only the sounds of Jake and Sarah riding up fast broke her from her terrified trance, and she threw her arm out to stop them. They hadn't seen the street sweeper at first, but when they did, they drew their mounts up with surprised cries. The driver and passenger seemed just as surprised to see the four horses as the trio was to see the vehicle, but the driver didn't alter course at all. If anything, he accelerated and turned right at them with the rollers spinning harder, the clatter of stones and pebbles loud in the carriage. The men in the baskets erupted into gleeful cries, pointing at them and slamming their palms on the cab's roof in encouragement. Alice guided Buck to the right, but the driver followed them, barreling down just twenty yards away, the vehicle surprisingly fast.

"Back the other way! Come on!"

Alice turned and raced back to the main highway, cutting hard right onto the road to go west again. Wind blasted her face and blew her hair back, strands whipping across her eyes as the kids rode furiously on her tail, Jake clinging to Hercules' tether where their backpacks and supplies bounced on his sides. In a burst of dust and flying rocks, the street sweeper banked hard onto the highway behind them, its tail sweeping around and throwing the men on the baskets around, the spinning brushes sweeping back and forth, knocking chunks of rubble and debris aside, scattering pieces everywhere. Alice slowed to avoid a pileup, weaving Buck between husks of car frames blocking their way, hooves pounding on the pavement as Sarah and Jake caught up with her, keeping well in front of the churning truck as it rushed toward them.

"We've got to get off the road, Mom!" Jake shouted. "Rocky is having a hard time on the concrete."

"Stormy, too!" Sarah called, breaking left around an economy car.

"I know!" Alice took a sharp angle to avoid a bucket seat in the right-hand lane with a corpse still slumped in it and Buck's hooves slipped and sent Alice's heart leaping into her chest.

"We're heading toward the city, Mom!" Jake shouted. "Shouldn't we stay away from there?"

Alice nodded, catching sight of an opening off to the right. "Follow me!"

She kicked Buck hard and rode him off the shoulder, leaping a ditch to land hard on the other side, shoulders thrown forward with the impact. Falling back into the saddle, she kicked Buck again and crashed through a thicket with a clatter of snapping brush and whipping branches, ducking a split second before a big one almost took her head off, jerking her face aside when a switch cut her chin. She dodged between a pair of massive tree trunks, leaped a log, and burst into a park with circular patches of artificial turf and jungle gyms all around. The grass was soft and green and overgrown, and they trotted across the vast field, angling northwest with the street sweeper's engine fading off to the left.

"What was their problem?" Sarah asked, moving up to her right and galloping smoothly ahead.

"They want to run us over," Jake said exasperatedly, "that's their problem."

"Well, they can't drive through all those trees to get to us," Alice said with relief. "Our best bet is to keep heading north and away from that infernal machine."

She snapped the reins and rode ahead over a baseball field, sprinting through the infield and exiting on the first-base side to head through a parking lot full of debris. Buck leaped part of a dashboard lying on the ground, landing smoothly and trotting by a baseball glove and several aluminum baseball bats sitting amongst the wreckage. They reached a road stretching west to east and stopped to check both ways, Sarah and Jake riding past her, turning their horses in a circle as they helped her search, Jake getting Hercules' tether wrapped around him.

The roar of the street sweeper's diesel engine jolted her stiff in the saddle, and the machine burst from between two city maintenance buildings on the left, turning up dust and pebbles, flying into the road and swerving as it drove right at them. A man in one of the baskets fired a shotgun blast into the air while his partners yelled at Alice and the kids to stop.

"Mom!" Sarah cried as Stormy whinnied and reared on his hind legs, touching down and leaping back the way they'd come on his own, running out across the parking lot toward the baseball field again.

"That way, Jake!" Alice shouted, leaning low over the saddle and urging Buck to go. "H'yah, Buck. Come on!"

The horse snorted and leaped into motion, Alice squeezing her knees as she tried to stay in the seat. Jake did an extra turn on Rocky to get untangled and raced right behind them, flying fast and guiding Hercules with quick tugs on the tether and reins. Another shotgun blast went off, followed by more shouts and whistles for them to stop. Alice ducked as they thundered across the baseball field, thinking they'd gotten away, but the street sweeper turned off the road and into the grass, churning up dirt and mud from its tires as it raced after them.

"Come on!" she growled. "You can't *possibly* follow us this way."

The massive vehicle continued onward, though, bouncing and jostling the men in the baskets as the driver angled across the walking path and rode the sloping hills up into the park, trying to cut them off. By then, Sarah had gotten control of Stormy and was glancing back for instructions and Alice rode up, trying to stay calm as another shotgun blast rocked the sky, the truck's horn bleating at them as the driver screamed out of his window.

"Should we split up, Mom?" Sarah's hair whipped around her head, cheeks rosy-red from the rush.

"No! Let's lead them off that way... to the southwest. Get them caught in some brush and woods, then turn around and run right past them. We can get back to the service road and fly north if we do that."

"Okay, let's go!"

"Stay with us, Jake!"

Determined, Alice leaned low over the saddle and fell into Buck's rhythm, pushing him hard around the edge of the park, flying across walking paths, cresting shallow slopes, and dashing past tennis courts to the wooded area on the other side. The street sweeper stayed nearby, the spinning brushes tearing up grass and dirt and throwing it high into the air, rocks and deadfall sweeping beneath it to rattle around in the undercarriage before spitting out the sides and back. More shotgun blasts chased them into the wooded patch, buckshot striking the trees and shredding leaves to pieces.

The brush was thicker the deeper they went, though, and soon they were forty yards inside, Alice pulling Buck up for a moment, drifting sideways as she watched the truck approach the wooded patch at breakneck speed. The men in the baskets were slamming their hands on the side and top of the truck, yelling for the driver to stop, but the diesel engine only revved louder, the broad front grill plowing right at them. It hit the first line of vegetation with a crunch, one sweeper arm catching a sapling and breaking off with the vicious jolt to the truck's frame, nearly throwing the men out of the baskets. Bushes and brush slapped the front windshield and rocked them back and forth, but the driver was so focused on Alice that he didn't see the magnitude of his predicament.

"Now, kids!"

She leaned forward and kicked Buck all in one motion, clinging to his back as he sprinted away from the high-throttling monster chasing them. They burst from the woods and flew around the tennis courts, heading due east toward the service road again. She raced on, willing Buck to fly faster, hooves pounding the ground in a flowing, powerful locomotion. Wind whipped into her eyes, forcing her to squint and turn her head to the side as his heaving chest worked like a massive furnace beneath her. They were a quarter mile distant when the truck finally reached the edge of the woods, rocking, tires spinning with big chunks of logs and deadfall caught up in its undercarriage, dragging along and slowing it to a near crawl.

A slow smile spread across her face as they flew past the swing sets and kept heading east, working their way through a stand of yellow poplars, weaving around a restroom facility and some basketball courts with the nets torn down. Bursting through the tree line, Buck leaped a shallow ditch and landed heavily on the service road, with the sounds of the other horses' clopping hooves right behind her.

"Whoa, Buck! Are you guys okay?"

Jake flew by without stopping, Hercules trailing behind with his tail flying in the wind. "Yeah! But why are we stopping? Those guys are trying to kill us!"

With a snap of the reins, Alice leaped forward and caught up with Jake, and they galloped north past city buildings, recycling dumpsters, municipal waste management, and the sanitation department. Gravel pathways branched out all around them and wove between the structures, many of them reduced to jagged sections of wall and the vague outlines of foundations to show they'd been buildings at all. At the city mechanic's shop, police vans and cars lay shattered and ripped apart by fuel explosions, parts of their flashing lights strewn across the road. Garbage, scraps of foam seating, and ash skimmed the pavement in front of them as the wind picked up and clouds moved in overhead. They slowed to a trot past the repair shop and came together in a straight line, the horses' sides heaving, heads tossing, snorting and twitching like they wanted to keep running.

Alice turned to an exasperated Sarah who was still panting and clutching her chest in disbelief. "Are you okay, honey?"

"I'm fine! Can you believe those guys, Mom!?"

"We're not out of the woods yet." The distant sound of the sweeper truck revved high and loud. "Come on, this road is turning east, so let's jump into that field there. H'yah, Buck!"

Alice nodded straight ahead and slightly left, angling Buck toward the field. The pavement turned to gravel and then dirt again as they pushed into a low stand of brush, the thin understory tugging at them as they squeezed through. Vines crawled up the tree trunks like they were massive trellises, and the scent of honeysuckle and sharp, bitter vegetation touched their noses. As soon as they were through, they broke into a gallop, crouching in their stirrups as the rain caught up to them and began to drizzle.

The shallow slope took them to a ridge line, giving them a decent view of their surroundings for miles. Alice glanced toward the road, half expecting the sweeper truck to come flying through the trees, dragging sticker bushes, ferns, and bits of deadfall behind them in relentless pursuit, but after a minute of catching their breath and letting the horses walk in peace, Alice turned Buck down the other side.

"Let's get out of here," she said. "The more distance we can put between us and those lunatics, the better."

They continued for another two miles, trotting into the rain, cooling the sweating horses and Alice's burning hot face. Finally, she drew Buck up, turning, laughing nervously as the kids came up behind her. They walked the horses up a moderate slope with spots of brush dotting the landscape as far as they could see and the sun came out through the clouds, golden rays bursting across the fields, turning the rain into a glowing mist.

"Look, Mom," Jake said. "A rainbow!"

Off to the left beneath the clouds, an arc of color spread from one end of the horizon to the other, orange, blue, purple, and green, vibrant against the saturated gray skies, the sweet smell of rain blotting out the ash and smoke as they crested the hill where wide plains stretched all around them. By the time they reached the far side, they were soaked, and Alice guided them into the tree line where they took protection beneath the tree cover.

"Why don't we rest here for a while?" Alice said, halting Buck and dismounting.

As Sarah and Jake got down, she noticed a red spot blossoming on Jake's back. "Son, come here. You've been hit."

"Wait, what?" Jake asked, tying the horses up to an oak branch while he glanced back. "I felt a sting, but it barely hurt."

"Sit down over here."

Alice knelt behind Jake as he took a seat on a rotten log, rolling his shoulder and wincing. "Ow! I guess I did get hit. Is it a bullet?"

She put her fingers through the shirt tear and tore it open, spreading the material and looking at the bloody wound beneath. "Not a bullet. Buckshot." Sliding her fingers over his slick skin, she found where the round pellet was embedded.

"Ouch!"

"Sorry, son."

"It's okay. Is it deep?"

"No. We should get it out as soon as possible and get this cleaned up, though. Sarah, get a first aid kit for me, please."

"On it."

Spreading the kit out next to her, Alice found a large tweezer and some saline rinse, which she sprayed on Jake's skin to reveal the silver lump just beneath the surface. It had made a small crater in his skin, like a miniature comet, the wound puckered and bruised around the impact site.

"Hold a flashlight on it, would you?"

Sarah stood behind her with the light, Jake sucking air through his teeth as Alice sprayed saline on the wound and picked at it with the tweezers. Plucking the piece out, Alice held it up for a moment and tossed it aside, then cleaned the wound more and spread some antibiotic ointment on it. Sarah handed her a bandage, and she dried the wound with gauze before covering it and pressing down with the bandage.

"There you go," she said. "Easy as you please."

"Thanks, Mom," Jake said, standing, rolling his shoulder with a mild wince. "Give me a minute to change my shirt and I'll be ready to ride."

Alice checked out their surroundings as Buck and Stormy found a pond-sized puddle near the trees and put their heads down to drink. "Like I was saying, why don't we just rest here for a while? The horses can drink and graze for a bit, and we can catch our wind."

They stayed just within the tree line, sitting on a couple of logs that were still dry, Sarah getting some snack bars from their packs and handing them out. Jake changed into a black T-shirt, one of their articles of clothing they'd washed during their stay at Nate and Elaine's. Once settled, they sat on the edge of the forest, listening to the rain fall around them with a soft patter on the leaves, drops hitting the forest floor with the shifting of branches and the sighing wind.

"Doing okay?" Alice looked over at her son as he winced and touched his shoulder.

Jake nodded. "It just stings a little. I'll be fine."

"We just need to keep an eye on it and make sure it doesn't get infected. Sarah, you're on duty for that. Make sure your brother gets his dressing changed at least once a day and tell me if it starts looking red and inflamed. You know he'll forget."

"I'm on it," Sarah replied. "Where do you think we are now?"

"I'd guess we're a few miles north of Columbus by now. Hopefully through the worst of it for the time being."

"Yeah, no more people, I hope." Jake snorted.

"No more people with street sweepers," Sarah added.

"What even *was* that?" Jake chuckled. "If they hadn't been shooting at us, it would have been funny. Running a street sweeper offroad and with a bunch of guys hanging off the sides."

"Making use of what they could find that still worked, I guess." Alice looked back in the direction they'd come from, the rain starting to lessen. "They were certainly no Wilford, Nate or Elaine, that's for sure."

After a short break, when the rain finally let up, Alice called for them to get moving again, and they mounted up and headed north along the tree line where birds chatted in low warbles and the staccato hammering of woodpeckers echoed through the woods.

CHAPTER SEVEN

James Burton
Chicago, Illinois

Holed up in the office on the third floor, warm in his soft camp clothes and with a blanket over his shoulders, James took stock of his position again, referencing the maps spread on the desk surface. It had taken an hour, but he'd finally relaxed, shaking off the shudders and shivers that had been constant at first, then tapering off as his cold bones warmed. Rain poured in sheets that were often too thick to see through, sprinkling off the brick, tinkling on the metal fire escape, splashing against his window, and running down in rivulets. There were sharp cracks of lightning, followed by lengthy waves of thunder that rolled lazily on for several long seconds. It was more rain than he'd experienced in a long time, giving the city a feeling of cold, dreariness, and hopelessness.

Sighing, he pulled his blanket around his shoulders tighter and chewed on a high-calorie double chocolate bar he'd found in his backpack, courtesy of the corporal in the refugee camp. The pistol he'd taken off of the man in the alley was beneath all the maps spread in front of him as he tried to develop a plan for where to go based off of where he'd been and where he was.

As best as James could tell, he was somewhere on the south side of Chicago, not a place he'd wanted to be, but driven there by fate and circumstance. Like Denver, the broad warehouse district and surrounding neighborhoods were a mix of intact and burned down, a twisting wasteland of buildings, wreckage, and decay. For the hundredth time, James traced a line from Hannibal to his current position with his finger, dismayed at what it had taken to get so far and what he'd lost along the way.

In circling Springfield, Missouri, he'd run into a sudden horde of refugees fleeing the city. The thousand bedraggled denizens had spotted him on his horse, and a group of able-bodied men had given chase, forcing him to kick Amber into a full gallop to get by, only to run into more people who'd grabbed at him and his supplies and Amber, trying to stop him and pull him off the horse. He'd run them over, fired on them with his rifle, and fought through the throng as they slashed and cut Amber on her flanks and shoulders with knives and machetes. After fording a wide creek south of the city, he'd lost the crowd and sprinted away, camping several miles east along the highway and well out of sight. Amber had grazed in a field that night while he slept outside in the moonlight and a sky full of stars with just a soft bed of sticks and fir branches beneath his bedroll.

He had next run into trouble in Decatur, Illinois, when he'd tried sleeping in an old, abandoned-looking barn only to find it was occupied by people when they returned late in the night from a scavenging run. The small group blocked his way out and demanded James give up Amber and his supplies, but he'd shot two of them after figuring out that they had no firearms, driving them back enough to hop on Amber and flee. They threw bottles and rocks at him, striking him and Amber both a few times before he got away.

He'd reached Champaign, Illinois and circled to the north after seeing massive glowing fires in the central and southern portions of town, and a motorcycle gang caught him on a strip of road between fields. Six of them on a combination of street bikes and dirt bikes chased him along the strip with roaring engines, and he barely made the next field before they overtook him. The dirt bikes pursued him through the rolling pastures and foothills, following James as he raced toward the nearest hill where he'd hoped the gullies and thick woods would be too rough on their machines. But the drivers kept coming, their faces impossible to see in the darkness as they throttled their bikes, spread out, and chased him. They could go almost anywhere he could, forcing him to drive Amber up a steep hill covered with loose deadfall, logs, and a ground full of stiff saplings. One bike had tried to follow him, misjudged a tree, and was knocked off by a branch to send him tumbling down the hill with his bike flipping on top of him. The other two met James at the top of the hill, and he turned Amber past them, narrowly avoiding being shot as a rider went by.

The motorcycles raced along the ridgeline with their engines spitting and sputtering, revving in increasing degrees of volume and pitch as they tore after him. They'd found James waiting atop the hill in a construction lot where several half-built new homes stood on the hillside. He had room to turn Amber and swing his rifle up, and when they flew up a dirt service road into the lot, he unleashed on them, missing the first man completely but hitting the second, first sending up sparks on the steel frame and then landing shots to the man's chest, causing him to fall off the motorcycle. The remaining driver sped to the end of the lot, turned, and stopped to pull out a radio. James assumed he was communicating with the riders on the road, and he fired at the man again, scaring him off and down the hill, dropping the radio under the wheel of his motorcycle in the process.

James had stayed around the construction neighborhood for the next few hours, Amber resting while he patrolled the area with the bit of ammunition he had left. Rain poured in a constant shower that lasted all night, turning the neighborhood into mud. Throughout the evening, motorcycles echoed through the hills, their engines revving as they closed in on him and formed a constricting ring to trap him. Abandoning his position and the temporary roof over their heads, James avoided the dirt road and carefully guided Amber downhill with only sporadic lightning bursts to illuminate the treacherous landscape. He discovered a deer trail leading him into a valley with a creek where Amber drank and rested and for the next hour they kept close to the stream and finally reached the road, using the compass on his staff to stay north, hoping to find an intersection to take him east again.

Two miles later, though, a burst of light came from nowhere out of the trees, and a powerful revving engine exploded to life, followed by the squealing of tires. James flew north again, and Amber's lagging response and heaving breaths told him she'd nearly reached the end of her endurance. After a mile-long chase, the other motorcycles joined in, cutting him off at the next intersection and sending him into the wilderness again, where the man on the dirt bike continued to harass him.

The rest was a blur of maneuvering, circling back on animal trails, flying fast, and sometimes hiding, all in the cold mud and rain as the headlamps pursued him. As Amber had continued to flag, James pushed her to a close cluster of storm-shrouded warehouses and neighborhoods at the edge of the woods. Seeking refuge in the town was pure desperation, but it was all he could think of, especially since the forests were failing him. Unfortunately, the decision had been one that had cost Amber her life in a dark back alley between the buildings. Finger sliding across the paper, he took in a deep breath, trying to fight back the tears as he traced his path one more time, trying to remember the signs he'd passed, the images blurry in his head as he had ridden in mindless panic. *Yeah, I'm in Frankfurt. I'm sure of it.*

Sitting back, he finished the last bite of his MRE, wadded up the packet, and tossed it into a nearby waste can. He hadn't noticed at first because of the boxes of papers and stacks of books on top, but a small couch rested against the east wall, the cushions comfortable and plush, if not threadbare from years of use. He made a bed out of it, putting down his bedroll and using some wadded-up clothes as a pillow. Standing and stretching his aching body, James took one last look through a crack in the blinds before he closed them and shuffled over to the couch, seeking refuge from his guilt and exhaustion.

There was no way he wanted to go out in the pouring rain, so his best bet was to stay inside for the night and possibly try to leave the next day or night, depending on what it looked like. Daylight travel could be safer in some ways and dangerous in others, and the night hadn't proven to be his friend, though he'd be less of a target without Amber. It would be a longer and more challenging road ahead, going on foot, but if he could stay beneath the radar and blend in with his surroundings, he'd still be able to make it. Appearing like someone too down on their luck to have anything of value would help, though would-be predators might not care.

He laid back on the sofa with a long groan and drew the cover over himself, then rolled onto his right side and stared at the dark and dismal room with the flickering shadows of rain on the walls and the slow drips like spiders dropping from strands of silken threads. His plan had always been to avoid entering cities, and he'd largely done that, at least until he was forced to do so – to his and Amber's detriment. Still, with as bad as his situation was, the last place he wanted to go was into Chicago proper and make things a magnitude or three worse. Of all the byways and highways, the cross-sections and adjoining roads, one stuck out in his mind, a long stretch moving west to east a few miles north of him: Highway 30. That was the demarcation line he'd decided meant the difference between being in Chicago and not in Chicago, and he promised himself he'd stay south of it at all costs.

With weariness dragging his eyelids downward and outweighing his frustrations and guilt, he let his eyes fall shut, brought his knees up, and curled up, pulling the cover tight and clenching his arms to his chest as a final shiver ran through him. Alice would tell him to be thankful for what he had. A quiet, warm room. Two exits should he need to escape. Food, maps, and water at his fingertips. Yes, he'd lost a lot of his supplies and he'd lost a fine animal in Amber, but he was still alive, and James wouldn't soon forget Amber or the kindness Eli and his people had shown him. The world had gone mad, but there was still kindness and hope left. Squeezing his eyes tighter only sent tears dripping onto his rollout mat, so he sighed and tried to listen to the rain, hoping it would lull him to a quick and dreamless sleep.

A smattering of distant gunshots and shouts woke him, and he laid still, blinking and listening in the quiet room to the slow drip of water outside his window, the stillness in the drifting dust, the tiniest sliver of gray light of day capturing the motes as they swirled in front of his face.

Another gunshot rang out, followed by two more in rapid succession. A shout of pain came afterward, then one of rage and anguish, causing his heart to beat a couple of paces faster. Swinging his legs off the couch, he sat and took several deep breaths, getting his mind around his situation, remembering where he was and that he was safe for the moment. James gathered his things, feeling his wet clothes to see they'd mostly dried out. The bathroom sink wasn't working, so he relieved himself in the toilet, then scooped out several handfuls of water from the tank to drink, then the rest went into a couple of plastic water bottles from his pack. Avoiding the mirror, James returned to the office and opened the blinds a crack, checking the dreary street with deep puddles everywhere, water glistening off the pavement as a low mist clung to every surface.

There were no signs of movement and had been no gunshots in several minutes, just a drizzle of rain that kept the rivulets on the windows fresh. With an uncertain shake of his head, he returned to the desk and began poring over the maps again. His next choice might be the difference between life and death, or failing to reach his family. He closed his eyes and thought about Alice, her beautiful dark hair running through his fingers like silk, her weight in his arms, and the smell of her body lotion. If she were there, she'd tell him to keep going no matter what and that it wouldn't make a bit of difference if he traveled during the day or night because every second of the road would be fraught with danger. The most important thing was to keep moving, to keep forcing his way through with each step carrying him closer to home.

With his mind made up, James got out of his soft, dry camp clothes and put on his travel gear, still soggy but tolerable. The second he put on his shirt, an unpleasant shudder ran through him. He circled to the maps again, memorizing the surrounding streets, studying the faint marks that were back alleys and the places he could hide if he got into trouble. While it had seemed like a vast city before, it was only a small suburb of Chicago and not the metropolis itself. He could get through it if he kept his head down and moved.

Maps folded and tucked securely away, James held his staff in one hand and tucked his newly-acquired pistol in his outer coat pocket along with the box of ammunition he'd gotten. He listened at the door for a moment, just to be sure no one was rooting around through the building, then quietly opened it and exited the office through the manufacturing floor. Descending the east stairwell, James paused at the bottom to peek through the square window. It was dark on the other side except for small streams of gray light spilling in the warehouse glass, and there were no signs of movement.

He stepped out of the stairwell and walked down the central aisle with machine equipment all around him as he crept to the south side of the building where he found a loading dock in the back, and exited through it to avoid the main street. Off the alley was a small patch of grass, and he suddenly changed course, walked over, squatted, and dug some of the moist ground up, smearing it on his coat and stick and then wiping it on his face. He'd cleaned himself up too much back in the office, he realized, and cleanliness would make him stick out like a sore thumb. Better to be dirty again and blend in than risk catching the eye of some lowlife.

Sticking to the narrow back alleys, James crossed from one block to the next, heart racing, breaths shallow as he kept one eye on the higher windows and one on the shadows. Dumpsters provided hiding spots whenever he caught a suspicious sound or something flitted at the end of the alley. He ran out of large buildings and jogged through back parking lots of still-standing warehouses, sprinting past those that had burned to their foundations.

At one of the corners he'd marked on his map, he found a gas station with its tank bays ruptured, the concrete split and peeled upward, the jagged edges of stone and metal jutting up from the ground. There was a minimart attached to the property, the front end scorched sideways across the brick front, glass shattered, insides gutted. James approached it with his head on a swivel, checking the dark shadows as rain swept in sideways, blown by a sudden gale tearing through the streets. He stepped inside through the blasted front door, searching the empty shelves for scraps of food. Everything had been stripped, but he fell to his knees and looked beneath the shelves, sweeping out several packs of potato chips, some wafer cookies, and loose hard candies. A few bottles of old milk rolled around in the bottom of the refrigerator, long gone bad, but his persistence was rewarded when he found a bottle of apple juice and several bottles of water in the bottom.

He drank the apple juice, the sugar surge giving him a burst of energy within a few minutes of finishing it. After collecting a few more items from the store, he topped off his backpack and started out the front door until two shapes flowed out of the shadows and slipped toward him. Turning quietly on his heels, he slipped out the back door and into an alley, circling back and going east again before they had a chance to pursue him. James stuck to the ruins like a rodent, becoming one with the husk of a city, keeping to the shadows and listening as another spattering of gunshots fired off to the north in counter to the closer ones.

Leaving the warehouse district, he entered smaller neighborhoods with strip malls and smaller buildings and businesses, and he kept to the rear lots and connecting streets to stay out of sight. A burst of violent gunfire ripped from the south, the echoes bouncing off the wet pavement, echoing across the buildings, distorting both the direction and closeness of their origination. The combination of bad weather and urban surroundings confused his ears, and for a moment he imagined being stuck in the city's grip forever, hunted by violence, unable to find a way out. Picking up the pace, James left the cover of a bank drive-through and sprinted for the next corner, seeing the first signs of trees and open fields in the distance.

When gunshots sounded again, they were much closer than before, so close the ricochets off the brick and the shouts of the combatants as they hurled obscenities at each other were crystal clear. When the sound of several pairs of running feet came down the street behind him, James fled the bank and ran for the next corner. Past the rubble of another gas station was a wide-open road leading out of town with the crowded buildings tapering off to subdivisions in the distance. Sensing freedom, he got out ahead of the throng, creeping quickly and quietly, glancing back repeatedly, losing the group in the misty morning streets.

James came to a corner of an intersection, a four way stop with the streetlights hanging from wires, the signs bent sideways from nearby explosions. In front of him, the sidewalk had cracked and fallen in, exposing the sewers beneath the street, raw sewage splashing around the edges as the broken and battered sewers over- flowed from the recent rains. A different set of gunshots came from a southbound street, shadows shifted in the gloom, and muzzle flashes flickered in the corners of his vision. They were moving parallel to him but edging in his direction, laughing, cursing and firing their weapons – though at what, he could not say.

The groups would soon converge on one another and James would be caught in between them if he didn't move quickly. In a desperate race to get off the road, James flew across the street and past a strip mall to a grassy lot with a ditch running along the side. With catcalls and whistles behind, James ran hard and jumped into the ditch, which turned out to be a grassy culvert embankment. Raising his feet, sliding down on his backside, he grabbed the edge of a concrete wall and flipped over to land in six inches of water flowing through the culvert pipe. With the violence closing in around him, James quietly squelched toward the circular opening and ducked, huddling on a narrow concrete lip just above the water's edge, waiting to see if the shooters would pass him by.

CHAPTER EIGHT

President Thomas Birk
Mount Weather, Virginia

Agent Harris stood at the door of a side conference room away from
Mount Weather's bustling staff. Inside were President Birk, General
Pulaski, Marine Colonel Crow, Marine Major Jasmine Spencer, and
staffer Cindy Strode. Missing a central table, it was more like a gathering of people about to watch a football game, with their jackets off
and hanging from hooks on the walls, sleeves rolled up, ties loosened,
sitting in foldout chairs arrayed haphazardly around the screen. Two
urns of coffee and a modest assortment of snacks sat on a table
against the rear wall.

The mood in the room was upbeat after the news about the
Saudis, relief rippling through those in the know over the fact that
they'd found the source of the attack, giving them a target for their
anger and dismay. Pulaski used a remote to filter through several
images on the screen, settling on a couple and discussing something
quietly with Colonel Crow. Cool ventilation and the distant rumbling

of some generators were the only noises audible outside of the room, reminding Harris of just where they were, deep underground with tons of earth, cement, and steel resting on their heads.

Harris took a step to the side and sipped on a styrofoam cup of tepid coffee before resuming his stiff position with his hands clasped in front of him. His job deep underground in a secure facility was nothing if not boring, and his thoughts turned once again to the loss of his family, filling his heart with warring emotions that clashed with his sense of duty. The few moments he'd had alone in his tiny quarters were a slight reprieve, and he used that time to reflect on his life with his family and shed his tears over their loss.

He'd loved his parents with all his heart. They'd provided him a wonderful atmosphere to grow up in, challenging him to do better and *be* better, supporting his interests as they'd changed over the years. His father had beamed when Harris had told him about being accepted as a Secret Service Agent, and while his mother hadn't been impressed about her son's new job, she warmed to it in the end, encouraging him to find a nice girl to date in Washington, get married, and make her a grandmother as soon as possible.

Losing his parents stung, but it was his little sister's death that cut him the deepest. Even when he was a senior at UVA, Veronica was the person who he spent the most time with, the scrappy tomboy who picked fights with the older boys in the neighborhood, played tackle football in the snow, and hit the gym hard. When he told her about his new career, she'd immediately asked, "When do I get to meet the First Lady?

"It doesn't work that way, sis."

"Then what are the perks of being your little sister, bro?"

A smile touched him, and his eyes turned glassy as a dozen such conversations ran through his mind, then he shook his head to rid himself of the haunting thoughts lest they draw him deeper into a pit of loss and despair.

"Hey, Harris. Get over here."

Harris stiffened and blinked as the President waved him over and patted the chair next to him. "Come on, agent. Have a seat."

"Pardon me, sir?"

"Sit, please. I want you in on this."

"Are you sure?"

"I'm sure. It's better than standing by the door all day."

"That's my job, sir. I—"

"I'm still the President, Harris. Park your ass."

The agent nodded and stepped briskly to the chair, circling it and sliding into the seat in one smooth motion. General Pulaski and Colonel Crow shot him odd looks but didn't argue with the President.

"What am I looking at, sir?"

"These are satellite feeds over Saudi Arabia we picked up over the past twenty-four hours."

"Don't we have an agreement with Saudi Arabia to refrain from aerial surveillance of their country based on a recent arms deal?"

"That," Birk laughed, "wasn't exactly ever adhered to."

"Mr. President, are you—" General Pulaski started to interrupt, but Birk put up a hand before he could continue.

"Harris has my complete trust, General. Relax. Anyway, prior agreements wouldn't mean diddly squat anymore anyway. We need to be positive they're not readying some attack to take advantage of this situation." Birk pointed to the screen. "And these images will show us exactly that." He nodded to General Pulaski. "Go ahead, General."

"Yes, sir."

The heavyset man edged forward on his chair and gestured toward the screen, which showed a saturated image of an area marked *Saudi-Iraqi Border*. All Harris saw were a bunch of criss-crossing highways, the vague outlines of large buildings, and miles of sand. Pulaski flipped through several similar images with unique structures and digital markings Harris figured were for some sort of internal, unknowable processes.

"What you see here is the border between Saudi Arabia and Iraq. Now, if they were readying for some kind of attack or preparing to send forces to aid their allies, you'd see a lot of buildup here, here, and here." Pulaski leaned forward and touched different parts of the screen where major highways seemed to intersect. "But we're not seeing any of that, which leads us to believe the Saudis aren't planning an offensive."

"They *aren't* planning one?" Birk asked, "Or they *can't* plan one?"

"I... wasn't ready to believe it, but we believe it's the latter. They don't have the mechanized divisions or air power to do it." The General clicked through pictures of what appeared to be urban areas with more buildings and streets clustered into sections and dark stains obscuring parts of the city. "This is Riyadh."

Birk gaped. "Is that smoke, General?"

"Yes, sir. It almost completely covers parts of the city and most of the outskirts. It's the same with Jeddah. We reached our embassy in Riyadh, and they've been locked into their buildings with basic communication cut off except for our ultra-secure satellite feed the Saudis aren't aware of. Our people described explosions and chaos in the streets, and we even received some shaky footage from a staffer in a second-floor window."

"What about the border between them and Jordan?"

"No activity whatsoever. These images were taken over two days, sir; we had to reposition some satellite assets after it became clear using strictly visible spectrums would be next to useless thanks to the cloud cover. We would've picked up any minute troop movements after that. There were none. We have images of every Saudi base, from Aziz Air Force Base to Riyadh, and there are clouds over all of them and no signs of armored units moving anywhere – or even left intact. The whole place is a dead zone. They were hit just as hard, if not worse, than everyone else in the world."

Harris raised his hand hesitantly.

"Go ahead, Harris," Birk said.

"I was just wondering. If they created this biological agent, why couldn't they keep it out of their fuel supply?"

"We asked ourselves the same thing," the General replied. "It could be they had a mix-up in their supply chain, or someone sabotaged them from the inside. Analysts are working on it, but between a lack of information plus the general situation in the world at large, we may never know."

"They're in worse shape than us," Birk whispered as he sat back, resting his coffee on his knee and shaking his head. "While we'd all love to exact some revenge for what they've done, I'll not authorize an attack. No sense in wasting resources on bombing a place that looks like *that*."

"I agree with that, sir," Pulaski nodded. "Glad we took our time and looked into it."

"Cindy?"

"Yes, sir?"

"Let's have Secretary of State Lewis reach out to the Saudis through our embassy. I want to set up a meeting with King Nayef and members of his staff to see if they need our assistance in any way. I want to keep our lines of communication open with them without letting them know we're on to them. I want to lean on them *hard* – any chances we have to get intel while keeping the moral high ground are ones I want to take."

"I'll talk to Secretary of State Lewis right away, sir," Cindy said, standing and leaving the room.

Birk turned back to Pulaski. "What about the Russians and Chinese?"

"Shitshows." Pulaski switched the screen view to a coastal region. "This is the East Coast of Kamchatka, where the Russians have several bases we're not supposed to know about. This is their biggest one, and all I see is a smoke cloud. Right there on the edge of the lake."

"Is that the Mengon Air Base?" Birk asked.

"The one and only, or what's left of it that's still burning. And look at this..." The pictures shifted south along the coast into what Harris recognized as China, Japan, and Taiwan. A red dot marked a spot southwest of Hong Kong. "This is China's Yulin Naval Base, which appears to be burning like the rest of the surrounding cities. But look here at these outskirts. See these lines along the highways near the hardest hit areas?"

"What are those?" Birk squinted at them. "Are those military convoys?"

Pulaski shook his head. "We thought so at first, but no." The images magnified with incremental clicks as the lines grew more pixelated. "Those are people and carts. Hundreds and thousands of them, pulled by humans and animals alike. None of it appears to be military."

"What are they doing? Trying to get away from the cities?"

"We think the Chinese government has enlisted the general population to clean up from the disaster. With most of the country being rural and living in what we'd consider to be squalor, they've got a lot more survivors than we do. Many don't have cars or trucks, and they move from village to village on foot or on pack animals."

Harris stared at the image.

"A built-in workforce," Birk said, with no small amount of awe. "And they look exceptionally well organized."

"Because they've been conditioned to be that way for generations." The General snorted. "Most wouldn't bat an eye if they were ordered to switch from farming to clearing rubble in a single day."

"So, the major players don't appear to be taking an aggressive stance?"

"It doesn't appear that way, sir. What we're seeing is a complete breakdown across the world."

"So, the Saudis screwed up," Birk said, "and the rest of the world has to clean up the mess? At least there're no threats from other nations, leaving us to focus on things at home."

"Looks that way."

Birk rested his elbows on his knees and looked across the room. "Alright. In light of this, I want the lion's share of our efforts spent here at home with minimal focus on surveillance of these other countries. Is that clear?"

The group collectively nodded, some referencing their notepads and jotting things in them.

"We're taking too damn long helping our people, and I want us to quadruple our efforts. Some of the reports from the cities have me scared out of my damn mind, I don't mind telling you."

"Law and order is exceptionally difficult right now, sir."

"I don't care." Birk began to stand up. "We're the United States of America. We're *not* going to sit around with our thumbs up our—"

The screen died, the images Pulaski had been showing snapping off in an instant as the lights faded, blinked, and flipped back to full power again. A slight rumble rippled through the walls, and a faint trace of dust trickled from a ventilation duct in the ceiling. Mumbled confusion filled the room as the group stood.

"What's going on, General?" Birk asked, turning as Harris stood as well, moving closer to his ward.

"I don't know, sir, but I'm going to find out." Pulaski took a radio from his belt and spoke into it.

Knuckles rapped hard on the metal door, jerking Harris to attention as he spun, hand resting on his pistol. The door flew open, and a Marine sergeant stuck his head in, face frantic, beads of sweat on his brow.

"Sorry to interrupt," he said. "but we're under attack."

Birk stood and pushed past the General. "What? Who's responsible?"

"I don't know, sir. They sent me to find General Pulaski, and to tell Agent Harris to get you to a safe room immediately."

Harris exchanged a look with Pulaski, and the General grabbed Crow and the others and cleared the room, jaws set as they rushed upstairs. Left alone with Birk, Harris gave him a quiet nod and gestured at the door.

"Right this way, sir."

CHAPTER NINE

Ryan Cooper
Somewhere Outside East Lansing, Michigan

"Can't we put them farther inside the tree line?" Helen panted, leaning on her shovel, wiping her arm across her brow.

They were out on the east side of the property with the five bodies stacked where Ryan had left them the previous day. He was waist-deep in a square pit he'd been digging all morning, sweating, arms and shoulders sore, hands sore in his thick leather gloves. The first two graves were completed, four feet deep and perfectly square on the edges. Ryan had made two more roughly shaped holes where Helen was standing, using the tractor's middle buster to churn up the soil and make it easier to get started, and Helen stood next to the pile of dirt he'd made, taking a break from her turn in the hole.

"I thought about it," Ryan replied, "but I want people to see these graves if they come onto the property again."

"But we can see them, too. Every morning, a reminder of what we did."

"A reminder of what we *had* to do, to defend ourselves," he corrected her gently. When she only glanced at the corpses with a sad frown, he slowly climbed out of the pit and put his arm around her. "I know it's not perfect, and it hurts to know we actually took people's lives, but these graves also serve as a different reminder."

"Which is?"

"It could easily be us instead of them," his tone darkened. "And if you think these people would have given us half the respect we're giving them, you'd be sorely mistaken. I imagine they would've just thrown us out in the woods along with the dogs after they put them down."

Helen's frown deepened. "That's a terrible thought."

"That's why I'm leaving the graves out here as a reminder. To their friends of what we'll do to defend ourselves, and to us that we must always be vigilant."

"I... this world. I don't like it, Ryan. I don't like what it's become and what it's turning us into."

He kissed her forehead and hopped back into the grave, staggering a little on the loose soil before plunging the shovel tip into the dirt and leaning on it. "Best way I know of to deal with it is to just keep digging."

"Move over. I want to keep helping."

It was Ryan's turn to frown. "That's not necessary, hon. I'd hoped to get this all taken care of before you even noticed it."

A tear streaked down Helen's cheek as she leaned her shovel against the tractor. "That's awful sweet of you, but we're equal partners in all of this, both the good times and the bad, the rewards and the burdens."

Ryan stared at her for a long moment and then nodded. "Fair enough. You can start moving that loose dirt out of the other two graves. Just drag it over to the main pile, and I'll use the tractor to push it over top of them after we lower them inside."

The next two hours were a grueling exercise in hard, unforgiving manual labor, digging being the hardest work he'd ever done, even more so than the farming, and by the time they had all five graves carved into the earth, Ryan was beyond sore, his wounded calf aching beyond belief, his arms and shoulders weak and shaking. Helen's white T-shirt was covered in dirt, the front of her jeans stained dark, her once white tennis shoes turned brown. The sun crept higher above them, filling the increasingly blue skies with light and glinting off the majestic red maples lining the lane. Birds kept them company as they labored, and the trees seemed reverent in their gentle rustling as the constant breezes ebbed and flowed to soothe their sweat every time they popped their head out of one of the holes.

"Why are you grinning?" Helen asked, stopping to lean on her shovel, wiping the sweat with a dirt-stained sleeve.

"Don't worry about it. It's silly."

"No no, I want some of that positivity you've got going on."

"Well," he smiled, "I couldn't help but think how fast the batteries are charging right now and how much juice we must have in the house."

Helen smiled and looked up, shielding her eyes with her hand. "It's a beautiful day. Prettiest one in a long while. Makes me want to just sit out back and relax, if we didn't have so much to do."

"We should be finished here soon, then we can get back on with what we *need* to be doing. Plenty left to get done so we're ready for when James, Alice, and the kids come home. I want them to be shocked by how well we've kept things here."

Helen nodded, winking at him. "The bullet holes will be a real shock, I'm sure."

Ryan laughed and the pair got back to their work, Helen clearing the last grave, then Ryan jumping in and digging deeper with the shovel, finding a rhythm to the work, fighting through the pain and discomfort, plowing through the last foot of dirt quickly and thoroughly. Finally, he leaned on the side of the grave with a groan.

"Are you okay, dear?"

"I'm fine," he replied, climbing out, unwilling to let himself rest. "I just want to finish with this and move on. Let's put them in now."

Ryan's shirt was soaked with sweat, and with both of them out there, he didn't bother using the tractor to lower the bodies in.

Instead, he took their arms while Helen took their feet, and together they moved them to their respective graves, stooping to lower them as far as they could before dropping them in. Ryan avoided looking at their faces and thinking about who they'd been before everything had happened, people with families, hopes and dreams who'd made enough bad choices to wind up being buried on the edge of a field.

He started up the tractor and used the bucket to shove the dirt over the graves, filling them to overflowing, then ran across the graves with the tires and bucket to tamp them down until there were five neat mounds sitting side-by-side, deep and covered well enough to keep the smells buried so that scavengers wouldn't be able to dig them up. After getting out and surveying their work, Ryan threw the tools in the bucket and started to climb into the tractor when Helen gently grabbed his arm.

"I... think we should say something, don't you?"

"We've done a lot for them already," Ryan said, pausing. "We could have left them for the coyotes—"

"But we didn't, because that's not the kind of people we are. They were our enemies, but they've passed beyond this world now. It's still our duty to try to be the better people, in some form or fashion. "

Ryan backed out of the tractor and eyed the graves warily. "I'm not sure I'd know what to say to them."

"You'll think of something. Anger, forgiveness, something in between... whatever it is you have to say, we shouldn't leave this unfinished." She took his hand in hers and squeezed gently, and he nodded and stepped over to the graves.

"I... know where I'm headed when I die, and I sure hope you all knew, too, because it's too damn late now. Ya'll might have been good people before all this started, or maybe not. This sort of a thing'll turn a good man bad before he even realizes it. But either way, I forgive you for trying to kill myself and my wife and take what belongs to our family." Ryan's throat constricted as the tumultuous emotions flowed through him. "And I hope and pray with every fiber of my being that we never have to kill like this again. I'll do my best to keep it from happening. But if we have to – we will. May God have mercy on you and keep your families from harm."

Helen was nodding by the time Ryan stopped speaking, and whispered quietly, barely loud enough for him to hear.

"Amen."

———

Ryan followed Helen from the chicken coop down to the house and into the kitchen, with baskets of eggs in their arms, faces and hands dirty from the digging, feeding the animals and doing some general cleanup. They placed their baskets on the breakfast bar and washed up, turning and smiling at one another as they dried off their hands and leaned against the counter.

"Another day's work done," Ryan said, crossing his arms. "And here I was thinking that we were done with farming when we retired."

"Just when you thought you were out, they pull you right back in." Helen laughed. "We've still got to bring down the milk from the barn. You'll have to run that ATV every day to bring those containers down. That'll make a lot of noise."

"I'll use the wheelbarrow from now on."

Helen frowned. "Oh, I wasn't saying that. You do not need to be straining those legs of yours, and if that means I need to help out or you need to use the ATV more, then do it. It's not like the gasoline is going to stay good forever, after all."

"Still... better to draw less attention. And the leg is feeling better, too; I should be able to walk them down without too much hassle."

"You're not as young as you used to be, Ryan Cooper," Helen crossed her arms. "You've got to let yourself heal. A *bullet* went through your *leg*. Even if it didn't do any permanent damage, it's still no minor injury."

"I'm not as young as I used to be, but I'm at least twice as tough."

"Tough? Ha!" Helen laughed. "Stubborn, you mean."

"Another truth," Ryan grinned before sobering. "But I can get the job done without running that ATV. The best thing we can do is to keep a low profile. If it means me going through more pain to do it, I will."

Helen wrapped her arms around him, resting her head on his chest. "I know you will. But don't overdo it. It won't do either of us any good if you run yourself into the ground. If you start hurting too bad, either use that ATV, or tell me so I can help you out, okay?"

Ryan hugged her and breathed in deep as she squeezed him back. "I'm glad the tough work is done... that was rough, seeing them like that."

"Sorry again about where we put the bodies."

"No, it's like you said, we want anyone else who tries to come out here to think two or three times before they pull anything. Still... doesn't make the process any easier."

Ryan turned to the sink to get a glass of water. "I'm glad we did it. When this all blows over we might have some explaining to do to the authorities, but, well... better to be judged by twelve and all that."

Helen nodded. "And, in cheerier news, my secret concoction got the bloodstains out of the carpet. It looks almost brand new."

"Whatever you used worked, though I won't easily forget what that woman's face... sorry." Ryan shut his mouth and took a sip of water. "Trying to get off the subject just brings it back around."

"The dogs did their job. It's all we can ask for from them."

"That they did. A little *too* well, maybe. How's Duke been?"

"Still limping, but more when he wants a treat."

"He knows how to play you. Don't fall for it."

Helen laughed. "I don't mind, really. He deserves it after what he did to help save us. Speaking of food, what would you say to me fixing us a snack? We need to finish up the leftovers."

"Only if you'll let me help make it."

They re-heated two half-eaten omelets from earlier and a large bowl of a boxed tuna meal they'd made the previous evening. Arms full, they took everything to the dining room and set it down, going back for cups of water and freshly pasteurized milk. Before they sat, Helen walked to the window and peered through the plywood pieces, gasping at something outside.

Ryan was chewing a bite of his omelet when he looked at her. "What is it, honey? Is something out there?"

"Not som*one*. But..."

Ryan threw down his fork with a clatter, grabbed his Winchester off the table, and kicked his chair back. Joining her at the still-intact window, he spread the blinds wider and glared into the yard through gaps in the wood. "Where are they?"

"At first, I wasn't sure." Helen tapped the glass. "Then I caught the movement way down by the fence."

"What in the world?" Ryan had been looking at the woods on the east side of the property but shifted attention to the driveway. "Is she waving a white flag?"

"I think so. Grab the binoculars?"

Ryan swept the binoculars off the table and pressed them to the window, focusing them in on a tall woman with brown hair down at the very end of the driveway, one hand resting on the gate and the other waving a stick with a white rag tied to the end.

He handed over the binoculars. "Any clue who that is?"

Helen checked. "Nope, I've never seen her in my life. Might be one of the neighbors from down the road."

"She looks young, maybe late twenties, but I can't be sure from here. Looks like she's alone, but impossible to tell with the tree cover."

"What are you going to do?" Helen asked, then shot him a skeptical look. "You're not going down there, are you?"

"Are you kidding? I'm absolutely not going down there. That's a trap if I ever saw one." He hefted his rifle. "I'll take the shot with the Winchester from the front porch."

Helen's eyebrows went up. "Wait a second. There's no need to shoot her."

"Isn't there?"

"How do you know she's with the group who attacked us? And you can't just shoot someone waving a white flag. What if she really needs help?"

Ryan pursed his lips and sighed in annoyance. "You know what I'm going to say to that."

"That we can't trust anyone, I know. So let's watch her for now,

101

Just hold off on doing any shooting until she comes onto the property, okay?"

"I..." Ryan's mouth opened and closed a few times before his
shoulders dropped. "Okay. We'll do it your way." He set the rifle and
binoculars on the table, grabbed his plate, and moved back to stand
near the window, watching the woman as he ate.

Helen brought him a scoop of tuna, and he finished eating while
on guard, occasionally putting his fork down to raise his binoculars
and check on the woman. When they were done with lunch, Helen
took their plates into the kitchen while Ryan remained vigilant, his
frown growing with every passing minute. The woman continued her
flag-waving, switching arms when one grew tired, her expression hard
to read from such a distance. Ryan watched her head movements to
see if she was checking for any accomplices waiting off to the sides
behind the trees, but she seemed singularly focused on their house
and getting their attention. Helen took his place for an hour while
Ryan cleaned up around the house, but when he came back to check,
nothing had changed, except that the woman was swapping the flag
between hands more frequently and the waving was done with less
intensity than before.

"If she wants to stand out there all day, let her," he fumed. "It's
nothing to us. Maybe she'll drop out of exhaustion."

"We won't get anything done standing here," Helen replied. "Why
don't you get the milk from the barn, and I'll keep watch."

"We can't be sure they're not waiting to take a shot at us. And in
case you didn't notice, I'm not exactly Flash Gordon these days."

She placed her hand on his shoulder. "It's the middle of the day,
and if they were going to attack us, it would have already happened.
Take Duchess to the barn with you. She'll sniff out anyone lurking in
the shadows."

Ryan frowned and rested his hand on his rifle. "You know what?
You're absolutely right. We can't let them scare us into hiding. We've
got animals to care for."

"That's right. Go on, and I'll keep an eye on her. Why don't you
take one of James' radios, too? I'll keep the other one with me. "

"I'll grab them." Ryan went into the kitchen where the radios were charging and brought them back, giving one to Helen while hooking the other on his belt. "You know what to do, Annie Oakley."

Helen gave him a bemused salute, and Ryan called for Duchess, attaching her leash and taking her out to the shed along with the wheelbarrow. The woods were still, a heavy silence settling over the farm as the breezes died down, making the woman down at the gate an even more ominous presence. Up at the barn, he picked up the containers of Bessie's milk and brought them to the house, setting them inside the door. By the time he returned to the dining room window, he was tired and sweating, and the expression on Helen's face told him the woman still hadn't left.

"She's still out there," she said, confirming it. "Hasn't moved and keeps waving her flag. I have to give it to her, she's got some endurance. My arms would be dead tired if I did that."

"That's it," Ryan snapped. "I'm going down there to run her off once and for all."

"What about the trap?"

"You can cover me, but this is getting on my nerves and needs to be put to a stop."

"You want me upstairs?"

"Watch me from the upper floor with your gun, just like before. I'll take Duchess with me in the back seat of the EV."

"You're taking the car?"

"They already know we have it, and it'll enable a fast getaway should I need to make one."

Helen looked back at the woman through the binoculars. "Promise me you'll at least hear her out, okay?"

Ryan groaned, starting to roll his eyes, then relenting. "Yeah, I guess I'll listen. If I don't like what she has to say, though, I'll run her off."

"Fair enough." Helen nodded while Ryan took Duchess outside and walked gingerly to the EV, putting the dog in the back before climbing behind the wheel.

His right calf was stiff, forcing him to put the seat back a few inches so he could stretch. The EV still had a twenty-five percent charge, an alert on the dashboard reminding him to charge it soon.

103

"Better plug it into the house soon. Doubt we'll need it charged all the way up, but better to have it and not need it." Ryan glanced back when Duchess whined. "There's a good girl. We're just going for a quick ride. Don't worry, it's not a vet visit."

He pulled around through the side yard and onto the driveway, rolling down the gravel road between the statuesque trees, a group of ducks fluttering out of the way from where they were crossing over the gravel. Ryan slowed and checked for movement in the woods and in the brush crowding the fences, but all was dark and quiet. Thirty yards from the gate, he pulled right into the grass and made a complete circle, staring at the woman as he passed. She'd quit waving the flag and stood there with both hands on the top rail, expression neutral as she watched him.

He'd been right about her age: late twenties, maybe early thirties, with dark hair, brown eyes, and a face full of fear and hope all at the same time. There were bruises on her arms and one of her eyes looked darker than the other; someone had put her through the wringer, or perhaps things outside the farm were even harder than they seemed. Once he had the EV pointed back toward the house, he paused and took stock of his surroundings, using his binoculars to check that Helen was sitting quietly in the second-floor window.

With a grunt of discomfort, he slowly got out and stood still with his gun in hand, hesitating another moment to listen and watch along the front fence and tree line. He popped the back door open, ordering Duchess to stay but giving her a way out if he needed her. The woman seemed vaguely familiar as he approached her, though he couldn't put a name to her face or say where he'd seen her before. Ryan came ahead with his rifle in both arms, keeping it loose and at the ready, stopping fifteen yards from the gate and the woman standing behind it.

"Who are you, and what do you want?" He was overly gruff, intentionally so, and pushed back the guilt over his impoliteness.

An uncertain smile tugged at the woman's mouth, and when she turned her head, he could see the remnants of a deep, old bruise on her left eye. "Glad you came out. I was getting tired. You'd think a stick wasn't all that heavy, but —"

"Who the hell are you, and what the hell do you want?" Ryan growled, looking around and still seeing no signs of subterfuge.

She stuttered. "I-I'm Sandy Crenshaw. W-wife of Chase. We live just down the road and—"

"Was Chase one of the men who attacked us the other night?"

She glanced away for a moment, hesitating, then the words came out in a rush. "I... yes. Yes he was. Look, sir, I've got a sick child. He's in a bad way and needs antibiotics, if you have any. I don't have anywhere else to turn—"

"Oh, that's rich," he laughed, genuinely amused at her brazenness. "Oh, you've got a lot of nerve, *Sandy*. Why should we help you when you attacked us?"

Sandy rested her hands on the rail, pleading with him. "I... what he did was wrong, okay? But I swear I wasn't involved. He was... I told him not to go, not to trust Jack, not to try and steal from other people but he did anyway and... I can guess what happened to him. He never came home, and my child is sick. I can't..." Her eyes turned glassy as emotion welled in her chest. "I can't lose him. He's a good boy, he's not like his daddy – I hope he never turns out to be like his daddy, truth be told – and he doesn't deserve to die like this. Please, if you've got any kind of heart..."

Ryan's curled lip slowly lowered as he listened to her, the mention of the boy short-circuiting his planned retort to the woman's begging. "Your son's sick?"

"Yes."

"Son of a..." Ryan groaned and sighed heavily. "What's his name?"

"Stephen."

"What are the symptoms?"

"He won't eat but a little soup and water. Cold even though he sits close to the fire and he's got a temperature pushing a hundred and one. Hasn't been this sick since he was a baby."

"Sounds like an infection. Could be viral, but how long's it been going on?"

"A few days now. Keeps getting worse."

"Probably bacterial, if I had to guess." Ryan rubbed the bridge of his nose. "And you say you live close by?"

"About six houses down."

"There a reason you came to us instead of friends of you and your husband's?"

"I-I didn't know what else to do. The others are... they're all bickering and fighting and don't have much in the way of supplies. Plus, I figured since Chase didn't come back, that ya'll were still standing."

"Bold of you to come seeking help from the people your friends and family attacked and tried to steal from."

"I—"

"What makes you think we'd help you after what your people did to us?"

Sandy's expression dropped. "I-I just thought I'd come down and ask nicely. Not for my sake. For my son's."

Ryan's resolve cracked, just a bit, and he searched her eyes for any signs of a lie before sighing. "All right, Sandy. Meet me here tomorrow, and I'll see what I can do. I'm not promising *anything*, understand me?"

Sandy's eyes widened at Ryan's unexpected response. "I understand. Thank y—"

Ryan bristled, his frustration boiling over, with Sandy the only person to direct his anger toward. "Your people – your *husband* – shot at us. Tried to kill my wife and me! Shot clear though my damned leg!" Ryan took a deep breath and released it slowly. "I should just put a round through your head to keep more problems from coming up." Sandy gulped, taking a couple of small, shuffling steps back before Ryan rolled his eyes and held up a hand. "I'm not going to. Just... I'm pissed off, understand, Sandy? If you people had come to talk *first* then we could have been working together from the start instead of dealing with this bull!"

"I'm sorry for that," she replied softly. "I can't make up for what my husband and the rest did. What he did..." Her voice dropped as she rubbed absently at her bruised arm. "Please, if you can, I'm begging you to help my son."

Ryan started to step back, shaking his head. "Not now. I need to think this over some more. Tomorrow morning, be at this gate, and come alone. Bring something to trade, and I'll try to see what I can do."

Her whole person melted in gratitude. "Thank you, thank you! Stephen and I both appreciate it. You bet I'll be here. Thank you again...."

"Ryan. And listen, Sandy? Just one more thing." Ryan spoke the words through clenched teeth, holding the butt of the rifle against his shoulder. "If I even *think* you aren't alone or that you're trying to pull something, I'll shoot you before you can make a move, and I'll bury you next to the rest of the assholes who tried to kill me. Got it?"

Sandy nodded as tears broke from her eyes. "Yes, I-I mean no. Yes. Of course. Thank you! I'll see you here first thing in the morning."

Turning and nearly tripping as she went, Sandy quickly walked back the way she'd come with her flag stuck in her pocket, up the road past the neighbor's house where she disappeared out of sight around a bend. After she was gone, Ryan closed the back door of the car, got in, and drove back to the house, swinging around the rear and parking between the solar panels and harvested crops they still had yet to process. Inside, Helen greeted him excitedly as the smell of fresh-brewed coffee began filling the air.

"Well, what did she say?"

Ryan leaned on the counter and released Duchess from her leash. "*She* is someone who claims to be named Sandy. Said her husband was involved in the attack on us. Said his name was Chase Crenshaw. Ring a bell?"

"Nope."

"I figure we must have buried him because he never came home, according to her."

"Well, what does she want?"

"She said her son is sick. Sounds like an infection. I'm guessing bacterial because it's been getting worse and worse, or so she says."

"Mm. Alice stored some broad-spectrum antibiotics upstairs in the hall cupboard. Could spare a few."

"True, but those are valuable pills, and we might need them someday."

"Fair. What'd you tell her?"

Ryan unslung his rifle and set it on the breakfast bar. "I told her I'd think about trying to find something her son could use, but it wouldn't be free. Thinking about it more on the way back up to the house... I figure she'll have to make us a great deal if she wants them."

CHAPTER TEN

Ricardo Braga
Rio de Janiero, Brazil

Sprawling favelas ran up the hillsides, brightly colored homes standing atop one another, filling in every nook and cranny both low and high, with terraced verandas jutting from the upper floors to peer out over the ocean. The skies were dark, yet the city was alight with both electric bulbs and candlelight that bathed the slope in a golden ambiance and glinted off the waves.

Boats out in the harbor had burned and sunk, the warehouses having gone up in flames or were already looted, many in the lower favelas living like despot kings. Along the shoreline, taxis, cars, and delivery trucks had caused raging blazes that had devoured entire sections of the city, leaving almost a million dead with fires still occasionally turning the skies orange several days later as some new source of fuel went up in smoke. Unlike those in western cities, the citizens of Rio de Janeiro had largely come together to keep the fires at bay, working in shifts to carry buckets of water up from the ocean and reservoirs, fighting tooth and nail for their homes and lives. Communities had absorbed displaced citizens even as the hotels and tourist spots along the shoreline curled with smoke and flames.

The worst had seemed to be over, but when the more affluent people living in the heights demanded harsh punishment for a poor boy who'd stolen from them, it kicked off a clash between the citizens. Underlying class tensions roared to the forefront, fights broke out, and genuine fear rippled through the city as it straddled a fine line between order and chaos. Unruly citizens overwhelmed the highrise homes out on Irmaos Point, looting, destroying, and putting them to the torch while the surrounding favelas remained unspoiled, Christ the Redeemer standing atop Mount Corcovado, overlooking the city with outstretched arms.

Ricardo Braga and his family sat in their home around a small kitchen table with modest decorations on the walls, a large wooden crucifix, and an image of Jesus above the doorway. Lanterns burned in the corners and sat on the windowsill, filling the room with a warmth that contrasted with the soft sounds of the ocean in the background. Marcia stirred a big pot of barbecued beef and corn, the rich smells drifting through their home. The short, dark-haired woman stood over the pot and sprinkled a few spices across the top, stirring, tasting it again, finally giving a sharp nod.

"This is ready, my loves," she said, using a pot handle to grab the cast iron pan and moving around the table to serve each one of their five children heaping spoonfuls of it, stopping at Ricardo's plate and dishing him an extra amount.

"Take some back and divide it between the children," he told her. "This is too much for me."

"Nonsense," she said with a smile. "Look at these round bellies. Everyone is eating well, thanks to you, Ricardo. Such a good and loving husband." She held the hot pan away, leaned in, and kissed him on the cheek before heading back to the stove and setting the pan down with a clank.

Ricardo's heart swelled with pride, watching his three daughters and two sons eat. "It is only by God's grace I have the strength to take care of my loving family. There is nothing I wouldn't do for you. Let us pray."

Ricardo gave his heartfelt thanks to God for their good fortune, their health, and the meal they were about to eat. With an "Amen,' he picked up his fork and ate while Marcia turned up the radio, and an official-sounding government voice filled the room.

"... Brazilian government continues to request all citizens stay indoors, shelter in place, and report any looting to the local authorities." Ricardo scoffed. "Looting of any sort will not be tolerated, and President Manuel has declared the act of stealing punishable by death..."

"Could you please turn that off, Marcia?"

"Why?"

"I can't stand hearing them prattle on about what *we* should do and all the promises they make to protect us. They only want to control our lives."

"It was a terrorist attack, Ricardo. No one could have seen this coming."

Ricardo scoffed louder. "But they should stop making empty promises. Nothing will change, and our people will always be exploited... more so now than ever!"

"I need to know what is happening. I need this radio on, Ricardo. Please?"

"Very well. Maybe they will say something worth listening to soon. But we would be fools to expect someone to come and rescue us. They will only try to save those at the top of the mountains first, while the rest of us are on our own. That's okay, because we don't need them, anyway. We're doing just fine."

"We're holding on by a string," Marcia reminded him. "And there are rumors of a mass relocation."

"Why would we move? We have everything we need right here."

Marcia shrugged. "They are only rumors."

The kids finished their meals and were excused from the table, and Marcia called after them to clean their rooms before they went to their cousin's.

Ricardo ate his last bite and started to get up to clean his plate when Marcia bade him sit. "I'll clean up. Rest a few more minutes before you leave."

"Thank you." He folded his hands in front of him as Marcia poured him a half cup of water from the jugs they kept in cool storage in the floor.

"I'll stop by the market today and buy a week's supplies if the prices are still low."

"The markets will continue to stabilize, and the vendors will have things under control again soon. The ships can't run, but we can do without imports. They've switched to local farms now. Beef will still be quite high, but pork will be cheap. Buy more of that until the price for beef comes down."

"I'll look for it," Marcia nodded, "and plenty of fruits and vegetables, too. The cost of corn has actually gone down. Can you believe that? I thought people would try to take advantage of the situation, but everyone has been so kind in the markets. No lines, no fighting, and everyone getting what we need."

"It is a testament to our people. We go through so much, but we always persevere."

"My only concern is the value of our money. What if the Real becomes worthless?"

"The vendors at the market will honor it still, out of pride. If not, we still have the valuables beneath the floor."

Marcia stood by him with her arm resting across his shoulders. "Heirlooms and things I'd rather not part with."

He patted her hand. "It should not come to that, dear. Ah, it's time for me to go." At the door, Ricardo hugged and kissed her. "Keep an eye out, dear. If you see looters, let Lucas know. He'll know what to do."

"I will. Have a good day."

Ricardo said goodbye to his kids, laughing as they all stormed in and hugged him, then he was out the door, descending the winding stairwell, crossing a short bridge to another landing, and smiling at the family sitting on their porch. He climbed down a steel ladder that creaked and groaned under his weight and at ground level he jumped off and landed on the cobblestone street, staggering a bit before heading along the winding lane to the construction site where they were clearing debris from a badly scorched collapse.

Dogs barked and citizens shouted up into the heights, and the distant sound of music came warbling in on the wind from the direction of the market area, filling him with a sense of peace he couldn't explain. People pushed carts packed with goods, carried baskets, and traded on street corners. They'd turned small warehouse buildings into hospitals where the injured could receive care. Nearby parks bustled with children and mothers. *It's truly a miracle,* he thought.

Ricardo moved with a hop in his step, entering the lower levels along the shoreline where the smell of char stung his nose and eyes. Around a bend in the hill where the tourist restaurants used to be, the scene opened to a blackened hillside with a spillage of bricks and steel, glass and furniture in an ever-shifting pile of junk. People stood on the outskirts with gloomy faces, watching and waiting and hoping beyond hope for their lost family members to walk out of the rubble. Workers just coming off shift dragged their feet as they left the work site, smears of dirt on their masks, their gloves pitch black, some bleeding from cuts and scrapes.

Ricardo waved to Darius and Miguel, took an air filtration mask from his foreman, and joined the work. As he entered, men stepped past him carrying timbers, scorched furniture, and sometimes a corpse on a bloody, filthy gurney, a thin sheet or piece of tarpaulin draped over the still forms. He fell into line with all the others, grabbing an enormous chunk of stone and handing it to the person behind him. More debris followed, an endless conveyor of rubble, winding like a snake into the thickest part of the collapse. While the bulk of the workers concentrated their efforts on one spot, others climbed over the hillside like insects, using blunt objects to bang on things, seeking out survivors and testing the stability of the structures.

Panting in the stifling mask, face hot even as the breeze off the ocean cooled his neck, Ricardo fell into a trance-like rhythm, becoming one with his fellows as the foreman guided them to new spots to dig. The head of the line turned upward, and Ricardo found himself on a steep part of the hillside with his feet spread apart, balancing as he handled heavy rubble, his hands sweaty and blistered inside his work gloves. After another hour, he was ready for a break, throat parched and desperate for a single glass of water. An explosion of noise and shouts filtered down, and word reached them that someone was buried alive in the hillside. All eyes shifted upward, sweaty faces hoping for a miracle. The second it was confirmed, workers ran up the treacherous slope, forming a new line where the foreman was pointing. Men with sledgehammers, axes, and a jack-hammer turned large chunks into manageable pieces, and wheelbarrows were brought up, filled to overflowing, and wheeled down on plywood ramps.

Ricardo worked his way up the hill, loading, carrying, and dropping big chunks of debris into the wheelbarrow until his hands were raw and bleeding even under his gloves. Off to the right, a group of people cheered and shook their fists as a woman was pulled from the wreckage, clothes torn, her face covered in dust, knees shaking as they led her to the waiting medical staff. Exhausted and applauding, Ricardo thought they were done, but workers raised their hands and flocked to another section as more soft bangs came from the rubble. Laughing giddily in disbelief, Ricardo stepped out of line and climbed up to be with the lead rescuers. An entire house had crumbled on the slope, spilling on top of several others, forming a bubble of wooden beams, chicken wire and steel rods they used to reinforce the structures, with bricks, mortar and dust everywhere.

The main body of workers stood off to the right, scooping aside big chunks, gesturing for more wheelbarrows to be brought up. As the minutes wore on, the workers grew impatient, throwing up their hands in frustration. Ricardo had worked in the caves and deep in the hulls of ships, and he knew how sound traveled. It could be tricky, and reverberations in steel and stone were difficult to track. He remembered searching through an entire ship for a half day before locating the origins of a mysterious pinging noise ringing up through the decks, narrowing it down to a steel shaft coming off the rudder.

He drifted off to the left by himself, staggering on weak legs, finding a flat spot in front of the spill, kicking random rocks and debris out of the way, falling to one knee, hands settling on the stones. Resting, breathing quietly, he prayed that whoever was stuck in there would strike something and make a sound that would reach him through all that rock. When it did a few seconds later, he could hardly believe it, the faint *clink* barely audible above all the rest of the din.

Whipping off his gloves, he rested his blistered fingers on the stone, whispering a prayer, begging them to hit it again. The next clink vibrated through his fingertips, metal on stone, the strikes weaker than before, and something deep within him told him time was running out. Ricardo worked his way back and forth across the ruins, touching different places and getting a feel of where the knocking was coming from. He fell to his knees and crawled beneath a lip of dangling stone, spotting the top half of a window frame, glass hanging off in jagged shards, the area beyond it pitch black beneath tons of rubble. There was only a foot of space, but he used a stick to knock out the sharp glass and thrust his head and shoulders inside.

"Hello! Is anyone in here?! Can you hear me?!"

The clanking came again, repeated whacks, Ricardo's heart leaping as he crawled in farther until his waist squeezed through the window frame and dust trickled on his head. He hollered again, but his air filtration mask muffled his voice. Lying on his belly, squeezed between tons of rock, he tried to get it off, but the space was too confined, and he had to back out and whip the mask off before diving forward again.

"Hello! Are you in here?" Remembering his flashlight, he unhooked it from his belt, flipped it on, and shined it into the darkness. A maze of piled stones stretched out ahead of him, just a few feet of space in any direction, shards of wood and steel jutting everywhere. "Hello? Answer me if you can!"

"Yes, I'm here," came the weak reply, a boy's voice filled with pain and fear. "Help me? *Please!* I'm here!"

A sudden rush of adrenaline hit Ricardo. "Are you hurt?"

"There's a rock on my leg, and Mama... she's dead, I think."

Ricardo's heart sunk, both for the boy's mother and in doubt that they could get the child out with a stone resting on his leg.

"Okay, I hear you. We're coming to get you. Don't move."

Despite the slim odds, Ricardo backed out of the hole, got to his knees, and stood. By then, a crowd had gathered around, the foreman grabbing him by the shoulders and shaking.

"Did you find someone?"

Ricardo embraced him and grinned wider. "Yes, there's a little boy in there. He's alive and talking."

The crowd roared with joy, and hands slapped his back.

"He is alive," Ricardo repeated, "but he has a rock on his leg, and his mother is in there with him, dead."

The foreman's face went ashen. "He's been in there the whole time with his mother's corpse? Poor boy. We must get him out."

The foreman stepped up on a tall stone to address the growing throng with a loud, booming voice. "This rubble has a rounded shape, so there must be some support below it. We will pull pieces off the top and try to lighten the load. Let's get to work!"

They attacked the hill of debris in a swarm, rolling off huge rocks, tossing the smaller ones way off to the side, leaving the longer beams jutting up to keep the support structure intact. From the air it would have appeared as though the mound took on a life of its own, the pieces of rubble shifting, the people groaning as a large section collapsed and fell in. Everyone stopped working, staring at each other until the mound finally settled into stony silence.

Ricardo fell to his knees and crawled in, shouting beneath the window frame. "Are you still with us? Are you there?"

After a painful pause, the child's voice graced his ears. "Yeah, I'm okay. What was that noise?"

"It was the rubble shifting. That was our fault. It won't happen again. What is your name, child?"

"Rafael."

"Okay, Rafael. Don't be afraid. I'll be right back." Ricardo stood. "He's okay, but we shouldn't move any more rubble. Someone must go inside and pull him out."

The foreman nodded and drew in some people around them, leaving Ricardo standing by the opening, eyeing it, shifting from one foot to the other as he measured up his chances of reaching Rafael.

Someone ran off and returned a moment later with a diminutive female worker who barely weighed a hundred pounds.

"This is Rosa," the foreman said. "She is the smallest of us. She volunteered to go inside and save the child."

Rosa stepped forward and stripped off her mask and gloves, staring at the narrow entrance with a determined expression. Workers behind her gathered some rope and started tying it around her waist, but the fear of crawling into the enclosed space - into the darkness beneath tons of rubble - finally got to her and tears began streaming down her face.

Ricardo grabbed the rope and took it off her, turning, tying it to himself. "I'll go inside."

"Ricardo, no," the foreman said. "You won't fit."

"I am no large man," Ricardo replied. "I've seen what it looks like inside, and I can fit. Plus, large stones might require my strength to move." He turned to Rosa. "Thank you... bless you... but I will do this, Rosa. Just remember to pull me out when I tug."

Rosa smiled and nodded, and as Ricardo faced the opening, the workers patted his back and shouted words of encouragement.

"Come on, Ricardo."

"You can do it!"

"We'll pray for you. God will go with you!"

Taking deep breaths like he was about to dive into a pool, Ricardo laid on his belly and flipped on his flashlight. The twisting curves of rubble looked the same, passages cutting into the pile of loose debris, like the tunnels of an anthill. Before fear and doubt could overtake him, he crawled inside, advancing past the window, wiggling ahead, pulling himself over tiny mounds of stone and squeezing beneath a wide beam of wood, stopping to shine the light around.

"Rafael, can you hear me?"

"Yes, I hear you," he called back with a whimper. "Are you going to get me out now?"

"Yes, I'm coming in now. No more delays. By the way, my name is Ricardo."

"Okay, Ricardo. Thank you."

Ricardo shook his head, admiring him for remembering to be polite despite the fact that he must be shaking with terror. As they talked, Ricardo had been tilting his ear, trying to pinpoint Rafael's direction, sensing he was off to the right. "Okay, son. I need you to keep talking to me so I can tell where you are."

"What should I talk about?"

Ricardo started crawling to his right with sounds close around him, trickling pebbles, the smooth sifting of sand and dust and a larger, deeper rumble reverberating beneath them, the shifting hillside, a tomb for the living and the dead. Shaking the terrible thoughts off, Ricardo crept along in increments, trying not to think more than a few seconds ahead at a time.

Have to keep moving... have to work deeper before you freeze completely. Talk to him... talk to Rafael.

"Tell me about your Ma —" He caught himself. "I mean, tell me about your brothers and sisters. Do you have any of those?"

"Yeah," came the timid reply. "I have one brother... Antonio. I have a sister, too."

"What's her name?"

"Emila."

"Oh, that's a pretty name. Where are they?"

"They were staying with my cousin when our house fell in."

Ricardo breathed a sigh of relief. "Well, I'm sure they're safe, Rafael. What is Antonio like?"

While Rafael talked, Ricardo focused on his voice, tuning out his fear and claustrophobia, imagining God's hand holding up the massive pile of stones above his head to soothe his mind. Where he crawled, he bumped and bruised himself, shoving rocks out of the way as he pushed on. With two more turns, Rafael's voice grew louder, somewhere off to the right, bouncing off the stones. But no matter how much he shined his flashlight around, he couldn't find the boy anywhere, and then he arrived at a dead end, forcing himself to wiggle backward until he came to a junction and took a hard right, chin brushing the ground as he edged into a wider space that gave him room to breathe and speak.

After a few feet, Rafael called out. "Is that you?"

"Yes! Do you see my lights?"

"I see it flickering. You're close."

"Keep talking to me... Tell me about Emila, and let me know if my light is getting brighter."

"Okay."

Ricardo estimated he was thirty or forty feet inside the rubble pile, the tunnels running deeper and farther than he could've imagined. Choking on dust, blinking particles out of his eyes, Ricardo reached the narrowest spot yet, forcing him to turn sideways, stick his arms through and suck his stomach in to draw past the sharp steel and concrete scraping his skin.

"Hi, Ricardo."

The voice was right by his ear, and Ricardo twisted, shifted, and sighed with relief when a pale face blinked back at him in the flashlight beam.

"Hello, Rafael!" He crawled a little farther and grasped his hand. "I found you. Now, let's see how you're stuck."

"It's my legs." He was sitting up but slumped over with the low ceiling atop his head, a large piece of concrete or stone covering the lower half of his body.

"Okay, let me see."

In the tight space, Ricardo worked around the massive slab, its shape roughly rectangular where it sat on a bed of smaller stones. As he worked his way around, his stomach sank, seeing how impossible it would be to move the rock without causing more damage to his legs. Coming around the other side, Ricardo stumbled upon the mother's body and jerked back, hitting his head on the ceiling with a sharp crack that sent waves of nausea through his stomach. Her entire left side was stuck inside a wall, her face covered in ash and dust, one eye staring past him into the darkness. He'd been so caught up in getting Rafael free, he didn't smell the rot until he was right on top of it, and he waited for the nausea to pass before he went on.

"Mama is dead, isn't she?" The boy's voice held the slightest bit of a tremor.

"I'm afraid so, Rafael," he replied, working on clearing the loose stones from beneath the slab. "And I'm sorry about that, son, but we need to get you out before we shed any tears for your sweet mama. Do you feel any pain right now?"

"No, no pain at all."

"Can you wiggle your toes?"

He thought about it and nodded. "Yes, I can wiggle them."

Shaking his head in confusion, Ricardo kept working, moving stones, unable to understand how Rafael could still feel his limbs. Soon, it became clear that the large slab was resting on the piled rocks, and the boy's legs were trapped at an awkward angle, but thankfully not crushed.

"I'm almost there," he said hurriedly as he cast more rocks aside. "Just a few more minutes."

"Okay."

Ricardo soon cleared enough stones to see the boy's shorts and his legs where they were trapped, feet spread where the rock had pinned him. More determined than ever, Ricardo finished maneuvering and reached to take Rafael's lower leg gently.

"Can you feel that?"

"Yes."

"Good. Now, we're going to pull that leg out first, and I want you to tell me if it hurts."

"Okay."

Tugging Rafael's leg and then his knee, Ricardo worked the limb free, making him shift to his left side and start backing out so that the other leg came, too. After some scraping and head bumping, with trickles of dust falling on their faces, Ricardo had him free.

"Excellent, Rafael. You're free. Can you move your legs?"

"I... I think so... yes..."

"We're not out of the water yet, son." Ricardo used the flashlight to inspect the boy's small form, finding some scrapes and bruises, but otherwise Rafael was unharmed.

"I'm so thirsty," Rafael said.

"Me too. I don't have any water with me, but there's plenty outside. Now, let's get out of here."

Ricardo gave the boy room to let him slide past, but Rafael paused to touch his mother's arm, her pale face bathed in the stark flashlight glow. Ricardo had tried to keep from shining it in her face, but in the enclosed space, there was no getting around it.

"Bye, Mama. I love you." He turned to Ricardo, his gaunt, dirty face holding more bravery than Ricardo had seen in his life. "Okay, I'm ready to go now."

With a nod, Ricardo gestured toward the rope. "I've got this rope attached to me. I want you to go out ahead of me and follow it to the exit, okay? I'll be right behind you."

The pile shifted as they started to move, dirt trickling more intensely, the low grumbling of stone vibrating through his whole body and jaws and teeth. Entire sections of the wall slid five or six inches, rocks clacking on the floor, voices outside calling in for them to hurry. The next few minutes were a blur, with Ricardo shoving Rafael out ahead of him, pushing on his backside and ignoring his complaints and cries as he bumped his head and elbows. Finally, with stones falling on him, Ricardo removed the rope from around his waist and tied it to Rafael, taking up the slack and tugging hard two or three times.

"Hang on to the rope, son! They're going to pull you —"

Rafael shot through the twisting passages, feet kicking, leaving a trail of dust behind him. Suddenly the boy was gone and Ricardo was alone. He shoved a pile of falling stone out of his way, fighting, spitting dirt, directionless. He slipped to his right where the ceiling dropped, clambering over it and sliding down the other side, cracking his head on a lip of rock before he was moving once more, elbows and knees propelling him like a lizard through the dust.

Crawl, man, crawl! For Marcia and the kids. By God's good grace, crawl!

Stones fell like rain, trickling in his hair, the dust so thick he could barely see in the dim light. A cool breeze touched his left cheek, and he turned toward it, pointing the flashlight ahead of him and pushing ahead. The window frame was five feet away, the clearance having shrunk by several inches since he last entered. Still, he crawled until his legs were pinned to his sides, and all he could move were his arms. He clawed at the rocks as the weight of the hillside pressed on his spine. Creeping the last inch, Ricardo tried to call out, but his throat was choked with dust, and the words died on his lips.

He thrust his hands through the opening to the sounds of cheering and celebration, but it wasn't for him, it was for Rafael.

Ricardo coughed and choked on his last breaths with a smile on his face, his last moments of life given to saving someone else's. Then firm hands gripped him by the wrists, tugging and pulling, inch by inch, freeing him from the mountain's hold. The cold air was a slap to the face as the workers hauled him free, and he slid another two feet, turning on his side and curling up his legs as the debris pile gave a final belch of dust and collapsed on itself.

Hands lifted him and patted his back, knocking the dust from his lungs, water sprayed his face, and someone thrust a bottle into his hands. He put it to his lips, drinking, washing out his mouth, spitting it to the side, then swallowing the rest. His legs were rubber, his back aching, bleeding from a hundred cuts and scrapes, but he turned his smiling face toward little Rafael where the crowd carried him around, cheering with joy. Rosa threw her arms around Ricardo, squeezing hard as tears streamed down her dirty cheeks and the foreman gripped his shoulders and hugged him, holding up his arm and shouting to the crowd.

"Cheers to Ricardo! Cheers, my friend!"

"Thanks," he said weakly, hand shaking as he took another bottle of water, drinking from it and spitting mud.

"God is truly good, Ricardo. The people will remember you for this."

"One thing, foreman."

The foreman leaned closer. "Yes, my friend?"

"It is good that Rafael is safe, but his mother..." Ricardo glanced toward the settling pile. "She's inside there and gone. He will need a place to stay, someone to care for him."

"Don't worry about it, my friend." The foreman patted his shoulder. "The boy will be well taken care of. Go home to your wife and kids."

"But I'm not even halfway done with my shift."

"Go get your day's pay from Juliana at the office. She will know what happened by now. Do not worry about it, Ricardo. Take your pay and spend it at the market. Take something good home for your family."

"Are you sure?" Ricardo asked, thankful when the foreman nodded and ushered him away.

He stumbled down the hillside, tripping over rocks and rubble. Hands took his arms and helped him until he stood at the bottom of the hill, and he turned to watch the workers crawling over it, still searching for any living souls. After collecting his pay, he passed through the favelas where savory scents drifted and music filled the air, the people still cheerful in spite of the dire situation. His dirty face and clothes showed where he'd been, and news of Rafael's rescue had spread throughout the favelas. People stared and smiled, grandmothers hugged him, younger women pointed and grinned and men clapped him on the back and shoulders.

At the market, a meat vendor threw in an extra cut of beef with the chickens, and another gave him a bag of candy for his children, expensive chocolate truffles for a fraction of their normal cost. By the time he left the market, he carried a basket of goods and a bouquet of colorful wildflowers and roses for Marcia. He made his way home, rounding the bottom of the hill where things were normal once more, music playing on the beaches, people dancing on a balcony way up high in the upper favelas. With his arms full, he climbed the steel ladder, crossed the bridges, and ascended the stairwell to his family's small apartment. He didn't mask his entry, putting down the packages of meat, vegetables, and candy on the counter with a loud thump. Footsteps came down the hall and turned into the kitchen, Marcia with a worried look that fell away when she saw it was him.

She clutched her chest. "You scared me, Ricardo. I didn't expect you home so early. Your shift —"

"Isn't even halfway over," he nodded. "They sent me home early."

"Oh, no, dear," her expression fell. "Did something happen? Did you get fired?"

Ricardo laughed tiredly. "Oh, nothing like that. Everything is fine. Well, I guess something happened..."

Marcia spotted all of the packages on the counter and her jaw dropped. "What is all this?"

"I received my full pay and made a quick trip to the market. Some kind people gave me some extra."

Marcia shook her head as she walked over, finally getting a good look at him, gasping as she reached out to touch his face. "Ricardo, what happened? You've got scratches and cuts... You're bleeding."

He nodded, remembering Rafael and the darkness beneath the rubble pile, the tight passages, the twists and turns and the rumbling stone, shuddering at the thoughts. "It's... a long story."

She took him by the hand. "I want you to tell me all about it. I'll get you a beer and take care of these cuts." She gestured to the things on the counter. "You didn't happen to pick up some bandages, did you?"

"In the bag."

Marcia checked. "There are bandages and antibiotic cream." She turned and held a tube up. "This is expensive, Ricardo. We cannot afford this."

Before she could go on, he pulled her close and hugged her tight. "Don't worry, Marcia. I didn't pay for that either. In fact, I got almost everything for free. I still have my day's pay. Here it is."

Bills and coins hit the counter, and Marcia blinked at the packages and her husband's grimy face. "Well, I expect this will be quite a story."

Ricardo shrugged. "Just another day on the job. When will the kids be home? I would very much like to hug them."

CHAPTER ELEVEN

Alice Burton
Talladega National Forest, Alabama

Water trickled over stacks of stones that dipped southward into the valley below as Alice and the kids stood on a flat piece of land just before a steep drop-off, the trail running parallel to it for a time before cutting back east the way they'd come along the hillside. The horses drank deeply at the creek's edge after their long ride through the beautiful, bug-infested woods, their tails swatting at the gnats and flies that had followed them out of the foliage. Red, orange, and gold leaves streaked the distant treetops like splashed paint on a canvas, and the slopes around them were covered with muted color as the changing season worked its magic on the flora.

The air was cooler than it had been during their trip through Florida and Georgia, though the sun still stood high and cast rays of golden light through breaks in the trees as it cut across the landscape. They'd entered an area of sloping forestland covered in low brush, crowded with hardwood saplings and prickly bushes, though the forest's denseness wasn't all that thick, and was interspersed with small meadows like the one they were taking a breather in while they waited for the horses to finish drinking. They could have ridden through the woods directly, but had come across animal trails that were much more accessible, three-foot-wide paths they'd been following for the entire day with no sign of humans, only the sharp hammering of woodpeckers, falling acorns from unseen squirrels and the snorts and chuffs from animals as they passed by.

"Would you look at that?" Jake stood a bit down the trail with his hands on his hips as the misty valley opened up at their feet.

"It's beautiful," Alice agreed. "We could live here if we had the right gear."

"No way!" Sarah was crouching near the horses, working on preparing an MRE. "There're way too many bugs up here. Almost as bad as Florida. Jake, can you find the bug repellent?"

"Coming right up."

Alice sat on the soft grass next to her daughter and opened an MRE. "Hrm. Beef patty and jalapeno pepper jack."

"We've been avoiding these," Sarah frowned, "but we're all out of everything else. Now we don't have a choice." She popped her beef patty into her heating pouch, poured in some water, sealed it, and shook it up, placing it on a rock beside her where it could cook, then she lifted a pack of crackers with a flourish. "And while that cooks, Chef Sarah will prepare the jalapeno dip for proper eating. Note how the chef breaks the crackers into bite-sized pieces *before* opening the packet." She smashed the package between her fingers, crunching the saltines inside, then broke the pack open and dug out a piece. With a squeeze of cheese spread on top, she ate it, shrugging. "Chef Sarah is not entirely displeased."

"We're getting pretty good at this MRE stuff," Alice smiled.

"Oh yeah. I've opened my share of MREs out here." Sarah spoke with a swagger as she chewed. "It's rough on us soldiers, but we'll get through somehow."

Alice laughed and got her MRE sorted out in her lap. There were crackers, a chocolate chip cookie, multicolored candy bits, and powdered chocolate drink. "Someone pass me some clean water."

"We need to conserve that in case we need it." Sarah held up a filter straw. "Today, we drink from the creek."

"Not for the chocolate drink." Alice groaned. "Please, tell me I don't have to use creek water for my chocolate milk. I know, it's filtered and just as good as the fresh stuff just... please."

Sarah eyed her. "You look desperate, mom. Fine. For you, a bottle of fresh water we got from..." She looked thoughtful as she handed over a bottle. "I'm not sure where we got it, but it's clean."

"Thanks."

"Found it!" Jake backed away from the horses and held up a can of bug spray. "I thought we might've lost it, but someone put it in one of Hercules' saddlebags."

"That was me," Sarah said. "I wanted it to be handy since I've been using it just about every day out here."

Jake walked over and tossed it to her. "Mosquitoes must really like you. They hardly ever bug me out here. Pun intended."

Sarah rolled her eyes and stepped away from the pair to stand back on the trail where she sprayed chemical mist all over herself.

"What about you, Mom?" Jake asked, sitting next to her. "Do the bugs drive you nuts, too?"

"I've been bitten once or twice," Alice replied, sealing her beef patty inside the heating pouch. "Not as bad as your sister."

"I'm not sure why they like her so much." Jake mocked. "She can't be that tasty...."

Sarah held up the bug spray can and threatened to throw it. "You want a dent in the side of your head?"

Jake laughed good-naturedly, holding up his hands. "Sorry, sis. I'm just playing around. I'm sure you're *extra* tasty to the bugs."

A moment later, after Jake had caught the flying bug spray can with a laugh, they were all sitting in a semicircle with the creek trickling nearby. Jake had filled their "dirty" water bottles with creek water, and they sipped from them with filter straws. The minutes passed lazily as they ate in silence, enjoying the peace and quiet, Alice wishing it was back home in the woods outside their house where they sometimes practiced camping on weekends.

"Your father would love this place," Alice said. "I miss being home, but that view is incredible."

"I wonder where we are?" Jake asked.

"It's hard to tell. After those guys chased us off the road, we could be anywhere. Feels like we've been following animal trails for ages."

"I'm not complaining about that," Sarah replied. "It's much easier than going through the woods blind."

"That's why I picked the trails," Alice nodded. "Much easier on the horses and us."

Sarah dipped her last cracker in her cheese and ate it. "Who do you think those men were back there? They were driving around a street sweeper. Can you believe that? They wanted to run us over so badly, but they didn't start shooting at us until we were about to get away."

"I wish I had an answer for you, honey. The way the world is now, I can't imagine what's running through people's minds. We'll never know what motivated them to be so mean. This is happening all over the place.... Society is messed up, and the survivors are a mix of good and bad."

Jake threw a pebble into the creek, where it bounced off another rock and splashed. "Mostly bad."

"You can't say that. What about Wilford, Nate, and Elaine? Those are all great people, and I'm sure we'll meet more like that on the way home. Need I remind you —"

"We've got a long way to go," Sarah finished for her.

"That's our motto, right?" Alice said. "We've got a long, long way to go."

"And a short time to get there," Jake added.

Alice finished her meal, folded up the empty packages, and placed them in a small plastic bag sitting between them. "Okay, guys. Let's get going."

They slung their packs on Hercules and mounted up with Alice leading the way north along the soft dirt path. Occasional tree roots cut furrows in front of them, and the trail edges grew steeper as they parted ways with the creek and entered the deep woods. The hillsides were bursting with pine and hardwood trees, purple flowers, and ivy scaling high up the tree trunks. The sharp scent of decaying leaves was turned up by the horse's hooves, and massive slabs of bedrock wore through the soil in great strips of gray. Other trails intersected with theirs, and she did her best to keep them moving north, but the trails inevitably wound west again, cutting through an endless expanse of wilderness as far as she could see.

After an hour, Sarah looked worried. "Are we even getting anywhere?"

"It's a trail, so I'd think it'll lead us *somewhere*, but these are pretty deep woods, and we haven't seen a house or a person anywhere for miles."

"And all we have is basic camping gear," Jake added. "No thermal blankets and stuff. It could get pretty cold out here at night."

"Keep looking, kids. There has to be an end to this. I'm only certain we're farther west than we wanted to be, and I hope we're not lost in the Appalachian Mountains somewhere. Those trails go on for hundreds of miles."

The next hour passed slowly, feeling like they were moving at a good clip but not getting anywhere. Cresting a rise, Sarah saw something and pointed, and they took the horses along the flat section of trail running smoothly into a gravel lot. A trailhead stood on the north end with a big sign next to it, and a few vehicles sat around gutted by explosions, leaving chunks of debris scattered everywhere.

"I think that used to be a camper." Jake pointed to a pile of junk sitting on its side with a long silver roof charred with fire marks.

"I think you're right," Alice replied. "And look past that... there's a service road that probably leads to a highway or main road."

"Should we take it?" Sarah asked.

"Let's go see what this sign says."

They turned their horses toward the sign across the lot, but Sarah got there first. "Talladega National Forest," she called out. "Okay, where is that?"

Alice frowned. "Alabama."

"Alabama?"

"Yep. I hate to say it, but we're off course." Alice started rummaging through one of her saddlebags. "But at least we know where we are, and I have a map that might help."

"Can we course correct?" Jake asked. "I mean, does this road lead to where we want to go?"

"Give me a second." Alice unfolded the map and placed it in her lap, pinpointing the Talladega National Forest. "According to the map, this main trail will take us through the hills and down the other side to another group of branching highways. It looks like a long shot, so we might have to do some camping."

"In the middle of nowhere?" Jake said. "Do we have the supplies for that?"

"We've got the supplies, though it might be a little cold. Still, we'll have access to all the firewood we'd need, and the road hasn't been too good to us lately anyway. Might be nice to go off-road for a while." Alice looked at the sign and then up the trail. "These trails are bound to be amazing, and the horses will have plenty to drink with all the creeks and streams running through these hills."

"But the bugs, Mom."

"You're going to get bugs no matter where we are, honey. Don't you want to avoid people?"

"And street sweepers?" Jake added.

"Ugh," Sarah groaned. "Okay, I guess going through the woods would be better than being on the road. And it would be better for the horses, too."

"It's settled. Let's go."

Alice walked Buck past the sign and onto the trail with a gentle breeze ruffling the low brush as birds chirped in the rustling trees, casting a peaceful calm over the forest. Off the trail on both sides were a spread of clearings, with iron grills jutting up and stone fire circles filled with pieces of charred wood.

"Looks like this place was busy at one time," Sarah said.

"This is probably for casual campers," Alice replied. "You know, those who didn't want to hike very far."

They rode for almost a quarter of a mile, spotting multiple camp-sites right off the trail. Abandoned, half-collapsed tents stood in a few places, flapping in the breeze, one spot with camping equipment strewn everywhere, blackened by flames, the edges of the clearing shredded by shrapnel. A handful of charred corpses lay sprawled around a squarish object with its top blown open and peeled back.

"Geez, what happened there?" Jake asked.

"A gas generator, I'd guess," Alice nodded. "Come on. Don't look at it." She picked up the pace and trotted up a short hill, popping over the other side but drawing up with a surprised cry.

A man popped out of the brush, stepping toward the trail with his hands up and waving. "Hey there! Hello!"

Alice grabbed her rifle as the kids rounded the hill behind her, pulling their mounts up short but pressing Buck forward with their collective bulk.

"Stop!" Alice said, training her gun on him. "Back the hell up!"

"Hey, no need for the gun, lady!" The man raised his hands straight up and took several paces back, bumping into a woman who'd stepped out of the brush behind him.

"Stay back!" Alice snapped, keeping her rifle pointed at the man's chest, holding the reins and controlling Buck as she did so. "Don't step onto the trail."

"I won't, I promise. The trail's yours."

Alice started walking Buck forward. "Okay, we're going to pass you, so don't try anything."

Glancing at the woman, he laughed. "Who's going to try anything? We saw you coming up the trail from our campsite and thought we'd say hello."

The man looked normal, early thirties with tussled brown hair and dark eyes, wearing a button-up denim shirt and jeans. The woman was short, with blonde, shoulder-length hair, wearing worn and dirty jeans and a light blue hoodie.

"Hello, and goodbye," Alice said, gesturing with her weapon barrel for them to move away.

"No need to be like that." The man's smile persisted. "We've been looking for good people out here for a while, and you seem like a nice family. That's why we came out of hiding to say hello. Can't... really say the same for others who've passed us."

131

"My name is Christine," the woman blurted and stepped forward. "And this is my husband, Mark. We're the Hubbards and we've got a couple of young ones, like you."

When they didn't move away from the trail but kept smiling, Alice said, "If you know what it's like out there, you wouldn't be walking up to armed strangers."

"I didn't know you had a gun until you pulled it on me," Mark replied.

"Surprising people on the trail like that is a good way to get yourself shot."

He swallowed hard. "Well, luckily you're good people because I'm still alive."

"Saving my bullets," Alice responded flatly. "Come on. Step back."

Mark did the opposite and stepped onto the trail in front of them, never dropping his smile. It only grew wider, and he lowered his hands to rest them on his hips. "I'm sorry, but we would be terrible people if we didn't offer you weary travelers some food and a warm fire to sit by."

Christine stepped to her husband's side. "Seriously, we could use some news if you have any, and Mia and Hunter are craving a little company. They haven't seen another kid in days." She gestured to Jake and Sarah. "It would do them wonders to talk to some other children for a change."

"We're not children," Jake replied.

"Well, you're close enough." Christine laughed. "They've been staring at our tired faces for the past couple of weeks." When Alice didn't immediately respond, she pressed on. "Stay for a few hours, please, we'd be thrilled just to have someone to talk to. There's plenty of food, and we could use the company." She gave Mark a sad glance. "A group passed the other day, but they didn't sound too nice, so we stayed away from them."

"Real rough-looking bunch," Mark said. "Big guys with guns and dogs. We hid down by the creek, hoping the dogs wouldn't smell us."

Alice backed Buck up a few paces and whispered to the kids. "What do you guys think?"

"We've got a long way to go to reach the other side of the woods,"

Sarah said. "We've been riding all day and... we could probably use a break."

"I guess it would be okay." Jake kept his voice low and didn't take his eyes off them. "And if they've got some kids, maybe we could help them out. Who knows, they could be like Nate and Elaine. Let's just be real careful, mom."

"Mhmm." Alice nodded and turned back to the couple. "Okay. We'll take a load off at your camp for a bit, but we're only going to stay a few hours before we get ready to ride through to the next highway."

"Great!" Mark said.

Christine smiled. "Oh, that's wonderful. The kids will be so happy, and they'll love the horses."

"Uh huh. Just... keep your distance for a while. Trust is hard to come by these days."

"Absolutely. Understood." Mark backed up a few feet and nodded understandingly.

"Where are you folks camping?"

"Oh, just right over here," Mark said, edging into the woods and pointing behind him. "Just forty yards off the trail."

"Lead on."

They followed the pair at a cautious distance, still staying on the horses as they went through the woods, picking their way along paths between the thistles and brush, finally coming to a clearing. Like the rest of the campsites, it was a circular area of about forty square feet with trails leading into the woods and a stone fire ring in the middle. Two large foldout chairs and two smaller ones sat around a modest fire with soft blankets thrown over the backs and bottles of water in the drink holders. A big blue tent and a smaller green one sat side-by-side close to a cluster of trees with their flaps open, thick covers and pillows folded inside.

On the far side of the camp, a boy and girl of around six played with an assortment of toys. Buck chuffed as he entered the campsite, and the girl dropped her dolls to stand and stare in awe, eyes wide as the four horses circled and stood at the edge of the encampment, keeping their distance from the couple. The boy gaped and clutched his toy cars, where he'd made a small town of ramps and roads in the mud, using rocks and stones as buildings.

"Hey, kids, we've got some guests," Mark said, gesturing to Alice as she dismounted cautiously and looked around, still holding her rifle, ready to use it at a moment's notice. "They haven't told me their names yet."

"I'm Alice. These are Sarah and Jake."

Christine walked straight across the campsite, turning as she got close to the children. "And this is Mia and Hunter. Kids, say hi to our new friends."

Jake and Sarah waved, but the new children only stared slack-jawed at the massive horses where they towered over everyone.

Christine laughed the kids' shyness off and gestured at the fire. "Mark, do we have any chairs for our guests?"

"We'll sit on some logs while they take our chairs."

"No thanks," Alice replied, handing her reins to Jake. "We'll pull up some logs. Don't want you folks to be put out."

Jake tied the horses up close by, while Alice, Sarah, and Mark dragged up some logs and spread them out opposite the chairs. After they had everything situated, they sat around the warm flames, Alice keeping herself and her two children on the side of the fire closest to the horses.

"What's cooking?" Alice glanced at a pan sitting on the grill over the fire.

"Just some country beans and ham I brought from home." Christine sat in one of the chairs and stirred the beans, moving the pan away from the center of the flames. "Have some."

"That's okay. We ate a little while ago." Alice gave Jake and Sarah a quick look, raising an eyebrow.

"Don't mind if I do." Mark found a bowl and dumped a couple of spoonfuls in, then grabbed a fork off a small table near the tents and sat in the other chair.

"You folks want some iced tea?" Christine asked. "There's plenty left."

"Yeah, I guess that would be okay," Alice replied.

"No thanks," Sarah said with a sidelong glance. "I'll just drink water."

Christine bent between the chairs, pulled up a large pitcher and some cups, and poured Alice, Jake and herself half a cup each. "It's unsweetened. I hope that's okay."

"It's fine." Alice put the cup to her nose and sniffed. "No offense, but you wouldn't mind drinking first, would you?"

Christine took a long drink while Mark chuckled next to her. "There's really no need to be so suspicious, I promise!"

"If you'd traveled the roads we have, you'd understand."

Mark sobered and nodded. "No, completely. I get it."

Alice took a sip and nodded, shoulders relaxing a bit for the first time since encountering the couple, hand slipping off of her rifle as she leaned forward on the log. "Thanks, Christine. This is good."

Jake sipped his and nodded in thanks while Sarah crossed her legs and put her hands out to the fire, watching the younger children who'd resumed their playing. Mia was fashioning clothes for her dolls out of twigs, grass, and wildflowers while Hunter drove his cars around the muddy freeways he'd built out of the knob of dirt. All four of them looked like they'd been at the campground for a few days at least, lending credence to Mark's and Christine's story. They also seemed to have more than enough supplies, and her worries over them potentially trying to rob her, Jake and Alice began to wane.

After a moment of silence, Alice gestured around at their camp. "So, what are you doing way up here in the woods?"

Mark finished his bite of beans. "We're from Ashland, about ten miles from here. Had a nice ranch house in the suburbs."

"It was a really great neighborhood," Christine said with a sad smile.

"After everything went to—" Mark looked at the two children, lowering his voice, "*hell*, we lost our house and most of our neighbors. A lot of great people died there."

"How did you survive the initial explosions?" Alice asked.

"Pure luck. We were out for a walk when it all happened."

"It was my day off from work," Christine said, "but I'd been doing housework all day. I was feeling pent up and wanted to get out for a little while. Know what I mean?"

Alice nodded.

"We were on the swings — I remember that so vividly — when the cars in the neighborhood started going off." Mark glanced at Mia and Hunter. "It scared the living daylights out of those two. Things were flying everywhere. People were screaming. We wanted to protect them, so we stayed put."

"That sounds terrifying," Alice said. "I can relate."

Mark shook his head. "It *was* terrifying, and I know you must have gone through the same thing. Anyway, we helped a couple of neighbors who were hurt in the explosions. We tried to dial nine-one-one, but all the emergency services were down. We stayed as long as we could before Christine suggested we get home. Our place was a few blocks from the people we were helping, and I saw it burning before we even got there." He took Christine's hand and squeezed. "There was nothing to salvage except a storage shed with some boxes of old clothes and stuff. I couldn't even get within twenty feet of the house until all the flames died down. Everything we had was taken away in an instant. We were destitute."

"I'm sorry to hear that," Alice said.

"I appreciate that. But you know something? It didn't seem so bad compared to what others had gone through. Not only had they lost their homes, but they lost pets and family members. From there, it took a while to adjust. Wasn't a single hotel standing in our area, and only a few barns, but we quickly learned how to survive. We scavenged, found places to sleep and stay warm, and somehow survived. We're working our way north to get to our family members up near Fort Payne. Figured the easiest way would be to take the forest route to keep away from people. Lord knows we've run across some bad ones."

"You're telling us," Jake snorted.

"We've met our share of bad folks on the road," Alice said. "Been in some pretty wild fights ourselves."

Mark took another bite. "Took us a while, but we hiked up here to the park and found the place all... well, I guess you saw all those cars down in the parking lot?"

"We sure did."

"And that site down there?" Christine clasped her hands on her knees and leaned forward. "It looks like it just blew up all the people. Must've been a generator or something."

"That's what I figured," Alice said. "They didn't stand a chance."

Christine spoke in a hushed tone. "We walked through there to see if we could scavenge anything, but I couldn't stay long. It was terrible."

"The reception isn't so great up here," Mark said, "but we tried to call the police. No response from them. Then a text came through from my brother up north – I guess before all the cell towers went dead – telling us to stay where we were and that everything had gone south in a hurry. We turned on our radio and heard the emergency broadcast system, but they've just been repeating the same thing for days."

Christine frowned. "Some kind of terrorist attack on our fuel, they said. Sounded pretty scary, so we decided not to take the kids out in that. We've been up here ever since."

Alice nodded and glanced at the little ones. "It was the best decision you could've made. There're still some good people out there, but there's a lot of danger, too. Having young ones like that makes it even more difficult. It seems safe up here, at least, which is good. What are your plans from here?"

"Still heading north, but we're giving it a couple of days to cool down. It's going to be tough, but we'll figure it out. The kids can walk fine, but not for very long."

"We've seen people struggling so hard with their children." Alice shook her head. "I can't imagine what it must be like to have to travel with little ones so young."

"Especially without those horses you have," Christine said. "Where'd you get them, anyway?"

"I promise we don't want to take them!" Mark held up his hands, chuckling.

"Oh gosh, no. We don't know two things about horses." Christine laughed. "

Alice smiled and recalled the events leading up to finding Monticello Horse Farm, including the man who'd tried to take their things on the beach and their short stint at Andrea's hotel. There was the shocking moment getting shot at by Wilford, who they'd eventually befriended, and talking about Wilford filled Alice with unexpected emotion, and she swallowed a hard lump, recounting the wild ride through the farm, shooting at people, and being shot at. "When it was all said and done, we've probably been forced to defend ourselves and shoot a half-dozen people and could've died several times over. Luck has been on our side, and the horses have made all the difference."

"What a crazy story," Mark said. "All those horses, and that old man trying to take care of them all by himself."

Alice gestured to the four horses tied up a short distance away. "That's why he offered to give us these to help us get back to Michigan."

"He turned out to be a pretty good guy," Christine said.

"He reads to his horses to relax them and stuff," Jake said. "I thought it was weird at first, but he's like a horse whisperer or something."

"And he can cook, too," Sarah added. "We had some great meals while we were there."

"We're going to miss him a lot," Alice said. "And we hope he's doing okay."

"Is that where you're headed?" Mark asked. "Michigan?"

"Yep. We've got a home outside East Lansing, and we'll hopefully meet my husband there. It already feels like we've been on the road so long, and we've got a way to go."

"We've got a *long* way to go." Sarah echoed their motto, and Jake grinned at the inside joke.

"Good thing we're only going as far as Fort Payne," Mark said. "That's a short distance compared to where you're going."

"Will the kids be okay walking that far?"

Mark chuckled and put his empty bowl aside. "We can get them pretty far, and we'll carry them for a while if we need to, at least until we find a vehicle to drive."

"That's easier said than done," Alice replied. "The only cars that work are electric ones. We had one for a little while—"

"Until someone shot it and made it catch on fire," Sarah finished for her.

"Oh, no!" Christine gasped. "You poor folks have been through a blender."

"It feels that way sometimes... but there were good moments, too."

"Like with Nate and Elaine," Sarah said, launching into what had happened at their house with the delivery of little Ethan and the night they'd spent there. Christine looked over at Mark with wide eyes when Sarah got to the part about Ethan popping out. "Mom was holding him, and I got to cut the cord. It was the most beautiful thing."

"That *is* beautiful!" Christine said. "I wish I could have been there to see it."

"You folks have quite the stories." Mark nodded and gestured toward a pack sitting at his feet. "Do you need any snacks or anything? I've got some jerky and cashews."

"Jake, would you get some of those granola bars from Hercules, and we'll trade the Hubbards for some of their snacks."

"Just not the peanut butter ones!" Sarah blurted, then looked around apologetically. "Sorry, but those are our favorites."

"Don't worry about it," Christine laughed and fell to a whisper. "We're not giving you the honey-roasted cashews, either. Only the plain ones."

Sarah chuckled and Alice grinned, feeling more at ease with their new friends, and by the time Jake had returned with the snack bars, she'd made up her mind.

"Hey, listen... sorry about the hostility earlier. It's been tough out here."

"Don't even mention it," Mark replied.

"If you're going to Fort Payne, why don't we travel together? Your kids are worn out, and we'd be happy to carry them, and you."

"That's so kind of you," Christine said, "but we couldn't impose like that."

"Nonsense. It wouldn't be a big deal. You can ride on the horses with the kids, and I'll go bareback with the equipment on Hercules."

"I hate to say it, Alice." Mark frowned, "but we'll have to turn you down. You folks have been through way too much to be put out like that. Those horses are about the most valuable thing out here now, and you need to treat them like gold."

"It won't hurt to share them until we reach Fort Payne. We'll drop you off and get right back on the road."

Mark and Christine shared a look before Mark finally broke down and smiled. "Well shoot, I guess if it's not too much trouble, we'll take you up on that offer."

"Then it's settled," Alice said. "When do you want to leave?"

"I guess we should go as soon as possible." Mark glanced at the sky. "It's getting pretty late now, though. Maybe we should hold off until first light?"

"That sounds good," Alice said. "We'll get a good night's rest, let the horses graze a little, and Jake... can you look around for a stream they can drink from?"

"There's one right over there," Christine pointed. "We've been taking water from it and boiling it."

"Perfect."

After slinging her rifle on her shoulder, Alice took their bedding off the horses while Jake and Sarah unsaddled them and led them to the creek to drink. Alice placed their bedrolls on the ground opposite the tents and prepped them for the kids, spreading blankets on top of them and rolling up old clothes to use as pillows.

"I hope you're good with that," Christine motioned at Alice's rifle as she bustled with some other chores. "I'm pretty nervous about guns around the kids."

Alice rested her hand on her pistol. "Gotta get used to it from now on, unfortunately. Chances are, you'll need one to protect yourself. You don't have any weapons?"

"Nothing at all." Christine sighed. "We've always been... against firearms. No offense to you or anything. I'm kind of rethinking that stance right now."

"Yeah, I can imagine. These are an absolute necessity out here with how things are right now. I'm shocked you didn't look for one before you left your neighborhood."

"Seemed kind of impossible since everything was burned down." She shrugged. "We just wanted to get out of there." Christine sidled up closer, lowering her voice. "And you've actually shot people?"

Alice nodded. "I didn't want to, but I had to defend us, and I'd do it again."

"I wouldn't want to mess with you guys."

Alice only smiled and marched up the slope a few paces to greet the kids coming up with the horses. "Did you find the creek?"

"Right where they told us it would be," Sarah said. "It was a little like the last creek we were at, and boy, were the horses thirsty. I think Buck drank my weight in water."

"Good. I want to make sure they're fed, watered, and rested before we move on. They'll have more to carry for a little while."

"There's a little field south of here a bit," Jake said. "Want us to take the horses down and let them graze?"

"That's a good idea, son." Alice turned back toward the camp and watched Mark and Christine talking to the kids quietly over past the fire and out of earshot. The woman bent low, speaking firmly to Mia as she brushed the dirt off her cheek, and Mark knelt in front of the brother, gesturing to him, also speaking too quietly to hear.

"Aren't they nice?" Alice asked.

"They're almost like Nate and Elaine," Sarah replied. "A little older, but their kids are cute."

"Quiet, though," Jake said. "I thought they'd be more curious about the horses. They haven't said two words to us since we've been here."

"Maybe they're just shy, or scared." Alice shrugged. "Anyway, it's nice to have met such nice people again. Helping them out feels good, and it's nice to be helped as well."

"I could get used to helping people," Sarah agreed. "Come on,

Jake, let's let the horses graze for a while, then we'll brush them. Maybe Mia and Hunter will want to pet them when we get back."

Alice watched them go with a wry smile. "Don't go too far, and if you need me —"

"Just yell!" they called back.

Sarah walked Buck and Stormy away from the fire, a satchel slung over her shoulder as they picked their way carefully through the woods. Christine was still speaking with Hunter and Mia, leading the kids by their hands and sitting them behind the chairs. Once out of earshot, Sarah focused on getting down the hillside, and they followed the creek down to a small clearing that was relatively flat where the water gathered in a pond before continuing its run over the bedrock. The forest was thick, but gaps in the canopy allowed sunlight to pour in like warm honey over the water.

"This place is incredible," Jake said, letting go of Hercules' and Rocky's reins, standing close by in case they started to wander.

"Yeah...." Sarah replied, guiding the horses over and letting them graze in the thick, vibrant grass. She strode to the edge of the woods where the forest floor was covered in moist deadfall and squirrels scampered up tree trunks to pause and watch them, insects singing in the shade, a rich chorus of sound that washed over them like a blanket of peace.

He came to stand next to her with his hands on his hips as he admired the sloping forest and the gray stones showing through the mossy ground. "What's up with you, sis?"

"What do you mean?"

"Well, you've gotten quiet."

"I'm always quiet."

Jake laughed. "No, you aren't. At least not for long. Come on, what's on your mind?"

"I'm not sure. Probably nothing."

"Is it something about Mark and Christine?"

"I'm not sure... I can't put my finger on it. Maybe it's because of all these abandoned campsites around, especially the one with the dead people. Maybe that's just creeping me out or something."

"Are you serious? After all the dead people we've passed on the road? I'd think you'd be used to it by now. I am."

Sarah scoffed. "I'll never get used to it, and I never *want* to get used to it. You'll be the first to know if I figure it out."

"Okay. What do you say we brush the horses out?"

"Yeah, sounds good."

They took the brushes from the satchel and brushed down the horses, working up a sweat, talking about Nate, Elaine, and Wilford, wondering what – and how – they were doing before switching to the topic of their missing family member.

"What do you think Dad's doing right now?" Jake asked.

Sarah shrugged. "It's funny. I can imagine what Wilford's doing, and even Nate and Elaine, but when I think about Dad... I can't think of anything. All I see is danger and...." Sarah trailed off with a whisper.

"Yeah, I know what you mean," Jake said. "Sometimes it's hard to remember what he looked like. I mean, I can't think of the last time I saw his face."

"Probably the morning he left for his flight to Denver. I barely told him goodbye. If I could have that moment back, I'd hug him and never let go."

When they were done, and the horses' coats glistened in the sunlight, they led them back up to camp where Alice sat across from the Hubbards with a rifle resting across her knees. The unsettled feeling in Sarah's gut returned, but Mia came running up with a smile and asked if she could pet Stormy, and the unease was dashed as the girl broke her silence.

Taking Mia by the hand, Sarah led her over, lifting her so she could reach up and pet the horse's beautiful, dark snout. It wasn't long before Christine came over with a smile, taking Mia from Sarah's hands and guiding her back to the camp, where she put her back with her dolls to play behind their chairs. Sarah watched for a moment, then she patted Stormy on the neck and hitched her to a tree branch with the others.

CHAPTER TWELVE

James Burton
Frankfurt, Illinois

Water trickled through the culvert pipe and swirled into the stagnant basin before flowing over a row of raised stones to race down the other side in a fast stream. James stood in six inches of the rushing water, pressed against the extended stone wall, grabbing the edge and pulling himself up to see who was coming down the road. It wasn't long before a group strolled into view; they were a rough-looking bunch, a couple dozen strong, men and women dressed in clothes that were too clean to be anywhere except from freshly looted stores. Tattoos decorated their bare arms, some with indigo blue markings visible on their necks and faces, undoubtedly members of a gang tuned to the streets who knew every shadowy alcove and back alley.

They pushed and shoved each other roughly, laughing, grabbing looted items from shopping carts and throwing them at each other. One man drew a pistol and took potshots at the remnants of the gas station, cracking rounds off the awning and then at one of the ruined pumps. Another man fired a shotgun at a building on the other side while a laughing woman kicked a chunk of debris and sent it sailing toward the culvert. James ducked as it skittered on the pavement, rolled down the hill, and plopped into the basin. Pressed to the cold, wet concrete, he waited for someone to notice him, ready to run deeper into the sewer system if necessary.

When no one came, James pulled himself up and peeked over the edge, rainwater dripping down his face. The gang was moving quickly and would be right on top of him before long, and James started to let go to get back out of sight but paused when someone shouted from down the road. Six figures jogged from a building behind the gas station and spread across the street, all of them big men, barrel-chested and wearing leather jackets with the arms cut off, symbols and emblems painted on the front in rough white and red scrawl, their heads shaved, beards hanging long from their chins. Taking up the width of the road, they gesticulated and flashed rude gestures at the much larger gang, one man casually swinging a chain as the others kept their hands close to weapons hanging from their belts. The potential confrontation heightened as the larger group turned to face them, spreading out two lines deep and brandishing more crowbars, pipes, golf clubs, pistols, and shotguns. The man with the chains shouted a challenge, and the leader of the larger gang, a lanky man with long dark dreadlocks that fell to his waist, turned and stared them down.

"Looks like some fools wandered into our territory!"

The big man wielding the chain stepped forward and spat. "Can't be your territory if you're dead."

"What d'you want?" The man with the dreadlocks barked.

"Everything," The other replied. "Just drop what you're carrying and step away, and you can live."

The man with dreadlocks turned to the people behind him, saying, "They want our supplies. Can you believe this?"

The others laughed and snickered, a few glaring at the smaller group.

"Just leave all the carts and backpacks," The man swinging the chain bellowed again, his smile growing wider. "It's pretty simple."

Dreadlocks scoffed and grinned before going dead serious. "We're not giving up anything, man. Tell you what. We'll give you ten seconds to beat it, or we'll beat *you*."

The smaller group's leader continued swinging his chain around casually, twirling it over his head and down at the ground where the heavy links bounced off the pavement. The rest of the group glanced at each other with crooked smiles, and James got the feeling there was something else at play.

The man with the dreadlocks had been counting down quietly, but then shouted the last part, "Three, two, one!" and started moving toward the other group. Before he made it two steps, figures rose on the roof of the building the smaller group had run from, rifles resting on the brick edging and aiming at the first group. Others appeared on top of the apartments across from them, and James shrank back as gun barrels flashed in a rapid-fire procession from rifles and hand-guns alike. Bullets struck the ground, ricocheting everywhere, a couple zipping by a foot above James' head while another snapped off some blades of grass on the embankment as it burrowed into the soil.

Rounds punctured flesh, peppering the larger group in a flurry of lead, and a handful of gang members screamed, clutching their chests, arms, or stomachs as they buckled over and collapsed to the ground. Others drew their weapons and were immediately targeted, guns clattering to the pavement as they gripped themselves and cried out in pain. Pinned between the two buildings, they took fire from both sides and only got off a few shots in retaliation. They jerked and spun, crying out, ducking and covering, running into and bowling over their carts as they sought cover.

Supplies spilled onto the pavement, and two cans of green beans rolled across the road to stop just a few feet from James. He was tempted to reach out and take them, but the shooting intensi-fied, and the leader of the larger group grabbed a gun from a fellow gang member and started firing at the rooftops from behind cover, sending the attackers ducking back and giving his still-living comrades a brief reprieve. He ran out of rounds after a few seconds, growling and throwing the weapon aside, turning to glare at the man in the street as he still stood where he had before the gunfire started, swinging his chain with a slow smile plastered on his face.

Standing in the middle of his decimated group, the leader started gathering survivors to him, getting the wounded up, shouting for them to move or they were dead. The head of the smaller group put his hand up, and the incoming fire halted. He gestured, and his people walked forward, preying on the downed group, beating them as they crawled and held their hands up, ignoring the cries for mercy. A crowbar struck a man's temple, leaving deep crimson splatters on the pavement and another man with a leather jacket kicked a woman in the side as she tried to stand, knocking her to the ground before swinging his ax in a brutal, overhanded blow.

The two leaders met in the middle of the bloody street, the chain whipping through the air, the one with the dreadlocks absorbing the blow on his arm, allowing the chain to wrap around it, grabbing it tight. Jerking his enemy toward him with his own chain, he swung a spiked bat at his opponent's side, sinking two inches of nails into his ribs with a thud.

James watched the engagement with a sinking feeling in his gut. If he stood, he'd be visible to the people atop the buildings, and when the winners of the brawl started picking up the loose supplies, they'd undoubtedly check the culvert pipe for survivors. Heavy objects struck ribs and jaws cracked as the groups descended into hand-on-hand violence, one battling for vicious, violent supremacy, the other for survival, both groups becoming more absorbed in the almost ritualistic fight.

It's now or never, he thought, slinking to the opposite side of the culvert entrance and starting up the moist embankment, staying low with his face pressed close to the ground, doing his best to hide in the knee-high grass and reeds. He made it ten and then fifteen yards, catching the end of the fight as the man with the dreadlocks took a punch to the side of the head, spun, and went down to the cheers and raised fists of the victors. Bodies lay everywhere, the rain carrying blood into the cracks in the concrete and washing it out in a pinkish flood.

James was just ten yards from the next block with two small

buildings, scattered dumpsters, a telephone pole, and a length of collapsed fencing covered in vines he could hide behind. Across the street, the crowded city blocks stretched ahead, more warehouses and buildings with narrow alleys and big stone stoops, old signs above the doors that were too weathered to read.

The victor raised his bloody chain at the people on the buildings, waving it as they cheered and celebrated their victory over the larger force. James was about to make a run for cover, but he caught sight of a grocery cart at the top of the ditch with its front wheels on the edge of the road. Inside were some food boxes and several gallons of water sitting in the basket. He started to move past it, then felt the light weight of his backpack resting on his shoulders with only a day or two of food remaining and no real way to get reliable, clean drinking water.

His decision-making and weighing of risks took a split second, then he was scrambling up the embankment, rising from the cool, wet grass, and grabbing the cart handle to push it down the road. The wheels made a clattering sound, louder than the rain but not as loud as the man waving his chain around as he bellowed and motioned to his group, receiving cheers and shouts in response. Stepping over to the man with dreadlocks lying in the street, he kicked him in the side, roaring at his people in victory as the rest of the gang laughed and picked up the supplies that had spilled in the road. The group above on the rooftops cheered louder, their collective shouts raucous as they celebrated their victory and spoils.

By then, James had made it almost a block away, shaking hands trying to keep a grip on the cart handle, his shoulders hunched over, shuffling at a steady pace to try and keep the wheels from clacking, but the sound was obnoxious, and it wouldn't go unnoticed for long. He winced when a shout rang out, and the cheering stopped, replaced by rumbles of surprise and faint laughter. James sank lower, staying as small as possible, trying to be invisible, a speck on the street. But the gang had spotted him, their curiosity roused into a growing murmur, six pairs of eyes staring at him from the street with others up on the roof reloading their weapons and taking aim at his back.

The man with the chain punched his fist in the air, bellowing, "Stop right there, man! I said, stop!"

James did the opposite, putting his head down and pushing hard, angling the rickety cart to the left as a spattering of bullets struck the asphalt behind him, the wobbly cart wheels making even more of a racket on the rough pavement. Pulling back on the handle, he got the front wheels on the curb and crashed up and over, pushing past another apartment building and warehouse as the gang gave chase, their feet pounding through puddles and kicking aside rubble as they ran, laughing and shouting as they yelled out what they were going to do to him when they caught him.

Adrenaline flooded his body and James tuned out their words and barreled ahead, looking quickly left and right, shoulders tense in expectation of a round to the spine. The gang closed on him, one woman with dyed blonde hair out in front, her skinny legs pumping, tongue sticking out from the corner of her mouth, a streak of violent glee in her eyes.

James banked hard left into a narrow alley, ducking as bullets shot past him, and as he rounded the corner too quickly, he hit a cobble-stone surface that caught the cart's wheels, flipping the backside up. The handle hit him in the chest as it sent him tumbling, the contents of the cart spilling everywhere. He landed on the cobblestones, arms pinned beneath him and chin smacking the ground. Stars shot through his vision as scuffling feet and shouts came closer, and the images of what he'd seen them do to the other gang flashed through his mind.

He forced himself up, starting to wholly abandon the cart and its contents, but stooped to grab a few cans of food in one hand and two-gallon jugs of water in the other. He ran for it after he'd picked them up, swinging the heavy jugs and tucking the cans in his arm like a halfback. The alley's length stretched on with no end in sight and no intersections to sidestep into and the gang reached the spilled cart a few seconds later, some laughing, while others continued the chase with growls and catcalls.

"Hey, buddy, you forgot something!"

"Come back, man... you left all this food back here. I'm gonna jam it down your throat until you choke!"

"Don't let him get away!" The leader bellowed, a cold streak of malice running through his voice.

Heart pounding in his chest, stomach sinking, James ran as hard as he could. The wind blew back his hair, and he considered throwing the jugs and cans down but stubbornly hung onto them. Finally, he reached the end of the alley and dashed to the right, sprinting head-long into a crush of dilapidated buildings that had caught fire, collapsed, and crashed together to fill in the alley with bricks and charred wood. He started to go back the other way but saw a path through, darting to the left between sections of piled rubble, ducking beneath toppled beams, jumping a crushed washing machine, and hopping through an ankle-twisting field of burned boards, wires and piping.

His knees and hips bumped sharp objects as he breathed in the stinging scent of ash and burned plastic, circling the piles to keep as many physical barriers as possible between himself and his pursuers. Shouts of frustration chased him as the group reached the end of the alley as well and saw what they had to go through to get him. Curses echoed off the buildings and into the neighborhoods beyond, and shots ricocheted off the rubble, though they were fired in frustration, and had no chance of hitting him, so he paid them no attention. Keeping his head down, he stayed low and ran hard, holding the water jugs and food in a death grip, trying to keep ahead of those hunting him.

While several tried to follow him through the ruins, others ran the edges, working to get around so they could cut him off once he came out the other side. James leaped and ducked and worked his way deeper into the moist soot-covered darkness, finding an old stair-well leading down into a basement, gently pushing aside the wet hanging flaps of insulation, reaching the subfloor, and seeking cover inside a darkened hall. He crouched behind a pile of drywall and wood, smoke drifting by, the softly glowing coals of smoldering materials stirred by the wind of his arrival, the smell acrid and nearly causing him to sneeze. He buried his face in the crook of his arm as footsteps reached the top of the stairs and stopped.

"Do you think he could've went down there?" a woman asked.

"Could have," the man responded, "but do you really want to go down after him?"

"Boss won't like it if we come back empty-handed."

"The boss won't know we didn't check every nook and cranny. Ugh, do you smell that? I ain't going down there and breathing that stuff in. Probably asbestos mixed with who knows what."

James kept his face covered, breathing through the moist material of his jacket, closing his eyes against the fog drifting through the hall, the broken pipes that had once been filled with who-knew-what creating a haze of fumes that mixed with the smoke. Feet appeared on the top step and descended a few paces, paused there, someone stooping and looking down the hallway past James and into the darkness. A flashlight's beam appeared suddenly and James held still, eyes shut tight as he tried to control his ragged breathing and keep from jostling the bottles and cans still in his aching arms. The figure seemed about to come down and look, but her shadow shook its head and headed back up.

"Yeah, you're right. It's pretty nasty down there. Let's head back with the others."

James waited until the footfalls faded far into the distance before he crept from his hiding spot, moving to the stairs, peering upward and half expecting the pair to be hiding somewhere just outside, waiting for him to poke his head up like a rabbit from its hole. At the top step he checked in every direction, creeping out of the condensed haze lightheaded and dizzy, stumbling ahead a few feet and ducking beneath part of the upper stairwell that had fallen and remained intact. He still caught the faint scent of fumes from the stairs and, beneath that, a more pungent sewage stench that was offensive but probably not nearly as dangerous to breathe as whatever was being churned up underground.

He remained there half the night, hugging himself, cold and shivering beneath the broken concrete, water dripping incessantly on his hood and off the front of his jacket. The gang moved through the shadows of the city around him ceaselessly, cries and whistles cutting through the chilly air as they searched for him but eventually gave up, their voices fading as late night turned into early morning. James fell into an uneasy, dozing state between sleep and consciousness, his head filled with flashes of dreams of Alice and the kids, their faces, mannerisms, and laughter shining through the murky fog like rays of sunshine. Eventually, James fell into a deep sleep, hungry, thirsty and yearning for home.

CHAPTER THIRTEEN

Ryan Cooper
Somewhere Outside East Lansing, Michigan

Ryan and Helen sat at the breakfast bar, each with a cup of coffee resting in front of them after finishing their chores for the day, going so far as to dust in nooks and crannies and even vacuum the floors. They'd taken their time, trading off shifts and listening to a bit of music on a CD player Alice had in the master bedroom. Soft rock, a little country, and even some old hits Helen had found in her carry-on she'd brought from home. The mundanity of the work was refreshing, bringing a sense of normalcy to the couple, and with the day's tasks done, they sat quietly, sipping the hot drinks tempered with a touch of fresh cow's milk and sugar.

"Those dogs eat as much as two people." Ryan snorted and took a sip from his cup.

"Good thing we have more eggs than we know what to do with."

The appliances hummed comfortably in the background, giving the place a sense of safety and security, but the feeling of sanctuary was only skin deep. The unpainted patches on the walls, broken dining room windows and damage to the loft were all direct reminders that violence could visit them at any time.

"The railings were chewed up by bullets," he said, looking up at the loft area, "and James doesn't have a lathe to make new spindles. We could search for some in another house, when it's safe to go out. Or we can just patch them up and do something more pressing. Personally, my vote's for that."

Helen ran her thumb along the smooth side of her plain white mug. "I'd like to get the place as close to normal as possible." She scoffed and shook her head sadly. "But I know that's not reality."

Ryan rubbed his leg nervously. "I would've expected Alice and James to be home by now. It's been too long."

"Don't you start worrying about them. You'll get me to worry, too."

"No, no. It's just hard not hearing from them, especially the longer this goes on, and with knowing what kind of people are out there and what they'd do to capitalize on an opportunity. Alice is alone with the kids...."

"Competent kids," Helen corrected him.

"That's true. But the world out there..." Ryan glanced at the blinds covering the rear bay window. "It's worse than it's ever been."

Helen grabbed his arm and squeezed. "See, now you've got me worrying again."

"Sorry, honey. I hate to sound pessimistic, but sometimes I wonder how long we can keep this up."

"Listen to me, Ryan Cooper, you've kept me going through all this, and I won't let you fall into despair. Can't afford for that to happen. Do you understand me?"

"Yes, honey." He sipped his coffee. "I should probably keep some things to myself, eh?"

"Not at all." Helen rested her head on his shoulder. "I always want you to be honest and let me know how you feel. But never forget – we've made it this far, and we'll keep making it just fine."

"We're just doing what we need to do to get by," he replied with a shrug. "Like with that young woman I'm meeting tomorrow. If she turns out to be a fraud, she'll pay a hefty price. I warned her I'll put a bullet in her head if she tried anything, and I think she understood. Still, I'd be surprised if she showed up at all."

"I thought you said you got a good vibe from her."

"Ugh. I'm basing that on my feelings about people *before* all of this. Who knows what's good or bad anymore. I'm trying to reserve my judgment for when I go meet her tomorrow."

"You think she'll bring anything worth trading?"

"That's the least of my concerns. I doubt she'll have much we need. No, I'm more concerned about her honesty. She seemed genuine, but that doesn't mean this isn't another tactic for them to get at us. A direct assault didn't work, so maybe they're trying something else."

"If they wanted to ambush you, they would've done it this morning."

"Maybe. Maybe not. I suppose it doesn't matter. If her intentions are false, we need to know exactly what we're dealing with here. She seemed to imply their group wasn't as tightknit as it had been, but it just takes one desperate person to rally a group of people to do some bad things."

"You should ask her more about that. Maybe she knows..." Something caught Helen's attention, and she raised in her seat and craned her neck.

"What is it?" Ryan asked, turning to his left to see she was looking through one of the windows on the rear side of the house.

"I thought I saw a flash of light out there."

"In the backyard?" Ryan pushed his coffee cup away and grabbed the Winchester, turning and popping out of his chair.

"I don't think so. It's out in the distance in the woods." Helen squinted harder. "On the highway, I think. You can just sort of see it through the trees."

"I'd wager someone's creeping around out there." He threw on his coat. "I'll take Duchess and check."

"Well, I'm going, too." Helen took her coat off the back of the chair and slipped it on.

"You don't have to. Might be best if you stayed here with Duke and Diana."

"Nonsense," she said, picking up her rifle and hanging it from her shoulder. "If it is those people again, you'll need some backup. We'll leave the dogs here to guard the house. Let's go."

Ryan got his boots from the foyer and sat on the stairs to put them on, and when he returned to the kitchen, Helen was standing at the window with her hand on the glass, looking through a pair of binoculars.

"Are they still out there?"

"I still see lights, yes. There's a lot of them flashing through the trees, but it doesn't look like flashlights. Too much greenery on the trees still to tell what it is, exactly."

"Now I'm more curious than ever," Ryan groaned. "If it's not the neighbors trying to circle behind us for another attack, maybe it's another threat. Can we not get a day or three's respite, please?"

They exited the house and walked to the barnyard gate, through the yard with the curious goats and sheep staring out from their enclosure, though not hungry enough or curious enough to come out and follow. The night was cool, their footfalls crunching on cold, stiff grass as the lights glared in the distance past the trees.

"You're right about them not being flashlights," he said. "They're all sitting at one level, not jostling around and pointing in different directions like a person would do. They're not moving around all that much. Looks like cars to me. Sounds like it too. Maybe somebody *is* out on the highway, like you said."

The sky was still cloudy gray, with the moonlight filtering through the gaps and giving them a little light to see by. Ryan kept his flashlight off until he reached the rear gate, using it in brief flashes to see in front of them. There were no trails to follow, only the forest floor covered with dead leaves, twigs, and deadfall big enough to tangle them or cause them to sprain an ankle. Thirty yards into the woods and his calf was stiffening again, the punctured muscles sending a deep ache up through the back of his knee to his hamstring, forcing him to favor it heavily. Approaching the end of the trees, they stooped and parted the bushes in a rustling of dry brush to reveal the short stretch of field and the highway beyond.

Humvees, APCs, and flatbed semi-trailer trucks with long tanks sat on the highway forty yards distant, moving west to east in an armored convoy that stretched out of sight. Off in the distance to the right, a Humvee with a wide plow on the front broke through the wreckage at a steady speed, shoving it off the right-hand shoulder with a crash of metal as it cleared a path for the line of military trucks following behind. Bathed in the glare of headlamps, the vehicles were a hodgepodge of old equipment riddled with dents and rust spots, broken windows with new pieces of plastic taped over them, entire sections of armor refitted and welded together. Old troop transports held the shadowy outlines of soldiers sitting in the back and three long, tubular fuel trucks brought up the rear, their seams rusted and worn but with bright new warning stickers plastered on the sides.

"I wonder where they're going?" Helen whispered.

"Somewhere East... maybe Detroit? Or heading to Washington eventually?"

"How do they even have the gas to move all those?"

Ryan shrugged. "It could be they've ramped up the production of new fuel. They've got a fair number of people in those trucks. Armed to the teeth, too."

"Protecting their fuel." Helen shivered. "Can we head back now?"

"Yeah. I'd rather not get spotted and have to answer uncomfortable questions." Ryan backed out of the bushes, guiding them back toward the house.

As they passed through the barnyard, Helen gestured toward the enclosure where the sheep and goats lingered. "We need to spend more time with the animals. Here, come look at something."

Changing direction, Helen led him over through the pack of animals and rested her hands on their heads as she passed them. "I noticed one of the female Southdowns was limping a little. Where are you, girl... ah, there!"

She guided Ryan through the bleating throng, the smell of manure thick in the cool night air. Finally reaching the trembling female Southdown in the middle of the herd, Helen nudged the others out of the way and crouched, holding the sheep steady with one hand while lifting her front right leg. Ryan shined his light on it and saw a series of short red cuts above the knee, the agitated animal kicking before Helen let her go.

"Might've gotten that wound on the brambles overgrowing the fences on the northeast corner. Darn it, I'd wanted to get to that earlier."

Helen stood and wrapped her arm around his waist. "We've been dealing with so much lately. You can't blame yourself for not getting to that. Besides, it's not that big of a deal. I think the bigger take-away is if we don't start spending more time with them, we're going to miss when more serious problems crop up."

"No kidding... I'll take care of that brush now. Do we have any supplies to take care of more serious injuries?"

"Alice has some things in a cabinet in the barn. Just some antibiotics and gauze in case of an event like this. We've got her veterinarian's phone number, too, for all the good that'll do."

Ryan snorted. "Yeah, not like we can call it. This brings us to another problem - how to get veterinary care for the animals. I guess we're on point for that, too."

"We never used vets much when we were just starting with our farm. We got by on what we had. If I remember correctly, you kept our farm animals in pretty good shape back then, mostly with bandages and antiseptic cream."

"Yeah, but without wormers, vaccines and professional help things could turn sour if we get some kind of disease that blows through the animals. But I guess we'll just have to deal with the situations as they come." He patted the sheep's head. "Well, no sense in letting her be uncomfortable. How about you bandage her up and I'll go cut down the brambles."

While Helen went inside to find antibiotics and a bandage for the sheep, James grabbed the rake, pruning shears, and a small hand ax from the shed. With his tools in the wheelbarrow, he rolled out to the northeast corner of the property where bushes and vines had overgrown the rails, creating a tangle of stickers and thistles the

Southdown had likely gotten caught up in. He went to work on the top of the greenery, cutting away the longer switches and branches, dragging the prickly vines off the rails with a ripping sound, and using his axe and shovel to cut out the more extensive roots that had embedded themselves deeper in the ground.

It took him forty-five minutes to get it all pulled, the strain in his back noticeable as he balanced his weight to keep it off his injured leg. He tossed the loose pieces over the fence to be burned later and got ready to go back. Wiping the sweat off his brow, he packed his tools back in the wheelbarrow and returned to the barn where Helen was checking out the other sheep, the Southdown with the injury easily noticeable by the bright white bandage wrapped around her leg.

"How are they looking?" he asked.

"Oh, most of them are fine," Helen said. "I found a few more scratches and cuts here and there but took care of those."

Ryan shook his head. "Just goes to show you how things can get away from us if we're not maintaining things daily around here."

"Did you get the brush all cleared?"

"It's taken care of. I dropped it over the fence so it'll be out of the sheep's way. I'll wait for it to dry and then drag it over to James' burn pile. Come to think of it, I should probably clear more of that brush that's been building up over the past few weeks and burn it, too. I reckon that's why a lot of the land around here burned so readily after all the fuel went up in smoke. Too much kindling everywhere." He nodded at the sheep as they wandered into and around the barn. "How much more work do you have to do up here?"

"I'm basically done, but I wanted to look at a few more animals before we went inside."

"I'll put the tools away and help you."

As the light faded, Ryan and Helen examined the remaining sheep, checked their hooves and coats, and inspected their eyes for any signs of injuries. For the most part, the animals appeared fine but for a few who'd gotten scratched up in the bushes.

"I'm kicking myself for letting that grow past the fence line," Ryan told Helen as they knelt beside one sheep and examined her legs. "I've heard stories about sheep getting strangled by vines. Not exactly the smartest of animals."

Helen shook her head. "I asked Alice why they'd decided on raising sheep, of all things."

"Ha, wouldn't catch me dead raising the things. Except now, I guess."

"Alice swears up and down by them. They were producing enough meat and wool sales to make it worth it, plus they clear the grass well enough that they didn't need to do any mowing. After getting more experience with them, Alice said they wanted to purchase some dairy breeds and expand the farm." Helen looked around. "At least we're not having to wrestle a whole herd of cattle between the two of us."

"That is very true. We should be able to manage what they've got so long as we don't need a proper vet."

"Alice has a few books on sheep-rearing." She nudged Ryan and winked at him. "So much for that retirement, huh?

"No kidding. Let's hope they're home sooner than later and can help. Looking at my growing list of chores is starting to get intimidating."

"Maybe if we can smooth things out with the neighbors with that woman's help and get some trading going, we might not have to work so hard to defend ourselves."

"Don't count on it. I'm pretty sure we're the only place that's mostly intact after what happened. House, vehicles, the whole nine yards. I think we'll be on guard for the long term."

Helen put her hands on her hips and stretched her back. "What do you say we get back inside?"

"Yeah, sounds good."

As they cleared the wandering sheep from the barn and locked up, the lights of the military vehicles continued blinking through the trees at the back of the property as they left the barnyard and returned to the house.

Helen held his arm as they walked. "I guess if we ever want to find out where those troops are going, we could follow the path they're clearing."

"I hope it doesn't lead to more highway traffic out there or people walking along. The last thing we want is more folks going by and noticing us."

"Time to tighten up the coverings on the rear windows."

"And I have to be careful not to run the tractor at night, and if I do, it's with the headlamps off." Ryan opened the back door and let her in. "Lights will be a death sentence if we're not careful."

Helen stepped past him and gave him a peck on the cheek. "I hope tomorrow won't be a death sentence for you when you meet that young woman."

Following her inside, he said, "I'll be careful, I promise. Besides, you'll keep an eye on me from up high."

"Absolutely, I will," she replied with a smile. "Want a warm-up on your coffee?"

Ryan shut the door behind him and took off his coat. "Absolutely."

The rising sun had yet to illuminate the horizon and Ryan and Helen stood by the back door, getting him ready for another trip to the gate. Belly full of coffee and breakfast, he finished slipping into his boot and Helen helped him shrug on his heavy coat.

"Do you have everything?"

He patted his belt line and jacket. "I've got my radio, flashlight, and pistol, and my rifle is out in the car with Duchess already."

"Don't forget these," Helen said, grabbing a small bottle from the breakfast bar and shaking the two dozen pills inside. "They've expired, but assuming he's got a bacterial infection, I'd guess they'll work, but make sure to emphasize that we're not promising anything."

"Thanks, honey," Ryan replied, putting the bottle in his pocket. "Don't worry, I will."

Helen squared up to him. "Let's go over the plan again. You go down there like yesterday...."

"And turn the car to face the house in case I need to make a quick escape. I'll keep the back door open so Duchess can come to me if I need her, too, same as before. Any signs of Sandy having a weapon or even the faintest hint there's anyone else nearby, I'll shoot her and make a run for the car. But as long as she's honest, I'll make a deal with her."

"Perfect. Be safe, okay?" Helen gave him a brief hug before stepping back.

With a confident nod, Ryan went outside into the brisk morning, his breath condensing into clouds of mist. The yard was quiet but for the occasional bird call from the woods or the chickens in their coop, scratching and clucking in the predawn light as glints of it began lighting up the yard. He zipped up his coat and walked to the car, climbing into the driver's seat and activating the vehicle. The dashboard lights illuminated Duchess' shaggy form in the backseat, her head tilting as she watched him from where she was sitting.

"We're taking another short ride. Ready?"

Duchess whined, licked her chops, and danced back and forth on her front paws. "Okay, let's go."

The EV rolled around the side of the house and down the driveway with its lights off, the gravel crunching beneath the tires the only sound the vehicle made as the electric motor propelled it forward. He turned a full circle in the grass down near the gate, then got back on the drive and pointed the front end toward the house. Once the vehicle was powered down, he slipped out with his rifle and moved to the passenger side, where he opened the back door a few inches and reassured Duchess with a confident pat on the head.

"Good girl. Stay here. This will be over before you know it."

The dog lowered herself with a whine and shake of her shaggy fur, showing no signs that she'd noticed someone hidden nearby, only staring at him with her big eyes as she whined again over being left behind. He scratched her between the ears and moved to the left-hand side of the gate where a drainage ditch ran along the fence line. It was only four feet deep, a mixture of moist clay and rocks along the sides which he slipped down, then he crouched and moved slightly closer to the gate where he'd have a good view of anyone coming up the road. Duchess stood in the back seat, watching him through the rear window as Ryan squatted in the darkness, the cold seeping through his jeans and jacket, calf stiff and tightening up, forcing him to reposition himself every few minutes.

As the first light of dawn crested the horizon and brightened the treetops to the east, the ducks began to make noise off toward the pond, and birdsong became louder and more varied. It wasn't much longer before a figure appeared out on the road, huddled in a thick coat, hands in her pocket, a plastic grocery store bag hanging from her arm. Duchess growled softly in warning, then louder, ears perked up and alert as the woman slowed her approach. Sandy stopped ten feet away, neck craning forward and searching for Ryan inside the car.

"Ryan? Are you there?"

Still crouched, he turned his head and called, "I'm here. What did you bring to trade?"

With hesitant steps, Sandy approached and rested the bag on the gate. "Batteries. We had a lot of spare batteries we weren't using, so I brought them. It's a mixture of double A and C... We're using the D ones in our lanterns, or I would've brought those. I also have some needles and thread in case you need to repair some clothing. I... I hope it's enough."

There had been no other movement on the road behind her, and the tree line to the east held deep shadows that shifted in the early morning light, though none seemed out of place. Duchess, too, was only fixated on Sandy, and showed no signs of having caught anyone else's scent, so he shouldered his rifle, rose and climbed from the ditch with his pistol in one hand and radio in the other, walking slowly toward Sandy as he thumbed the transmit button.

"Helen, do you see anyone hiding?"

"No. I haven't spotted any movement in the trees on either side of you, and there's no one in the road or around the Jones' house."

"Thanks. Keep watching. If anyone so much as sticks their heads up, you know what to do. I'll make sure this one gets it, too."

"Got it."

Ryan put the radio back on his belt and approached the gate, slipping his pistol back into his pocket and gripping his rifle in both hands.

"You don't have to threaten me like that," Sandy said, taking a few steps back. "I came alone. There's no one hiding anywhere."

"Trust comes hard, Sandy, especially with what happened the other day."

"Believe me, you did a number on them... on us. They've been licking their wounds and no one wants to mess with y'all ever again."

"Good, though I highly doubt they never want to try something again. If they get desperate enough, they'll come again... and I'm sure you can guess what'll happen if you're part of that."

Sandy gulped nervously. "I just want to help my son." She returned to the gate and put the bag back, expression flat yet hopeful as she awaited his judgment.

After another once-over of the surrounding area, he pulled the bottle of pills from his pocket and put them on the gate, stepping back and nodding at them. "These are expired, but only by a few months. Should be plenty potent. Obviously I have no idea if they'll work, but they're broad-spectrum and I'd think they'll work assuming this is a bacterial infection. Two a day for ten days is what's on the instructions."

Sandy glanced at the bottle before taking the bag off the gate and holding it out to him. "Here are the batteries and sewing stuff."

Ryan shook his head and turned away, walking back to the car with a slow gait.

"Wait, don't you want this stuff?"

He stopped and turned at the back of the car. "Of course I do. Given what's going on around here, I want all I can get my hands on." He glanced at his leg and let out a deep sigh. "I'm old, my leg hurts and what I really want, at the end of the day, is just to be able to work together with the folks around us. Trust, Sandy. That's what I want. This is a good first step, you coming to meet me like I asked. Keep your supplies – you and your son probably need them more than we do."

Sandy took the bag and grabbed the pill bottle, staring at the label and turning it around to read the instructions. With glassy eyes, she held the bottle and bag aloft and shook them in his direction. "Thanks for this, Ryan. I'm... I'm so sorry my husband was—"

Ryan shook his head and waved her off. "Yeah, yeah, I don't need to hear it again. And you're welcome. If you want to keep building on this trust, meet me here again in the morning after you've medicated your son. I'd like to know how he's doing and if the meds are helping him or not."

"Absolutely. I'll be here in the morning. Thank you so much," tears streamed down her cheeks as she clutched at the bottle of pills. "I won't forget you for this."

Ryan nodded and muttered an 'mhm', shut the back door, and climbed into the car, watching Sandy hurry down the road. Before she passed out of sight, she broke into a jog, flying with her hair bouncing on her shoulders. Duchess whined and leaned over the seat to nudge and lick his face.

"Good girl," he laughed and rubbed her ears, then he turned on the car and crept back up the driveway.

Helen met him at the back door, letting Duchess in and joining him at the kitchen table where she warmed up his coffee and sat across from him.

"Well, what happened? I saw you let her keep her bag of whatever she brought."

"It was a productive exchange, I think." Ryan related the conversation, describing how appreciative Sandy was of the antibiotics, and how he'd refused to take what she'd offered and why. "I couldn't bring myself to take her supplies given how much we've got here."

"You could've taken it out of principle."

"Maybe."

"What's your angle, Ryan?" Helen's eyebrow went up.

"Like I told her, I want trust." He thumped his fist on the table, growling in frustration. "I'm tired of being on guard twenty-four seven. Even one more person we can trust would do wonders for us, and for them."

"Will we be able to trust any of those people, after what they did to us?"

"I doubt it... but you know me, always holding out hope."

Helen reached across the table and patted his hand. "You've made some pretty good decisions, and I trust you've got a solid plan."

"The important thing now is to keep working hard and maintain our patience, both with ourselves and the neighbors. And you know that's something I run thin on sometimes."

"I'll help you with that," Helen smiled. "Are you ready to go do some work?"

"Yeah... let's fill the thermoses with coffee first. It's going to be a long day."

CHAPTER FOURTEEN

Sarah Burton
Talladega National Forest, Alabama

A rustling near her head brought Sarah out of a deep, dark sleep, the exhaustion of riding all day on the slanted forest trails leaving a deep soreness that penetrated her hips and lower back. She blinked wearily at the campfire, the flames having died down to orange and gold flickers as grogginess clouded her head. All around her, insects chirped and the brush rustled, the wilderness crackling and snapping to the light snores of those lying around the fire ring.

Christine and Mark were across from her with Hunter between them, three bundles mixed in with a variety of blankets and red and blue sleeping bags. Jake was at Sarah's feet with Mia near her head where the rustling had come from, the young girl behaving restlessly all night and struggling to sleep.

Mark and Christine had kept the two children busy, making it hard for Jake and Sarah to spend time with them, but at least Mia still hadn't been worn out enough to sleep out of pure exhaustion.

Sarah closed her eyes again, clinging to the grogginess, hoping to get a few more hours of rest before Alice woke them up to get packed up and move out. Just before she drifted off, a light tapping on her shoulder brought her out of it, and she stirred back awake with a subtle flicker of alarm in the back of her head. Sarah pushed her sleeping bag down and started to turn when a small hand gripped her shirt and a soft, timid sound came into her ear.

"Sarah? Are you awake?"

"Yeah, um..."

"Please, help us." It was Mia, her request urgent, voice barely above a whisper. "*Please*."

"Wha...?" Jolting awake, Sarah got her elbow beneath her and turned, expecting Mia to be right next to her, but all she saw was a rustling of blankets and a small form shifting, rolling over, and disappearing in the folds near Mark, Christine and Hunter. She started to say something, but Christine and Mark were up and moving across from her, whispers passing between them. Christine got up, checked on Hunter, then crawled around the fire in the opposite direction. Sarah sank into her sleeping bag, closed her eyes, and pretended to be asleep as more covers shifted and rustled near her head, then Christine whispered something Sarah barely made out.

"Be good... understand...?"

Mia responded in a quiet, tiny voice. "Mm hm."

Christine stood and circled the fire to lean over Mark. "I'm going to help Alice keep watch. I'll be back soon. Keep an eye on things here."

"Okay."

After Christine had gone, Sarah tried to recapture the grogginess of before, but an irritating nausea clung to her stomach, and she only half dozed to the forest sounds that had suddenly grown cold and sinister for reasons her sleep-addled brain couldn't quite figure out. When she finally slept it was fitful, with explosions and angry faces chasing her through her dreams, weapons firing from the darkness and shapeless forms trying to drag her and her family off their horses. A short time later, the sun crept above the trees, casting a fragile glow over the campsite and making it impossible to sleep.

Alice appeared a few moments later, shaking her and Jake's shoulders. "Come on, guys. It's time to get up and get moving. We'll help them get their bedding and tents packed up and buckled to Hercules, then we'll divide up the riding between the other three horses. Sarah, make sure your brother gets up."

"Okay, Mom," Sarah replied, pulling herself out of her half-sleep and slipping her boots on, hips and back feeling even worse from lying on the hard, uneven ground.

She went to wake Jake, but he was already up and moving, shoes on and kneeling by his sleeping bag, slouching as he rolled it up and tied it into a firm, round bundle. When she turned back the other way to find Mia, she'd gone off with Mark and was busy gathering the toys she and Hunter had been playing with the day before. With a grunt, Sarah rose and got moving, rolling up her sleeping bag, stuffing it into her pack, and buckling it to Hercules' saddle with automatic movements driven by exhaustion. A few minutes later, Mark had stoked the fire and had something cooking on it, the rich aroma helping to drag her the rest of the way out of her sleep.

"What *is* that?" Jake said, heading back over to the fire. "It smells amazing."

"Just a few leftovers from the week," Mark said. "The ham and beans from last night and some sausages packed in tinfoil. I just toss them into the fire along with onions and peppers. Let them cook for about ten minutes and you've got a meal."

"That sounds delicious, Mark," Alice replied. "It's good to know we found some more new friends with cooking skills."

"Oh, we do a lot of camping, so I guess I've learned a thing or two."

They ate off tin plates, Sarah sitting on her log with her knees together, head down as she focused on eating when Jake sat next to her and nudged her with his elbow.

"What was all that about this morning?" He kept his voice low, and Sarah checked to see that Mark and Christine were standing by the horses, where Alice was helping them strap their tents and campfire equipment to Hercules.

"I thought Mia might've whispered something to me, but it feels like a dream."

"Whatever she was doing woke me up," Jake said. "What was she whispering?"

"I think she said..." Sarah shook her head slowly. "I think she said she needed help, or maybe her brother did. I can't remember right."

"Maybe they both did." Jake gave a pointed nod to where the kids stood off to the side, holding hands with toys tucked under their arms. "They seem way too quiet to me. You should tell Mom what you heard."

Sarah took a deep breath. "I'm... I'm really not sure if I heard anything, but something doesn't feel right about the situation. I'll tell Mom as soon as—"

"Sarah. Jake. Let's get moving. Please help Mia and Hunter onto the horses. They'll ride with you on Stormy and Rocky, and I'll let Christine and Mark ride on Buck."

"That's unnecessary, Alice," Mark said. "We're more than happy to walk beside you guys."

"Seriously, I don't mind. Do you know how to ride? If not, I can help you."

"Absolutely not, Alice." Christine took her arm. "We wouldn't think of making you walk. It's enough that our little ones will be off their feet and up high where it's safer. We've seen snakes around, and there are predators everywhere, so we'll help make sure the horses don't get spooked."

"I heard a story about someone's kid getting snatched while they were up here," Mark said. "A mountain lion had dragged them several yards to the woods when the father finally caught up with them and shot the darn thing. The kid, though...well. It was a tragedy."

"Oh, that's terrible," Alice raised her eyebrows. "I think we're strong enough in number to keep everyone safe, though."

"We appreciate that," Christine said, then turned to Mark. "Come on, honey. Let's grab our packs, and we can get moving."

Sarah kneeled in front of Mia and held out her hand. "Come on, honey. You can ride with me."

Mia nodded and allowed herself to be led to Stormy, and Sarah mounted and held out her hands for Jake to lift the little girl. After Mia was situated in front of her, and while everyone else was busy, Sarah whispered in her ear. "Are you okay?"

Mia nodded.

"What did you say to me this morning?"

Mia shook her head.

"But—"

Christine stepped past them, glancing up with a smile.

"Is this your first horse ride?" Sarah asked Mia, matching Christine's smile.

"Yeah."

"Are you scared?"

"Yeah." Sarah's heart nearly broke as the word came out in a small, soft whimper.

"Well, hold on to the saddle horn in front of you. I promise I won't let you fall off."

"Okay."

"Stormy would feel better if you petted him. Want to pet him?"

"Okay..."

"I'll hold on to you, and you can just reach down and pet him. Go ahead."

Mia put her hand on Stormy's muscular neck, stroking his sleek coat and when he snorted, she snatched her hand back and giggled wildly.

"Did you like that?" Sarah laughed.

"Yeah."

"See, this'll be fun!"

Mia's giggle cut off when Christine stepped over and held Stormy's bridle, drawing an annoyed grunt from the horse. She gave Mia a lingering look before shifting to Sarah. "What a beautiful horse. Is he gentle?"

"Oh yeah, Stormy's great. I promise I'll take good care of Mia. I've got a lot of experience riding now."

Christine's smile faltered before the corners of her mouth lifted with a nod. "Good. Now, Mia, stay in the saddle with Sarah, and do exactly what she tells you, okay?"

Mia nodded back and settled against Sarah, and Sarah hugged her and took up the reins, staring at Christine as she joined Mark up front with Alice and Buck. Soon, everyone was ready to go, and Alice, Christine and Mark took the lead, walking slowly through the thickets that crowded their pathway, kicking up a dust cloud as they headed back toward the trail.

Alice swayed on Buck's back as the seemingly endless trail wove over a string of spurs that skirted the southern tip of the Appalachian Mountains. The path cut north again along the edge of a narrow ridge that gave them astounding views of the sweeping valleys, with bright pink coloring the horizon, and the sun glinting across the tree-tops, countless trees standing at attention like spears pointed at the sky. Conifers were standouts in the forest as many of the other trees' leaves were beginning to change color, the pines growing thicker where creeks ran through the flatlands and becoming thinner up on the valley walls. Wide streams wound down from the heights, pouring over cold stones to the bottom where they cut through pastures filled with tall grasses.

"Oh, check it out!" Sarah pointed into the valley at four specks lumbering alongside a narrow creek.

"Are those bears?"

"I think so," Sarah replied.

Jake shielded his eyes from the sun. "It's a mother and some cubs I think."

"See them, Mia?" Sarah asked with hushed excitement.

"Yeah, whoa!"

"They're pretty cute," Alice said. "At least from this distance. Won't be so cute if we get between mom and her cubs, though."

"Yeah, Mom," Jake said, and Sarah chuckled.

Alice smiled at Mia seated in front of Sarah, hanging on tight and wearing a wondrous expression. "How's she doing?"

Sarah forced a smile. "Pretty good, I think. At first, she was a little scared, but she's enjoying the ride now."

"The kids have never been around horses before," Christine said, walking up quickly and patting Stormy on the neck. "They might act a little weird until they get used to it. If she starts to bug you, let us know, and we'll get her right down. That goes for you, too, Jake."

"We're good back here," Jake replied.

"And Mia's doing fine," Sarah said, "right, honey?"

Mia nodded faintly and looked in the opposite direction, her tiny mouth forming a thin line.

"Are you sure you don't want to ride?" Alice asked Christine. "Seriously, you can ride with me on Buck. You and Mark can take turns."

"We're fine walking," Christine replied, looking back at Mark.

"Yeah, don't worry about us," he added from where he hiked beside Jake and Hunter, having drifted back from the lead.

"Have it your way." Alice shrugged and faced forward, focusing ahead as they descended a deceptively complicated switchback that hooked them south and then north again, pulling them deeper into the valley where the slopes rested in the dark, cool shade of the trees and mountains above.

Acorns fell with sharp cracks, and the woods creaked around them as unseen creatures scurried through the branches above and the undergrowth below. Flocks of birds launched high and turned in perfect synchronization, painting the sky in moving shadows before alighting in the treetops. A squirrel ran across the path, dodged back and forth through the thickets, then scampered halfway up a tree to stop and stare as Alice and Buck slowly ambled along. She gave the woodland creature an amused half wave, and it shot up into the higher branches at the movement to disappear into the leafy vegetation.

They walked endlessly, taking only brief breaks to rest or drink where the trail was wide and flat, coming upon ample creeks and small ponds where the horses could refresh themselves. By the third hour, Alice noticed Mark and Christine panting and sweating as they all ascended a treacherous incline, barely able to lift their feet, leaning against the horses and nearby trees for leverage.

The soil crumbled beneath them in places, thick roots stretching across the trail that stood inches above the dirt, easy to trip on for anyone not paying attention. At the top, they reached a shoulder of the hill with a massive stone monolith, its chiseled gray walls towering over them. The path wound around it to the north and continued on the other side, and Alice waited for everyone to join her at the top while she looked out across the extraordinary view.

"Are you sure you guys don't want to swap and ride for a while?" Alice asked Christine as she stumbled to the top, stopping to lean over with her hands on her knees.

"No... it's... fine." Sweat poured down her face as she sucked air, and it took a good minute to catch her breath. "We're doing fine."

"It doesn't look like it." Alice mumbled as she turned Buck away to give the others more room to fit on the shoulder.

Sarah and Jake joined them, leading Hercules up with Mark coming last after falling behind. He took the same position as Christine, leaning over and holding his side.

"I'm fine," he waved. "Just have a cramp, is all."

"We'll rest here for a minute. It looks like the trail winds around this big outcrop and continues down the other side. It's going to be just as hard going down as it was going up, maybe harder. So, let me know if you want to ride." Christine and Mark stood to the side in quiet discussion but didn't accept her offer. Sarah and Jake dismounted with the younger kids and started to give them water, but Christine and Mark pulled them to the side and gave them some from their own supplies. Alice allowed them a few extra minutes to rest before calling for everyone to mount up again. She gave up on offering Mark and Christine a ride but watched them as they descended the hill, half staggering over rocks and branches, forced to grab the horses' saddle straps or harnesses to stay close to the kids.

"You're going to get yourself stepped on if you keep that up," Alice warned them, but they paid her no mind and stuck to the horses' sides, checking on the kids every few minutes until Sarah finally looked at Alice with a helpless expression and got a shrug in response.

It took them an hour and a half to get down the hill with the midday sun brutally beating down on them, and Alice was sweating just watching the others try to keep up. After a tricky descent, they reached a floodplain that sloped straight to a crystalline lake surrounded by a stand of pines above a windswept forest floor. Alice marched them to the edge of the lake where Mark and Christine stooped over with their hands on their knees, gasping and beyond winded. Sarah started to help Mia down when Christine came out of her tired stance and snatched the young girl out of Sarah's hands.

"I can get her..." Sarah said, exasperated. "And I was going to ask my mom if we can rest in the shade for a while."

"Yep, that's what she needs," Christine said. "Come on, Mark. Let's take the kids in the shade and let them rest a while."

Mark and Christine took the kids and sat them on the shoreline where the trees arched over the lake, handing them their toys and some water and sitting tiredly next to them. Alice slouched in her seat, sliding off Buck and staggering a couple of steps, leaning on him so she didn't fall.

"Good boy," she said, leading him to the water's edge. "Come on and get yourself something to drink."

Sarah and Jake brought their mounts over to stand in line and cool off in the shade, then together they gathered lake water in bottles and drank it through filter straws, standing around quietly while a soft breeze blew through and dried their sweat. Alice went to the shoreline, stooping and wetting a rag to place against her cheeks and neck while Jake and Sarah squatted by the water, glancing over at Mark and Christine as they came up.

"Those are pretty cool," Mark said. "Are those filter straws?"

He'd taken off his heavy coat and looked miserable and wet, his sweaty clothes hanging off his shoulders, pants loose on his hips. Christine walked up behind him, a ring of sweat around her T-shirt, beads of it trickling down her face, strands of lank hair clinging to her cheeks.

"Yep," Alice replied. "We got them a long time ago from a warehouse just before someone tried to rob us."

"I guess you don't need any of our waters," Mark said, holding up an unopened one.

"No, we're fine. The straws work well."

Christine pushed a strand of hair behind her ear. "That's got to be a pain, having to suck on the straw so much."

"Eh, it's not hard, especially when you're thirsty," Alice smiled, watching Jake and Sarah strolling over to the kids, Jake side-arming tiny stones so they skimmed across the water. "You two seem to have plenty of supplies for people who've been up in the mountains for several days."

"We used Hunter's toy wagon to haul our supplies up here," Mark said. "Saved our butts."

"Until the wheels fell off," Christine said, accepting the wet rag Alice offered and going to the edge of the lake.

"We started out with a few cases of water and have less than one now," Mark said. "I guess we should have picked up some filter straws, too."

"Camping supply stores would have them. Before we leave you at Ft. Wayne, we'll look for some."

"Oh, wow. We'd really appreciate it." Mark wiped off his forehead with a rag. "Maybe you could give us a list of stuff in general to pay attention to."

Alice patted Buck's flank. "I mean, it's good to have an idea of where you're going and what supplies you have on hand and need, but most of the lessons we learned out here are from experience. We were never what you'd call preppers or anything like that, but we've adapted and just rolled with the punches." Alice crossed her arms and laughed. "The world doesn't care about lists or plans."

"But you've done well compared to a lot of people we've seen.

"Well, you haven't seen the kind of people *we've* seen if you've been up here so long."

"No, that's true. But we survived."

"Don't get me wrong," Alice crossed her arms. "You made the right decision coming up here, especially for your kids. But off these trails, the world is a different place."

Mark turned his face away and rubbed his chin. "Yeah, well, um... I'll pick your brain a little before we get out of these woods if you don't mind."

"Sure, maybe on one of these breaks—"

"Hey, kids! Get back here!" Christine shouted as she got up and started around the shoreline where the four kids were sitting together. Sarah was stooping by the water and using a stick to poke around at something while Hunter and Mia were nearby, leaning on Jake, watching, and smiling as he spoke quietly to them. Christine rushed over in a panic, snatching Mia up and taking Hunter by the arm, turning them roughly back to their original spot and sitting them down hard, leaving Jake and Sarah standing there gaping.

"I-I was just showing them some tadpoles," Sarah stammered confusedly. "They weren't even close to the water."

Christine reeled on Sarah, fist clenched, her eyes flashing with anger briefly before the look faded, and she shook her head and smiled thinly. "I'm sure they were fine, but I just don't want them that close to the water. Neither one of them can swim... so, please just keep that in mind."

"Yeah... okay... sorry again," Sarah replied in confusion.

"Oh, my..." Mark put his hand to his forehead and started to walk away. "Sorry about that, Alice. Christine is super protective of the kids."

"That's okay," Alice frowned. "I totally understand. I'll make sure my kids don't take yours too close to the water. Jake. Sarah. Over here please."

"Mom, we didn't do anything," Sarah whispered, coming over with Jake as she defended herself. "They were three feet from the water the whole time, and Jake was right there next to them!"

Alice gripped Sarah's shoulder. "I know, honey. I saw them. You're fine."

Sarah's aggravated look faded into bewilderment. "I thought they were nice people, but... they're starting to annoy me."

"We're all under some stress from being on the trail. Tell you what, just stay away from them for a little while and let them cool off a bit. In the meantime, let's check out the horses for cuts and abrasions. We passed through some pretty rough thickets growing up on the trail. And remember what Wilford said about scratches. If you see any breaks in the skin, we have to use that antibacterial ointment he gave us to gently clean them. Just report anything you find to me before you try and treat it."

"Yes, ma'am," Jake said with a brief salute, while Sarah stared across at the Hubbards for a long moment.

"Mom, there's... something else."

"Hm?" Alice pulled Buck away from the others and moved down each leg carefully, running her hands along his forearms and knee, all the way to the hooked pastern, remembering what Wilford had told her about pale legs being more susceptible to sun damage and chaffing. "What is it?"

"It's the kids, they're just...."

"I know, hon. Mark and Christine are an odd pair."

"No, I mean... I had this... nevermind." Sarah sighed and headed off to tend to another one of the horses.

Alice watched her go for a long moment with a raised eyebrow before finishing up her once-over of Buck. "Looks like you're perfect, boy." She patted his hip and had a handful of cashews from their pack, watching the Hubbards closely where they sat off to the side, Mark and Christine crouched on the lakeside, talking quietly amongst themselves, occasionally gesturing to the children who continued to nod in response.

Not long after, Alice cupped her hands over her mouth. "Okay, folks. Let's move out. This time we'll keep going until it's dinnertime. We're talking a good three hours or more of tough terrain. Mark and Christine? Are you going to be okay? Sure you don't want to ride?"

"Oh, yeah," Mark called, standing and stretching his arms over his head. "We're good. Looks like it'll be flat forest trails from here on out."

The trail followed the lake shore to the north and cut eastward through the trees again. "It looks that way," Alice nodded, keeping her voice positive. "Just let me know if you need some help."

"We will."

They mounted up the same as they had before and walked along the glimmering shoreline to where the trail cut east, stepping into a narrow tract of sun-baked dirt with few roots or stones in the way. Mark was right about the area; the path was broad and flat, with thin stands of pines and good visibility for forty or fifty yards in any direction. Mark jogged ahead, confidently calling out spots where the trail dipped or turned and once out of the woods, they descended even deeper into a valley, moving along the edge of a pine forest with vast, sweeping grasslands off to the right.

"Mom, can we stop for a bit?"

Sarah and Mia were riding close behind them, and Christine had fallen back a little to talk with Hunter, resettling him in his seat and shaking her head as she spoke with him.

"I said we're riding through to dinner."

"I know," Sarah winced, "but we really need to stop now."

Christine had let go of Hunter and was shuffling ahead, catching up with Sarah and Mia.

Jake chimed in, "Seriously, Mom. My legs are killing me from being on this horse all afternoon. If we could rest a few minutes so I could walk it off, that would be great."

"Yeah, Alice, a short break for the kids wouldn't be bad!" Christine called out.

"I was hoping to get farther," Alice replied, "but we can take a quick break. Hey, Mark, we're taking a break."

He'd gotten about twenty yards ahead but came jogging back, hand raised and nodding. "Sounds good to me!"

Pulling the horses off the trail and a few feet into the woods, they tied them up so they wouldn't wander and sat on the leaf-covered trail edge. Christine and Mark took Hunter and Mia off to the right, sitting them a few yards away from the group, speaking and gesturing to them as they had been throughout the trip. At some point, Hunter said something loudly and punched Mark in the arm. Mark's face turned red with anger, and he drew back his hand but let his arm fall at the last second, chastising him quietly instead. Alice watched the exchange closely, eyes narrowed, sipping on a bottle of water.

"Jake, let's get some snacks," Sarah said, and the two stood beside Hercules and rifled through his saddle bags for some high-calorie protein bars. The pair talked quietly for a moment before Jake wandered off a few yards to the right near the Hubbards and the horses, eating his protein bar while staring into the woods.

Sarah sat heavily on Alice's right, head low and whispering. "Mom, we've got a problem."

"What's going on?" Alice accepted a protein bar and tore open the package. "Besides how those two treat their kids, I mean."

Sarah shook her head. "Whatever you do, don't look over at them, okay? Just try to be natural."

Alice stiffened slightly but nodded. "What is it?"

"Mia and Hunter? They're not their kids."

"What in the world are you talking about?"

"Mia and Hunter aren't theirs. I had my suspicions last night when –"

"Hey, Alice, do you have any extra snack bars?" Mark was walking over, smiling at her.

"We've got some here." Jake swept in and cut him off, turning him toward Hercules and their saddlebags.

"Jake's running interference so I can talk to you." Sarah's voice dropped another octave, and her words came out in a rush. "Last night, Mia tried to tell me something, but Christine interrupted her. I was so tired I thought it was just a dream but I'm sure of it now."

"Is that what you were trying to talk to me about earlier?"

"Yeah!"

"What did she say?" Alice asked, picking up a twig and twirling it between her finger and thumb as she sipped from a bottle of lake water.

"She said, '*help us*.'"

"Help us?"

"Yeah. I was confused at first, but now it's making a lot more sense. The way they've been overprotective of the kids but being just awful to them. And every time I try to talk to Mia about *anything*, Christine is right there, interrupting us."

Alice smiled as if Sarah had told her a joke. "I wonder why she's doing that?"

"Well, she's looking at us now, so don't look."

"I won't. Go on."

"When we first met them, Christine *seemed* friendly, but her smile creeps me out now."

"I won't lie, I've been watching them a fair amount since the lake... something definitely seems off."

Mark and Jake walked over with a handful of snack bars and gave one to Christine, and the three stood talking together.

"Jake is keeping them busy," Sarah said, "so we have to talk fast. What have you been noticing?"

"Everything, now that I've been paying attention," Alice replied. "They won't ride even when they're near to keeling over, and ever since the lake, Mark really seemed to know the trails. A little too well, if you ask me..." Alice shook her head. "But... why?"

"I don't know *why*, Mom. I just know something's wrong."

While Jake was talking with Christine, Mark stepped away and had turned to watch Alice and Sarah. Alice and Mark locked eyes, and Alice saw something sinister in them, something she hadn't quite picked up on herself, not until Sarah had made them stop, not until she'd colored in some lines and asked a few more questions of herself. Mark's eyes shifted as he glanced toward Buck, and Alice's heart sank as she saw him shifting to move toward the beast, realizing that she'd made a horrible, terrible mistake in letting her guard down.

Her rifle was no longer in her arms, but was instead strapped to the side of Buck's saddle.

She leaped up and launched herself toward the horses, slipping on the loose leaves and almost going down. Buck was in the middle of the horses, forcing her to skirt around Stormy's flanks and circle to the right side where the gun was sheathed. She squeezed between Buck and Rocky and lunged for the weapon, but Mark was already there, hand on the stock and drawing it free from its sheath.

With a desperate gasp, Alice grabbed the gun barrel and tried to shove it back down into the scabbard while simultaneously reaching for her pistol. Mark saw what she was doing and struck out awkwardly with his left fist, landing a weak blow, though it caught her on the jaw, sending stars spinning through her head as she fell and rolled beneath Buck. The horse shifted his massive weight above her, hooves stomping close to her head and Alice rolled to the opposite side, grabbed Stormy's stirrup, and hauled herself up, wrestling her pistol free.

There was a scuffle near the trail, and Alice slid in that direction, gun pointed at Christine where she struggled with Jake, pushing, pulling, twisting with grimacing faces as they each tried to gain control. Gone was the timid, seemingly friendly woman of before, replaced by a wildcat who glared and snarled at Jake, the tendons in her arms and hands standing out as she wrestled with him. Sarah rushed in screaming and flailing, striking Christine in the head with a wild punch, then hit her again, knuckles cracking hard across her neck and shoulders and arms, but unable to knock her off of Jake.

Unable to fire unless she wanted to hit one of her kids, Alice shifted in the other direction, looking for Mark when the butt of her rifle flew toward her face, smashing her in the side of the head, sending her staggering to her right, twisting, tripping, and falling on her backside at the trail's edge. Rocking backward and then forward, she swung her gun up, focusing on Mark's blurry form, and firing half-blind, barely holding onto the weapon. The pistol's kick threw her off balance as the rifle butt sailed by two inches from her nose, and her head cracked the dirt hard, sending arcs of light shooting through her skull all the way to her eyes, clenching her head in a fist of pain. She brought her gun to bear for one last shot, but through the blur in her vision she realized she wasn't holding it anymore. Before she could scrabble around for it, Mark was on her, his knee in her chest, pinning her to the ground while she gasped and gripped his leg, squirming and kicking weakly.

"Knock it off, Alice!" Mark growled, putting the rifle barrel against her forehead and pushing back to the ground. "Knock it off, or I'll blow your head off!"

Alice gave another kick, and the rifle barrel slipped to her cheek, pressing the side of her face against the dirt.

"I'm *serious*." She heard the safety tick off. "Settle down right now, or you *and* your kids will get it!" He half turned. "Christine, you got things under control back there?!"

"I've got them," she said. "Just give me a second to get them tied up!"

Mark stepped aside enough for Alice to see, and a slow-burning anger grew in her chest and twisted her guts with hatred as she stopped struggling, blinking away the dirt in her eyes. Christine had a gun pointed at the back of Jake's head, forcing him to slump forward where he sat on the trail. Sarah lay on the ground nearby, holding her stomach and nursing a bloody nose and lip while glaring at Christine with revulsion.

Christine's hair sat in a tousled bun, strands hanging loose from their clips to frame her red, puffy face as she panted and screeched at Sarah. "You come at me again, you little bitch, and I'll put a bullet in the back of your brother's head!" Forcing his arms behind his head, she used a piece of rope to bind him, eying Sarah the entire time, daring her to try something.

"I... I don't understand," Alice murmured, each word like a gong going off in her head.

"Of course, you don't." The rifle barrel pressed harder into her cheek as he laughed. "Because you're stupid. Hurry up, Christine."

"Almost there."

Brandishing Jake's pistol, Christine walked toward Sarah, who'd gotten to her knees and looked like she was about to lunge. Christine lashed out with a kick and Sarah cried out in pain as she tumbled over, holding her face as blood poured from her nose. Jake tried to move toward her, but Christine side-stepped him and pistol-whipped him, sending him tumbling over next to his sister.

"Now, y'see, that's the kind of foolishness that's gonna get you all in trouble." Christine tutted, wagging the pistol at the pair. "Let me go over the rules real fast. *We're* in control now, and we got the weapons. If you do something stupid, I'll put a bullet in you both and your mom, too. Play nice, and you'll get out of this just fine. We don't want to shoot anyone if we don't have to. You're no good to us lame or dead."

"You're... you're liars! I knew it!" Sarah stammered as drool and blood dripped from her chin, her face smeared with red.

"Ohhh, come on now. We're not *that* bad. If we wanted to just shoot you and take your things, we'd have already done it. Now, the pair of you get up and come over here. Sit down nice and easy together."

"Jake... Sarah..." Alice croaked, "Just... just do what they say."

"That's right," Mark purred. "Even your mother knows when you've lost. Come on now. We don't have all day. This charade has put us *massively* behind schedule."

Emotions battled behind Sarah's eyes, her jaw working back and forth as tears streamed down her cheeks. Finally, she looked at Jake who had rolled over onto his side and the pair nodded and she helped him stand, then they moved over to where Christine had indicated.

"Now, put your hands behind your back," Christine said. "Good girl. I'm going to put the gun down for a second, and I know what you're thinking, but if you make so much as a twitch to try and get it, Mark'll put another hole in your pretty mommy's head. Are you going to make any trouble?"

Sarah's whole body sagged and she bowed her head and shook it.

"Fantastic. See? We *can* get along! One second, hon."

While Christine bound Sarah and tightened Jake's rope, Mark removed his knee from Alice's chest, gesturing with the rifle barrel. "I'm going to need you to flip over, too."

Hatred flashed in her eyes and she glanced over, trying to find her pistol, gauging how long it would take her to lunge for it. Mark chuckled and shook his head.

"Your gun got knocked about ten feet in that direction. If you think you can get to it before I shoot you three or four times, well, I mean hey, try it and see where it gets you."

"Don't do it, Mom," Sarah rasped. "They said they wouldn't hurt us. You won't hurt us, will you?"

"Of course not." Christine's words were saccharine as she finished with Sarah and Jake and came to assist Mark, getting on her knees, rolling Alice over, and binding Alice's hands while Mark stepped back. Taking her by the shoulder, she flipped her back and retreated a few paces to survey her handiwork with Mark.

"Dang, Christine," Mark laughed. "We finally got 'em. That rest break was perfect. Kudos to you kids for insisting on it."

Christine whooped and slapped him on the back, waving the pistol around in Sarah's direction. "I wasn't sure we could do it. That little bitch is pretty strong, but an elbow to the gut was all it took to knock her down."

"C'mon, let's get Alice over by the others." Together, the pair took Alice by the arms and lifted her, half dragging her to the kids, and throwing her down next to them.

"Now, let's see what they've *really* got on them." Before he stepped away, he aimed the gun at Jake's face. "Don't try anything stupid, you hear? Your kids will suffer the consequences of your mistakes. Ya get me?"

Alice clenched her teeth, taking a long breath and nodding before Mark and Christine went over to Hercules and began rifling through their bags.

"Are you kids okay?" Alice spoke softly to them, and Sarah sniffed and nodded.

Jake leaned forward, glaring intensely, jaw flexing. "I'm going to kill them, Mom."

"I heard that!" Christine called, taking the nearly-empty bug spray and two used water filter straws and tossing them over her shoulder into the woods.

"I'm just glad we don't have to put on that act anymore," Mark snorted. "Took forever for the bitch to let her guard down."

"Right?" Christine replied. "Maybe we should just shoot them all for annoying us so much."

"Now, you know we can't do that, so don't get too excited. We've still got a way to go. But, hey, we just doubled our workers for the camp up north. Want a snack bar?"

"Sure do. What about the brats?"

Mia and Hunter sat quietly a few yards away with their heads low and holding hands, Mia clutching a doll to her chest, both of them avoiding even a wayward glance in Mark or Christine's direction.

"They can go hungry for all I care," Mark shrugged. "They nearly gave us away anyway."

Tears stung Alice's eyes and ran burning down her face. "How can you say that?"

"We can say – and do – what we please." Mark stepped away from Hercules and stood in front of Alice with his feet spread, mouth twisted in a contemptuous grin. He stared at her for a few seconds before raising the rifle and pointing it at her chest. "Or are you deaf *and* stupid?"

"If you lay a finger on any of their heads," Alice spoke through bared teeth, "you'll wish you didn't live to regret it."

Mark's smile dropped for a moment, his eyes opening nervously for a few seconds before he dropped the charade and laughed uproariously. "Nah, Alice." The laughter ceased without warning and there was a slight *click* as his finger ticked the rifle's safety off. "You won't be doing a damn thing about *anything*."

Alice's eyes registered the briefest flash of light from the end of the rifle's barrel, though both it and the ear-splitting boom were instantly cut off when a meteor struck her chest and sent her flying backward into a pit of darkness.

CHAPTER FIFTEEN

Raj
Industrial Area, Doha, Qatar

Dawn broke over the city of Qatar, the sun's rays streaming across the rooftops and the telephone poles, seeping in through the window to give the first glimpse of the day's heat. Raj finished his morning tea in the one-room apartment he shared with fourteen other men, the workers packed in on cots lining every wall, the bathroom only a bucket in the corner, leaving the room soaking in a perpetual reek that choked his lungs. Foremen outside shouted for the workers to get up and moving, their voices booming above the quiet din, eager to force their workers to get back to clearing Qatar's streets and rebuilding what the flames had destroyed. Once rolling in gas and oil money, the ultra-rich city had been brought to its knees just like the rest of the world by the explosions that had broken out in its refining factories and neighborhoods.

The slums where the workers stayed had been spared the worst of the explosions since they couldn't drive vehicles or operate gas-

MIKE KRAUS

powered machines. But the ruling class of Qatar - the business owners and foremen who owned the workers' "contracts" - were determined to keep them moving every hour of the day in constant, grueling shifts. Several men in the room were on their knees in the middle of the floor, praying as a voice from a radio chanted softly beside them, while others poured themselves tea from a small stove in the back, burning scraps of lumber they'd picked up from the previous day's shift.

Bali, an older man who'd been in Qatar for three years, sat up in his bed and held his feet, gently touching the blisters covering them. "I don't think I can work today."

"You must keep working." Akash, a younger man who hadn't been in the country working for long, leaned against the bunk pole, "or you won't get fed."

"What does it matter when all we eat is dirt and water?"

Raj couldn't disagree with the older man. The food, which had already been bad before, was more rotten and bland than ever, and regular supplies of rations had dwindled. The men in his work crew were withering away more each day, losing muscle mass, energy, and the will to live. Tea in hand, he walked over to talk to Bali and Akash.

"It doesn't matter what you feel or think," he said. "If you do not show up at the roll call, they will come looking for you."

"What are they going to do?" Bali replied. "Beat me more?" He turned to show long open sores across his bare back and shoulders.

"I understand, my friend," Raj said, trying desperately to find something to motivate the man. "But if you don't get up, you will lose the money you've made, and they'll send you home."

"What money? They haven't paid us for weeks – and the pittance from before? Barely worth it anyway!"

"Perhaps they will make it up once we're out of this." Akash shrugged and gestured. "How can we expect them to pay us when everything has crumbled?"

"Then how can we afford to work?" Bali continued. "If only they would send us home." He grabbed Raj's arm. "And why don't they send us home, you wonder? Well, I know. It's because they can't. The

188

planes no longer run and even if they did, we are nothing but slaves to them anyway."

"You don't know that," Akash said, shooting Raj a doubtful look.

"I do know that, in fact," Bali replied. "The company office burned to the ground. That's where they kept our passports."

"Is this true, Raj?"

Raj shrugged. "I don't know. And we may be slaves, but at least we have a place to sleep and some kind of food to eat. What can we do but keep working?"

Bali squeezed Raj's arm harder. "We could fight back. They were strong before, too strong for us to fight against. Now, though, we may stand a chance." He broke down, his expression twisting miserably. "As it stands, I may never speak to my wife again, much less see her. They promised us so much, and lied about it all, but now...." His words trailed off into sobs and tears.

"All of that may be true," Raj said, the first stirrings of anger and resentment welling up inside him, "but all we can do is keep going. They cannot abuse us so badly that they lose their workforce! They could get more of us before, but they can't now!"

"Yes, that's right," Akash agreed. "They must take care of us."

"Oh, they don't care." Bali fixed them both with a glare. "There are so many of us here already. It doesn't matter. Where one of us falls, another takes his place. We're going to die here, my friends, and I will be the first."

"Hush, old man," Akash said, noticing others in the room watching them, a danger if one of them was spying for the company. The mere hint of a complaint or workers making demands would bring whips – or worse – down on their heads. "Come on and get up. Raj and I will help you."

Raj was nodding. "That's right, old man. We'll help you get there, but you're on your own from there. Here, now. Where are your shoes?"

They got Bali dressed, fed him some tea, and helped him walk outside to the booming voices of the foremen. Workers formed lines in the two-story apartment slums, marching like zombies to the stair cases and into a wide lot where foremen tapped heads and called names, ensuring everyone was on hand to work. The reek of so many unwashed, sick bodies clung to the air, burning Raj's nostrils and filling him with hopelessness.

Raj's story was like so many others, lured from India by a recruiter who promised a fine contract to come to Qatar and work for a company, though as soon as he arrived, they'd taken his passport and swapped his contract for a new one, extended by an extra year with only three-quarters of the promised wage. Raj had been warned of such practices before he signed up, but with no jobs in India, he'd had to take what he could get and hope things wouldn't be as bad as people claimed. But it hadn't turned out the way he'd wanted, and life had become more dismal with every passing day, only compounded by what had happened to the fuel supply.

"What kind of work will it be today?" Bali asked as they reached the ground floor and shuffled across the court where a smoky haze covered everything.

"The same as yesterday," Raj replied, "We will clear rubble until that is gone, then we'll rebuild their city."

The foremen counted the marks on their arms drawn in permanent ink, checked off their lists, and waved them through. They walked east along a boulevard toward downtown Doha, the once pristine high-rises glowing in the desert sun turned to tall spikes of char still giving off clouds of soot. The sun crested the horizon and bathed them in its warmth, the temperature reaching close to a hundred well before noon. On the way, they were handed lukewarm bottles of water with broken seals and at another line, workers gave out bowls of cheap, fatty pork and oatmeal, a combination that tasted like lumpy sawdust to Raj, though he forced himself to eat it anyway. By the time they reached the work camp, Raj was sweating, his stale clothes moist, and the several men walking near him were barely shuffling along, shirts pulled up over their heads and shoulders slumped.

Under the watchful eye of a few Qatar guards in their clean brown suits, the line moved between husks of buildings that had fallen in on themselves, narrow paths cleared through the streets so they could trek deeper into the ruins. Their worksite was a block of shorter office buildings, fourteen floors, most of them collapsed into a pit of rubble like a tooth rotted to its root. Raj fell in line with other workers picking up debris, dropping it into wheelbarrows or sending it down a conveyor run by men turning cranks. There were no trucks or heavy machinery to move anything, just a few hastily constructed pulleys to lift the bigger pieces, shifting them to large trailers to be pulled away by more workers.

Foremen shouted insults and threats to keep the pace up, and the workers hurried at first, but their energy quickly faded by midday when the sun's glare spiked temperatures upward of a hundred and seventeen degrees. Despite the thousands of workers picking away at the pile, things moved at a painfully slow pace, the dent in the building's side slowly carved out to reveal the guts of the place; its stairwells, pipes and wiring were all cut into smaller pieces, rolled up, and stacked in trailers for reuse.

A little after noon, the first man collapsed on a pile of bricks and was carried away by some other workers, but instead of calling a break, the foreman pressed them harder, using belts and sticks to whip the men and keep them moving as they slowly cut through the rough mound. Only a few wore gloves they had been able to find, Raj not being one of them, and his hands were soon raw and aching, not even the calluses he'd built up offering any protection. The workers wore rags on their heads and shoulders, glistening bodies sweating and dusty beneath the sun's heat, clustered beneath patches of shade at every possible opportunity to keep cool.

A short time later, two other men collapsed from heat exhaustion, adding to the murmurs of disgruntlement. The worst injury of the day occurred when a makeshift pulley failed and dropped an I-beam on a worker's head, instantly breaking his neck and drawing cries from the men until the foreman amplified the threats and abuse, forcing everyone back to work. They continued their grueling labors, working beneath the cruel sun and the foreman's whips and curses. Raj wiped the beads of sweat off his forehead and stayed close to Bali and Akash, the two younger men watching over and helping the older one as he picked up huge chunks of rock, turned, and shuffled over to the wheelbarrow to drop them heavily inside. He was a robot, expres-

191

sion slack, eyes blank as he trudged on until, finally, they came to their first break of the day.

Carts were pushed up with dozens of water bottles stacked on top, the seals broken and the liquid cloudy, but it didn't stop the workers from grabbing them and drinking them in two or three gulps. A few splashed the last bit into their faces, washing away the sweat for only a moment before it came back twice as strong. Raj and Akash helped Bali over to the cart of water, but he was mumbling, hands shaking, eyes rolling back into his head.

"Here you go, old man," Raj said, taking a bottle for himself and Bali, opening it and feeding him so it dribbled down his chin. "No, Bali. You must get it in your mouth. Don't spill it." Bali felt blindly for the bottle, almost knocking it from Raj's hands. "There you go, man. Drink."

Raj opened his own bottle and drank deep, his nose curling at the dirt and grit and the faint whiff of sewage.

"All right, men! The break is over! Back to work now!"

Raj turned as the foreman grabbed the water cart and shoved it to the side. He held a belt wrapped around his fist, and he glared blood-shot at the group as he pointed to the pile of debris he wanted moved.

"Can we get some good water?" Raj asked.

The foreman turned his gaze in Raj's direction. "What is that? Who spoke?"

"It was me," Raj replied, holding up the bottle, particulates floating inside. "I asked if we could have some good water. This is dirty."

The foreman stared at the bottle for a moment before snatching it out of Raj's hand. "Oh, I am sorry your water is not adequate for you. I would hate to have you drink poor-tasting water."

With a widening grin, he turned the bottle upside down and drained it into the road to the groans of the workers.

"You didn't have to do that," Raj said. "I just wanted —"

"No, no, no!" the foreman cried, throwing the bottle into the air and raising his hands. "This man has exposed a grave injustice. We will only have the *best* water for you from now on. We will immediately send back all the water planned for you on the next break and dump that into the sea. Then we will look for the best water in the city for you. It might be a couple of days until we get the pipes working again, but I'm sure you will be fine holding out until then."

The crowd groaned even louder, and someone shoved Raj from behind as the members of Qatar's official guard laughed and nudged each other behind the foreman, who spoke louder, addressing the crowd.

"Do all of you feel the same? Do you want fresh spring water in a few days after you've died of thirst, or are you happy with what you have?"

Many shouted apologies to the foreman, begging for forgiveness and to allow them to get back to work, though a few voices cried out in dissent and cursed him.

"Who said that?" The foreman's eyes widened with rage, spittle flying from his mouth as he screamed. "All of you will pay for the remarks of a few! No more water until the evening for all of you!"

"Please," Raj pleaded. "There is no need for all this."

"No need for all this? You are the one who is causing problems, and you're disrupting everyone's work."

"I wasn't —"

The foreman slapped him in the face, the sound cracking above the murmuring workers, their voices fading as they stared. Raj touched his hand to his burning cheek, mystified at his own swelling rage, a volcanic pit of lava rushing from his stomach and up through his chest. Shoulders rising on a sharp breath, Raj flexed his fists, surging with strength, opening his hands so they formed claws. Before he knew what he was doing, he lunged forward and wrapped his hands around the foreman's neck.

Growling, the foreman grabbed Raj's arms and tried to remove him, but the grip was too tight, some unfathomable power coursing through Raj's fingers, digging into the man's neck to squeeze off the airway. His only satisfaction would be killing the man who'd made his life a living hell, and no one tried to stop him as he dug his thumbs into the foreman's windpipe and crushed his voice box with a sharp snap. The foreman crumpled, eyes bulging, cheeks turning red, gasping as he dropped to his knees and slipped from Raj's grasp, collapsing on the hot pavement where he kicked weakly, clawing at his throat for a moment before he lay still.

Raj stood straight, staring at the foreman and then at his hands, flexing them as strength still surged through them. Squeezing out tears, Raj waited to be shot or dragged away immediately, but the crowd had fallen dead quiet, hundreds of men standing in the rubble who'd seen Raj strangle the foreman. The two guards came forward, their rifles sliding off their shoulders and into their hands before they paused as if sensing a change in the air. There was a moment of calm, a pause between what had happened and what would happen next, Raj's life already gone in a blink, nothing left to lose and everything to gain.

One guard moved to help the foreman while the other pointed his rifle at Raj's chest. "Kill them," Raj spat, his voice rising on a quivering note of rage. "Take them and kill them! Do it now, or we'll all die here and never see our families again."

No one moved, the weight of their servitude heavy in their minds, the idea of rising up such a foreign concept that it seemed impossible to grasp. Uncertainty flashed across the workers' faces as they glanced between the guards, Raj, and the foreman on the ground. With the foreman dead and his whip silenced, something shifted in the crowd. Eyes narrowed, bodies tensed, and fists flexed like Raj's, the sentiment among the workers shifted in the face of the guards' hesitation, wanting to punish the people responsible for their misery.

One guard pressed the barrel of his rifle against Raj's chest and started to squeeze the trigger, but hands reached in, grabbed the weapon, and pushed it upwards. Two shots fired into the sky before the crowd dragged the guard down and took his rifle, viciously striking and kicking him until he no longer moved. They turned the other guard's gun on him, shooting a quick burst of rounds to his stomach, blowing blood across the hot pavement as his agonizing screams were muffled by the bodies pressing in around him.

Men raised the rifles into the air while others lifted the dead foreman's body, tossing him back and forth, cheering as they punched and kicked him before throwing him into the pile of rubble, his body impaling on twisted rebar jutting out of the ruins. Raj grinned grimly as the crowd swept forward to the next worksite where the confused guards and foreman came running up only to be overwhelmed by the throng, who beat them, stomped them, and took their guns before they could open fire. More guards in spotless brown uniforms were trampled in the flood, and one soldier fired back, killing two workers before he was disarmed, the smell of blood enraging the throng as they spilled into the streets and tore apart anything left standing, showing no mercy. Raj turned and found Akash, clasping his hand and pulling him close.

"What did you do!?" Akash cried. It wasn't an accusation, but a question of wonder as he grinned madly into the rage-fueled faces shouting and cursing their masters. "What did you do, Raj?!"

"I have set us free!" Joy and bewilderment rushed through Raj as they were swept away in the sea of humanity.

The crowd squeezed into empty streets where there'd been no fire or destruction, quickly overwhelming the guards before breaking into the foremen's apartments, taking fresh bottled water and food, liberating them of the fancier pieces of furniture, snatching up their clean clothing and carrying their spoils above the crowd, cheering as they celebrated. They rushed over to long tankers with clean water sloshing inside, at first taking turns at the spigots, but in their haste to drink, breaking them off so that everyone squatted to get hit full in the face, gulping what they could as they washed off their filth and sweat.

Raj and Akash were shoved forward into a gush of fresh water that hit them in the chest, splashing, cooling their heated skin but not the flames of their rebellion. Laughing, Raj pushed his way to the front and took several gulps of the foamy spray before he was knocked out of the way. The throng finally began to settle, men milling around, raising their fists and cheering for their victory.

When the loudspeakers erupted with a foreman's voice demanding the rioters stand down and return to their hovels, they grew quiet, cowed as the inevitability of their servitude weighed on their minds once more. When a new group of guards and mercenaries in black riot gear ran in, Raj gritted his teeth, jumped on a trailer, and swept his arm at them.

"Take them down quickly, or they will kill us. Do it now before it's too late!"

The crowd shifted uncertainly toward the guards, fists raised and shouting but not attacking, merely forcing them back with threats and curses. When a nervous mercenary fired a burst of rounds into the throng, dropping a handful of workers, the flames rose again, hotter than before. Teeth gritting, heart pounding, Raj encouraged them with sweeping motions, yelling words that seemed to come from another person, not himself.

The first few mercenaries were trampled, and the rest quickly dropped their weapons, turned tail and ran for their lives, begging for mercy and receiving none. The crowd swept on, growing to almost ten thousand angry voices, spilling into elite Qatari residential neighborhoods that had been spared the destruction, dragging family members of the guards and foremen from their homes, beating them in the roads and leaving them bloody and bruised. Workers leaped atop expensive cars that were fresh from the factory, devoid of fuel and thus having survived the devastation, jumping up and down on the hoods and violently tearing them down to their individual components.

As the Qatari citizens got wind of the uprising, they fled their homes, rushing to escape the angry throng, men defending their families with rocks, knives, and sometimes guns, only to be consumed by the hungry mob. Akash thrust Raj atop a shining white car, and thousands packed in the narrow street, raising their fists to him, shouting encouragement, and waiting for their next orders. Raj lifted his hands and motioned for quiet, then a foreman's bullhorn was pressed into his hands, and he turned it on with a squeal of feedback.

"My fellow workers, we have been slaves too long. They lured us here with false promises, lying contracts, and slave's wages. They have treated us worse than animals!"

The crowd cheered as one, the sound so deafening Raj was sure they could hear them back in India.

"They made our fathers, mothers, brothers, and sisters promises of a better life only to grind them into the dirt beneath their heels. They would do the same to us if we let them. It's time for the tables to turn! Show these monsters what we have lived under for far too long! To the docks!"

Like a sea of humanity breaking upon the stones of injustice, the crowd shifted and followed intersecting lanes to the Qatar dock area, where ships lay sunken in the bay, a graveyard of passenger boats, cargo vessels, and tankers. They were cracked open, capsized, their hulls blown out and breached, and the oil and fuel that hadn't burned slicked the waters in giant black patches that had captured fish, seagulls, and garbage in the glistening rainbow waves.

The people who had been driven from their homes were pushed to the docks, squeezing to the edge, turning to face the rising swell of workers who swarmed after them. Raj's people chased hundreds of them up to the heights where tall cliffs loomed above rocky shores, where a simple waist-high stone wall was all that helped to keep people from straying out and falling to their deaths. Still, the press of the throng pushed some too close, and they were shoved over, windmilling into the open air to crash on rocks that crushed their bones and cut off their screams in an instant.

The workers jeered at them, sticking and poking them with weapons they'd fashioned out of rebar and pieces of wood. Grim-faced men stood in front of their families, yelling back while women with silken hair and well-manicured fingernails crouched behind them, holding their children close as they were pressed to the edge. At the docks, the workers surged forward, shoving hundreds into the bay to splash and flail, their oil-covered faces searching for their loved ones in the brackish mess. A worker threw a lighter into the bay, and flames arose with a tremendous whoosh that swept across the waters, consuming everything in its path, screaming mouths sucking in the flames as they gasped for air.

On the cliff, Akash grabbed a man and pulled him away from the wall, and the workers behind them threw him to the ground and beat him. A woman fell in front of Raj, hands pressed together, begging for mercy as more plunged from the heights in a chorus of howls. Raj could only see the friends and family who'd died for the benefit of the rich, his brother, father, and many others worked to death, lied to, and cheated by the Qatari government, her pleading eyes and prayers doing nothing to quench his simmering rage.

Raj grabbed her hand and helped her to her feet, the woman's expression changing to gratitude until Raj stripped the golden rings off her fingers and the jewel-encrusted bracelets from her wrists, then shoved her toward the edge. She hit the wall, flipped back, and went over, flailing as she plummeted, striking the sheer cliff face twice before smashing against the rocks below.

The ocean crashed over the dead in a blood-oil spray, patches of it aflame as it consumed thousands of bodies, the waves clutching them and dragging them out to serve their endless sentence in the cold and ruthless sea.

CHAPTER SIXTEEN

James Burton
Frankfurt, Illinois

James cowered beneath a pile of wreckage, a cold concrete slab that had fallen from some upper floor looming over him, supported by stacks of rubble, protecting him from the storms rippling across the city. It was drizzling, and the pipes in the building were gurgling as water passed down through the ruins, finding every nook and cranny it could to escape into the sewers. He held a can of peas on his knees, one from the spilled cart, using a can opener from inside his collapsible stave to open it. The jugs of water sat by his side, and he'd already drunk and spat back out half of one of them to wash the smoky particulates from his throat.

The food went from can to mouth automatically, shoveling it in with his fingers, so focused was he on the edges of the ruins and the shadows that lurked there that he disregarded the fact that the food was cold. People wandered out in the gloomy early evening, faint movements out in the fog, though none had ventured toward him, held back by either the thick smoke drifting around the ruins or the potential of the whole place to collapse at any moment. While he hadn't heard anything from the gang, he wasn't out of the woods yet; escaping the congested and violent city was paramount. Shoving the last handful of peas into his mouth, he chewed them into mush and swallowed them down, then had one final swig of water, stood, and packed everything up.

He shrugged his pack on and picked his way through the wreckage, crouching to sneak between the rubble and fragmented walls, squeezing through cracks and ducking when he heard sounds on the perimeter. Near the edge, he got on one knee and waited, listening, observing the darkness before rushing into the night. With his stave in his left hand, he used the compass end to stay heading east, breaking into a narrow alley and stopping at the end to look both ways. When he didn't see anyone, he sprinted to the other side, barely catching a glimpse of the street sign as he flew by. He couldn't remember Rosen Street from his map studying back in the warehouse district, so he continued slinking through the darkness, his footsteps hidden by the sounds of pattering rain and grumbling thunder. Whispers and the occasional shouts bounced off the brick walls and old wooden siding of the surrounding buildings, making it impossible to know where they came from.

He slowed to check each street sign, not recognizing any until he came to a major intersection with Dixon running west to east, a street that was far too close to the Highway 30 demarcation line for his taste. Going by his compass, James angled south by southeast, heading toward a long block of wooded areas cut by winding lanes and a spattering of buildings. When the road turned back to the north, he went off-road and passed through a vast park with children's play sets and slides. The soft pink padded turf under the swings and slides had been burned and melted, the surrounding grasses turned brown, and the treetops stripped bare of leaves and healthy branches by a firestorm that had swept through.

He pointed his flashlight toward the parking lot off to the left, which had been turned into a field of hot slag by explosions. Bent car frames littered the pavement in a scatter of shredded metal and parts, already showing rust spots and decay from the intense rains. Bodies had fused to the seats, crushed and burned, hair lank, skin hanging loose off their bones, organs liquefied into thick puddles that mixed with the rain. A reek of death lingered in the air, and James wrinkled his nose and moved on through the park at a steady clip, cutting between two buildings that had collapsed in a mountain of black coals. When he shined his light across the rubble, he gasped, stomach churning at the pile of dead bodies around the doorways turned to charred sludge.

Clamping his teeth to hold down the rising bile, James bent his head and continued, keeping his flashlight pointed at the ground and searching for a path through the darkness. With no trail in sight, he pressed past the brush and pushed between sticker bushes, tripping over chunks of black wood and crunching dead leaves and twigs. The gray mist rose off the forest floor, reflecting his flashlight beam into a glow so bright it forced him to turn it off in order to keep moving. Stumbling into the darkness, he came to a patch of thinning trees and moved from one to the next, touching his palms to them as he passed to keep his balance through the unsteady, mucky terrain. On the other side of the woods was another park with a pond in the middle, rain sprinkling the surface where the remains of a half-dozen bodies floated at the edge of the water, surrounded by burned branches, the details of their forms mercifully too obscured by darkness to make out.

James came to a street heading due east and south, taking it despite the distant cracks of guns echoing from ahead. Soon, the squarish forms of buildings stuck out above the treetops, and he entered another small township on the edges of the larger city. The storm had started to pick up, whistling between the buildings, howling in gales like ghosts trapped in a concrete limbo, destined to haunt the shadowy stoops and darkened windows forever. Rain struck him sideways without warning, forcing him to put his hands in his pockets and slump forward, head low as he stared at the pavement slipping by beneath him. Water gathered in his hair and dripped off his chin, creeping down his neckline and getting his semi-dry shirts wet once again while the eyelets on his worn boots leaked like sieves, and soon his feet were wet and cold as well.

James kept to the center of the road, walking with a wide stance to stay balanced as the wind punched him like a prizefighter. He stopped looking for signs and focused on staying upright, squeezing between piles of junk and spilled bricks, stumbling toward a line of sawhorses stretched across the road, covered in tarps and flapping in the breeze.

Sandbags stood in stacks on both ends, like a military checkpoint, though it appeared abandoned, with no lights or soldiers anywhere. When he reached the barrier and tried to squeeze through, though, dark figures rose from behind the sandbags, water dripping from their helmets, green ponchos fluttering in the breeze, a half-dozen guns pointed at him.

"Got another banger!" someone called from the left-hand side, aiming a rifle at his face. "Stop right there!"

James had frozen at the first signs of movement, and he threw his hands up when he saw the soldier's finger slip beneath the trigger guard. "Don't shoot! I'm not a—I'm not one of them! I'm just passing through, I swear!"

Another soldier grabbed the rifle barrel and shoved it down, the tall, cowed figure stepping forward to get a better look at James. After a second, he nodded. "Hold your fire, people. I recognize that stick he's carrying. They give them out at the refugee camps." Shifting his attention to James, he said, "Okay, buddy. Who are you?"

He stood in the cold with his hands up and water dripping down his arms. "My name is James Burton. I'm coming from Denver, Colorado, heading to East Lansing, Michigan. Yeah, I got this from one of the refugee camps back west."

"I guess I shouldn't have mentioned that," the soldier replied. "You could've stolen it from someone leaving those camps. Show me your arms and neck."

"My... arms and neck?"

"Tats. Do you have any?"

"No." James rolled up his sleeves as a flashlight beam cut across him, then he unbuttoned his shirt and moved back and forth, exposing his chest and neck.

The light flashed across his face and moved back and forth before lowering.

"Okay, you're not in one of the gangs. Or if you are, you're the only one I've seen who isn't all inked up."

"Definitely not. Is this a military checkpoint?"

Chuckles rose from the group as they lowered their weapons and relaxed.

"Some might call it that. Some might call it hell on earth." The tall figure rested his hand on a sawhorse. "We're the remnants of a group from the Illinois National Guard. I'm Captain Fred Lister, and the young woman who almost shot you is Lieutenant Dawn Washington."

James put his hands down. "Thanks for not firing, ma'am."

"You're very welcome," Washington replied. "You should be more careful next time walking headlong into a checkpoint like that, though, especially with it being so dark and rainy out."

"Yeah, that's my fault," James chuckled nervously. "It's been a hell of a week, and I'm just trying to get out of the city. I hadn't meant to come this far north."

"None of us did, man," Lister replied.

James shivered and put his hands in his pockets, hugging his coat tighter around his waist. "How long have you guys been here?"

"Way too long. You said you came from a camp back west?"

"Outside of Denver."

"Any news?"

"I'd ask you the same thing about conditions to the east. I've got a long way ahead of me. Maybe we can trade information."

"That sounds like a good idea," Lister replied. "Come on through."

The guardsmen parted, and James stepped past the barrier, nodding respectfully to Lieutenant Washington before following

Lister onto a sidewalk along a series of dilapidated buildings. One of the older apartments gave off muted light from the covered windows, and the captain guided them up a set of stone stairs and through the front door to stand in a large foyer area with a raised ceiling and an old chandelier hanging above them.

Without taking off their coats, they entered a side room with a table, chairs, and a short stack of supply bins with more empty ones sitting on the side. An electric lantern rested on the old wooden windowsill and gave off a dim light, barely enough to see by. Near the window, which was cracked open a couple of inches, a two-burner propane stove sat on a table with a pan on one side and a coffee pot on the other.

"Have a seat there." Lister gestured at the chair nearest the window. "You hungry?"

"I could eat something." James nodded and sat. "If you've got any of that coffee left, I'd welcome it. Haven't had anything decent in me in days."

"I'll get it," Washington said, shouldering her rifle and heading that way. She was a squat, burly woman with ink-black locks stuck to her cheek.

The captain sat across from him, falling heavily into his chair and pushing back his wet hood to reveal a sharp-eyed young man with a troubled brow, face smudged with dirt, taller than James by a few inches, and lean under his bulky National Guard poncho. He ran a hand through a dark buzz cut, whipping water onto the floor.

"I'll have a cup of coffee, too, if you don't mind, Lieutenant."

"No problem."

Lister sat back with a sigh and gestured at James. "I'll let you go first. I'm sure your story is a lot more interesting than mine."

James shrugged. "It started back in Denver; I was waiting for my airplane at Denver International, to fly down to Florida to meet my family for a vacation. Everything started exploding on the tarmac... planes, fuel trucks, just everything. It was a horrible, bloody scene."

Lister leaned forward. "How did you survive all that?"

"It was insanity trying to get out of the gate. People were screaming, and chunks of debris fell on our heads and crashed through the windows. I hitched a ride on an employee cart, got to the concourse, fought my way downstairs, and got outside. It wasn't much better there; the parking lot was one big ball of flames, and the debris was hitting everyone and cutting them to pieces. I saw..." James shook his head, remembering the people taking luggage out of their trunks when their vehicles exploded. "Just a lot of stuff I never want to see again as long as I live."

"I'll bet. Obviously, you made it out of there."

"Hid beneath an underpass with planes falling from the sky. A jet engine almost hit me."

"Damn," Washington said as she set a cup of black coffee and a bowl of what appeared to be chicken noodle soup in front of him. "Sounds like a war zone."

"It felt like one. I was just trying to get away from it all. There were fires everywhere, and I talked to some folks on the way in who were supposed to pick up people on incoming flights. Don't think they made it." He picked up a spoon and took a bite of the soup, which amounted to a thin broth with a few noodles and small chunks of chicken. "Anyway, I made it through the city and hitched a ride on a cargo train heading east. It was actually your people running the train, at least for the first stretch."

"Colorado National Guard?" Lister asked.

"Not sure if it was Colorado or not, but they were a good group of people. We stopped once to pick up some Army troops and vehicles, then continued until we reached a refugee camp outside Kansas City. Couldn't tell you exactly where, but it seemed to be a train junction somewhere."

"Maybe the Sims Junction camp," Washington said, bringing the Captain his coffee. "We call it camp ten-twelve."

"Sounds like it. Thank you, Lieutenant."

"Not long after I showed up, the place fell under attack —"

"Attack?" Lister leaned farther forward with concern. "What kind of attack?"

James shrugged. "Couldn't tell you who it was, but I jumped in and tried to help them out. I followed a corporal around for a few hours and helped lug ammunition to the tanks and Humvees."

"So, they found some armored vehicles that work," Washington stated, standing beside the table with her arms crossed.

"Equipment they'd gotten out of the junkyard motor pool. The tank crew mentioned they were old machines on the verge of decommissioning."

"You talked to the tank crew?" Lister glanced at Washington. "How'd that go down?"

"I sure did." James slurped the rest of his soup. "Helped them fix a firing mechanism problem in their tank. While I was inside, they mentioned all that."

The Captain and Lieutenant exchanged another look. "Seems like you were pretty involved over there," Lister said. "I'm not sure how you fixed a mechanical problem the crew couldn't."

"I've got a doctorate in mechanical engineering and tinker heavily at home, and their mechanic was indisposed. Not a complex problem, but easy to miss and not know how to fix."

"I'm sure they appreciated the help."

"They loaded me up with some good gear, including an M4 I lost somewhere around Champaign. Luckily, I still had my walking stick." James motioned to where he'd leaned it up against the wall. "That thing has saved me more times than I can count. Probably the only reason why I'm still alive."

"Yeah, they've been handing them out at all the camps, last I saw."

James settled back and sipped his coffee, the hot brew warming his belly and sending a chill up his back. "Other than that, I met some nice Amish people and hitched a ride to Hannibal. We pushed our way across in a pole barge, and that's where we split up. Took a horse all the way here, getting chased and harassed the whole time. I'm surprised I made it this far. Amber – the horse – didn't."

"Sorry to hear that," Lister said, leaning back in his chair. "That's quite a story."

"Now, I'm just trying to get back to my family. My in-laws are in East Lansing and I'm hoping my wife and kids will be able to make it up by the time I get home, otherwise I'm going to have to go searching for them. I've got a homestead with some supplies that might carry us through this, but if not, I've got some farmland I can work to keep us going."

"Your wife and kids are down in Florida?" Washington asked.

"They *were* down in Florida, waiting for me to meet them for a vacation when all this started. Couldn't say where my family is or if they're even safe. I signed up for some database thing back in Kansas City, but they weren't in it."

"Most communications are down or spotty at best. Everything except for military radios and some AM-FM channels."

"I guess I just have to hope they're on the way, then." James sighed, finishing the soup before continuing. "How about you folks? How'd you end up here? Shouldn't there be more of you?"

"We're the remnants of a group sent into Chicago to search for survivors," Lister sighed wearily, "back at the start when finding survivors was a priority. We were supposed to meet up with another group at O'Hare International Airport. Didn't make it past Oak Lawn. We got cut off by fires — boy, the city was blazing — and had to seek shelter nearby. We were holding our position and helping people where we could when a gang attacked us out of nowhere. They overpowered some guards on the perimeter, took their guns, and wreaked havoc on the rest of us. Took down half my damn squad before we could get out of there."

"We've been heading south since then," Washington added, "hoping to link up with a rail line. We've got some wounded in the other room. Things are slow going what with the rain and injured, plus having to deal with bangers coming out of the woodwork."

"I believe it. The rail lines are the way to go, and I wouldn't mind finding one myself, especially after seeing the people running around these neighborhoods."

"I take it you ran into some gangs?" Lister asked.

"Ever since I showed up in this area. The first people I ran into were a couple of junkies, and the next day I ran into the gangs while trying to get out of town. I was stuck in a ditch while they fought." James shook his head and released a low, whistling sigh. "I'll tell you what, the people living in these streets are as violent as they come. Slaughtered each other right in front of me without a care in the world. Small group ambushed a big one and took them down like it was nothing."

"Yeah, numbers have very little meaning anymore," Lister said. "The stronger are getting taken out just as easily as the weak."

"It's a madhouse," James agreed, "and it's hard to find hope in any of it. But getting home to my family is what's keeping me going. It's the one light I cling to."

"So, how'd you get away from the gangs?" Lister asked.

"Ah, they spotted me when I tried to grab some food they'd abandoned during their fight. Almost caught me, too."

Washington chuckled. "Hear that, Cap? James here tried to steal supplies from right under their noses."

Lister grinned. "That takes some balls, for sure."

James laughed. "Turns out it wasn't such a great idea. Almost got myself killed over a couple gallons of water and some cans of peas, but I hid in the ruins until they lost interest. I wandered around for a few more hours trying to find my way out of the city until I found you guys."

"Look, James," Lister said after a pause and a slight nod of agreement from Washington. "We're getting out of here soon and heading south. Want to come with us? We could definitely use the help, and it sounds like you've got some experience under your belt."

"I'm no soldier," James replied, "but it sounds like you're heading my way, and I can hold my own, so yes. Absolutely."

Lister slapped his palm on the table. "Good man. We'll leave first thing tomorrow morning. Until then, you can take a bunk in the next room and get some rest."

James was already shaking his head. "No way. I'm way too hopped up, especially after the soup and coffee. If you don't mind, I'd like to take a watch, maybe help relieve someone here? I can handle a firearm, but as I said, I lost my rifle a few nights ago." James removed the revolver he'd taken off of the junkie from his pocket and set it on the table. "I took this from one of the folks who attacked me. It's all I've got as far as weapons go, but I'm happy to use it."

Lister gave James a nod. "All right, friend. Washington, go get Rodriguez."

THE RUINATION

"Yes, sir."

The Lieutenant stepped out and came back with a haggard-looking woman who staggered in and gave a weak salute, water dripping from her helmet and poncho.

"You wanted to see me, sir?"

"Get this man a weapon and get some shut-eye."

Rodriguez stiffened. "Get him a weapon?"

A mischievous smile played across Lister's mouth. "James here is the man we heard tell about over in Kansas City, Rodriguez."

"The tank man?"

"One and the same."

"Wait a second," an eyebrow went up as James looked at the trio. "You knew who I was? Why all the questions?"

"Sorry, not sorry. Had to make sure you were who you claimed. Not every day a civvie fixes a mothballed piece of armor and helps save lives. Your name was passed around by a few folks who said to keep an eye out for you should you pop up. Said you were good people. Anyway, Rodriguez? James'll take your shift until morning."

The guardswoman looked at James with uncertainty.

"Trust me. Hit the bunk. You've been up forty-eight hours straight, and I don't want you shooting your foot off or letting some banger sneak up from behind and shank you because you're exhausted."

"I... thank you." Rodriguez's shoulders sagged as an untold weight was lifted from them, then took off her helmet to shake out a thick mane of soaking-wet black hair. Without another word, she walked into a back room and disappeared into the shadows, briefly reappeared with a rifle, then vanished once again.

James checked the weapon over, taking a couple of extra mags from the captain, then slung it on his shoulder and gave a brief salute. "Private James Burton, reporting for duty."

"Very good, James," Lister and Washington both laughed. "Follow the Lieutenant, and she'll show you your assignment."

James started after the Lieutenant before she turned and handed him a long poncho. "Put this on," she said. "It'll keep you dry, mostly."

209

James thanked her and put it on, buttoning it tight around his neck and pulling it down to cover his midsection and upper legs. From there, he followed Washington outside and marched to the barrier, crossing the street to the left-hand side where two guardsmen squatted behind the stack of sandbags.

Washington spoke loud to be heard over the pouring rain. "This is your spot for the night with me, Wiseman, and Pugh. Wiseman and Pugh, this is James. He's sitting in for Rodriguez tonight."

"Are we still moving out in the morning?" Pugh asked, the dark-eyed blonde squinting beneath the brim of her helmet, not bothering to question the unusual arrangement.

"That's the plan," Washington replied. "We'll get Rodriguez up in eight hours so you two can get some shut-eye before we move out."

"Righteous, Lieutenant." Pugh pulled her helmet lower and leaned against the wet sandbags.

"Appreciate that, ma'am." Wiseman nodded and took up a position next to Pugh. James and Washington squeezed in on the outside, and James peeked around the sandbags into the wet, dismal streets. For the first time in days, his heart settled, his mind stopped racing, and a sense of peace rested on his shoulders.

He turned to Washington. "I'm sure glad I ran into you, Lieutenant. It's good to be among friends."

"It's good to have you, James. As Captain Lister said, we can always use the help."

"You know how to use that thing?" Pugh asked with a glance at his M4.

"Well enough," James replied. "The Captain said you ran into trouble around Oak Lawn."

"It was a rough and tumble for a while there," Pugh replied. "We got called out of a training session to kill fires at our motor pool. Half our training buildings went up in smoke and there was nothing we could do about it. We were standing around in the rubble, pissed off about losing some of our buddies, when we got the order to head to O'Hare. I guess the Captain told you how that worked out."

"Lots of fires and gang trouble?"

"Yeah, we were on fire control the whole way there, trying to work with some local departments to save some city buildings and the police station. We were dragging hoses through the streets and trying every hydrant we came across." She laughed sadly. "We had a little water pressure for a while until the treatment plants lost power and the pressure stopped. All we could do after that was run away."

Wiseman grunted. "The fires were moving fast, and we got surrounded pretty quick and had to get out of there, but some of those firefighters hung around and kept fighting. Don't know what happened to them, but by the time we got north of the area, it was nothing but an orange fireball everywhere you looked."

"Not a pretty picture," James frowned.

"Not even close," Wiseman replied. "I guess we finally wised up and got our butts out of there. Wandered south for a while, tangled with the local gangs who'd somehow survived. Then out of nowhere, it started raining. Damndest thing."

"That was a miracle," Pugh said. "One minute, we were breathing smoke and ash, the next minute it was clear. I used to hate the rain. Not anymore. Well, maybe not so much now that it won't let up. Can't keep my socks dry for the life of me."

James recalled his ride through the back woods and hills, barely escaping the motorcycle riders before ending up in the torrential rain in the city where he'd lost Amber. "I can't say I love it so much, but I can see your point. It's certainly a blessing in a lot of ways. How about your families? Have you heard from them?"

"Not a thing," Pugh replied, while Wiseman only shook his head. "My parents are in Ft. Wayne, and Wiseman's people are in Columbus. I tried calling my mom and dad every ten minutes at first but gave up. My phone ran out of juice days ago. How about you?"

"I was supposed to meet my family in Florida for vacation. In fact, I was about to board a plane just before everything on the tarmac blew up. If things had happened ten minutes later, I would have been aboard and wouldn't be kneeling in the rain with you fine folks."

Pugh grinned. "Lucky you, James."

"Yeah, welcome to the club," Wiseman added.

James nodded and sat back on his heels with rain falling on his poncho, the moisture somehow seeping in around the neck. Light-ning cracked and illuminated the bottom portion of Washington's quiet visage, jaw firm as she searched the gloom with the other guardsman standing vigilant. With a heavy sigh, his worries muted for a little while, James hunkered down and guarded against the night and their enemies.

CHAPTER SEVENTEEN

Ryan Cooper
Somewhere Outside East Lansing, Michigan

It was early afternoon, and Helen and Ryan were out in the chicken coop after feeding and tending to the rest of the animals. They'd milked Bessie and wheeled the containers to the house, placing them just inside the door to pasteurize later after they went in. A brisk breeze rustled the treetops, sending leaves and pieces of garbage skimming across the yard. The flying garbage had been a steadily growing sight over the last few days, growing as it was caught up along the fence line and in the woods, and Ryan grumbled as he pointed at it.

"I haven't seen so much garbage blow around in all my life," he said.

Helen narrowed her eyes. "No more garbage collection and lots of places burned down... it'll probably get worse before it gets better."

"Yup. I imagine this stuff is being carried for miles across the town, especially with the kinds of winds we've been seeing." He sighed wearily. "Just more things on the to-do list. I'll get to it later if I can. It might be a good idea to walk the fence line anyway and ensure there's no funny business happening."

"Well, let's get the eggs and get back inside. My hands are freezing."

"This whole not having weather forecasts anymore kind of sucks."

Helen chuckled and poked his side. "You used to complain all the time about how wrong they always were!"

"Yeah, well... you don't know what you've got till it's gone and all that jazz."

When Ryan opened the chicken coop door, the birds rushed at him, clucking and squawking to get past his feet and he stepped aside and let them go flying out into the yard where Duchess and Diana were chuffing and loping around playfully.

"You not feeling good or something?"

"Hmm?"

"You just let all the birds out, or are you so caught up in thinking about trash you missed that?"

Ryan grinned at the chickens running around as they circled to the right and settled down to peck at the grass and dirt. "Eh, I figure we can start letting them out again and feed them out here."

"You sure about that? Someone could still run up and snatch them."

"Well, given all that happened, I kinda doubt that'll happen again, but we can put them back up in the evenings. Regardless, they need some fresh air and running around space."

"Agreed."

"Hey, look at that," he said, pointing to Duke who was sitting and watching as the other dogs ran around with the birds. "Duke really must be hurt if he's not chasing them. Hey, Duchess! Leave the rooster alone!" Ryan shook his head and went inside, nudging aside the lingering birds and heading for the roost.

They put their rifles down so they didn't bump things in the confined space and Ryan reached in to get the eggs in the top row while Helen knelt and got to the bottom. Soon, their baskets were filled with golden brown eggs, and they were ready to head back.

As they left, Helen checked the lock. "Way to go on the latch; it's still holding up strong."

Ryan smiled and nodded, and they walked back to the house, with Ryan taking a detour over to the solar panels. He handed Helen his basket and kneeled at the end of the row, checking them for evenness and angle, ducking beneath them to verify the wires and cabling were still firmly connected and the poles hadn't shifted in the recent wind.

"Everything looking okay?" Helen asked.

"So far, so good." Ryan looked at the sky. "The clouds are staying away this week, and we're getting plenty of sun. The batteries are nearly full, and the appliances are running just fine."

"I'll need a nice hot shower to chase the cold out of my bones." Helen shivered. "It seems like it'll be a frosty winter if it's this cold already."

"Let's hope it evens out," Ryan nodded, taking his basket back and gesturing toward the house.

He gave a low whistle. "Come on, you old mutts. Get over here."

The dogs came running, except for Duke, who walked behind them, still favoring his shoulder with a slight limp. They piled through the back door, dog claws scratching on the hardwood, slavering and nosing at the egg baskets, causing Helen to turn away.

"Shoo, you nosy animals," she said, "or you won't get any of these in your food tonight."

The dogs gave up on Helen and turned to torment Ryan. "Oh, no you don't," he said, gesturing to his right. "Go on. Now!"

After the dogs went off, Ryan and Helen placed their baskets on the breakfast bar, leaning forward and looking at each other bemusedly.

"Those animals have the energy of five-year-olds."

"Someone around here needs to have some energy," Ryan replied, "because mine's running low."

"Me too." Helen paused reflectively. "I was thinking about what you said about Sandy today. Don't get me wrong, I'm glad it all worked out, but you're so dead set on getting something in return, then you just let her keep what she had. Sometimes I don't get you, Ryan Cooper."

"I'm a man of mystery."

"Seriously," she frowned. "What was your goal with all that?"

"Well, the way I see it, whatever this is..." He gestured all around and at nothing in particular. "It isn't going away anytime soon. If anything confirms that, it's the damn military trucks we saw."

"That much is true. We've seen no signs of any aid coming from anywhere, nor power coming back on – have we even seen a plane in the sky?"

"Nope. And aside from some bruises from the brawl and a little nick in the calf, we managed to survive just fine. We've proven to everyone left around us that we're strong. At the same time, showing some generosity to Sandy will go a long way to show that we're not total assholes and that we can work with other folks as long as they respect us. With any luck, that'll lead to folks wanting to work with us and not against us."

Helen grinned. "Smart man. Look at you, playing the long game."

Ryan winked. "Of course I am. When don't I?"

"You want some dinner?"

"I'd love some dinner." He smiled warmly. "I'm enjoying our meals together again. Not the best situation to make it happen, but I'm very grateful."

Helen circled the breakfast bar and moved to the refrigerator, resting her hand on the handle. "We've tapered off a bit over the years.... You had so many projects you wanted to work on, and I had my shows. But we always had dinner every night."

"That's true, but it's nice starting the day with you again. I missed it." Ryan shifted uncomfortably. "What I mean to say is, I love you. I always have, and I always will. I wouldn't want to go through this with anyone else."

Helen's expression reflected his love, her eyes glassy as she returned to his side, wrapping her arms around him and resting her head on his chest. "And I'm just as in love with you as the day we met. I'm so proud of you, Ryan Cooper. I'd be helpless if it weren't for you."

Ryan hugged her tight and smiled in the still moment. "What we taught the kids enabled us to be here when all this happened. I just wish they were here with us."

"They will be. Soon." Helen selected a boxed meal from the pantry, noodles and a parmesan sauce. "This is supposed to take chicken. Want to go dress one?"

Ryan laughed. "Not right now, but I've got another idea."

Helen got some water boiling while Ryan took a handful of eggs out of the refrigerator, cracking them, scrambling them, and slowly cooking them in a pan, stirring frequently. Once the noodles were done, Helen put in the sauce mix and Ryan chopped up the eggs with his spatula and dumped them in the pot, stirring everything up in a rich mixture with the garlic-parmesan aroma drifting through the house.

"Not bad," Helen nodded. "Good use of the eggs."

"We need to put the blasted things in everything, so I figured hey, why not try it."

By the time the pair had nearly prepared their food, the dogs had all lined up in the great room, ears perked up, used to hearing eggs cracking before going into the gravy and dog food mixture they'd been getting for dinner.

"I guess I should feed these monsters, too," Helen said.

Together, they fixed the dogs their bowls and put them off to the side, then Ryan stewed tomatoes from their harvest and made mashed potatoes with butter and milk, salting them lightly.

"How are we doing on spices?" he asked.

"We've got plenty of salt and pepper and some other odds and ends. But we'll have to find some more eventually."

"I can't imagine life without them," Ryan agreed. "Let me add them to my list, though I don't have a clue where we'll get them long term without coming across a stash or something." As he sat down with his plate, Ryan pulled his notepad over and wrote *salt and pepper*. "At least we've got our own garlic bulbs and rosemary. That stuff grows fast."

"We can grow the garlic all year round, but the rosemary and other leafy spices will struggle if it drops below twenty."

"Garlic is my favorite anyway, so I'll be fine if we keep our supply up." Ryan wrote garlic on his list. "You know, Michigan is one of the largest producers of salt in the country." He tapped his pen on the tablet as he thought. "From what I remember, there are salt companies in St. Clair, Manistee, and Detroit."

"I know we had a lot of salt companies in the state," Helen said as she brought her plate over and sat next to him, steam rolling off of it. "But I didn't realize we were one of the biggest producers."

Ryan shook his head absently. "I remember reading it somewhere, but that's something to think about if we talk about gathering resources. Salt is critical for us to live, so it might be worth a trip over to the east to look around. Maybe we can do that after we check in at Grand Rapids once the kids get back."

"Oh, you're talking big quantities, huh?" Helen said, talking around her food. "I was thinking an easier way would be to scavenge from some local markets or homes in the area. Could get a lot of essential spices that way."

"We can start there, but it's hard to say where all this will take us, so I'm going to put that idea on the back burner. Think about what we could trade for salt if we had enough. Also, we'd need it to make butter, which we need to start working on soon.

"Speaking of Grand Rapids, I'd hate to think what would've happened if we were back there when this all took place...."

In Grand Rapids, Michigan, the skies loomed cloudy and gray, flat and elongated as if pressed against a glass tabletop. There was no sun like in East Lansing, a bitter cold layer of cloud cover floating in off Lake Michigan to keep the temperatures down. Miles of destruction stretched in every direction, vast patches of scorched neighborhoods and smoking warehouse districts with just a few clean-standing buildings and homesteads glowing like diamonds in a box of coal dust. Around many of those oases stood people with shotguns and crowbars, pieces of rebar and knives, guarding what few supplies remained, the lone survivors of the vast waves of fires that had swept through the region.

Dogs barked throughout the ruins as they meandered, ratty-eared and skinny through the rubble, dragging out food scraps and nibbling on cooked corpses, roaming in small packs as the former pets slowly turned feral. Turkey vultures swooped in big lazy circles overhead, diving, gathering in flocks to pick bones clean, tearing through char and ash to get at rotting flesh underneath. Shouts rang out to chase them away, and a sporadic shotgun boom sent them flapping and squawking.

In the middle of a field straddling two properties was a wide, brown barn where light peeked through cracks in the walls. Off to the side, a few crates of supplies were stacked beneath tarps held down by bricks. Shopping carts with bottled water, canned vegetables, soggy boxed meals, and two-liter soft drinks were parked in a neat row under an awning with backpacks lined up next to them. Inside the barn, lanterns stood in every corner, filling the room with a dirty yellow light, wind howling through the barn windows. The place had a dusty, musty feel thanks to the years' worth of accumulations of old hay and manure. Around a dozen farm folks with graying hair, scraggly beards, and oil-stained overalls had gathered, rugged people who hunted and farmed, all of whom wore camouflage jackets, flannel shirts, military coats and hats and thick leather and rubber work boots.

Women locked arms with their husbands, all wearing mixed expressions of determination and frustration. One man threw back a shot of whiskey while others drank from a five-gallon water cooler against the north wall, or picked at the small tray of crackers, cheese, and beef jerky. All of them were quiet, their attention focused on a tall, older man standing on a platform on the south side of the barn floor. He wore a long-sleeved shirt with a camouflage fishing vest over it, blue jeans and work boots, and a pistol on his hip. A neatly trimmed white mustache sat above his thin upper lip, and his face was long and lean with weathered features that betrayed the number of years he'd spent out in the sun.

"Settle down now, folks. We're about to get started." Red Fletcher motioned, waving his hands as the crowd noise faded to murmurs and grumbles. "Now, I'm not going to waste everyone's time. We know from the government broadcasts that this is some kind of terrorist attack, and it's been more devastating than we could have ever imagined. We've all lost something. Even Martha and I lost..." A sob hiccupped from his chest, but he quickly controlled himself. "Well, you all know we lost a son and daughter-in-law and two grandbabies. Sorrow runs deep in all our hearts."

Any remaining mumbling fell dead.

"Now, we've managed to survive thus far by pulling our resources together with what remained after our properties burned down and doing what we had to do in that regard. And we've scavenged everything we can from the ruins of the surrounding farms, even harvested some crops. But the fire has claimed almost everything and left us with next to nothing. Jed Reese slaughtered the two cows we had left, and we thought that would help get us through the winter, but most of that was stolen by those sons of bitches a few nights back. And they killed Jed, too. Good news is we got three of them—good shooting Reynolds and Hansen—but the rest got away with our meat. Chasing them down is going to burn more resources than we could retrieve so we're going to leave that particular avenue unexplored.

"We've got some supplies left, but they won't last us long. I've talked to all of you, and none of us has any other family around. That means no help unless we come by it on our own, by peaceful means or violent ones." He paused and rubbed his forehead. "The bottom line is that we're in trouble, down on supplies, and things aren't going to get any better. We need to find someplace permanent to go if we're going to get through this."

Murmurs ran through the crowd, followed by nods and affirmative whispers.

"What I'm saying is, we need to leave this area. There's nothing for us here but trouble. Bigger gangs are moving in all around us and, well, we're crafty – but they've got numbers on us."

"Why don't we join up with one?" Jim Brunson spoke from up front, a former Army grunt with a firm jaw and slicked back white hair.

"Really? You think they want more mouths to feed? Especially older folks like us?"

"What about planting crops in the spring?" Nancy Likely asked, a tough, wiry farmer who owned what remained of the next property over. "We've got two or three fields ready to go, and if we start early in the spring and don't get any days of frost, we could be well stocked up by the middle of summer."

"That's just it, Nancy," Red replied. "We don't have that much time. Everything we've got is right here, and it ain't much. Martha and I estimated we've got maybe a week's worth of food, tops, and barely any ammunition after that last fight we had to secure a couple days more food. I figure we can use what we've got to get someplace better rather than sitting here and starving."

"What about the shopping plaza downtown?" Tyler Reed asked, raising his hand. "That place is packed with stuff."

"I'd warrant they're the same people who took our cows, too. I can't prove it, though. You think they're going to help us? Or that we've got enough ammo to neutralize them?"

Angry murmurs rippled through the crowd, mostly between Tyler and the two other retired Marines he had in his group. Tyler conferred with them a moment before turning back to the front, red-faced and angry. "Well, maybe we do! Why don't we march down there, shoot the bastards, then take our stuff back?" A few people cheered and clapped.

"That would be great," Red conceded, "but they've got us outnumbered ten to one, *and* I heard they raided the police armory right after everything went south. I reckon there are about a hundred people in that camp, most of them heavily armed and a hell of a lot younger than us. We go walking into a place like that, we'll last about ten minutes. Our advantage is being smart, not numbers or brute force."

The crowd grew quiet and shared uneasy looks, then Tyler broke in again. "Okay, let's be smart about it. We come up with a plan, sneak in, and steal what we need."

"Okay then," Red snorted. "Who here's the fastest of us?"

The aging crowd measured each other up before frowning and shaking their heads.

"That's right. We've got three people in their forties, and the rest of us are older than that, a couple of us with one foot in the grave. We've got joint problems, bum legs, and more than a few hip replacements."

The response gave way to a ripple of grumbling laughter from the crowd, and most nodded in agreement with Red's assessment. He'd taken on the role of de facto leader near the start of the whole deba-cle, his neighbors coming to him right away as his reputation for being a man of action put him head and shoulders above most. He'd accepted the position with some reluctance at the start, taking responsibility for their failings and accomplishments with a firm jaw and a willingness to learn from his mistakes.

"What do we do then?" Tyler asked, thumbs hooked into his belt.

"Well, like I said. We move to a better place."

"That's bound to be a lot of walking. Maybe shooting, too."

"Any way you measure it, yep. I figure we've got a week to get wherever we need to go, and we may be able to stretch our supplies if we scavenge along the way. Take what we need from anyone who we see along the way. Put 'em down if necessary."

"Where are we going?" Jim asked. "Is there some kind of Garden of Eden no one knows about?"

"I don't know about that, but there is a place close by that might give us a lead."

"*Might* give us a lead?" Tyler spat. "A lead doesn't get us anything, Red. A lead sounds like pissing in the wind to me, not a permanent roof over our heads."

"A lead will get us to that place, Tyler. We sure won't find it around here."

"What's your lead, then?"

Red glanced at Martha. "I know this guy named Ryan. A friend of a friend. Play – played – golf with him from time to time, and he lives just a few miles away in a townhouse with his wife, Helen."

"He got a farm in that townhouse, Red?" Tyler asked, a few in the crowd smirking.

"There's not a farm in his townhouse, Tyler, but they *were* farmers their whole lives, just like us, and they've got relatives not too far away who have property. Just last week, he told me about how they'd be spending a few weeks outside East Lansing to house sit for their daughter's family. Apparently it's a big, nice farm on a solitary road, shared with just a few neighbors. Sort of place that might have survived the fires, much like this building we're in."

Tyler spread his hands in a helpless gesture. "And what makes you think it's still standing?"

"I'm not saying it'll be standing for sure, but Ryan made it sound like his daughter and son-in-law were real sharp folks. Not preppers, but homesteaders, if you know what I mean. They've got supplies, farmland, and animals. Even some kind of backup power system or something that could keep appliances running for a good long time."

"Sounds like a great place!" Nancy said.

"Sign me up!" Another person in the group shouted.

"Unless they're Amish, they drive cars like the rest of us," Tyler smirked, looking around. "That means their in-laws house probably went up, too."

Red shrugged. "They're house-sitting. Means the daughter probably drove their car to the airport and left it parked out there. And I happen to know that Ryan and Helen have an electric car. Now, an electric car wouldn't have blown up, would it, Tyler?"

Arms crossed, and a few people rubbed their chins while others whispered excitedly among themselves at the prospect.

"Okay, you got me, Red." Tyler shook his head. "It sounds like a nice place, but risky. Why can't we find something like that around here?"

The crowd broke into mumbles and disagreements, uncertainty and dismay as they gestured and discussed the predicament heatedly.

"We'll be in deep shit in a week if we stay here." Red raised his voice to quiet them again. "And you know as well as I do how good the prospects around here have been looking. The way I see it, this is our shot. If we find something good on the way, so be it, but if not...."

"You know where the farm is?"

"No, but I bet if we go to Ryan's house and see if there's anything left of it, we might find a clue. It isn't that far, so if it doesn't pan out, we won't be that much worse off. Folks, this is our best bet at getting to a solid place. In fact..." He paused and looked grimly across the group. "This may be the last walk we ever take. We'll need to keep going right on through. No stopping for anything unless we come upon a good scavenging spot. We take what we need, even if it means killing everyone in our way – well, so far as our ammo holds out, anyway. All right, I've spoken my peace. Let's hear how you feel about it."

Red stepped back and waited for the mumbling voices to discuss what he'd proposed, and after a few long minutes of debating, Tyler stepped through the crowd in his red coat and scruffy, brown-gray beard.

"Okay, Red," he said. "Most of us agree with you. You've shown some darn good leadership so far, so we'll go."

Red smiled and glanced at Martha, then shook hands with several people in the front row as the buzz of excitement rippled through the group.

"All right, everyone, there's no time like the present. Let's get packed up and head out. We'll need everything we can carry, in case we find somewhere between here and there that looks suitable to stop in for a while. Load up the carts and wagons and let's get a move on."

The group packed up the food and water that was inside the barn, put out the lanterns, and stepped out into the cold. Carts were loaded up, tarps folded, ropes gathered, bundled, and put away. Red and Martha took the lead, pushing their carts ahead of them on a dirt track with all the possessions they had been able to rescue from the remnants of their home: a motley collection of canned goods, a back-pack with a couple of changes of clothes, their shotgun, a box of shells, two jugs of water, and some odd pieces of camping equipment. The lack of extra firepower had been Red's greatest regret from his house fire. A stockpile of gasoline and a generator had been near the outside of the house directly opposite the interior wall where his gun safe had been, and the conflagration cooked off the ammunition and caused catastrophic damage to every firearm contained inside the safe.

Reynolds and Hansen were near the front with Red and Martha, the pair of retired Marines each carrying a shotgun along with backpacks with some pistols and the bulk of the remaining ammunition. Tyler slogged behind the group with an oversized backpack on his shoulders and a pistol on his hip, leaning forward, arms hanging forward to balance his weight. The others pushed carts or pulled small brush or firewood wagons behind them, rusty things with wobbly wheels, packed with goods and held down with bungee cords.

More than a few of the group were already walking with limps, having long had problems with their hips or knees or not being in the greatest shape to begin with. They all wore the same haggard expressions, a tired and worn-out bunch, but as they turned east on the main highway and left the burned-out husks of their homes behind, an energy overtook them. Hope and desperation both drove them, each knowing they had to be strong if they were going to reach their destination. A woman wept and staggered along, crying about everything they were leaving behind, her husband replying that they weren't leaving anything behind because there was nothing left. Miles passed by swiftly to the jangling song of wobbly wheels and rickety aluminum, shadows moving with the huddled forms of people still around, stray dogs getting bolder, and people watching warily from porches of half-torched homesteads.

"Reynolds, Hansen, and Tyler," Red pointed. "Go on up to that string of houses there and see if they have anything worth taking."

The men nodded, checked their weapons, and went on up while Red and the others formed a perimeter around the carts. People ran from the first two houses, and Red's men brought back a couple of garbage bags full of canned goods and assorted supplies.

"Not bad," Red said, nodding for them to give the bags to Martha. "How about those other houses? I'll go with you this time."

Checking his pistol, he led the three men up to a house with a burned-out garage that had taken part of the house with it. It was a small ranch model with aluminum siding and a small garden and porch. Red went up first while the men went to the front windows and put their hands to the glass.

"Anyone home?" Red asked.

Tyler shook his head and tried to look through the cracks in the blinds. "I don't see anything—Wait! Yeah, I see someone inside there. They just ran to the back."

Red backed away from the door. "Were they armed?"

"Unknown. But if we're going in, we should go now."

Reynolds stepped up to the porch, hauling his two-hundred and sixty-five pounds with him. "Step back, Red. I'll knock it open."

Red came down off the porch with a glance at the others, then he got his pistol out and held it at the ready. Reynolds held his shotgun in his right hand and opened the screen door, putting his ear against the door for a moment before rearing back and slamming his foot against it. The frame cracked and bowed but didn't break, then on the second try it exploded inward, and Reynolds ambled inside, followed by scuffles and something crashing, glass breaking, and a grunt and shout. Tyler and Hansen flew inside next, but Red came up slower, taking his time to enter carefully as shadows fought and staggered across the living room, smashing a table and hitting the wall with a thud. Reynolds pinned a man half his weight against the wall by his neck, shotgun in his right hand as he pressed his bulk against the homeowner while Tyler was laughing and Hansen grinned with his shotgun half raised.

It was an open floor layout, and Red saw into the kitchen where several cardboard boxes sat filled with supplies. He went straight over, nodding to Reynolds to hold the man still while he put his pistol to the stranger's head.

"We just want your supplies, not your life, though we'll take that if we need to. Just quit struggling and you'll get out of this more or less intact."

The man relaxed his grip on Reynolds' arm, though there was little else he could do with the larger man's forearm pressed to his chest and pinning him to the wall.

"That's all the supplies we have," he wheezed and struggled weakly. "You take those from us, we'll starve and die. Please, don't."

Red was struck by how guiltless he felt, wondering when those vestiges of humanity had slipped away before he shrugged off the thought and pushed the weapon the harder against the man's head.

"Settle down, son. You're young. You can find more supplies us old farts can't. Hey Tyler, check in back, would you? Don't want any surprises."

The man gasped, struggling a little to break free but stopping when Red raised an eyebrow. A long hallway stretched to the rear of the house, and Tyler started down it but was drawn to the kitchen table where the boxes were, picking through them and pulling out some canned goods, rice packets, flashlights and batteries.

"Hey, man. There's some good stuff in here." Tyler flipped a can and caught it with a laugh.

Red growled. "Tyler, would you do what I told you and —"

A thin woman in a white T-shirt slipped from the hallway, crouched low and dashing past Hansen to grab Reynolds' gun, jerking it out of his hand, fumbling with it, but getting it to her waist as she backed into the kitchen. "Let him go!" She shouted at Reynolds and then swept the gun menacingly from Tyler to Hansen. Red shook his head at Hansen, who looked about ready to make a move, and held his hands up.

"Hey, lady," he said. "No one needs to get hurt."

"You've got no right coming in here, threatening us and taking our things, you damn thieves." She spat every word, her dyed blonde hair striking a contrast to her angry red cheeks.

"We don't want to hurt you," Red said, "and we won't take your things if you put down the gun."

She scoffed. "You think I'm stupid? No, y'all get your asses out of here now! I swear I'll shoot you!"

Reynolds loosened the pressure on the man's chest enough for him to slide down the wall and stand unsteadily on his own two feet. The retired Marine looked back and forth between the woman and Red, one eyebrow arched in question at his leader.

"Why don't you put down the gun first, lady," Red said, "and we'll just—"

"No! We've been told that before and still got robbed! Took us

227

three days to get what's on that table, and we won't have it taken again!"

"Honey, why don't you put the gun down?" The man licked his lips nervously as he looked at the men standing in his home, undeterred by his wife flailing a shotgun wildly back and forth. "Maybe... maybe we can work something out."

"See, your man's got a good point there. He can see you're outnumbered and —"

"No!" she snapped. "I won't let it happen again! I just won't!"

She jerked the shotgun to her shoulder and got a bead on Reynolds, squeezing the trigger, though Reynolds dove out of the way faster than his age would have suggested him capable of. Hot buckshot hit the woman's husband in the chest and he slumped against the wall as blood drenched his shirt and the wall both. Red raised his pistol without hesitation and fired four times, each round hitting her square in the chest. She fell to the floor still holding the shotgun across her lap, gaping at the crimson stains spreading throughout her shirt. She tried to say something but slumped flat onto her back with a sob, and Red fired once more into her head, sending a spray of blood across the wall.

The room hung in silence for a few long seconds before Red wheeled on Tyler with a snarl. "Man, you were supposed to check the hallway!"

Tyler stared at the dead people and shook his head. "Sorry, Red. I, uh, —"

"Just do what I say, when I say it, and things will go smooth. This did *not* go smooth. Do you not realize that every round counts? That's six less than we had before, dammit! And who the hell knows who heard all that commotion."

He shook his head as Reynolds used the kitchen table to get back to his feet, feeling across his shoulder and back where a few pellets had grazed him. The rest of their group outside were shouting, and Red crossed to the door to see Jim Brunson and a few others coming up into the yard with their guns out while Martha stood on the sidewalk looking concerned.

"Everything's fine," Red waved. "It's all under control. Y'all just stay there, and we'll bring out some supplies in a minute." When everyone relaxed and milled back to the street, Red turned back to those left inside. "You okay, Reynolds?"

"Yeah, Red. Just a few scrapes. Better'n those two."

"I was wrong about you," Red nodded. "You move pretty damn fast for a big boy. Okay, let's get this stuff loaded up and get out of here before those shots draw more attention than we bargained for."

They packed everything up and took the five boxes out, Hansen and Reynolds each carrying two while Red and Tyler got the rest. Outside, they handed the supplies to the others who started putting things away in their carts.

"It won't last us very long," Red announced, "but every little bit helps."

Martha took his arm and pulled him aside, whispering. "What happened?"

"That got ugly, but nothing we couldn't handle. It's all good now."

Martha fixed him with a lingering look, and Red nodded firmly. "I said it's all *good*."

"Is it? I heard a woman in there yelling."

Red's eyes narrowed. "Martha. You and I've had this discussion before. It's a dog-eat-dog world now, and we've got to play hard if we want to survive this. You know it."

She stared at him for a long moment before nodding and gripping his arm harder, marching onward down the road out of town.

"Reynolds and Hansen," Red called as the convoy got back underway. "Walk the edges and watch for anyone moving in. Shoot first, ask questions later. You know how hard and fast things can turn."

The two men nodded and took up their positions, shotguns at the ready while others spread out and lingered on the edges of the group, protecting the supplies and one another as they moved through the midday gloom. They passed once vibrant neighborhoods decimated by fires, looking like they'd come under attack from bombers, guts of houses and cars strewn everywhere, leaving only a few beams or brick walls standing.

The recent rains had turned everything into a dark sludge that carried debris to the sewers which had quickly clogged and created wide, swirling black ponds that covered the streets. The water was dank and gave off a pungent, rotting reek, and Red shook his head and picked up the pace, moving out ahead of the group. He stayed out in front for a quarter of a mile, surprised when he turned and saw that the group was keeping pace with him.

"It won't be long now," he called. "Just another mile and a half past the golf course where we played."

The group chatter picked up, and a few smiles showed as they helped each other along. There was a hardness about the members of the group, the kind of toughness that only came from living and fighting through hard times their whole lives, sharing wounds, tragedy, and victories and bearing hardships that would have killed anyone weaker years prior – say nothing of the last few weeks.

A sudden swell of baying, barking and yelling pulled their attention to the rear of the group, all eyes on Tyler where he was lying on his back, legs kicking, reaching to punch at a pack of dogs as they tore at his backpack and thick jacket. Reynolds and Hansen moved into position on either side, Hansen closing and squeezing his shotgun's trigger as a dog spun and snarled at him, the shot removing the animal's face and scattering it across the pavement. Reynolds fired at another dog that looked like it hadn't eaten in weeks, hitting it square in the side, causing it to break off and crawl for a few yards before lying dead on the pavement. The pack took off as others in the group came forward and began swinging hand tools at them, yipping and howling as they fled down the street in a scrabble of claws. Reynolds fired again at the pack, hitting a few of them in the backside, stinging them with birdshot as they hurried after the group.

"Hold your fire, dammit!" Red yelled. "Save the ammo! Are you okay, Tyler?"

"I'm fine," Tyler replied, getting up with help from the others and brushing himself off.

Red glowered at him, his voice low and serious. "You need to get frosty quick, Marine. I'm serious. That's two times you've screwed up and almost got someone else *or* yourself killed, and two times I've overlooked it. There won't be a third."

Tyler's normally brusque expression had turned soft in the face of the reprimand, and he replied softly. "I hear you, Red. I'll do better."

"Damn straight you will." Red glared at him and turned to address the group as a whole. "He's lucky it was just a few mangy old dogs. Next time, it'll be people, and it'll be a knife in your back or across your throat, and you'll be left to bleed out in the street while the rest of us carry on. I'm telling you, folks. Be on the lookout and ready to act instantly." He shrugged. "Otherwise, you're just going to die, and the rest of us will have more food as a result."

Martha came and walked next to Red as they marched on, taking him by the arm to the front of the procession, and the group continued their march east past the golf course with its expansive, overgrown greens and unblemished woods, still remarkably beautiful with their gold and rustic red colors coming with the weather change.

Soon, they'd gone farther away from their neighborhood than they'd been since the disaster, the protective ring around their supplies growing tighter, their gazes warier, senses elevated and on the alert for any threats. Beyond the golf course were more neighborhoods, and Red stood at each intersection ahead of the group, trying to read the signs and figure out which road would lead to his destination. Everything was unrecognizable, though, the houses and townhouses having turned into darkened squares beneath the gloomy skies and fog, the streets hardly streets anymore but riverbeds of wreckage and murky puddles.

They came to one neighborhood Red recognized, and he moved up the lane, shuffling out ahead of everyone else, heart pounding with the expectation of failure since there was hardly a house left standing, and those that were had fire damage to their exteriors or had been broken into.

He superimposed what he remembered about Ryan's townhouse over the wrecked area and stopped at the end of the street before it curved left, standing in front of a line of five homes with the remnants of garages and stoops marking each one. The foundations were placed so close together it made a single long structure with fire breaks between them, though they had made little difference since almost all the garages held the remains of gas-powered vehicles, their burned-out frames half covered in collapsed roofs. The smoke grew thicker on the far end of the street, clinging to everything, swirling through the gaps with every uptick of wind.

"Are you sure this is it?" Martha asked, coming up next to him.

"I'm positive." Red gestured to the left. "I remember because when I dropped Ryan off, I turned around in that driveway over there to get back out to the main road. His house would've been..." He stepped to the middle garage and front porch and held both hands up perpendicular to the ground to frame what would have been the townhouse's sides. "Right here. They were right here."

"Doesn't look like they're here anymore, boss," Hansen said. "What should we do now?"

Frowning, Red growled. "I figured they wouldn't be here, on account of them visiting their daughter's home. But there's a fair amount of wreckage to look through. We should dig through it, see if we can find any kind of—"

"Red?" Hansen's demeanor changed, and he turned, gesturing with his shotgun pointed at the far-left end of the homes. "Looks like we've got company."

Shadows approached through the gloom, slinking between the piles of rubble and an engine block lying in a driveway.

Red stepped back and unslung his rifle, hissing to the rest of the group. "Anyone with a gun, get up here. Form a defensive line."

The defenders moved into position with their weapons raised, keeping those who were unarmed behind them with their supplies. Red placed his hand on Hansen's back and stepped to his right, tracking a figure coming toward them.

"Best slow up and show yourself before we open fire!"

A man rushed to them from the ruins, hands up, weaponless as far as Red could see. "Please! Can you spare some food? Please?!"

"Step back, mister," Red growled when the man kept coming, seeming to ignore the firepower arrayed against him.

The firing line moved a couple of paces backwards, waiting for Red's orders, all except for Hansen who took a step forward, lining up a shot. Still, the man was undeterred, and he hurried across the stretch of burned grass separating the driveways where Red and his people were standing. He wore ragtag clothing, a chewed-up poncho that hardly kept the rain off, his pants soaked and dirty, stomach lean and wide bloodshot eyes stark against his gaunt frame. Others moved behind him, forms creeping through the shadows with flashes of loose garments, and Red felt a ball of nervous tension creep into his gut.

"I said stop!" Red took a step forward, leveling his pistol at the man who refused to heed his warnings. "Stop or we will fire!"

Hansen's shotgun barrel flashed in a blast of smoke and flames, buckshot spraying the man's face and chest, tearing his plastic poncho to shreds as he screamed in agony. He staggered to the edge of the grass and fell to his knees, blood dripping from his wounds, then more gunshots flashed as the defensive line continued what Hansen had started, firing at the remaining shadows in a barrage that made them dance and cavort until the three or four shapes pitched backward into the driveway, falling motionless to the ground with cries of pain.

Martha ran forward, her flashlight sweeping across the downed figures, screaming, "Stop shooting! Stop it!"

The gunfire sputtered to a halt, and she rushed through the clearing smoke to the fallen man, but it was too late. He was lying in the grass, body twitching and arching upward as he breathed his dying breath and fell flat. Red rushed forward to her side, his near-empty pistol still trained on the bodies farther away, kneeling next to Martha as she touched his neck to try and find a non-existent pulse.

"Dead... they're... they're all dead." Martha stammered, moving past him and shining her light on a mother and children who were lying dead beyond the person Red presumed was their father. The woman was face down in the driveway, reaching for a smaller, curled-up figure off to the side, and another child, a teenager, lay against an old piece of furniture near the mother's feet, hair hanging lank on her shoulders, staring at nothing, body slack. Blood soaked the driveway, running through the cracks, over the side, and into the street.

Martha knelt between the mother and first child, looking back and forth before turning to Red. "It was a family, Red," she gasped. "We... just killed a family."

Red stiffened, working his jaw for several seconds before turning back and giving Hansen a near-unnoticeable nod. "It's a damned tragedy, but they should've stopped. We warned them and they kept coming. It's just how it is."

Martha broke down with a sob. "Don't say that, Red! These were kids and a mother, unarmed and innocent! We didn't have to kill them in cold blood!"

"Sorry, Martha," Hansen said, watching Red as he spoke, "but your husband's right. I didn't want to shoot him, but who knows what they would have tried to do. Been on enough tours to know that kids are just as dangerous as adults."

"Don't give me your war bullshit, Hansen!" Martha choked out the words, hissing at the pair of men before turning back to the fallen figures. "These people... we didn't have to do *this*."

Red placed his hand on Hansen's shoulder. "You did good. We *did* have to shoot, and we'll have to do that a lot more if we want to survive this. They could have been anyone with any number of intentions. Hell, there's no way to know if they even *were* innocents. They should've stated what they wanted from a distance and not rushed us..." He shook his head. "No, my conscience is clean."

Red stared at the girl pinned in Martha's flashlight beam, resolve hardening his heart, a stone wall growing over the tender muscle, the pulsing beat clenched in a cold hand. It had been a crying shame, but the worst of it was the disapproval in Martha's eyes, and he had to turn away or be consumed in it.

"We can't show anyone any quarter," Red announced, speaking louder to the group. "No one showed *us* any. Remember that." He nodded and wiped the moisture off his nose with the back of his hand. "Now, let's start going through these ruins and see if there's anything we can find to help us. Look for supplies, but more importantly, look for things that might tell us where Ryan went. Letters, address books – anything. Got it?"

Turning away from the bodies with murmurs of agreement, they approached the house, the right side of which looked like it had

234

almost melted and broken away, leaving some of the left side intact. They wandered through the rubble, picking through pieces of Ryan and Helen's lives with the soggy black furniture, fallen ceilings and part of the second floor hanging off the stairwell which was crushed and twisted.

"No one goes upstairs yet," Red announced, standing at the edge as the others went inside. "Let's check this floor and the basement first. Check and triple check what someone else searches. Leave no stones unturned. Canned goods and supplies are likely down in the basement if they've got one."

Red stepped into the living room, feeling his way around with the tip of his boot, making sure the floor was still stable before he went on. He shoved a couch aside, clearing a path for those coming behind him and working toward the kitchen. The kitchen table was still mostly intact with debris piled on top, and the cooking island was covered in wet drywall and wood. He was about to start checking the cabinets and drawers when Hansen called out.

"Over here, Red! I think I found the basement."

"Martha, can you check the drawers, please?" He forced himself to speak softly to her, trying to undo some of the damage from earlier.

"I'll... I'll do it now," she confirmed with a nod, barely looking at him.

Red worked his way out of the kitchen, stepping over a chair and coming around to where they were gathered by the door. Hansen tugged at the door, and it came open, grating against the floor. The steps had collapsed in a few places, though they could see the basement at the bottom.

"Want us to go down?"

"I'll go," Red said. "I won't ever ask any of you to do anything I wouldn't do myself."

Flashlight out and shining toward the bottom, Red led a couple of people down, bringing sacks with them, stepping precariously and calling out stable footholds and holes in the wood. At the bottom, he walked across the carpeted floor of the basement, shining his light around what had once been a comfortable living space, though its walls were covered with soot and black mold, the floor wet from water still dripping from the pipes. Working his way around, he found a small bar with some whiskey and soft drinks, gesturing for one of the people behind him to collect them while he went through another door on the far side of the room. His smile grew wide as he shined the light around at a couple of shelves with some canned goods stacked on them.

"It's not a lot," he told the person behind him, "but it makes this trip worth it, at least."

Red and his helper filled up their sacks and left the basement to the excited murmurs of everyone upstairs. He stepped into the kitchen, holding up his sack. "Not quite the goldmine I was hoping for, but we got something, anyway. A couple of cases of corn and green beans, some baked beans, and tomato sauce."

His helpers held their sacks up, one saying, "Whiskey, soda, and a few boxes of spaghetti and pasta, too."

The group nodded appreciatively, though all eyes had turned to Tyler and Martha, standing in the kitchen with all the drawers pulled open, papers and pens and drawer junk strewn everywhere.

"That's great," Martha said, coming to the kitchen table with a thin smile, still avoiding meeting her husband's eyes. "But I think you'll be happier to see what I found stuck to the side of the refrigerator."

Red put his hands on his hips. "Well, do tell. What did you find?"

"This." She held up a half-burned, soggy piece of paper and waved it at him, and Red stepped over and took it, reading it with a confused expression that faded into pleasant surprise.

"Well, I'll be. An envelope. This what I think?" He took the remnants of a red card out of the envelope, flipped it open, and read it. "A birthday card for Ryan, signed 'Your Loving Daughter.' Hmmm..." He threw the card on the floor and looked at the envelope again. "The half with the address is burned off, but... ha!" Red's smile broadened and he chuckled wildly as he grabbed Martha's stiff form in a bear hug.

"What're you so excited about, Red?" Tyler grumbled. "No address on it, so it's useless."

"Are you kidding me?" Red gawked at Tyler. "I swear, you need your head looked at." Holding up the envelope, he pointed to the postmark. "It's postmarked Elsie."

"What's that mean?" Hansen asked.

"You idjits... you'd think you hadn't ever been farmers in your whole life before." Red rolled his eyes. "It's a farming town, just outside East Lansing! And the card was to *Ryan* from his *daughter*, who...."

Hansen and Tyler both looked at each other, their looks of confusion slowly vanishing as realization dawned.

"Now you're getting it," Red laughed as he tucked the envelope into his front pocket, his aches, pains, emotional distress and exhaustion melting away. "Ladies and gentlemen – we have what we came for. It's time to get a move-on!"

CHAPTER EIGHTEEN

Agent Alan Harris
Mount Weather, Virginia

Harris guided President Birk through the bunker's inner passages, the long concrete hallways painted green with bold white markings. Military personnel hustled by, running to their posts while alarms blared throughout the facility, a voice booming from speakers in the walls, ordering various groups to different locations. A distant explosion rippled through the building, the concrete trembling ever so slightly from the blast, dust trickling from the ceiling vents as Harris instinctively grabbed Birk around the shoulders.

"Right this way, sir," he said, still moving, gesturing for the President to turn. "The safe room is at the end of this hall."

As they walked, Harris received updates from Security Chief Westbrook over his earpiece. "Attention all security teams. Hold your positions. General Pulaski is sending Marine units into the woods in a hard formation to scatter the attackers. I'm patching everyone in."

A Marine's gruff tone cut through the line along with scattered bursts of gunfire and a distant explosion. "Enemy units have struck the comms tower, and Bravo and Charlie teams are moving into the woods to counter."

"Who's hitting us?" Colonel Crow asked. "Saudis?"

"Negative, sir," replied the Marine. "They appear to be civilians."

Harris let go of his earpiece and turned to Birk. "I'm hearing it's a group of civilians, and they've taken out the comm tower, which explains the disruption in our feed."

"Civilians?"

"Seems to be. They're hitting us around the perimeter. Hold on a second... I'm listening in." Harris walked and listened as the spotty feed filled his ear with static and bits of transmissions. "Okay, Colonel Crow has sent Alpha team led by Sergeant Timmons around to the east wall...."

"Colonel Crow, this is Alpha team. We're halfway along the east wall and found a box that used to hold explosives. It's some heavy stuff the civilians shouldn't be playing with. We'll leave it by the fence line for someone to secure."

"Roger that, Timmons," Crow replied. "They may be trying to distract us before attacking the gate. Get your asses moving."

Harris leaned closer to Birk. "They've found some explosives and dead civilians, so they think they're trying to rig up something to take down the gate."

Harris and Birk reached the end of the hallway, a door guarded by two armed Marines who saluted and stood aside. Birk stooped and punched in his keycode, and the magnetic locks popped the door open. Harris pushed through and checked the room over, a small space with a stripped-down bathroom, a desk with a computer on the north side, and a few sparse pieces of furniture and crates of supplies on the east wall.

"Can we hold out?" Birk asked as they entered the room. "This place is hardened as far as I know."

"Assuming they don't breach the entrance, then yes. The barriers around the facility were mostly chain-link fencing and barbed wire when we got here," Harris replied. "They put up a few more barriers since then, but that's clearly not deterring them. And the hardening on the entrance isn't anywhere near the level of more robust facilities."

"Is that supposed to make me feel better?" Birk chuckled as he slipped into the computer chair.

"No, sir."

Birk pressed a key, and the computer screen lit his face in its glow. "Well, I appreciate the honesty, Harris. I'm tapping into the communication channels now." He read the display and rolled backward a foot. "I don't get it. We've been making supply drops all around the country. Why are they coming here and attacking us?"

"Good question. I'd say..." Harris hesitated.

"Go ahead, Harris. Speak freely."

"In my opinion, people are pissed at our response to what's happening. The supplies were a good first step, but people are looking for long-term answers. At least, that's my best guess. I think they're here to vent their frustrations on whoever's in power."

Birk snorted. "Well, they could've just knocked or filled out a complaint card or something. We don't have *that* many people here, but they can't imagine that getting to the President is going to be easy, can they?"

"No clue, sir. Hold on, there's more coming in..." Harris touched his earpiece and listened. Timmons was panting over the line when it suddenly opened up to the Sergeant's entire team.

"What's this, Sarge?" a Marine asked.

"It's explosives, rigged to blow," a female Marine replied. "But I've never seen it set up like this before. Looks demented."

"Will it work?" Timmons asked.

"You got me. It's a clusterf—"

"Focus. Can you disable it?"

"No way, Sarge. Not without a lot more time to trace this mess of wires... and we've got fifteen seconds left, if this alarm clock is the timer."

There was a brief pause, then Timmons' next words were shouted into his radio between him running and panting. "Back away, now! Colonel Crow! Brace for detonation. I repeat, brace for deton—"

Harris nodded to President Birk. "This doesn't sound go—"

An explosion rocked the facility, far greater than the one before, sending light fixtures rattling and the floor shifting beneath them as a brief swell of claustrophobic panic ran through Harris' brain. He forced himself to settle down, breathe deeply, and remember that the facility – while not built to NORAD specifications – was still designed to withstand an enormous amount of firepower. Next to him, Birk gripped his desk, grimacing until the rumbling and dust had stopped.

"Are you okay, sir?"

"I'm fine." He chuckled and raised an eyebrow. "Whoever they are, they sure know how to introduce themselves."

A few minutes earlier...

Sergeant Timmons stood behind a wall of sandbags on the north fence line of the Mount Weather facility, pacing and watching the murky tree line with its shifting shadows and fog. The sky was cloudy, with an ambient glow clinging to the soft edges and spreading halos across the Blue Ridge Mountains.

"You sure the attack is going to come from this direction, sir?" Private Tori asked, the assistant gunner squatting in a corner while she finished wiping down their M249 SAW.

"It doesn't matter what we think, Private. Our orders are to make sure nothing comes over that hill."

"They'd need to be mountain goats to get up here," Private Ramakrishnan replied derisively. "Or birds."

"Birds, mountain goats or flying unicorns – I don't care. Shut your traps and focus!"

Where the hill bent toward the north, the ground became treacherous and rocky, with only about twenty yards of flat space before it dipped almost straight down, with trees and foliage clinging to the hillside. Their visibility wasn't much better, made worse by the sweeps of floodlights from the towers, only serving to fill the woods with an impenetrable glow where shadowy branches waved. The insects were particularly loud as well, forming a chorus of chirps and

241

creaks that echoed all around them, blocking out any hope of picking up potentially important sounds, except for the occasional order bellowed from loudspeakers set atop poles.

Timmons spoke after a long pause. "Colonel Crow's orders are to guard this piece of fence line, and that's exactly what we're going to do."

"I know, Sarge, but —"

"I said *that's exactly what we're going to do.*"

"Yes, Sarge."

The small group was part of the squad guarding the Mount Weather perimeter, run by Colonel Crow from inside the command center. Sergeant Timmons paced inside their small four-by-twelve-foot barricade, which sat just outside the fence line with a gate right behind them and more guard towers spaced along the three-hundred-yard length. Through gaps in the woods, the faint orange glows of fires pulsed across the valley and spurs. Smoke drifted by, the byproduct of cities and towns long since burned to the ground, leaving a fog that carried across the miles with no signs of dissipating.

"How long do you think those fires will rage, Sarge?" Tori asked.

Timmons stopped pacing. "Your guess is as good as mine and worth about the same, too."

Samson took the rag from Tori and finished drying off his weapon. "With no firefighters around, the fires from the cities will probably carry on for weeks. Probably have to wait for everything to burn itself out."

"That's going to destroy...everything," Tori replied.

"Yeah."

"Do you think it's this way everywhere, Sarge?"

"Oh, it's everywhere. At least that's what they said at the last officer's meeting, but they're keeping things under wraps. They want us to focus on our jobs, and that's what we'll continue doing until someone comes to relieve us." Timmons raised an eyebrow. "But since you all seem so bored and chatty and unable to focus, let's do a complete equipment check. Right now."

"Yes, Sarge," Tori sighed and received grumbles from the rest of the fireteam as they found their equipment packs and began going through them.

They hadn't gotten more than a few moments into their check when an explosion erupted from the west side of camp, drawing surprised cries from the team and causing them to stagger back in surprise. A fiery plume crawled over the high fencing and rolled up into the sky, billowing black and orange flames pluming upward with blasts of sparks flying off to the sides. The buildings just inside the fence line blew apart in the explosion, and the shrieks of the dying followed close behind.

Marines from other sections sprinted toward the fires as a smattering of machine guns erupted from the corner positions, lighting up the night with tracers in brilliant flashes of red. The communications tower, a one-hundred-foot-tall steel construction with heavy beams and crossbars, satellite dishes, and antennas jutting from the top squalled as the metal twisted and bent. The structure continued groaning as the top third cracked in slow motion, broke downward, and finally toppled to the ground. Marines dove out of the way as it crashed and threw flames and debris into the sky, the heat rolling across the grounds.

His Marines started to leap the sandbags when Timmons grabbed them and pulled them back behind cover. "Get back here!"

"But, Sarge!" Sampson argued. "They're getting hit hard!"

"Sit down, Marine!" Timmons jerked him by the arm. "We don't move unless we're ordered to."

Grabbing his radio, he crouched down, speaking quickly into it. "Central, this is Sergeant Timmons on the north fence line. We've got an explosion on the west side, multiple casualties, incoming enemy fire and a breached perimeter. Please advise."

Flaming debris rained across the grounds, and more gunfire was exchanged, shrapnel and stray rounds flying in their direction, pinging off buildings and poles, zipping by like hummingbirds in the darkness. His radio erupted in a spattering of commands, cries for help, and requests from other units for direction until Colonel Crow came on the line and barked orders for Bravo, Charlie, and the reserve units throughout the facility. Marines gathered and charged toward the west side of camp in a flurry of running boots, and while Timmons expected the gunfire to fade and stop, it only grew more intense, the rat-a-tat of small arms fire chattering with machine guns, and two heavy thumps he took to be grenades.

"Who the hell... get ready, Marines," he growled, hand on his rifle. "I have a feeling—"

"Alpha team..." The rest of Colonel Crow's order was lost in a flash of white noise, a hiss, and a crackle of static.

"Say again!" Timmons shouted at the radio.

Puffs of dust erupted all along their sandbagged position as rounds embedded themselves in the barrier. The Marines instinctively ducked, falling flat as the nearby tree line sparked to life with muzzle flashes that deepened the approaching shadows. Forms ran between the trees in a surprisingly organized fashion, stopping in staggered formations to shoot at them from behind the thick trunks, keeping them pinned.

"Suppressing fire!" Timmons howled, wincing as rounds zipped above them. "Give them something to think about!"

"Yes, sir!" Sampson called, crawling to his M249 sitting on a crate, the barrel pointed out at the woods.

He slid up to the weapon, put the stock to his shoulder, and ripped off a return barrage, sweeping the barrel from left to right in a burst that sent their attackers ducking, diving aside, or flying back. The forest blossomed in high-pitched screams as a few of the rounds found their marks, and a spray of wood chips and shredded foliage erupted into the air. Tori and Ramakrishnan flung themselves against the sandbags on either side of the machine gunner, dispersing fire to the edges in a withering response, keeping their attackers pinned down.

"Colonel Crow!" Timmons shouted into his radio. "Alpha team is under attack at the north gate. Say again, we are under attack at the north gate. Small arms fire coming from—"

A spark of flickering light flew from the tree-line, arcing through the air, falling just short of their position, glass shattering and releasing its flammable liquid in a splatter of fire and heat that ran up the front of the sandbags and billowed skyward. The Marines flinched and pulled back for a few seconds, waiting for the wave to dissipate. They quickly resumed shooting at the tree line, though the break in suppressive fire had given the attackers time to scatter, making them too hard to pin down.

Timmons tossed his radio to the ground and crawled to Tori's side, resting his weapon across the sandbags to join in firing at the running figures moving along the tree line. Another arcing firebomb flew at them, hitting the ground five yards away and spreading liquid flames right at them, a potent concoction that stuck to the sandbags and kept burning.

"Is that gasoline and Styrofoam?" Timmons yelled, rising to the sandbags, firing bursts through the flames. "These assholes are dropping homemade napalm on us! Don't let it get on you, whatever you do!"

"Incoming!" Tori shouted, and the Marines dropped again as another bottle soared into the air, flying over them and tumbling end-over-end where it crashed into the gate and erupted in a ball of flames that crawled up the fencing, rolled around the barbed wire and licked at the sky.

"Damn that was close!" Samson shouted.

"Suppressing fire! Do not let them throw more of those!" Timmons ejected his mag and slammed a new one home, crouching back down behind the sandbags as the SAW began to fire next to him.

Samson picked out shapes along the tree line and opened up again, sending more bodies jerking and rolling back in the thick foliage. "Got two, Sarge! I need another belt soon!"

Bringing all their firepower to bear, shooting long bursts with their carbines and the SAW and alternating to swap out mags, they turned the treeline into mulch, cutting limbs to pieces so that they crashed to the forest floor, dust and smoke billowing up in plumes. The attackers fled the tree line in the face of the onslaught, and the muzzle flashes faded until there were none left.

"Bastards!" The last of Samson's ammunition rattled off in a rain of brass casings, the 249 clicking dry.

Tori was beside in an instant, loading in a new belt, then Samson slammed the cover over the feed assembly before pulling back the charging handle. He knelt back down, sweeping his weapon through the smoke and dust still filtering through the air, finger resting on the trigger guard as he squinted, looking for any hint of movement.

"I think... did we get them all?" he asked quietly.

Only silence answered from the tree line, and as their adrenaline began to drain, the dark edges around their vision lightened, and they began to hear other noises from around the camp as they filtered in. More Marines and various Army units were pouring from the bunker doors through the breach in the fence line, heading into the western woods where muzzle flashes flickered like fireflies.

"Alpha team, are you there?"

"I'm here, sir." Timmons fell to one knee. "We're all present and accounted for."

"Sitrep?"

"We engaged a small force of maybe two dozen armed with light arms and Molotovs and repelled them."

"Were they soldiers? I need identification."

"It was too dark to make them out, and we haven't swept the area yet, but my impression is they were civilians. Well-trained, but still civilians."

"Did you get a bead on what kind of weapons they were using?"

"Pistols and AR-style rifles, sir."

"Did you hear any automatic weapons?"

Timmons glanced at the others, who all shook their heads. "Nothing we could hear."

"Very good, Timmons. I want you to bring your team to the south gate, via the east fence line."

"Sir? That would leave this area unguarded."

"We've got some reserves coming up to take your place. We need you to make haste toward the south gate and hold that position until told otherwise. Understood?"

"Absolutely. On our way." There was a squelch from the radio, and Crow began addressing other teams as Timmons strapped the radio to his hip. "You heard the man," Timmons told the team, who were already packing up their gear. "Grab ammo and get your asses moving."

"I need another belt," Samson said, taking a belt of ammunition for the SAW from Tori and looping it around his neck.

As he wound a strap for the SAW around his shoulder, Tori and Ramakrishnan got their remaining magazines stuffed into their vest pouches and inside a duffel bag, and they slung all they could carry on their shoulders.

"Let's go, Marines!" Timmons straddled the sandbags and climbed over. "We're already late to the party."

He cross-stepped along the fence line, using the flashlight on his barrel to sweep the area as his team trailed behind him. Blinking and flashing lights from broken light poles flickered behind him, combining with the burning buildings to cast an eerie orange glow over the area. Bodies lay at the edge of the woods, some caught in brambles and thick brush, all of them with tattered clothing and gaping wounds after being hit with Samson's M249 and the others' carbines.

"Ramakrishnan, get up ahead. Watch the fence line and we'll cover the woods. Double time."

Wordlessly, the scout swept past them and got out in front, nearly jogging to the northeast corner as the others watched the woods. When Ramakrishnan fired in three bursts at something up ahead, Timmons broke into a run and caught up.

"Use your words, dammit! What do you see?"

"People running down the hillside to the east; I gave them some parting shots. Should we pursue?"

"Negative. Stow the gunfire unless I say. Just keep moving."

They crept along the east wall, getting farther away from the main battle, which seemed to have gone deeper into the hills to the west. Fires were spreading, and thinly-manned emergency crews were trying to put them out, but Timmons stayed focused on the tree line. It was flatter on the far side, with sparse clusters of trees and brush, the moon bright behind the clouds, its sparse rays that broke through the cloud cover highlighting a rise that swept south and curved out of sight.

"Watch that little valley. If there was any place for an ambush, that would be it." Timmons' shoulders clenched as he jogged, sweat dripping down his neck and back as he waited for someone to hit them.

Tori followed close behind him with Samson, the squat woman carrying the heavy duffel bag full of ammunition over her left shoulder with her carbine resting on her hip. The privates worked as one, sweeping their weapons across the trees, focused and silent as they searched and moved. Halfway along the eastern fence line, Ramakrishnan stopped to squat over a pair of dead Marines and Timmons swept his flashlight across the sprawled bodies, illuminating the gunshots and bloodstained fatigues.

A pair of civilians in jeans and dark jackets lay a short distance away, one with a shotgun, the other with an older Winchester rifle lying in the grass nearby. Spotlights from the near watchtowers swept in and stopped on the Marines, and Timmons turned and waved, then the lights moved on.

Tori kicked one of the attackers. "Must've been a militia or something."

"I wonder what they were trying to do? They lost a *lot* of guys." Samson leaned over, looking at the bodies.

"The answer might be right there." Timmons nodded to a plastic bin lying on its side, the lid thrown off, its contents spilled across the grass. "Have a look, Tori."

"On it." She circled smoothly to the bin and knelt. After a moment of rummaging, she held up a block of gray clay. "This is not good, Sarge."

"What?"

"Take a look."

Timmons moved where he could see and shined his light near the spilled contents, which amounted to more gray blocks, timers, wires, and switches. "Son of a... that's C4. Civvies wouldn't have that."

"If they raided an armory, they might," Tori replied. "Plenty of 'em left to raid, I'm sure, especially if they're a militia. Whatever they're up to, it can't be good. I wonder if this is what they used to destroy the guard positions on the west side."

"Bigger question is – is there more of the stuff?" Timmons shook his head, lips pressed firmly in a tight line. "Put all that in the bin and set it against the fence, out of sight."

"Yes, Sarge."

While Tori worked, Timmons got his radio. "Colonel Crow, this is Alpha team. We're halfway along the east wall and found a box that used to hold explosives. It's some heavy stuff the civilians shouldn't be playing with. We'll leave it by the fence line for someone to secure."

"Roger that, Timmons. They may be trying to distract us before attacking the gate. Get your asses moving."

Ramakrishnan led them to a section of the perimeter reinforced by concrete walls and higher fencing. The air was still, the sounds of fighting growing distant, the cracks of rifles, the sharp *pop* of pistols drawing the Bravo and Charlie teams away. Wind blew gusts of smoke past them, Timmons feeling vulnerable out in the open with their backs to the wall, chasing shadows that flitted at the edge of the darkness.

Near the southeast corner, Ramakrishnan stopped again. "What's this, Sarge?"

Timmons moved past Ramakrishnan and shined his flashlight at a blind spot along the wall where groups of gray blocks were lined up at three-foot intervals, connected with wires and small junction boxes. Tori dropped her ammunition sack and strode over, feet spread as she took in the configuration with a glance. "It's explosives, rigged to blow. But I've never seen it set up like this before. Looks demented."

"Will it work?"

Tori shrugged. "You got me. It's a clusterf —"

"Focus. Can you disable it?"

Tori took out her flashlight and examined them closer, tracing the path along the cables to reach a junction box with glowing red numbers. "No way, Sarge. Not without a lot more time to trace this mess of wires... and we've got fifteen seconds left, if this alarm clock is the timer."

Timmons sidestepped and watched five seconds tick down, brain trying to process what he was seeing before he grabbed Tori and threw her toward the sweeping lowland, clutching Samson and Ramakrishnan next, shoving, pushing, and screaming at them to take cover. As he ran, he snatched his radio off his belt and shouted into it. "Back away, now! Colonel Crow! Brace for detonation. I repeat, brace for deton–"

The explosion came with a sharp thud so thick and deafening that it sealed out all sound around him, filling his ears with throbbing pain and high-pitched ringing as his ear muffs were ripped off by the force of the blast. Pieces of dirt, rock and concrete stung the back of his neck as his body was picked up and hurled through the air by a blast wave of heat. His rifle and radio flew out of his hands, stomach doing somersaults as the world rolled around him. He defied gravity, windmilling his limbs until he met the ground feet and knees first, then rolling, arms and legs limp as he flailed and tumbled.

Chunks of concrete zipped past him and thudded like lobbed softball pitches, an enormous cloud of dirt and smoke filling the area. His mind was numb, lungs heavy as he gasped for an elusive breath that refused to come. Flipping onto his back, panting, he blinked at the sky as a column of fire and smoke swelled high above the complex, its top rounded and oozing across his field of vision. For a moment he clung to consciousness, then darkness claimed him, sealed his eyes, and dragged him down to a world of black silence.

CHAPTER NINETEEN

James Burton
Frankfurt, Illinois

James woke up on the cold, hard floor with a thermal blanket over him and a backpack for a pillow. The room was chilly and musty, and two wounded soldiers were lying head to foot against the north wall, stirring awake as well, stretching and groaning in pain.

Washington stood over him. "Come on, James. It's time to go."

James nodded, threw the cover off, and swung his legs around. His body was not only sore from the previous day's chase through the streets, but he'd slept awkwardly, and a stinging pain radiated up the right side of his neck.

"Ugh," he grabbed his neck and massaged the spot.

"You good?" Washington asked.

"Yeah, just a crick in my neck. I'll be fine."

"We move out in fifteen. Did you want to help carry some of these crates out?"

James had left his boots untied but still on, and he leaned forward to tighten the laces. "Yeah. I'll start bringing out some crates. Do you want everything?"

"Leave anything marked 28B. That's all camp gear. We'll be moving fast, so we want ordnance, food, and water. Start with the MRE bin over there against the wall." The Lieutenant nodded to the south side.

"Got it. No twenty-eight bravo. Start with the MRE bins."

James stood and stretched his arms over his head, then bent and touched the ground, swinging his upper torso back and forth to loosen up his stiff muscles as one of the wounded guardsman sat up against the wall.

"Tough sleeping on the floor, huh?" she asked dryly.

James nodded. "Probably doubly so for someone with a wounded leg. Got shot?"

"I wish. Sprained my ankle carrying equipment with this genius." She rolled her eyes and jerked her chin toward the soldier at her feet, who was getting up.

"We were carrying our crates through the ruins," he said. "Could have gone around, but Cap wanted us to go right through." The guardsman shook his head and raised his arm, which was in a sling. "Plenty of places to get hurt. Bunch of stuff fell on us. Oswell hurt her ankle, and I busted my arm up."

"Good thing we're not taking all the stuff," James said.

"Screw the gear. I just hope we get out of this damn city soon." Oswell winced as she kept one leg straight and edged up the wall. "This place has been a death trap since the day we entered."

"You got that right, sister," her partner said.

While a pair of soldiers came and helped their wounded comrades, giving the woman with the hurt ankle a makeshift crutch made from an iron rod, James started carrying out the MRE crates and set them outside where the guardsmen were gathering. The troops began emptying them and stuffing everything they could into their backpacks, readying their carbines and ammunition pouches. James' breath plumed in the cold misty morning and he yawned repeatedly while trying to force his sluggish body into action, but the dozen guardsmen seemed energetic, eager to escape the crowded and violent city. Back inside, James adjusted his pack, organized his remaining supplies - which weren't much - and grabbed his pistol and walking stick before joining the troops. Lister was rounding everyone up and climbed onto the hood of a car to address them.

"Okay, people. Listen up. We're getting out of this town ASAP. I want Washington and Witkowski on point and the rest to keep good spacing and know where your friends are. I want eyes on the rooftops and searching every nook and cranny. Let's not get caught with our thumbs up our asses. Any questions?"

The guardsmen all stood silent, feet spread, expressions focused; twelve, plus the two wounded, and James. Grubby, wet, and cold, they stared nervously at the imposing streets as if expecting something to leap out of the shadows and strike.

When no one spoke, Lister hopped down. "All right, people. Let's move out."

Washington took point with Witkowski, a broad-shouldered redheaded man with stern gray eyes. They fell in line, marching up the right side of the street, leaving behind the sandbags and tents, assorted crates of camping equipment, and an old radio with the parts stripped clean. Every step they trekked south, away from James' self-imposed demarcation line, left him feeling a little better. Still, the township stretched around them with old buildings and architecture from another age, a block of warehouses with bold writing. James lingered toward the rear with the wounded as they marched, the man with the broken arm holding his carbine in his left hand while his companion hobbled on her crutch, already breathing heavy but focused ahead with a set jaw.

"I'm glad to be getting out of there," James said. "I didn't want to get any closer to downtown."

"No kidding. Never got your name, by the way. I'm Oswell." She held out her left hand. "Emily Oswell."

"James Burton. Good to meet you." James started to ask a question, but she was panting and struggling with each step, looking for a place to put the end of her crutch and careful not to fall.

"You want a hand?"

"It's all good," she said with a head shake. "I can handle it. Just don't want to fall and break the other ankle. Cap would never let me live it down."

The crew traversed narrow streets and moved through an endless field of wreckage, where blown-out vehicles and piles of bricks mixed together. Where he could, James walked ahead of Oswell and knocked chunks aside with his staff, doing what he could to make it easier on her. It had stopped raining, but everything was still dripping and wet, the buildings glistening and stained, dark scorch marks up the sides wherever fires had licked at them. Boots splashed through puddles and crunched across shattered glass, kicking bricks and garbage aside as Rodriguez walked up ahead with Pugh and the ever-quiet Wiseman.

The line suddenly stopped, Washington and Witkowski standing in the middle of a major intersection with the corner buildings shattered and fire-scarred, car parts and metal strewn across the cracked pavement. Stock still, rifles shifting to the east where fog choked off their visibility, they searched the gloom as echoes of kicked rocks and scuffling feet came from that direction.

Captain Lister pointed to three guardsmen, and they rushed to where a pair of cars sat sideways in the middle of the street. James circled to the right-hand car and stood by the trunk where a taillight dangled loosely by its wiring. Rifles flew up when a group of people strolled from the fog, dark figures led by a massive man James recognized, one with a wide chest and huge gut, his clothes bloodstained from his fight – and victory – over the man with dreadlocks and his gang. A chain dragged the ground behind him, the links stained red with chunks of hair and flesh, held in a huge hand with bruised and scraped knuckles.

The leader's hair hung limp, beard smeared with blood, eyes filled with malice as he walked straight toward Washington and Witkowski. The guardsmen backed up, carbines raised to their shoulders, fingers slipping within the trigger guards, bodies clenched as the rest of the gang filtered in behind him. They'd grown since James had last seen them, numbering two dozen or more, and their piggish eyes sized up the soldiers before catching James where he was hiding, turning his insides to liquid beneath their malicious grins.

"Stop right there!" Washington shouted. "Don't come any closer or we'll blow you away."

The leader growled from behind bloody lips. "I like our odds."

"It's not just us," Washington said. "I've got another dozen rifles pinned on you assholes. One wrong move, and you're dead."

As if noticing the guardsmen crouched down behind the cars for the first time, he only snickered. "I still like our odds."

James slipped around the car and walked to where Lister was about to step out and confront the man. He grabbed him by the arm. "Wait a minute, Captain. I've met these people before. It's one of those gangs I told you about."

Lister ducked back under cover. "What can you tell me?"

"Up there." James nodded upward. "They'll have people up on the buildings ready to ambush us. I watched them pick apart an entire gang from up there. They're a lot smarter with their tactics than they look, trust me."

Lister pointed at Rodriguez and Wiseman and then at the rooftops, the two guardsmen splitting off and moving down the street with their guns sweeping the heights. The Captain stepped from cover and strode out to stand next to Washington, sizing up the gang leader and the dozen people behind him, their own hands bloody evidence of their violent rampage.

"I'm Captain Lister of the Illinois National Guard. Stay where you are, and we'll move through this intersection without any problems. Make any sudden moves and we'll put you down. Get it?"

The leader stared at Lister for a moment before his thick tongue came out and licked his lips as he glanced in James' direction. "You got a man with you who stole from us. We've got no beef with you, but with him... that's another story. Give him up, and y'all can pass."

"Can't do that," Lister said. "Everyone with me is going to pass through this intersection, and you're going to take your people and move back. This isn't a request. It's an order."

"If you won't give us our man, then you'll have to pay full price to cross... in bodies."

Lister's finger slipped inside the trigger guard. "Back the hell up, or I'll open up that fat belly of yours! We've got people watching the rooftops; you won't even get a chance to try your bullshit on us! You *will* lose this fight! Now move back!"

The gang leader watched Lister closely for a long moment, seeming to contemplate the weapons arrayed against him and his odds of winning when he finally backed his people up several steps, holding his hands up in a mocking gesture, the chain scraping against the pavement. "Go ahead, soldier boy. Go on by."

Lister didn't move his eyes off the gang leader or his finger off his trigger as he called to the rest of the guardsmen. "Move out. Single file. Let's go."

Pugh went first, stepping between the vehicles with the remaining guardsman following. James gestured for Oswell to go next, and she hobbled out ahead quickly with him right behind her, his insides curling as he locked eyes with the gang leader and noticed the thin woman who'd chased him into the alley standing nearby, snickering loudly.

"That *is* the slimeball who got away from us," she said with a malicious grin. "He's going to pay first."

The leader snickered. "They'll all pay in the long run."

"Shut up," Lister growled, backing up with Washington and Witkowski as Rodriguez and Wiseman filed in behind them, crossing and slipping onto the right-hand sidewalk, heading east and continuing their trek through the wreckage.

The crew navigated the foggy streets with Washington and Witkowski on point, the Captain and James guarding their rear, and as they tried to pick up the pace, it was clear where their weakness was; Oswell was hobbling in an upright position, rifle swinging by her side, unable to keep up with the guardsmen who moved faster and were able to better stay in cover, with a full range of movement.

Sounds echoed around them, drawing James' attention everywhere and nowhere: every dark alley, every cross-section of narrow lanes, and up above where the enemy might shoot from the rooftops. A breeze blew from an alleyway ahead in a burst of fog, and a shape rolled out in a clatter of plastic wheels. Washington and Witkowski stopped and raised their rifles to fire, and the rest of the troops hit the walls, only for the mist to clear to reveal a small gray wagon packed with dolls and kids' toys.

"What the hell is this?" Lister stepped to James' side. "IED?"

"I think it's just... toys. These people are kind of messed up in the—"

A brick hit the ground two feet in front of the pair, breaking in half and scattering shards. The guardsmen pressed harder against the walls or threw themselves behind piles of junk and then another brick fell, then another, high-pitched whistles and cheers from above shrieking through the gloom to accompany the bombardment. A rock bounced off the back of Rodriguez's helmet and knocked it crooked on her head, and when she looked up, another landed directly on her uplifted face, crushing her nose and cracking her teeth, sending blood flooding down her front. She fell against the wall and dropped straight to the sidewalk in silence, a single burst from her carbine firing into the sky. James slid next to her as bricks rained around them, striking the ground, one glancing off his forearm as he tried to protect himself. Flipping Rodriguez over with one hand, he winced at her bloodied face and crushed forehead, blank eyes staring up at the sky.

"Lister, s-she's gone" James' face was pale.

"Son of a *bitch!*" Suppressing fire, *now!*"

Washington was the first guardsmen to start returning fire, aiming upwards and dispersing several bursts toward the rooftops, chewing at the brick and sending more shards raining on their heads. Soon, the air was filled with dust, and the guardsmen cursed as they searched for targets while a seemingly limitless supply of bricks dropped on them, all without a solid angle to return fire on their attackers. To the west, the leader of the gang and his people jogged after the group, taking their time as they took up positions behind the cars and piles of fallen concrete and brick.

"Lister, we've got a problem," James called out as Lister knelt over Rodriguez's fallen form.

Lister saw where James was looking. "Keep moving forward,

people," he called ahead. "Someone help Oswell. James and I will cover our retreat."

James held up his pistol. "I've only got a few rounds for this thing."

"Take Rodriquez's rifle. Ammunition pouch in front. C'mon, man, hurry up!"

The weapon had become tangled in her arm, and he had to lift her and slide the strap off her shoulder, setting it aside and trying unsuccessfully to unhook her ammunition vest. With a grunt of frustration, he grabbed several magazines from it and stuffed them into his pockets. Bullets cracked the brick above his head, shots coming from the west forcing James lower, crawling, pulling the M4 across the pavement, staggering to his feet, and throwing himself onto a pile of debris next to Lister. The sputtering of the Captain's rifle set James' teeth on edge, and he raised his pistol and emptied six bullets into the shadowy mist, draining the weapon.

"Aim for the fat one," James called. "Take their leader out and they'll crumble!" He stuffed the dry pistol into a pocket and brought the M4 to bear, picking out targets, clutching tight to the bucking weapon as he fired in bursts, trying to keep the shadows at bay. Where one fell, though, two more took their place, barrels flashing in return, thudding into their cover and sending fragments of brick bursting into James' face. He aimed directly at the flashes, catching one man as he sprinted from one car to another, knocking him off his feet while Lister pinned a second man against the brick wall across the street.

"Let's go, private!" Lister patted James' shoulder, shoved himself off the brick, and chased after the moving guardsmen.

James got up and staggered behind him, past the toy wagon someone had kicked over, stumbling, turning, and firing west to keep the gang on the street pinned down honest. As he spun back to follow the Captain, he nearly tripped on Pugh who lay sprawled with her helmet crooked, a fragment of something embedded in the side of her face. He stooped to grab her ammunition, but the pack had already been taken, and Lister was urging him onward.

"No time, James!" he growled. "We're all dead if we don't move!"

Bullets pinged and sparked off the metal husks of cars, ricocheted off the walls, and zipped by, a horde of angry hornets with deadly stingers. Ducking and scrambling, he kept up with the Captain to the echoes of laughter and high-pitched whistles, bricks and bullets plaguing their retreat. Finally James and Lister caught up with the main group and they pressed on, sidestepping, sweeping their weapons upward and back with Washington calling out possible escape routes and angles of future attacks. James ran up beside Wiseman, who was helping Oswell hobble along, grunting and groaning whenever her sprained foot struck something.

"Are you guys okay?"

"We're good," Wiseman mumbled. "Just watch our backs."

Lister surged ahead with Washington, leaving James alone to guard the rear. The gloom closed in behind them in slow swirls of smoke with no moving shadows or signs of pursuit, and his hopes began to rise that they'd gotten out of the worst of the trouble. It was only when Lister shouted and a flurry of bullets sprung at them from the other direction that James shed that hope. He fell to his knees instinctively as chaos exploded in front of them, the guardsmen retreating from a group who'd cut them off. Two were shot before they could get to cover, spinning and running into each other before toppling onto the pavement, their uniforms shredded and dripping red.

Washington and Witkowski crouched in the open, spraying bullets at shadows rushing at them in a horde of shapes, cutting them down even as incoming fire flew at them. A round struck Washington in the shoulder and another hit Witkowski in the leg, and he collapsed to his good knee as he ejected his spent magazine and jammed a new one home.

"Into the alley!" Lister called. "Come on! Washington, Witkowski, let's go!"

Guardsmen angled into the narrow passage, one struck in the neck, clutching the gushing wound as he hit the corner and bounced to the ground, dead before James could try and reach for him. James got behind Oswell and pushed her and Wiseman toward the opening when Wiseman's head rocked back, and he collapsed beneath

Oswell's arm. Another guardsman was there to take his place, and the two disappeared into the passage. James and Lister reached it, waving the other troops inside and waiting for his point men. They were backing up, firing in alternating intervals, Witkowski somehow staying on his feet as rounds hit him in the arms and chest.

"Come on! Let's go!"

Witkowski turned, stumbled, and took another handful of rounds in the back, his face a mask of pain as he collapsed to his knees and hit the pavement. Washington sprinted past them, and James followed Lister as they dove deeper into the passage, dodging rocks and stones still falling from above but escaping the withering gunfire that had cut them to pieces. He stayed on Lister's heels, weaving between the garbage piled in the alley with aluminum trash cans and dumpsters everywhere. One lid flew up, and a man jumped up like a jack-in-the-box to fire on Oswell and Lister, the wicked thuds of lead plunging into flesh, bits of fabric and blood popping off Lister's body as he collapsed against the wall. James aimed at the figure with his arms stretched over the edge of the dumpster but his aim was off, and he shot the side of the dumpster before raising the sights and burying a string of rounds in the man's chest and face, rocking his head back.

Oswell wasn't where she'd initially fallen, but had kept hobbling ahead into the narrow passage. Lister was tumbling backward, and James switched his rifle to his right hand and caught him, bearing his weight for a few steps before pushing on. Staggering, clinging bloodily to each other, they pitched forward into the gloom as it rained rocks, bricks, and garbage from high above their heads. Something light struck the back of James' head, and a heavier piece crashed on Lister's foot, causing him to yowl in pain. Through the smoke and chaos, light appeared ahead at the end of the passage where the rest of their group ducked and fired in wild, panicked bursts. Bricks and bullets rained on their heads, and the forms ahead staggered and fell with waving, windmilling arms as they were taken down.

"Stay with me, Lister!" James shouted. We're almost there–"

The Captain jerked in his grasp, slipped to his knees, and took them both down. They hit the ground, James crawling from beneath him and rolling him over. Lister was spitting blood, gasping, seizing James by the shoulder and squeezing as he tried to say something. James leaned forward to hear the whispers sputtering from his mouth, but the racket was too much, the calls and whistles and shapes closing in on them, finishing the guardsmen and stripping them of their weapons, ammunition, and the few supplies they carried.

When the light left Lister's eyes, James laid him gently on the ground and faced the onrushing figures surging toward him, who were so caught up in their assumed victory that they had ceased firing. Clenching the M4 to his shoulder, screaming at the top of his lungs, James fired through them, putting three-round bursts back and forth to shred their flesh, drawing howls and curses as he cut them to pieces. James turned the narrow alley into a kill box of their own creation. His scream ended as his magazine emptied, and he quickly exchanged it for a second, leaping bodies as he ran, firing with abandon, continuing to fire until he reached the other end of the passage and stopped. Part of him wanted to keep going, to keep shooting and cutting them down for what they'd done, but as the heat of the battle fled along with the adrenaline, James lowered his weapon and slowed to a halt.

Spinning, he sprinted back down the passage, leaping the dead, reaching the end where the rest of the guardsmen had perished. He glanced around at the corpses helplessly, checking them for signs of life, tears stinging his eyes as he found no one left alive. Operating on pure survival instinct, he got on his hands and knees and collected spare magazines, stuffing them and an extra pistol into his pocket. When he was finished taking all he could, and with the worry of the attackers gearing up for another assault on his mind, James started to run but stopped when he heard a groan nearby.

"Oswell?" James called, rushing to a dumpster with its lids flipped open and hanging over the cobblestones. Behind it, Oswell had taken cover, a rifle in her lap, her teeth grinding in pain. James kneeled next to her, checking her for wounds. "Are you okay, Oswell? What hurts?"

"In the hip," she replied in a pained voice, face twisted in agony. "Leg, too."

James bent closer and parted the torn material of her fatigues, unable to see the entry point between the blood and swollen flesh. He searched the dead bodies, tearing off a guardsman's belt and wrapping it around Oswell's leg directly on the wound, double cinching it tight to her pained groans.

"I can't do anything about the hip, but maybe the pressure will help stem the bleeding in your leg. We need to get you somewhere safe. Come on."

Getting beneath her arm, he started to lift her but stopped when she clenched his shoulder with a red-stained hand, shaking her head, distraught, tears running down her face in despair. "No, it's no use."

"What do you mean? Come on, Oswell. We're the only ones left, and we've got to get out of here before they come back."

Oswell dropped her weapon, grabbed James' jacket, and pulled him close. "I'm not going anywhere. It's because of me all this happened. We couldn't move fast enough. Everyone had to wait on me."

"That's not true and you know it."

"No..." She shoved him away. "I didn't want them to take me. I should've stayed back there at the camp and let them go ahead. Now, look at them." She stared at the corpses, familiar faces turned lifeless and dead. "I went through basic with these guys. Saw them every weekend. I don't deserve to be alive when they're all —"

"Shut your mouth," James growled, grabbing her and trying to lift her again. "There'll be time for self-pity later. We've got to go. Come on!"

"What's the point?" she whimpered, settling like dead weight. "What's the point in any of this? Everything we had is gone. I don't know where my family is... they're probably dead like everyone else. And these animals in the streets..."

"Get a grip, Oswell! That's not true at all. I've met good people since airplanes were falling from the sky in Denver. And I know there's more, including my family and yours. We're going to get out of here for *them*!"

Oswell shoved her rifle into his chest and started taking off her ammunition belt. "No, James. You've got a family to get home to. You don't need me slowing you down. I won't have it. I have nothing to fight for anymore, but you do."

"How do you know what I have to fight for?"

"I heard you talking to Lister and Washington. About getting home to your family in Michigan. I know you'll make it, but not with me in tow. Now, take the gun and ammo and go. I'm gonna bleed out here soon anyway. Just go!"

James crouched with the equipment lying at his feet, the sounds of shuffling boots coming from behind them, dust trickling on the metal dumpster lids as their enemies prowled the rooftops. They shouted back and forth to each other, hunting for their prey in the smoke and dust, reinforcements looking for their fallen comrades and those responsible for the slaughter. If James and Oswell weren't gone by then, there'd be no repeating his victory; they'd be dead. He picked up the belt, buckled it around his waist, shouldered her rifle, and stood over her, watching her sob quietly with the pistol resting in her lap.

"When they come for me, I'll be ready," she said. "I'll take a few of them out before they get me or I bleed out." She wiped tears away. "Go on, man. Get out of here. Get back to your family."

James nodded gently and started to turn, then stopped, fist clenched at his side and heart torn with indecision. He recalled his time on the train, at the camp, and then with the Amish and wondered, for the hundredth time, what might've happened to them, hoping they were okay. All of his regret over the train, his pride over having helped at the camp and the advice he'd given Eli and Clara about making hard decisions to stay alive, even if it went against their religion, came back to him in a flash.

Oswell was right, of course. It would be a suicide mission to assist her and think he could escape unscathed; the gangs were fast and knew the streets too well. He'd be a sitting duck, slow and helpless, likely getting them both killed, and ruining his chances of being reunited with his family.

"Son of a...." Sighing, shaking his head, he kneeled by Oswell.

"What the hell are you doing?" Her breaths came hard as she struggled to focus. "Every second you waste is —"

"Shut *up*, Oswell," he snapped. "Listen, you're probably right. I stand a much better chance of getting out of here alone, but I *won't* do it. Getting back to the people I love is important, but it won't mean anything if I leave a friend behind. Survival has to be for... something more. More than just living. And if I don't walk that walk, then there's no point in *any* of this."

Oswell glowered at him, but James chuckled darkly. "If you won't get up off your ass, I'm just going to sit down next to you and we'll see what happens. I'm putting the choice on you, like it or not. Now, make it."

Her jaw tightened as she considered his words, finally shaking her head and snatching her weapon back. "*Asshole.* Help me get my gear back on."

"That's the spirit."

Stooping, he got under her arm and used the dumpster to leverage her to a standing position, laying the ammo pack over her shoulders and buckling it around her waist. She leaned against the dumpster as he did it, putting her weight on her left foot and wincing at the slightest movement.

"I can't find my crutch."

"It's right here." James stooped and snatched it up, handing it over and waiting for her to rebalance. "You got it?"

"Yeah. I should be able to go on my own."

"Great. I'll provide cover." James rested his hand on her shoulder. "We're going to get out of this. Or take a *lot* of them with us."

Oswell nodded, set her lips in a firm line, and gestured for him to go. James stepped into the passage, swinging his rifle in both directions, mimicking a soldier's crouched firing stance he'd observed from the guardsmen.

"Okay, follow me."

They moved south, getting only a few yards before someone on the roof spotted them and shouted. The shots were sporadic and off-target, though, the rounds merely peppering the pavement nearby. A moment later they were at the end of the alley, staring across an expansive open dirt yard with several large buildings behind it. A dilapidated crane with a leaning arm loomed above a bloody battlefield in the yard with dozens of people on both sides, knives flashing and pistols rattling as they fought and died. Their gang colors were indistinguishable from one another in the fracas and their methods were beyond barbaric. Combatants waved knives and lunged while others swung bats and crowbars like cavemen, smashing bones and cracking skulls, spilling blood on the dirt.

"Are they the same gang?" Oswell grunted.

"I don't think so," James said, jaw dropping as a man stalked a woman with slow, deliberate steps, arm extended, pistol firing only when he was on top of her and she turned on him, backpedaling when he shot her, staggering a few more paces before pitching onto her back. "It's another group... these people are crazy."

"See what I mean?" Oswell shook her head. "We've got insanity behind us and in front of us. We'll never get away."

James followed a trail of old cars, most of which were rusted out and stripped down, not blown up or burned like he was used to seeing. They were parked nose to tail, forming a lane leading into an enormous junkyard with rows of crushed vehicles stacked ten high as far as he could see.

"I see something. Follow me. Quick."

"Quick ain't in my vocabulary at the moment, in case you forgot," she replied with a grunt, shouldering her rifle and grabbing the loose pant material of her right leg to help keep it elevated enough to walk on the crutch.

They moved west, keeping close to the brick wall, rushing for the next crushed vehicle to hide behind, casting glances back at the battle. James stepped away from the building, exposing himself as he got a better look at the yard and how they could get just a hundred yards down and across the street.

"What are we looking for?"

"See the junkyard? I think a couple of people could get lost in there pretty easily."

"Yeah, I see it now. Good call."

"It's as good a place as any. We have to cross the street, though. Let's go. Quickly!"

Angling between a pair of cars and leaving their cover, they crossed to the other side of the road and moved west, then south along the junkyard's curved dirt lane. James cringed at every shout and gunshot, expecting them to turn on Oswell and himself, their luck finally turning somewhat when no one fired on them or gave chase.

They hobbled toward a corrugated aluminum wall, rusted and flimsy with wide-open gate doors hanging from their hinges. The place was massive, a cityscape of towering stacks and heaps of metal atop each other with smoke loosely drifting above the top layer. The gravel path through the yard was filled with puddles, pieces of car parts and old oil slicks that clung to their boots and pants as they shuffled along. Oswell was practically dragging her leg behind her, grunting as she gripped her pants leg to keep it elevated, every step pure agony.

"Just a little farther, Oswell." James kept watch behind her, rifle at the ready. "Just keep pushing!"

They made it to the first row when their luck finally ran out and the first bullets struck the metal car frames with sparks and dings. Lead ricocheted with sharp whizzing noises as rounds buried themselves in crushed engine blocks and doors and shouts and curses followed them, boots pounding pavement as the gangs gave chase, the victors of the battle looking for more blood to shed. James and Oswell moved deeper into the rows, cutting left to get lost in the massive stacks that were quickly turning into a maze. The smells of oil, antifreeze, old gasoline and grease clung thick to the air, and they splashed through rainbow-colored puddles, hurrying to find a place to hide.

Taking Oswell's arm so she could lean on him, James' back strained to keep her upright, grunting and panting with every step as he searched for a place to go, anywhere to hide from their hunters. James stopped them at an intersection with nothing but rows of crushed and dismantled vehicles stretching in every direction, massive towers of rusted hulks with hoods thrown open, their parts stripped out and sold. Several stacks appeared ready to fall, the top layers leaning precariously atop the groaning steel, water from the recent rainstorm still dripping from the fenders and off the chassis to add to the greasy puddles around them.

"They're still coming," Oswell said, looking back. Something zipped through the air and exploded behind them, sending flames climbing a stack in tendrils of orange and dark smoke, the heat gusting against their clothes, blowing their hair around.

"We need to get lost *real* fast," James growled. "Come on... this way!"

CHAPTER TWENTY

Ryan Cooper
Somewhere Outside East Lansing, Michigan

Rays of golden sunlight bathed the frosted ground, burning off the moisture into a fine haze that covered the property, spreading to the high boughs where robins and sparrows huddled and waited for the coming warmth. Some flew in agitated patterns, flitting across the treetops, bickering with the others in sharp chirps and piping warbles, chasing each other from one tree branch to another. On the ground below, sheep and goats bleated for their breakfasts, crowding Ryan as he pushed the wheelbarrow to the gate and entered, each trying to be the first to get their morning meal.

Despite the chill, Ryan had worked up a sweat after collecting eggs with Helen and making another minor repair to the fencing where it had separated from the frame. A couple of chicks had escaped in the process, and he and Helen had spent a few long minutes chasing them around, a process made much more difficult with his wounded calf. Ryan had kept stooping and grabbing at the running balls of yellow fluff, only to have them slip out of his hands at the last second. When Duchess cut the lightning-quick birds off and sent them flying back in his direction, he'd managed to catch them and put them back in the coop.

"Ryan, one. Chicks... twenty-two," he mumbled as he wheeled the wheelbarrow up to the barn and popped the front door open.

Taking a bale of hay from inside the door, he dragged it to the enclosure and dropped it into a hay trough, the barnyard animals surrounding it and nibbling at the roughage. For additional nutrients, he took a bucket of feed and spread the pellets around the yard in wide tosses to keep them from crowding the barn entrance, where he hoped to pull out the tractor and perform some maintenance. Once everyone was fed, he walked inside and took care of Bessie, refilling her trough with fresh water and leaving her a good portion of hay to eat.

He patted her side. "Helen will be out in a little while to milk you, old girl. Hang in there."

Bessie lowed in response, and Ryan took that as an "okay," after which he pulled the tractor out in the yard, cutting the engine off to kill the noise. Taking a folded piece of paper out of his pocket, he looked over the list of maintenance items to prepare the tractor for colder weather. James had maintained the tractor well, but the battery terminals were caked with potassium carbonate, and he used the terminal cleaner to scrape them off before reattaching the cables. The oil had a dirty sheen, so he changed it, started up the tractor, and let it run for ten minutes to spread the oil throughout the engine block. One fan belt was dry and cracked, and the tires looked like dry rot was just starting to set in on them.

"Hopefully these get us through this next season, but we'll have to look for some new ones in the spring."

Hands and arms smudged with grease, Ryan began to wipe down the tractor, cleaning it from the dirt and grime that had caked on over the last several days. The woods were quiet around him, the shadows still deep in the early morning light and fog, and the robins flitted actively in the warming air, coming down to pick at pieces of feed the sheep and goats didn't eat. Duchess chased a few before

269

getting bored and lying in a patch of sunlight, her furry tail swishing back and forth in the grass. In a sudden jerk of movement, the dog twisted to her feet, head high and ears perked up, nose pointed at the front gate.

"What is it, girl?" Ryan reached for his rifle sitting in the wheelbarrow. "Do you see someone?" When he got to the barnyard gate, he saw the reason for Duchess' distress. "Someone at the gate, eh? Looks like Sandy again. Wonder what she's doing here... c'mon girl, let's go back to the house."

Ryan waved to let Sandy know he'd seen her and then slipped his coat on, squeezed through the barnyard gate with Duchess, and headed to the house.

"Back already?" Helen stood at the stove, canning the remaining produce they'd harvested. "Or maybe you're looking for something else to eat?"

"Food sounds great," he replied, ignoring his groaning stomach. "But that's not why I came in. Sandy's down at the gate again."

"Were you expecting her?

"Not today." He shrugged. "At least not that I remember. I'll go down and see what she wants."

"Well, take Duchess and Diana with you. Diana is fidgety today and has been driving me crazy. Are you going to take the EV?"

"Not today. I'll walk them down. Do you have a sec to watch my back?"

"I've got jars in the pressure canner, so I've got nothing to do for another forty minutes. I was thinking about milking Bessie, but she can wait a little longer."

"She looked fine when I saw her," Ryan agreed.

After Helen went upstairs with her rifle, Ryan left through the front door and walked down the long driveway, passing the majestic maples as they swayed in the gentle breeze. The warm smells of decaying leaves and mulch drifted by, and the ducks quacked as they floated on the ponds, flapping and flicking water off their wing tips at the sight of Ryan and the dogs.

Reaching the gate, Ryan nodded curtly. "Sandy."

"Hi, Ryan."

"What brings you here this morning? We didn't plan to meet today, did we?"

"No, we didn't. I'm sorry about dropping in like this, but it's not like I can text you or anything."

Ryan allowed a slight smile. "You certainly can't. I don't have a problem with you stopping by as long as you stay behind the gate."

"Fair enough," Sandy brushed a lock of dark hair behind her ear. The haunted look in her eyes from the last two meetings had been replaced by something like relief, a smile tugging at the corners of her mouth. She held up a small plastic bag. "I brought this for you."

"What's in it?"

"A dozen eggs... and a thank you letter from my son, who's recovering very well right now, thanks to those antibiotics you gave me."

"Oh, that's good. Let me see." Ryan opened the bag and unfolded the note written in blue-crayon scrawl, which he read out loud. "Thank you for the medicine, Ryan! You're the best!" Chuckling, he held up the note and waved it. "That's awful sweet of him. I assume he's doing much better?"

"Miles better. His fever broke overnight, and he had a gigantic appetite this morning."

"Well, there you go. That's wonderful, Sandy. I'm happy to hear he's doing all right."

"The antibiotics really kicked whatever he had in the butt."

Ryan nodded. "Make sure you keep taking them for the full regimen of ten days. You don't want it coming back stronger."

"Will do. It's amazing how a little thing can go so far." Sandy gestured to his leg. "I saw you limping. Is your leg healing okay?"

"It's a little stiff, is all, and it'll be that way for a while. The bullet penetrated clean through, though it didn't hit any arteries, thankfully."

Sandy covered her mouth. "Oh, my. I... I didn't realize that. Is there anything I can do to help?"

"Unless you've got a spare leg, not much." Ryan pulled up his other pant leg to show her his prosthetic. "I mean that literally."

Sandy gaped. "Is it just your foot, or is it cut off higher? If you don't mind me asking."

"Foot and a bit more. Came off just above the ankle, but the prosthetic rides all the way up to my knee. Gives it a little more to hold on to, if you know what I mean."

"How'd that happen, if you don't mind me asking?"

"We were farmers back in the day, and accidents are a way of life. This one happened to be bigger than most."

"Well, I'm sorry that happened to you. It's got to be hard getting around with your legs injured like that."

"I'm tougher than I look," he chuckled. "I get by. What about you? What's your story?"

Sandy raised her eyebrows and sighed. "I was a teacher at the middle school, and my husband was a plumber. When everything happened, he was on a job site, and I was at school. One minute things were fine, and the next the parking lot was a wall of flames. The windows blew out, glass sprayed everywhere, the kids were crying and screaming... we thought it was the end of the world."

"Close enough," Ryan nodded and rested one arm on the fence.

"Anyway, we watched out the windows for a short time, thinking it was some terrorist attack or something. I just wanted to keep the kids safe and away from the windows. The fire spread pretty quickly to the building, though, and that's when everyone started panicking.

"I packed the kids into the hallway to join some other evacuating classes. The smoke was so thick, and everyone was choking and crying. I've got to tell you, Ryan, my heart was racing like it's never done in my life." Sandy's eyes turned glassy as she dove deeper into the memory. "We'd gotten to the end of the hall, and kids were filing down the stairs. I thought we were home free, then I heard crying from back the way we'd come. I went back to look for them —"

"How did you keep from suffocating on the smoke? That stuff can kill you in just a few minutes."

"No kidding. It took me about a week to recover. I used my shirt to cover my mouth and stayed low like they say in the fire videos. Didn't take long to realize that the boy crying was my Stephen."

Ryan's eyebrows went up. "Your boy?"

"Yes. Ryan, I... I've never felt fear grip me like it did then. A list of class schedules ran through my brain, trying to remember which room he'd be in. I ran straight for Mr. Westerly's class and got halfway there before remembering he'd taken a study hall at the end of the day, which started a couple of months ago. I rushed to the end of the hall, but it was all one big blur. I don't remember any details, but I eventually found Stephen under a desk with another little girl. Smoke was much thicker in the hallway, so I checked the windows to see if there was a way to climb out from there, but there were no fire escapes on that side, and it was a three-story drop. I took my shirt off, ripped it in two, and covered their mouths, then I snatched them by the arms and took them back into the hall. Luckily for us, the stairs were right there, and we joined a bunch of other people trying to leave. We made it out but..." She shook her head, smile fading as tears began to fall. "I heard later that most in the preschool building didn't make it."

"Good heavens." Ryan used his finger and thumb to rub his wet eyes. "That's horrific."

"It was hell. We waited for emergency services but obviously they never showed up, so we helped as many people as we could, then walked home."

"So, you're all by yourself with your son now?"

"Sort of. A few of us have gotten together, had communal meals, and traded with each other. At least until Trace got involved with Jack and his buddies... we're kind of on the fringe now, just staying nearby for safety's sake but not participating with the group very much. It's complicated."

"I can imagine."

"It's just one more tragedy in a string of them." Sandy looked past him to the farm. "Nobody's fared quite as well as you all have, though. Especially since you have that tractor."

"I reckon that's what's got people worked up."

"That's part of it, for sure. You've got what nobody else has... a tractor, dogs, plenty of farm animals, a standing house and barn...."

"Well, none of it's mine, remember. It belongs to my daughter and son-in-law. And, listen... I won't promise we'll be best friends, but I wouldn't mind contributing to a potluck of sorts, if that's the kind of thing you're doing."

"That'd be nice." The smile returned. "I'll tell the others you're amicable to something."

"No, no, no. Hold on a second. I want to take it slow with everyone after what they did to us. Despite you and me getting along fine, I still don't trust most anyone these days."

"No, I understand."

"And I triply don't trust anyone in a circle of folks who tried to steal from us and kill us. It could just as easily be us in those graves we dug."

"I understand completely."

"Let's keep these meetings going for a few more days and continue sharing information. If I'm comfortable with what you say, and you're comfortable with what I say, we'll see about joining in for a meal together and maybe even working together. If that goes well, we can see about talking to the other folks, too. I like to help folks and I'm open to the idea of second chances, but I won't take any unnecessary risks."

"I can't disagree with you there, Ryan. And I think I speak for the group – well, the few who I talk to from time to time – when I say we all understand that. They know you're not to be trifled with."

"Good."

"Tomorrow morning, then?"

"I'll be here. Is there anything else your son could use?"

"No, I think we're okay for now."

"I'll figure something out to return the favor for the eggs."

"Great. Until tomorrow."

"Tomorrow."

Sandy waved, turned, and headed back down the road with a hop in her step. Ryan watched her for a long moment before calling the dogs to him and heading back to the house, contemplating the conversation and hoping the tightrope he was trying to walk wouldn't end up backfiring on him. When he reached the front yard, he waved up to Helen to meet him around back, where she shrugged on her coat as she came out the door.

"How'd it go, dear?"

"Better than I expected." He showed her the bag's contents and handed her the note. "She gave us a dozen eggs, and this is from her son.

"Isn't that sweet? Not that we need the eggs, but that's very kind of her." Helen read the note with a growing smile. "This is so great, Ryan. It really feels like we're making some progress here."

"Seems that way. Do you want to go up and take care of Bessie now?"

"I'll just take the cans out of the pressure canner real fast."

Helen hurried off, then locked arms with him a few minutes later as they walked. "What's Sandy like?"

"Seems nice enough. A teacher, apparently, or she was. Been through a lot, just like everyone, I guess. She almost lost her son twice."

"How so?"

Ryan told her about what happened at the school and how Sandy had heard Stephen crying from a classroom down the hall, recalling the smoke and flames she'd mentioned. "A place like that with the generators gone and the sprinkler system not working would go up like kindling. Sounds like she saved those kids in the nick of time. Feel awful hearing that there were a lot who couldn't be saved, though."

"Oh, my."

"I have to say, I've got a good feeling about her, and she seemed genuinely remorseful about her husband's actions."

"So, you trust her?"

"Hell no. For all I know, she's playing the long con. Good feelings don't get you far in my book these days. We'll see, though. It'd be nice to have an ally."

They reached the barnyard gate and slipped inside with the dogs, Duchess and Diana walking toward the sheep and goats, barking low, cutting them off when they tried to get around them, and herding them away.

"I'll put the tractor back, and you work on Bessie. We'll use the ATV to drive the milk to the house; my leg's sore after all this walking."

They finished the day's chores with Ryan pulling the tractor inside the barn and fetching the ATV. He straightened up around the place while Helen collected a single large five-gallon container of milk, ready to be pasteurized. Legs tired, calf stiffening from the day's work, Ryan brought up the ATV and pulled it to the barn entrance where Helen waited.

"Do you need help with anything else?" she asked.

"Afraid so. Today's chores wore me out. I could stand for a night on the couch with a movie."

Helen put her hands on her hips. "Are you suggesting we skip guard duty shifts tonight and enjoy a night together?"

"Not really, but you know, with the dogs around and the neighbors appearing to be kept in line, we can probably afford a couple of hours of semi-relaxation. I'll go through Alice and James's DVD selections and pick us out something good."

Helen grinned. "Feels like ages since we've had a good movie night."

Ryan grabbed the five-gallon container handle and started to lift it when the sounds of engines caught his ear. "You hear that?"

"Yep." Helen scanned the treeline. "I think it's coming from the north side of the property."

"Someone's on the highway again."

"The military?"

"I don't know, but we should have a look. We'll drive out this time. I don't feel like walking that far."

Climbing aboard the ATV, Ryan drove it up to the barnyard rear gate where Helen got out and let him through, and he waited for her at the edge of the woods. Once she was back in the passenger seat, he moved ahead, sticking to the thin patches of birch saplings and avoiding the heavy undergrowth where they could get stuck. It was a bumpy, jarring ride, and working the pedals with his injured leg sent aches running from his knee to his hip, but he finally pulled to a stop about three-quarters of the way through the woods.

"C'mon, let's walk from here."

They got off and trekked the rest of the way, crunching over the deadfall as nuts hit the forest floor and the high boughs rustled. At the edge of the tree line, roughly in the same spot as before, Ryan spread the stiff branches to reveal another line of armor moving on the highway, wide APCs and Humvees with mounted guns manned by military personnel. The convoy stretched far to the west, a hundred units long at least, more of the same older equipment and gas tankers.

"This one's even bigger than the other one," Ryan said.

"More fuel and supply trucks, too."

"I count seven fuel trucks so far... they either have a cache of older fuel, or they're refining it."

"Should we try to talk to them?"

"I don't think so," Ryan shook his head. "But we should start monitoring the radio more often. If they've got a way to make fuel, or at least transport it, then maybe they're attempting to try and start some recovery operations."

"That'd be nice – a bit of potential good news would be welcome."

"Exactly." Ryan pulled back from the bushes. "Let's go."

Ryan drove them to the barn, taking his time and easing them over the bumpy terrain, tired from the day's work and mulling over the situation with Sandy and the military's recent movements. The situations left him with mixed emotions, fear and uncertainty clouding his thoughts, pressure to make the right decisions intensifying as things continued to progress around them.

At the barn, they teamed up to get the milk container back onto the ATV, Ryan grunting as he bore most of the weight, his calf screaming in pain by the time he got it situated and dropped it into the cargo tray.

Helen noticed his discomfort. "Let's get you inside with some warm compresses on that leg of yours."

Ryan climbed into the driver's seat and went to start it up, then paused when the hairs on the back of his neck stood up. "Did you hear that?"

Helen got in next to him and tilted her head to listen. "What?"

Ryan shook his head, still listening but only hearing the wild woods and fluttering birds, the soft bleating of the barnyard sheep, and the gentle gusting of wind across the yard. "I thought it was an engine...."

"The convoy?"

"Pretty sure they're gone by now. No, it was loud and clacking, kind of like a diesel truck." Ryan raised his head and gazed into the distance. "Sounded like it was coming from the west."

"More people who got older vehicles running, maybe."

Ryan stood still for another moment, then shrugged and chuckled. "Or maybe it was nothing at all. I'm old; hearing things is what I'm supposed to do, right?"

Starting up the ATV, he drove them back to the house beneath steel gray clouds pressed flat and stretched thin, with sunlight coating the edges in bright highlights. Ryan took it as an omen of an uncertain future, a reminder to remain vigilant in a world torn asunder.

CHAPTER TWENTY-ONE

Dappled sunlight filtered through the towering boughs of the loblolly pines, casting warm patterns on the humid, dank undergrowth below them. A trio of songbirds, unbothered by the cares of the outside world, chased each other from branch to branch, swooping beneath each other with elegance unmatched by fighter pilots, their tittering warbles their own miniaturized version of gunfire. The sight of a few insects skittering across the pine needles of the forest floor distracted them from their rivalry and they dove low, landing and devouring their food, hopping back and forth in search of more. A low groan emerged from a misshapen lump near the songbirds and they scattered, not knowing what had made the noise, driven by pure survival instinct back into the trees where they sat silent for a few moments, watching the forest floor with newfound caution.

Death wasn't supposed to be painful. A warm loving embrace, a release from life's pain and an eternity somewhere better, yes. Side-splitting chest pains, sore arms and legs and a headache to beat the band, no. For several long, agonizing moments, she lay still, trying desperately to return to the dark sleep where pain receded to some back corner, her mind fragmented and unthinking of anything except the physical pain until one tiny tendril emerged. A single thread that, when tugged, unraveled the curtains and sent Alice Burton bolting upright, the lightning bolt of agony ignored as she forced words from her dry, ravaged throat.

"Jake?! Sarah!?"

READ THE NEXT BOOK IN THE SERIES

The End Of All Things Book 4
Available Here

books.to/BhiYs

WANT MORE AWESOME BOOKS?

Find more fantastic tales at books.to/readmorepa.

If you're new to reading Mike Kraus, consider visiting his website (www.mikekrausbooks.com) and signing up for his free newsletter. You'll receive several free books and a sample of his audiobooks, too, just for signing up, you can unsubscribe at any time and you will receive absolutely *no* spam.

Special Thanks

Special thanks to my awesome beta team, without whom this book wouldn't be nearly as great.

Thank you!